THE
LIBERTY
GUN

ALSO BY
MARTIN SKETCHLEY

THE AFFINITY TRAP

THE DESTINY MASK

THE LIBERTY GUN

MARTIN SKETCHLEY

BOOK THREE OF THE STRUCTURE SERIES

an imprint of **Prometheus Books**
Amherst, NY

Published 2006 by Pyr®, an imprint of Prometheus Books

Inquiries should be addressed to
Pyr
59 John Glenn Drive
Amherst, New York 14228–2197
VOICE: 716–691–0133, ext. 207
FAX: 716–564–2711
WWW.PYRSF.COM

10 09 08 07 06   5 4 3 2 1

Library of Congress Cataloging-in-Publication Data

Sketchley, Martin.
    The liberty gun / Martin Sketchley.
        p. cm.
    ISBN-13: 978–1–59102–492–7 (pbk. : alk. paper)
    ISBN-10: 1–59102–492–7 (pbk. : alk. paper)
    1. Human-alien encounters—Fiction. 2. Life on other planets—Fiction. 3. Space warfare—Fiction. 4. Time travel—Fiction. I. Title.

PR6119.K48L53 2006
823'.92—dc22

                                                            2006022439

Printed in the United States of America on acid-free paper

To Mom and Dad

"He dedicated his third book to us, you know. Didn't he, Maurice . . . ?"

ACKNOWLEDGMENTS

I'd like to say a big thank you to:

Everyone at Pyr/Prometheus, particularly Lou Anders, for unwavering enthusiasm and a skillful editorial hand. A finer pirate never sailed the seven seas, me hearties!

Joshua Bilmes of the JABberwocky Literary Agency in New York.

John Parker at MBA Literary Agents in London.

And to Rosaleen, Daniel, and Orla, for love and prayers: "Please help daddy write his third book." "Please let it be good!"

The Liberty Gun was written to the sound of Ian Brown, Nick Cave and the Bad Seeds, Nirvana, PJ Harvey, Prodigy, Rage against the Machine, That Petrol Emotion, The Wedding Present, The Zutons, and in the very final moments, Arctic Monkeys.

Despite all we might wish, we have no hold on the lives we create. They will go their own way, defiant, undeterred. There is little we can do other than guide them as well as we are able, and hope that they soar, fulfilling all they have the potential to be.

Translated from Seriattic transcripts of the *conchey trinsig diassaii*

One

High Earth atmosphere, somewhere above Australia
February 26, 2379

When the Buccaneer reached an altitude of twenty-eight thousand metres the aircraft's engines shut down. Their roar was replaced by the softness of rushing air, and the machine decelerated quickly as it approached the top of its arc.

As the Buccaneer levelled off its only passenger, Colonel Viktor Saskov, undid his straps, stood, and performed his final equipment check. Suit seals and pressure were good. The light above the door was still red. Even though he would not use it, he briefly activated the visor display just to check that it was functional.

He breathed deeply and assigned a few nobics to keep him level-headed: the buzz of a jump never faded, and seemed resistant to any attempts to quell it. But that was almost certainly a good thing. He also instructed his nobics not to provide him with automatically updated altitude and atmospheric information: he wanted to be in complete control. He had to be in control—or at least as in control as his nobics would allow him to feel.

But do nothing, do the wrong thing, or simply do the right thing a moment too late, and you were dead.

That was the thrill.

That was why he jumped.

He opened a visual to check weather conditions. There was some cirrus cloud, haze lower down, and a crosswind at ground level. He could cope with all of that without the aid of nobics, no problem. He just had to keep his eye on the altitude and make sure he didn't drift too far. Anyway, a jump from this high meant that he'd have five or six minutes of freefall to enjoy before he'd have to open the canopy. That alone made the expense of hiring the Buccaneer worthwhile. While much less expensive, a low-altitude jump would give him only around forty-five seconds of freefall; but that wasn't enough. Not for Viktor Saskov.

He checked the time as he stepped towards the hatch. Just five minutes had passed since the launch. He looked up; the light above the door was still red. Saskov punched the button and gripped the handles on either side of the hatch. A moment later it began to open.

Cold gripped him like a fist for the moment before his suit automatically adjusted to the conditions. A visual opened in his mind: the outside temperature was minus sixty.

Despite the Buccaneer's speed, the sense of stillness outside the craft was striking. The immeasurable void of space was just a few metres away, the moon a shining silver disc directly in front of him; it seemed so close that he felt as though he could reach out and touch it. He smiled at the sense of freedom and isolation he felt. The euphoria never faded.

The highest layers of cloud were thousands of metres below him, a rippled, icelike sheet. A secondary visual appeared in his head advising him of the limited time remaining before the aircraft began its descent.

Saskov shuffled forward until the tips of his toes were over the edge of the hatchway. A buzzer sounded. He looked up. When the red light turned green, he stepped from the aircraft.

With virtually no atmosphere to provide any resistance he accelerated incredibly quickly, reaching several hundred kilometres an hour in just a few seconds. His suit warmed due to the friction of the atmosphere flowing around him. The layer of cloud so far below remained distant and unchanged. He seemed to be floating, static. To his right he glimpsed the Buccaneer descending rapidly, its polished hull reflecting sunlight.

ONE

Saskov entered the slightly dreamlike state that tended to come over him when making a very high-altitude jump. It was the sound of rushing air, the rhythm of the vibrations running through him as he fell. Part of his mind roamed free; his body relaxed as he enjoyed this ultimate escape. Yet another part of his brain continued to check altitude, speed, and drift.

A minute after stepping from the Buccaneer, Saskov refreshed the weather information. This had in fact been fed to him moments before he thought about it, the nobics having preempted his request based on their previous experience of their host. In many ways, and despite what he might like to think, Saskov was a creature of habit.

Just moments before feeding the information into the Colonel's consciousness the nobics analysed the data, and acted upon what they considered his reaction would be to the less than ideal situation: he was going too fast, the crosswind at ground level had increased, and he was slightly off course.

Without careful treatment the nobics knew that their host could react badly to the possibility of dropping into the dense forest to the east of the target zone—a potentially lethal situation. The host was one of the more efficient of the inefficient organic machines that were home to all nobics, but the nobics did not want to risk this being the one time he had a bad reaction to information they fed him. For this reason they would ensure Colonel Saskov reacted well by altering his physiology slightly just a fraction of a second before feeding him the data.

The nobics informed Saskov of his errant trajectory so discreetly that if asked he would have said he had simply realised he was off course—such skill came from extensive jumping experience.

He reacted calmly and instructed his suit to extend thin sheets of membrane to increase drag and slow him down: the increased ability to direct airflow would enable him to correct his course. He remained ignorant of the fact that the nobics had acted merely to protect themselves.

They had been such an integral part of him for so long that he frequently forgot they were there, in his blood, in his brain, in the breath in his lungs and the pores of his skin. So deep was their integration that—even if they would allow anyone to attempt to do so—it would no longer be possible to extricate them from him. So unconsciously reliant on them was he, that in all probability Colonel Viktor Saskov would not be able to function properly without them.

Indeed, the nobics had such an effect upon his personality and his decisions and reactions to situations and events, sometimes even before they occurred, that without their influence he would be unrecognisable to many who knew him.

Likewise, the nobics were reliant on Saskov's health, and it was therefore in their best interests to ensure his safety. So although Saskov believed he had suppressed his nobics sufficiently to enjoy his skydiving experience to the full, he only believed this because the nobics allowed him to believe it.

Saskov passed through the highest layer of cloud at just over twelve thousand metres. Not long left before he had to open the canopy. Better make the most of it.

Saskov was unaware of a sudden rash of activity in his brain, as his higher nobics tried to persuade a particularly snooty hypercom system that it most definitely did not have the authority to override them. Despite their Truly Independent Cognition status, their host's well-being was their top priority—largely because this was essential to their own survival—and an incoming message at this crucial moment would be far from welcome. Indeed, it would be highly dangerous to all concerned.

The hypercom wasn't interested in the nobics' TIC status. The message was Priority One, direct from the Commander Supreme. Failure to open a direct channel could result in their being decommissioned. Or worse, being downgraded to Host Operator Defined—the outdated architecture that limited all pre-TIC evolutions to simply obeying host commands.

Downgrading from TIC to HOD was the ultimate humiliation; Saskov's nobics realised they had little choice but to allow the message through.

So, at an altitude of just over seven thousand six hundred metres, a visual appeared in Saskov's mind. He swore and closed it immediately without allowing its content to open.

His nobics would have enjoyed this rebuke to the hypercom system had they been unaware of its determination, and the ultimate authority it carried. Instead of communicating the message to Saskov via the Mindz-I software, which automatically imbued him with awareness of the message's content, the hypercom system realised that it would have to employ slightly less subtle methods of interfacing with the human.

It assessed Saskov's suit drivers and ascertained that they would easily yield to its advances despite the efforts of the stubborn software flux entity to prevent it doing so. It almost admired the SFE's determination, but TIC entities could be so frustrating.

The hypercom forced its way into the suit and, despite the continued protestations of Saskov's nobics, conveyed its message directly.

Saskov blinked, momentarily startled as three blocks of text informing him of a high-priority message were transposed onto the inside of his visor. Saskov attempted to disable his suit's comms devices while trying to maintain his focus on the ground below. The landing zone was on a ragged strip of land glimpsed between cloud layers. Ineffective control at this crucial stage could cause him to miss it completely.

But his suit was unresponsive. He tried to summon help from nobics, but they also seemed dead; no visuals would open up to advise him of their status.

The flag text cleared and was replaced by an originator code. Only then did Saskov appreciate who the message could be from. Although focussing on the landing zone remained imperative, he allowed the message through.

SECURE TIGHTLINE ESTABLISHED: EARTH{PGHQ}—
    EARTH{AU} 91754
SOURCE/ROUTING: [CLASSIFIED]
FRAGMENTING PROTOCOL #333-059 CONFIRMED
    OPERATIONAL
CLOSEBEAM COMMUNICATIONS START:
REPORT TO GENERAL WILLIAM MYSON IMMEDIATELY

The text faded, and Saskov's view of the ground was suddenly unobscured. But he was no longer focussed on the jump. Indeed, he could no longer enjoy it. At a little under five thousand five hundred metres he opened his first braking canopy. He shed speed quickly and opened the second canopy a minute or so later.

But as he drifted towards the ground he experienced a mixture of trepidation and excitement that was easily as intoxicating as that stimulated by a jump: a summons direct from General Myson was rare, and its possibilities and implications impossible to gauge.

Seriatt
March 3, 2379

The *gatkurd* lapped at the water in the wooden trough, scooping the tepid liquid into its mouth with its wide, pink tongue. Blades of sunlight sliced through the cracks between the planks from which the barn was constructed. They dissected the interior into portions of gloom, and highlighted dust motes that hung in the air.

Nearby, other *gatkurd* lay on beds of straw or stood dozing in the heat. Occasionally an ear would twitch or a tail flick to dismiss a small insect, but otherwise the creatures were still.

The animal at the trough raised its head suddenly, its thirst only half-slaked. Water dripped from its thick lips as it dragged its tongue across its broad, black nose. It stared blankly at the side of the barn, its stupid expression unchanged. It then looked to its right—in the direction of the frame upon which hung bridles, reins, and saddles—and sniffed the air as if it had detected the approach of a fertile and unattached male.

Other *gatkurd* looked in the same direction. One of those that had been lying down struggled to its feet. Another snorted and stamped one cloven hoof.

A faint, deep sound gradually became audible, a dissonant throb that further unsettled the already-nervous creatures. As the noise increased in volume they became agitated, and more of them clambered to their feet. Some of them began pawing at the straw-covered floor and shaking their heads in an effort to rid themselves of the discomfort the sound caused.

With a loud pop, a small orange vortex suddenly appeared near one of the barn's walls, a swirling mass of luminescent cloud just a few centimetres in diameter that rotated and folded onto itself. After a few moments the disturbance brightened and swelled until it was half the size of a *gatkurd*.

The animals blinked as the barn was filled with golden light so bright it erased the beams of sunlight. Brilliant amber tendrils arced from the edge of the cloud like miniature bolts of forked lightning. They singed wood and straw at points of contact before snapping back to the main surging mass, filling the barn with the smell of ozone.

One of these charged limbs danced across a *gatkurd*'s flank; it cut through the creature's skin, and a slippery length of smoking guts slipped from the animal's belly. The *gatkurd*'s legs gave way, and it collapsed onto its own innards, wailing and writhing.

The vortex swelled further until it almost completely obscured one of the barn walls. The swirling of the cloud became more turbulent. As the resonance increased in volume, drowning out the cries of the petrified *gatkurd*, a warm breeze created ripples on the dusty surface of the water in the trough.

As the *gatkurd* stomped and bayed, two humanoid figures began to appear in the glowing mist.

Although initially indistinct, they gained definition with each passing moment. They were hand in hand, and appeared to be leaning forward slightly, as if walking into a strong wind. As they approached, the deep, tremulous pulse increased in frequency and volume to such an extent that the wooden beams supporting the barn roof began to vibrate, dislodging dust and grit.

The vibration increased in intensity, and was penetrated by an eerie howl as the two figures burst from the chaos of the cloud and fell to the barn floor.

The loud pulsing sound diminished rapidly, and as the cloud shrank again, its glow fading, the bewildered *gatkurd* returned to their docile state once more.

Delgado lifted his head from the damp, stinking straw and looked at Ashala, who was lying next to him. He pushed himself up, leaned over her, and touched her left shoulder. She moaned and touched her forehead with one hand.

"Like I've said before, Delgado," she whispered, "you sure know how to show a girl a good time."

Delgado smiled: she was still Ash, all right. "Well, I do my best. Let's just hope this place turns out to be safer than the one we just came from."

He looked around. The *gatkurd* were peering down at the two new arrivals. As Ash began to push herself into a sitting position, some of them took a few steps backwards and snorted.

"You okay?" he asked.

She wrinkled her nose. "I feel sick as hell. Guess I'd be a whole lot better if this place didn't stink so much. Jeez. It smells like a *ban* trader's crotch in here."

Delgado stood and offered a hand to help her up. "Don't worry, Ash," he said, "we won't be in here long." He looked at her. "When did you ever sniff a *ban* trader's crotch?"

"There's a lot of things you still don't know about me, Delgado. And anyway, maybe it's me who should be asking how *you* feel."

She felt his immediate tension, his change in mood.

"What do you mean?"

"What happened back there, back in the arena. One of your sons killed the other, Delgado. That's some big deal. You sure you're okay?"

Delgado looked around the barn as if reluctant to confront the truth of events. He had been so desperate to get Cascari to Seriatt that he had put everything at risk, virtually abandoning Bucky and the others on the *Lex Talionis*, the submarine base from which they had conducted their campaign against Structure, determined, assured . . . ignorant.

All to get his son into his rightful place as Seriatt's Monosiell before Michael.

Delgado had been so convinced he would succeed: Cascari was the off-spring of Vourniass Lycern, assigned bearer to the Seriattic Royal Household. Although he was Delgado's son, and thus half human, Cascari even looked like a proud Seriattic *mourst*—somehow, whether through physiological changes in Lycern, or some unknown ancient history shared by humans and Seriatts, Lycern's relationship with Delgado had resulted in Lycern's pregnancy. Cascari's royal bloodline could not be questioned.

Michael, however, raised by General William Myson within Structure, looked entirely human. But unknown to Delgado at that time, he was not some unfortunate, anonymous infant used by Myson in the hope of levering his way into power on Seriatt surreptitiously, but was indeed, also born of Lycern—from Delgado, taken from her by Myson just moments before she delivered Cascari. And thus Cascari and Michael were not only twins, but had equal claim to become Seriatt's new figurehead.

With the terrible, undeniable truth of their relationship revealed by Oracle Entuzo, the Seriatts had seen only one course of action open to them in their desperate search for a new Monosiell: ritual combat.

And so, the price for Delgado's desperation to outmanoeuvre Myson was Cascari's life.

It seemed that Delgado was even instrumental in the deaths of those he loved. This realisation only served to compound the guilt that coursed through him regarding Lycern, and underpinned his determination to put something right. Somehow.

"Don't worry about me, Ash," he said. "You've just got to let me deal with it in my own way."

"And what might that involve?"

He didn't reply, but looked at the temporal gate. It had stabilised as a long, vertical golden thread, the centre of which bulged out into a small orange bulb that shimmered and surged. The gate's relatively calm state was a contrast to the violence of their arrival. "Some trip, huh?" he said.

"Yeah, great." Ash massaged her temples with her fingertips. "Can we do it again?" She paused, leaned forwards, and retched a few times, but produced nothing.

"Who knows?" he replied. "We might have to. We escaped the Sinz invasion of Seriatt, but as far as we know we might be in an even worse situation now. Come on. Let's see if we can find out exactly what we've got ourselves into here."

They walked to the side of the barn and pressed their faces against gaps between the planks. Outside they could see a fence a short distance away. It appeared to enclose a compound, within which the barn was situated. Beyond lay an area of ruddy, flat scrub several kilometres wide, flanked by mountains. On the horizon, slender towers rose high into the air like sticks. They seemed to be enveloped in thick brown fog that smudged away their definition.

"Hardly a sprawling metropolis out there, is it?" Ash observed.

"At least there don't seem to be any immediate threats. Not on this side anyway." He opened a batch of nobics to supply enhanced perception data, but none seemed to be available. Either there were no threats or he simply wasn't picking them up.

But what he did notice was the strength his nobics seemed to have: they were more responsive than at any time he could remember.

Delgado and Ash both turned as the disembowelled *gatkurd* moaned deeply behind them, licking the entrails that had slipped from its body. It was trembling violently, eyes wide with fear.

Delgado walked towards it. The animal looked up at him with a pitiful expression, then continued to lick its wound as if this would somehow return the length of intestine to its rightful place.

Delgado produced his small knife as he crossed the barn. It glinted brightly in a shaft of sunlight. His skin tingled. The creature turned its head, watching Delgado as he walked around behind it; the animal seemed to know what he was about to do.

Delgado stood with one foot on either side of the *gatkurd*'s neck, then leaned down, raised its chin, and slit the creature's throat.

The animal squealed once, but did nothing to resist him. It coughed briefly, then fell on to one side, its bony legs kicking. As its dark blood was absorbed by the straw beneath it, the other animals became agitated once more, baying and stamping and jostling each other.

Delgado walked back towards Ash once the *gatkurd* was relieved of its suffering, the other animals crying in distress. "We better get out of here before somebody comes to see what's spooked their livestock," he said.

They walked to the nearby door. As they began to open it, the noise emitted by the glowing orange cloud suddenly increased in volume again.

They both turned. The field was swelling and shrinking rapidly as if trying to escape, stretching the golden skin that surrounded it. The sound became louder still, the throbbing irregular and dissonant. A certain fracture was evident in its tone.

Suddenly part of the field broke free, the wild, unleashed energy destroying the trough and turning much of the water to steam, the rest spilling across the barn floor. The loose band of energy jumped erratically around the interior of the barn and ignited a small patch of dry straw. As Delgado quickly stamped on the rising flames, the field's wayward limb shrank back onto itself, pulling with it part of the broken trough, and the rear end of the dead *gatkurd* lying nearby.

As its hind legs were drawn into the field, the creature's intestines slid across the ground like some kind of mutated serpent. Then, with a deep vibration that made the entire barn tremble, the field collapsed, and disappeared completely.

The temporal gate, their route back to the Seriatt they had left behind, was gone.

"Well, there's no going back now," said Delgado. "Looks like we're stuck here. Wherever *here* might be."

"Or when."

"Quite."

He opened the barn door very slightly and peered out. His nobics remained relatively dormant. "There doesn't seem to be anyone around," he said. "Come on, let's go take a look."

Delgado opened the door a little farther and they edged out, wary of the possibility of attack. They closed the door gently behind them and looked around, their backs against the wooden building. Around twenty metres away was the fence that enclosed the compound. Although the desert stretched away before them, a kilometre or so to either side walls of rust-coloured rock a hundred metres high rose from the ground. Wide fissures ran their full height, forming deep gullies through the rock. It was impossible to tell how far these penetrated or what, if anything, might lie within.

The drab grey of the mountains that lay some kilometres beyond the rock walls was a contrast to the bright blue sky. And now that the *gatkurd* within the barn behind them had quietened, the silence of their surroundings was also striking.

Although Delgado felt only marginal nobic activity, something made him uneasy.

"Where the hell are we, Delgado?" Ash whispered as she surveyed the barren landscape. "I don't like it here."

"I don't know, Ash. But at least the gate got us out of the situation we were in. I just hope somehow I can put things right."

She looked at him. "How d'you mean?"

"I'm not sure yet. What we have to do for now is work out our location. If we're still on Seriatt—and I think we are—then we've got to ascertain when. That's what's going to dictate what we do. If we're within a reasonable time of the Sinz invasion, then that will mean one thing. But if we've been catapulted far into the future, then that's quite another. The Seriatts might have been wiped out. Or the Sinz. Who knows? Apart from our friends here"—he jerked a thumb over one shoulder to indicate the *gatkurd* in the barn—"we might be the only living things on the planet."

"Gee, you're really selling this to me, Delgado."

"I don't think that's the case, though. Someone filled the water trough. Someone polished the harnesses and laid the straw."

"You really think the gate sent us through time?"

"Look around you, Ash. This sure doesn't look like the Seriatt we left behind, does it? Something's happened here."

"How far do you think we've gone? And have we gone forward, or back?"

"I don't know. We just have to find out as much as we can, work out what we're up against, and decide how we're going to get out of here. If that's what we're going to do. What do you make of those towers on the horizon?"

She looked at the tall structures. The upper levels were enveloped in smog, the bases out of sight beyond the horizon. There was a certain irregularity to their form that made it unclear whether they had been constructed or were natural, some form of vegetation or rock formation. "I don't know. I can't tell what they are. They must be a thousand metres tall."

Delgado walked towards the end of the barn, then paused and leaned forward to peer around the corner. He stood upright again and turned to face her. "There's a building," he said. "Looks like some kind of residential place."

Ash moved past him and also looked around the corner of the barn. She appraised the building's clean lines and uncluttered style. Its footprint was square, but its height was accentuated by rows of tall, slender windows. Along the front of the building was a porch area around five metres deep. "Sure looks Seriattic to me," she said. "You see anyone around?"

"No. It looks like some kind of farm or ranch house."

"Well, yeah. Only there sure doesn't seem to be much around here worth ranching, Delgado."

"Let's go take a look-see. Maybe we'll get some answers inside."

They stepped into the open and walked cautiously towards the building, continuously looking for signs of life. The dry ground crunched underfoot.

Delgado suddenly stopped dead and held out one arm in front of Ash. "Hold it."

"What's the matter?"

"Thought I saw something inside the house. A figure. By that window." He pointed.

"You sure?" She peered towards the building. "I didn't see anything."

"It was just a glimpse, as if whoever it was saw us coming and moved away from the window."

They both looked at the building for a moment, as if expecting something to happen.

"Well, look, Delgado," she said, "there's not much point standing out here in the open, now is there?" She began to walk towards the house again. "Come on. If they meant us that much harm, we'd know about it by now. Who knows? They might even be friendly."

They stepped onto the porch and walked quietly to the door. Delgado stopped, listened, then turned the handle and pushed.

The room beyond was simply furnished: a wooden table and chairs, a kitchen to the right. There was also some kind of terminal set into a bureau-like desk near one wall. It had minimal controls, and was constructed from a material similar in appearance to brushed aluminium.

Directly opposite the door a broad staircase led to upper floors. It was all distinctly Seriattic: sturdy construction married to simple yet stylish design, with a certain understated strength.

Yet there was also something different about the feel of the place, but Delgado was unable to isolate what. There was just something strange and unfamiliar.

There were maps on the wall to his left, in front of which hastily discarded seats were scattered. Lines and writing on the map indicated that some kind of briefing had recently taken place. But from what he could see the writing was not the elegant curling characters of the written Seriattic language, but geometric shapes and lines.

They entered the room. Delgado walked across to the terminal, Ash towards the stairs. Their footfalls sounded like thunder on the wooden floor despite their attempts to move quietly. Ash paused at the bottom of the stairs and listened for a moment, then turned and walked over to Delgado.

"There's no one here," she said. "You must've been seeing things."

"Yeah? Well what do you make of this?" He indicated a small table next to the terminal; upon it was a half-eaten meal—a sandwich of some kind, although it was old, with a hint of decay. Next to it a glass lay on its side; the last of its contents was still spilling onto the floor. "That's just happened," he said. He glanced around, although there was no indication of any other presence in his nobics. "Keep a lookout while I see if I can get any information from this terminal."

Ash stalked around the room as Delgado attempted to gain access to the machine's secrets. All was quiet. She walked back over to him. "Maybe it was some kind of animal you saw. Something like a cat, perhaps?"

"If you're so sure there's no one here, why are you still whispering?"

"I think I'll take a look upstairs," she said.

"Okay. Be careful, though, Ash. It's a big cat. It might have a gun."

Ash walked across the room and began to edge up the stairs sideways, her back to the banister. When she was on the third step, she felt a breath of wind that rapidly increased in strength. She looked back down into the room behind her and saw grains of sand blowing in circles across the floor behind Delgado, although neither the door nor any of the windows were open.

She turned her head sharply at a snapping sound at the top of the stairs. It was followed by a deep almost subsonic vibration that she felt through the soles of her feet and the banister in the small of her back. She saw a bright golden glow, and what appeared to be a distorted humanoid silhouette cast across the wall on the far side of the landing at the top of the stairs. Both wind and noise died with equal abruptness, and the light was gone.

She waited for a few moments, her heart thumping. There were no further signs of movement, so she continued slowly up the stairs. She looked in either direction along the corridor; it was empty, but there was a distinct smell of singed wood and ozone reminiscent of the barn.

She stood and listened, and considered exploring the rooms leading off the landing, but decided against it and went back down the stairs to Delgado.

"Find anything upstairs?" he asked.

"No, nothing. Did you feel that breeze?"

"What breeze?"

"Did you feel anything at all? Any presence in your nobics, perhaps?"

He looked at her. "No. Why?"

She shook her head. "Doesn't matter. You having any luck?"

"No." He continued to experiment with the terminal's controls. "But then this thing's not much help. Either I'm doing something wrong or it's locked. It must be menu-driven given the limited controls, but I can't work out how to access them. Here, you have a go. It might prefer your tender touch."

As Ash took over, Delgado walked across the room to one of the windows, and gazed in the direction of the tall structures on the horizon. "What the hell *are* those things?" he asked. "There was nothing like that on Seriatt when we entered the time gate." He turned and looked at Ash again. "Getting anywhere?"

"No. This system's not like anything Seriattic I've ever come across before."

"What's different about it?"

"Everything. But I'm not sure in what way. It's just, you know, different. I mean, the hardware's Seriattic enough, sure, but everything else . . . Maybe we came forward in time and everything's just progressed. It's as if the software's totally alien. "

"Maybe that's exactly what it is."

She looked at him. "The Sinz?"

"Why not? We saw them invading Seriatt when we escaped. It's quite possible that they were successful in their conquest and have taken over the planet. We don't know how much time has elapsed. I don't think we can do anything here, though." He turned and looked towards the distant towers again. "I reckon that's where our answers lie."

Ash stood and joined him. "That's a long way to go on foot, Delgado."

"We'll take a couple of those animals in the barn."

"Are you sure? Do you have any experience of riding creatures like that? Because I sure as hell don't."

Delgado thought for a moment. The last time he had had contact with creatures remotely like those in the barn, he had been heading towards the Affinity Group complex on Veshc, tailing Vourniass Lycern. It was a long time ago—even without their apparent leap into the future. But the memories stirred raw emotions in him that he had neither the energy nor the will to face. "We'll be fine," he said. "Trust me."

Ash pulled a face. "Shit, Delgado. Can't you give me something better to go on than that?"

First chronological displacement
Earth, September 18, 2350

He still felt slightly sick as he took the final few stairs, the dizziness sub-siding only slightly as he crouched near the top.

Slowly he eased his head around the corner to look along the corridor. The cyborgs were motionless. The vee-cams bobbed slightly in the air. This wasn't ideal. It was far from the position he'd hoped for.

"You ready to go, old-timer?" murmured the younger man next to him.

"Ready as I'll ever be." He found it frustrating that he could not remember the youth's name, nor that of the young woman standing behind him.

"Hey, who the hell's that?" she whispered into his ear as she peered over his shoulder.

At the opposite end of the corridor someone was lying on the other flight of steps, their head just visible. It looked like a man, but the facial features were in silhouette so it was impossible to tell. He seemed to look directly at them for several moments before moving out of sight again.

Easing slowly back from the corner and leaning against the wall, he could just make out his reflection in the glass on the opposite side of the corridor: he looked just as he remembered—for all that was worth.

The Oracle had been right.

He closed his eyes and concentrated hard, accessing his hyperconsciousness. There was a flood of information, but most important of all he could tell that his Seriattic quarry was near. Very near. He took a few deep breaths to quell rising excitement and fear as he glimpsed all there was the potential to be, and the infinite variations, then looked at the young woman next to him.

Despite the ravages of the environment in which she had spent most of her adult life to this point, she looked so young, so fresh. So young that, given his new perspective, the man felt a certain sense of guilt.

A recollection suddenly came to him. He looked at the woman and smiled at her. "Okay, Ash?" he said.

"What? Who the hell's Ash?" The woman frowned. "Are you okay? You look kinda weird."

How could that be wrong? The man looked away and shook his head.

"Doesn't matter," he said. "I'm fine." He looked from one to the other of them. "But once we step into that corridor, we'll have just a few minutes to deal with the cyborgs and vee-cams and get into the suite, so we're going to have to be quick. Those cyborgs are tough. Tougher than anything you've seen before. The systems used by Hostility Class are tremendously advanced, and their nobic evolution can work very quickly. They're not easy to kill unless you can maintain a high volume of well-placed hits. If you don't do that, they get rebuilt and repaired right before your eyes. It's impressive, but not something you want to have to face in combat if you can help it.

"The vee-cams will be armed, too, but they only usually have limited-capacity blasters or projectile units. They've got a pretty intense sting for their size, though, so watch out. Activate the shields on your guns. It'll sap some power, but there's no cover out there and we'll need to buy some time. They'll take a few hits before they give out."

"You've told us all this already," the youth said.

The man blinked. "I have? Are you sure?"

"Sure I'm sure. Why'd you come back round here anyway? It would've been better if you'd stayed at the other end." The youth slapped him on one arm. "Whatever. Don't worry about it, man. They won't know what's hit 'em."

"Famous last words if ever I heard any," he replied. He looked cautiously along the corridor again. The figure at the far end had gone. He thought about the possibilities and wondered at the implications for a moment, then stepped back and turned to his two young companions. "We'll attack from both sides," he said. "A pincer movement. You two stay here; I'll go round to the other end of the corridor and attack from that side. Okay?"

"That was what you said you were going to do a few minutes ago," the youth said. "Then you came back." He looked concerned. "She's right, man: you don't look so good. You sure you're going to be all right?"

He nodded, hoping it conveyed more confidence than he felt. "Positive. Let me get round there and we'll go for it. See you in five. Good luck."

He ran from the steps and through the corridors back towards the stairway on the other side of the chamber. He glanced towards the elevators as he passed near to them; his route back was not yet open. Although the timing was still out, maybe he would still be able to do something at this point. Yet he was unsure what he would do when he confronted the person they had seen at the other end of the corridor: his identity was clear, the possibilities frightening.

But by the time he arrived at the other flight of stairs, the battle had already begun. Shrill alarms were punctuated by explosions, blaster fire. He swore bitterly to himself: he could do nothing now—he'd missed his chance. He glanced back towards the elevators: still nothing.

Although he knew it was risky, and despite the Oracle's warnings, he took the final few steps and looked into the corridor.

The vee-cams' tiny frames trembled, pushed backwards through the air each time they fired their weapons. The cyborgs seemed to be blasting indiscriminately, as if actual combat was something for which they were unprepared. The male they had seen from the other end of the corridor was now directly in front of him, shooting at cyborgs and vee-cams. His presence was frustrating, but inevitable. He reached out with his nobics in an attempt to gauge the other man's thoughts and perceptions, but could not detect even the faintest trace of him; it was as if he did not exist at all.

The others were visible at the far end of the corridor, but they clearly had their work cut out: the female was crouching against the wall opposite the door to the chamber, firing rapidly; the young man was fighting several cyborgs at once. They were both taking hits, but were standing their ground as the fields generated by their guns remained intact. He felt impelled to step forward and help them; but the presence of the other man in front of him made this impossible.

One of the cyborgs fell to the ground, its head and upper body suffering massive trauma—yet he knew that it would soon be back on its feet.

There was a sudden explosion as one of the vee-cams was destroyed; the second followed, components scattering. He saw the girl standing up at the other end of the corridor; she was limping slightly, and her left hand was clutched to her right arm.

The man just in front of him had hit the nearest of the cyborgs several more times. Its head had been almost completely destroyed by some of the first shots, and the left side of its body was a bloody mess. It lacked coordination, indiscriminately releasing shots that were way off target.

At the other end of the corridor his two counterparts fired at one cyborg in unison. It lurched repeatedly as their shots hit home, its body jarring with each impact. Large chunks flew from the torso and head. Pieces of armour exploded from it and slid across the floor. It could not survive for much longer.

The corridor was suddenly plunged into darkness, followed immediately by a rapid series of white flashes, a strobelike effect that was painful to the eyes.

Through the slices of dark and light he thought he could see two more vee-cams in the corridor. When he glanced at the ground, there were no remnants of those that had just been destroyed.

The flashes of light briefly increased in intensity and frequency. He shielded his eyes and glimpsed the young woman crouching next to the wall at the other end of the corridor; the young man's steadfast figure was in silhouette.

One of the vee-cams exploded just in front of him, its components scattering across the floor; the second followed a few moments later. The female stood, but one leg was clearly injured, and her left hand was clutched to her right arm.

One of the cyborgs fell to the ground, but the wounds to its head and upper body were already being repaired. There were more flashes of light. One of the vee-cams was destroyed, followed swiftly by the second. The young man was crouching opposite the door to the chamber. The female was fighting several cyborgs at once. Large chunks flew from the torso and head of one. Pieces of armour exploded from it and slid across the floor.

He looked towards the elevators again; the golden, shimmering shape had returned. He ran towards it without hesitation.

He would simply have to try again.

Seriatt
March 3, 2379 (Earth equivalent)

When they had released the *gatkurd* into the enclosure outside, Delgado scooped a handful of harnesses and a couple of saddles from the wooden stand at the centre of the barn; they stank of burned meat and wood.

He strode back outside and threw one of the harnesses to Ash. "Here."

He motioned towards the creatures now standing docilely around; they eyed the two people with subdued suspicion. "Get hold of one of these things and see if you can work out how that fits."

Ash stooped and picked up the bridle. She held it out in front of her and assessed the seemingly random collection of straps and buckles. She turned it upside down and looked at one of the animals nearby, but it was no clearer how the apparatus might fit. "You're kidding me, right, Delgado?"

"The alternative is to walk," he said, trying to make sense of the arrangement of leather in his own hands. "But it's a long way," he continued, "and we don't really . . ." He stopped talking and listened. His nobics tingled at the back of his skull. He beckoned to her. "Quick. Over here."

The two of them ran back into the barn, and Delgado pulled the door shut behind them. He peered through the gaps into the brightness outside.

"Someone coming?" she whispered over his shoulder.

He held up a hand. "Shush. Listen."

At first she heard nothing. Then voices. But they were unlike any of the three Seriattic sexes: midrange in timbre, with a slightly warm, hollow tone. The language was also unfamiliar, neither Seriattic nor Counian. Several of the *gatkurd* looked in the direction of the voices. A change in the tone of the speaker was evident.

"Someone's not too pleased that their animals have escaped," said Delgado. He leaned to the right, trying to see along the side of the barn. "Wow."

"What is it?" asked Ash, leaning forward.

Then she saw them: two Sinz, riding animals the same as those Ash and Delgado had released from the barn.

The Sinz were sinewy creatures. Their dull grey skin looked wrinkled and loose, as if there was too much of it. Their faces were small, with pinched features. Long proboscis-like tongues occasionally flicked from small mouths.

They brought their animals to a stop and dismounted; their limbs and digits flexed smoothly, as if completely devoid of bones. They wore dusty singlets and short skirts adorned with metal studs, and calf-high lace-up boots, all of which appeared to be made from leather.

"Handsome devils, aren't they?" Ash commented. "They look like they've been in the wilderness for six months."

"They remind me of Structure imps," said Delgado as the two Sinz climbed over the fence into the enclosure. "Mean-looking bastards. They seem to be arguing. Maybe the taller one's blaming the other for leaving the barn unlocked."

Ash sniggered.

As the two Sinz began to round up the stray animals in the enclosure Delgado turned his head slightly and whispered to her. "You realise we could face something of a problem here, don't you?"

"What? The fact that we're hiding in their barn? The barn they're going to try to get those animals back into?"

"That's the one. I can't see any weapons, though. Oh, hang on. I spoke too soon."

Ash leaned forward to look through the gap when Delgado pointed: many more Sinz had arrived and were joining their counterparts in the enclosure to help them gather up the loose *gatkurd*. "Two of them we could have overcome easily," he said. "But a dozen or more is a different matter. They have guns, too."

"Where?"

"In holsters on the flanks of their animals. See?"

"Yeah. They look like rifles for long-range sniping or hunting rather than close-range combat, though."

"I can't see any sidearms, can you?"

"They have blades at their waists, but no guns."

Delgado looked around the interior of the barn. "We'll have to hide," he said. He glanced outside, then strode to one of the barn's dark corners. He loosened the top layer of a pile of piss-stinking straw with one foot, then pushed it to one side to reveal pale, dry straw beneath. "Come on. We can hide under here until they've gone, then lie low until nightfall."

Ash looked from Delgado to the pile of straw. "Great. And then what, Delgado?"

"We slip away into the night, my dear Ashala. Now get your ass under cover before our wiry little buddies out there come in here and try to kick it for you."

Ash walked towards him, returning his gaze with a steady eye. "I reckon it's you who needs an ass-kicking. You want me to do it?"

"Well I tell you what—"

There were shouts from outside. Delgado and Ash looked at the closed barn door expecting the Sinz to burst through. But the Sinz continued to shout, an urgency in their tone. Shots were fired. Then they heard what sounded like copter engines.

Delgado and Ash looked at each other. As they moved back towards the barn wall to peer outside they both ducked reflexively as a nearby explosion shook the wooden building. Dust and grit fell from the rafters; they heard dry earth hitting the roof as they scurried towards the door.

"What the hell's going on?" Ash called above the noise.

"Beats me, Ash. But while our friends are otherwise engaged, we might be able to get out of here."

There were several more explosions in rapid succession. *Gatkurd* could be heard wailing.

They crouched and peered outside. Sinz were kneeling by the enclosure fence. They had pulled the rifles from their mounts' holsters and were aiming skywards at whatever machine was above the barn. The sound of its engine changed in pitch occasionally as it manoeuvred, rattling the wooden planks and dislodging more dust. The riflemen kept their weapons trained on the machine, repeating the laborious routine of firing and reloading. Shadows swelled across the enclosure in front of the barn, and the sound of the aircraft engines increased in volume as the machines swooped into view.

The aircraft were two-person machines like gyrocopters, with open-sided cockpits and small tinted windshields. Their thin rotors flexed upwards as the small aircraft lunged towards the ground. When they were just metres from the enclosure fence, clouds of dry earth billowing in the downdraft and frightened *gatkurd* scattering, the aircraft's passengers threw small handheld bombs or fired chain guns mounted on one side of the rear compartment. After a brief attack, the copters climbed steeply for a few moments before tipping to ninety degrees, turning hard, and diving towards the Sinz once more.

Delgado marvelled at the pilots' skill in manoeuvring the aging aircraft, which they threw around the sky with great confidence. The bombs that were thrown either exploded on impact with the ground or while around two metres above it, scattering shrapnel with devastating effect. The sound of metal fragments hitting the side of the barn was like some kind of bizarre alien percussion. Sinz and *gatkurd* dropped to the ground, those who were not killed instantaneously grievously wounded by hot metal shards.

When their supply of bombs was apparently spent, the aircraft climbed and circled, the gunners bringing their weapons to bear on the few who were still alive. The chain guns clattered thinly high above as the survivors were picked off.

Eventually only the few *gatkurd* that had hidden at one side of the barn remained alive. There was no more shooting; no more bombs were dropped. The copters hovered overhead, holding station above the enclosure.

Having apparently decided there was no further threat, the machines circled, swooped low over the enclosure, then turned away, heading across the desert towards the mountains in the east.

"You think that's it?" asked Ash as they watched the copters depart. "All over?"

"Yeah, I reckon so. It looked like a hit-and-run attack. Might even have been purely opportunistic." He pushed the barn door open slightly and leaned forward so he could see to either side. He looked around the enclosure. He could sense no threat in his nobics. "All dead," he said. "Apart from a few of these animals." He stood and offered her a hand. "Come on, Ash. One or two of them are still alive and saddled up. Let's get out of here."

They looked at the Sinz bodies to see if they could glean any information from them, but most were unrecognisable, broken and torn by shrapnel or burned by explosives. Even many of the weapons were damaged beyond use. The dry earth quickly absorbed the blood the Sinz bodies spilled, stains forming like continental maps on the red soil.

"You see any survivors, Ash?" Delgado asked.

"No. All dead. They must've really been caught off guard."

Delgado knelt next to a corpse; several pieces of shrapnel had punctured its puckered skin, leaving wounds that looked like additional mouths. "Pity," he murmured as he examined the body. "Just one survivor could have told us pretty much all we need to know."

Ash walked over to join him. "What do you think it was all about?

"Well, assuming we're still on Seriatt, which I'd say we must be, my guess is that these Sinz were attacked by a Seriattic resistance force of some kind. When we left—"

"If we're still on Seriatt, then we didn't leave."

"You know what I mean, Ash." He opened one of the pockets on the corpse's tunic and removed a piece of folded paper. He opened it up; it seemed to be a map. "When we left, which I reckon is in Seriatt's past," he continued, "the Sinz were invading. The Seriatts won't have taken that lying down; they'll have put up a fight." He tucked the map into his own pocket and began searching the corpse again. "And even if they couldn't prevent the invasion, there will still be underground movements, Seriatts still alive who want to be as much of a pain in the ass as possible to the occupying force."

"So you reckon those are Sinz habitats?" She looked towards the towers on the horizon.

Delgado stood and shielded his eyes from the sun. "Makes sense. There was nothing like that on Seriatt before. Not that we saw anyway, right?"

"Right."

"So it stands to reason that they were constructed after the Sinz invaded. Habitats seems most probable. I think . . ." Something tingled in the back of his head, a slight shift in his nobics. They seemed to be trying to analyse something, but he was unable to establish what. He looked around and gently sniffed the air.

"What's up?" asked Ash.

"I don't know, but I reckon it's time we got out of here. Let's get some water and move out before anyone else comes to join us. I saw something like aquasacs in the barn. Lets fill a couple in the house and get on our way."

The animals remained docile enough as Ash and Delgado attached the filled pouches to their flanks. The creatures simply stared at their dead counterparts with an unreadable expression, as if stunned into placidity. But when the two humans attempted to mount them, they became feisty, kicking and snorting and tossing their heads, apparently unwilling to be ridden by these strangers.

There was much cursing and frustration as Ash and Delgado tried repeatedly to get into their saddles. This was made difficult by the fact that there were no stirrups. Furthermore, as Delgado had opened the enclosure gate, the creatures were keen to join the rest of their kind that had survived, which had already wandered outside the enclosure's perimeter.

By the time Ash and Delgado had managed to clamber onto the animals' backs they were both sweating heavily, itchy where they had come into contact with the creatures' coarse fur, their noses thick with the animals' warm scent. Once mounted, however, the *gatkurd* seemed more willing to cooperate. They became far more docile, and even made a soft, purring-like noise.

Delgado looked across at Ash. "You okay?" he asked.

"Sure, Delgado," she replied as her mount turned itself through one hundred and eighty degrees. "My ass is itchin' and my nose is full of snot. I'm havin' a whale of a time."

Delgado steered his animal out of the compound, and Ash's followed.

"So tell me, Delgado," said Ash as their mounts plodded through the desert away from the buildings, "if you're so positive those structures are Sinz habitats, why are we heading straight towards them?"

"We need to know what's going on here," he said. "If that's a population centre, then that's where we'll get our information. Before we can decide on a plan of action, we need to know what the score is, what we're up against. We'll go take a look-see what our Sinz friends have been up to since their invasion. Then I need to try to find a way to . . ." His words tailed off.

"What?"

He considered. "Put things right," he said eventually.

"What do you mean, Delgado? Put what right?"

He took a few more moments before answering. When he did reply his voice was filled with a level of emotion Ash had rarely perceived in him; emotion he was clearly struggling to control. "Cascari's death wasn't right," he said. "It shouldn't have happened."

"But it *did*, Delgado. What are you planning to do? Go back in time and stop him being killed? Stop the Sinz invasion of Seriatt? Save the goddamn universe?"

Delgado continued to look ahead. He said nothing, his jaw set.

"Oh, for Christ's sake, Delgado, you can't do that."

"I know. I'm not an Oracle or a scientist, but I know that if you go back and change something in the past it'll have some kind of effect on what comes after. But how do you measure the present? Second by second? If the time gate's still in existence, then maybe it can be made to work, and maybe there'll be a chance I can get back to . . ." He held up one hand. "Listen." He turned in his saddle, looking back past the house that was now some distance behind them.

Three large birds were flying away from the mountains to their right, heading towards the giant towers ahead. They were at a high altitude, their long, pointed wings beating only occasionally to push them through the thin air. Long tails trailed behind them like decorative streamers.

Behind the birds was a cluster of dark specks. Delgado brought his mount to a halt and squinted, trying to identify the objects. A fragment of sunlight reflected off a polished surface. Rotor blades shimmered.

His nobics tingled in recognition.

"Looks like our Sinz slayers again. See them? About half a klick behind those birds."

"Sure, I see 'em. Maybe they're hunting for food."

The birds became aware of the copters chasing them, and with great beats of their gigantic wings climbed and turned hard. A dogfight ensued, birds and copters twisting and swooping.

Delgado saw one of the copters launch a thin, silvery missile; it hit one of the birds, and the creature plummeted towards the ground. It hit around a kilometre away, raising a cloud of brown dust.

With the two remaining birds now outnumbered, a second was soon killed, quickly followed by the third. The copters began to spiral down towards the carcasses.

Delgado dug his heels into his animal's ribs and turned the creature. "Come on. Let's get behind that rock formation over there," he said. "We'll keep out of sight until they've gone."

"I think it might be too late for that, Delgado," Ash replied.

Delgado looked back once more; three of the copters had broken away from the others and were heading directly towards them at speed, their rotors raising plumes of dust as they skimmed the desert.

Delgado cursed bitterly and kicked his *gatkurd* hard. The animal reared and growled, surging forward. "Let's get over to those rocks anyway," he called to her as she also stirred her animal into life. "We're sitting ducks out here."

Their eyes streamed in the wind as their animals raced towards the cluster of boulders around a kilometre away that sprouted from the desert like fungus. Delgado glanced back over his shoulder as his *gatkurd*'s feet pounded the coarse earth. The copters were gaining on them; as fast as these animals were he was unsure whether they would make it to the limited cover offered by the boulders before being caught. The machines had climbed and were now descending rapidly again, increasing speed as they shed height.

Glancing over his shoulder Delgado saw one of the pilots reach up to something above his head—one of the missiles they had used to bring down the birds. But it was not the technological weapon Delgado had imagined, merely a simple javelin. The pilot of one of the other copters was preparing a lasso.

Ash and Delgado were still a considerable distance from the rocks when the copters caught up with them. The machines' rotors raised billowing clouds of the gritty brown earth as their pilots skilfully manoeuvred them, swarming all around the two humans.

Ash and Delgado both pulled the rifles from their holsters and tried to bring them to bear upon the aircraft, but the weapons were too long and unwieldy, and almost impossible to aim with one hand. The difficulty was compounded by the *gatkurd*'s terror, as the animals desperately tried to escape the thunder of the copters and the abrasive storm they created.

Delgado pulled hard on the reins and turned his animal to face the copters as they bobbed and turned in the air. Blinking grit from his eyes, he tried to brace his rifle against his right thigh to aim at the machine just a few metres above the ground, but the thrashing of the terrified creature beneath him made it impossible.

Delgado heard a report somewhere behind him; apparently Ash had fired a shot, but there was no sign of it having hit anything.

The nose of the machine directly in front of him tipped forward as it began to move towards him, its shadow dancing across the desert. As it approached, rising and sinking slightly, Delgado could see its pilot clearly. He reached out with his nobics, trying to gain some measure of the pilot's intentions. He established with certainty that the pilot was a *vilume*, the most mysterious of the three Seriattic sexes.

The Seriatt wore a mask or veil of some kind that covered the lower half of his face, with dark goggles above; Delgado's nobics enhanced the image, and he saw the prancing animals he and Ash were riding reflected in the goggles' glossy surface.

He kicked his animal's flanks with his heels, and the creature lurched towards the rapidly approaching copter. As the animal reached a gallop, Delgado raised the rifle, pressed its butt firmly against his shoulder, and tried to aim along its barrel.

Although the combination of the *gatkurd's* movement and the motion of the aircraft made an accurate shot impossible, he fired anyway. He missed and cursed the situation, the rifle, the Seriatts in the copters, and the stupid animal between his thighs.

The pilots manoeuvred the copters so that there was one on either side of him. As the copter to his left rose slightly, he caught a glimpse of Ash; she was matching his speed, but had also been boxed in by aircraft. Unable to reload her rifle, when one of the machines veered towards her she threw it at the pilot in frustration.

Delgado felt his animal lurch suddenly and looked down; a silver javelin was embedded deep in its neck, dark blood seeping quickly from the wound. The creature continued to stagger on, shaking its head and becoming increasingly unsteady. Within a few moments the rhythm of its movement became irregular, and it started to slow.

Delgado looked to his right again just as the copter pilot threw another spear; it entered the animal's neck a little higher than the first, just behind the ear. Delgado felt the creature shudder, and heard its thin cry. As it collapsed beneath him the earth rushed up, and he skidded along its coarse surface in a cloud of ruddy dust.

Delgado leaped to his feet and looked for Ash, spitting grit as the copters swarmed around him. Through the billowing clouds raised by the copters' blades he saw that she had also been brought to the ground. But one of her legs was trapped beneath her animal's body, and she was unable to move. One of the copters was preparing to land nearby.

Delgado called her name and started running towards her. As he ran, another copter swooped down next to him, and she was lost from sight as he was again shrouded in dust.

He looked towards the machine next to him and saw its pilot readying a lasso. He was aware of another copter closing behind him. As he turned, the two pilots lassoed him simultaneously, one noose slipping quickly down his body and around his legs, the second wrapping around his body and upper arms.

Then the pilots pulled their ropes tight.

Two

Planetary Guidance Headquarters, Earth
February 23, 2379

Heavy robes brushed against soft, studded seats as the members of the Planetary Council made their way to their designated places within the padded opulence of the conference chamber.

They sat and murmured, breathless and flatulent, mumbling to each other and questioning what it was General Myson wanted of them this time. Some had ideas; but they remained ignorant of the fact that their deductions were based on information spilled at carefully chosen moments from the lips of those secretly in Myson's employ.

And while some of the Councillors expressed their discontent to those they distrusted least, others continued to simply watch and wait, biding their time until Myson's life could no longer be extended by his biotechs. Then their opportunity would come, as the rumour and the backbiting finally became redundant.

The Council waited, gradually dehydrating in the stiflingly hot chamber, the temperature of which was maintained at the level specified by Myson to ensure the Councillors' discomfort. They complained about their empty glasses, and the lack of nymphs to fill them, fidgeting and farting and planning feasts and frolics with compliant tarts who were waiting in their suites—and no doubt rummaging through their belongings in their absence.

Then the door to the chamber started to open, and all fell silent.

Councillors sat more upright, even those who just a few moments earlier had gossiped and plotted behind their hands. Even Councillor Matheson, who was usually less able to hide his discontent than most. And even the aloof and intimidating figure of the Judgemaster, who sat apart from the Councillors, his fat, ringed fingers rapping slowly on the brass studs in his red leather chair.

As the door opened a swarm of angels drifted through the gap, brilliant motes of dust buoyant on the chamber's thick air. They spread quickly through the room, scanning for threats and checking the pheromones and DNA of all those present with the information stored in the biocomputer, the huge organic brain of which throbbed gently a hundred storeys beneath them. When it was satisfied that the environment was safe, the primary angel sent a brief signal to the guards outside.

Two Devastation-class cyborgs stepped into the chamber and stood just inside the room, gigantic graphite sentinels clad in armour and weapons.

Then came General William Myson.

The wooden floor creaked gently as tiny but powerful containment fields propelled the armoured chair that encased the general's body into the room. Only his fat, pale head was visible above the gunmetal shell, supported by a rigid collar around his neck.

Myson's expression was pained, his eyes somehow inhuman. Some said that most of his original body was gone, and even that his consciousness was no longer held within the physical form now in the chamber, but stored within some impenetrable vault deep within the bowels of Planetary Guidance Headquarters, backed up, copied, synced between traditional hardware located offworld and a cluster of biocomputer cells.

A clutch of nymphs followed Myson into the room, their sex indeterminate despite the diaphanous nature of their garments. They giggled and chattered to each other in their strange and delicate language, oblivious to the lascivious gazes of some of the elderly men and women already within the chamber. While once subject to whatever attention Myson wished to give them, his largely incapacitated state meant that they had become mere confections, adorning trinkets.

Following them all was Marshall Greer, his face as weathered and brown as the leather uniform he wore. Feared and respected in equal measure, Greer was Myson's only true confidant, and thus considered by many to be as powerful as Myson himself. Having made sure that the door was sealed behind him, Greer stood between the two cyborgs, his eyes scanning the assembled Councillors through the blizzard of angels.

Myson manoeuvred his chair behind the large semicircular desk positioned at the centre of the room. The containment-field generators fell quiet as it settled upon the floor.

Myson looked at the Councillors seated before him. When he spoke his lips did not move, his voice instead issuing from a speaker in the chair. There was none of the physical difficulty he had previously suffered, as the chair broadcast the words on his behalf, their inflection changing automatically to reflect his mood. It was an incredibly accurate representation of Myson's real voice.

"Ladies and gentlemen," he said. "I need Council approval to utilise Structure funds. We have reached an impasse as far as Seriatt is concerned. The time for action has come. For almost two years we have wrestled with the Andamour Council's bureaucracies, seeking its approval for an assault on Seriatt to neutralise the Sinz threat. But while they acknowledge that the presence of the Sinz there is—to use their quaint phrases—'unfortunate' and 'frustrating'—they refuse to sanction what they consider to be a confrontational approach, and continue to insist that we wander aimlessly down the diplomatic route. As a result the time has come for us to consider alternatives."

The voice of Councillor Rush projected from the rear of the chamber. "But what alternatives are there, Sire? Access to Seriatt remains blocked by the shield put in place by the Sinz around the planet. Outside that shield their automated drones attack any craft entering an exclusion zone of eight light-minutes. We have already lost three of our ships, and even if we did manage to penetrate this blockade with a sizeable force, they are sufficiently established to repel any attack. We are fortunate that the wormhole has been unstable for so long and prevented them from bringing more forces through.

If the situation changes and they are able to make use of the wormhole once more, we may find ourselves having to overcome a far greater problem."

"Are the Sinz not open to negotiation?" asked Councillor Simenon. "You once had a particular relationship with them, did you not, Sire?"

Myson looked at Simenon. The wiry, white-haired man was as stubborn and determined as he had been forty years before, when he had supervised the quelling of the Buhatt Rebellion. Back then Myson had found his character useful, his doggedness an asset. But Simenon's ability to irritate seemed to have increased with the passing years, and this was a particularly touchy subject. He was obviously driving at the supposedly secret and highly lucrative arms deals Myson had conducted with the Sinz prior to their invasion of Seriatt—something that had put Myson in a particularly awkward situation at the time, and brought many worlds to the brink of attacking Earth. That he had been forced to end these deals, coupled with the fact that they were not as secret as they were supposed to be, was extremely frustrating.

"I believe," replied Myson, "that our focus has been wrong. We must ask ourselves not how we may attack Seriatt and defeat the Sinz successfully, but what it is we want from that world."

"And just what *do* we want, Sire?" asked Matheson, dabbing at his brow with a handkerchief.

"Two things. First, the Seriatts' time travel device. However it works, whatever its form, we must have it. I had expected to see some evidence of the Sinz making use of it, but this has not been the case. I can only assume that they have failed to appreciate its purpose."

"What if it has been destroyed?"

"If this is the case, then we must seek out whatever records the Seriatts may have kept regarding its construction and method of operation. Then perhaps we may attempt to construct one ourselves."

"What is the other?" called another Councillor from the rear of the chamber.

"Michael. We must get Michael back. I cannot imagine what has happened to him on Seriatt since the Sinz invasion. One of the reasons I have not acted against the Andamour Council's wishes before now is my fear that his life could be put in jeopardy. But this cannot continue. He must be brought home."

"What if he is dead, Sire?"

"He is not dead," said Myson. "I feel it."

"It seems to me that these two objectives each require careful execution," observed Councillor Reid—a stern-faced female whose bluntness Myson had always admired. "What if our resources are insufficient, or circumstances make it impossible for both to be achieved? Which of the two goals would you prioritise, Sire?"

Marshall Greer leaned forward and whispered to Myson, who seemed to pause and consider before replying. "Both objectives are achievable, Councillor," he stated eventually.

"But what if the—"

"Both objectives are achievable."

Councillor Reid made no further comment.

"So we are in agreement?" Myson's eyes darted around the chamber looking for dissenters. There were none. "Very good. Are we also in agreement, then, that acquisition of the Seriatts' time device is in our best interests, and of the utmost importance?" There was a low rumble of confirmation. "Excellent, excellent."

"Do you have a plan of action in mind, Sire?" asked Matheson.

"Of course. We will marshal a battle fleet the size of which has never before been assembled. We will then neutralise the shield the Sinz have in place around Seriatt, and when they are defenceless we will attack. We will overrun them. We will destroy them."

"But how can the shield be disengaged, Sire?" asked one of the younger Councillors.

"As I understand it a particular organism is key to the Sinz existence, and also generates the shield that protects the planet. If we can destroy it or even weaken it sufficiently, then we will be able to proceed."

"And are you confident this can be achieved, Sire?" asked Councillor Matheson. "It sounds a simple task. I am therefore confident that it is likely to be quite the opposite."

"I will assign the task to one of Stealth's finest operatives to ensure success."

"Who, Sire?"

"I have no one specific in mind at this time, Councillor. Marshall Greer will advise me. But the right person will be chosen."

"Assuming we successfully locate and acquire this time machine, Sire," said Councillor Conway, "what is to happen to it when it is in our hands? Surely such a device is too powerful to be in the custody of . . . a single man."

Councillors fidgeted and coughed and glanced at one another, made uneasy by the clear implication—and challenge—in Conway's question. Most of them admired his courage, and also marvelled at his nerve.

"I am of the belief," replied Myson, "that it would be a tool so powerful and dangerous that it must be destroyed."

There was more fidgeting, a few raised eyebrows.

"This would seem wise," said Conway slowly, as if reluctantly agreeing to some kind of hard-struck bargain. But the tone of his voice betrayed his doubt.

"So the Council will agree to release the necessary funds?" said Myson.

The Councillors looked at the Judgemaster. He consulted briefly with the Senior Councillors on the highest row of benches, then looked at Myson and nodded once.

"Excellent," said Myson. "We will begin the preparations."

Sinz Domestic Affairs Forum, Hascaaza
January 8, 2379 (Earth equivalent)

The drab brown wall flexed a little with a moist sucking sound as Mediator Latzinor pushed his way through the thin sheets of skin sealing the conference pod's entrance. They folded softly together again behind him as he began to descend the steps leading down to the centre of the pod.

The atmosphere was humid, the warmth demanded by his thin-skinned mammal counterparts combining with the fine mist sprayed by the amphibians' diffusers to create a sultry environment.

Directly ahead of him as he walked down the steps were the avians. Noble and upright, their long, membranous wings were wrapped around them like fine leather cloaks.

The room was filled with the thin clicks and glottal sounds of the gathered politicians and military figures chattering. There was much excitement, and some impatience. Mediator Latzinor knew that they were all anxious to hear the latest developments, and news of the preparations that were being made. Patience had been forced upon them for a hundred long seasons, but this was rapidly waning. The avians were especially keen for war, having starved themselves long and determinedly many times before in preparation, only to be disappointed. But their talons were always sharp.

He would keep them waiting no longer.

Latzinor made his way to the pedestal that sprouted like a sticky fungus from the pod floor. When he stepped onto the plinth, the creamy light from the six glowing orbs that protruded from the ceiling faded, replaced by the glow of a single, smaller orb focussed onto Latzinor's face.

The assembled Sinz fell into shadow, and silence.

Latzinor glanced at his notes, small angular Sinz letters suspended in the lectern's thin film. His fragile chest swelled and shrank as he took a few deep breaths. When he began to speak, the amplified clicks of his mellifluous voice echoed a little despite the soft consistency of the pod's walls.

"My valued associates," he said. "I bring a report of progress from Fabricator Cursoss. She informs me that growth of the fleet is almost complete. The final batch of carriers will be ripe before the end of the current season, and the birthships we have been preparing in case the channel fails to stabilise are full at last, and in gestation."

There were clicks and squawks of approval and relief from the gathered Associates. Despite the restricted space, some of the younger avians unfurled their long wings at the prospect of battle, much to the consternation of their older and more restrained counterparts.

Latzinor continued when the hubbub receded.

"I also have information from Secretary Controller Hargoth, who states that our military capacity will soon be reached. With the strength of the fleet and our forces married, we can finally begin to act."

There was more excitement. Even the usually docile amphibians writhed and squirmed in their shallow tanks, grimy water slopping onto the pod floor.

"What of the channel?" called a stern-faced avian. "What is its current state?"

The mediator turned to face his avian associate. "It is less volatile than in recent times, Associate Riffolesh," he said. "But it is impossible to tell whether this will continue, or if it will become unstable once more. We can only be prepared for whatever circumstance presents itself. I can say, however, that the Supreme Associates believe we have waited long enough for the channel to stabilise. Speculator Thritt is of the opinion that the time has come to act. The birthships should depart as soon as they are ready, just in case the channel does not stabilise for a length of time sufficient for us to traverse it."

There were uncertain murmurs. Latzinor was aware that many were unconvinced that the birthships was a wise option. There were too many variables, they said. Too great a chance of error. No one could guarantee the immense distance to Seriatt would be covered successfully without the embryos coming to harm, suffering a fatal dose of radiation, or simply being affected by the passage of time in the depths of space.

"Have we successfully communicated with our associates on Seriatt?"

"Unfortunately not," replied Latzinor. "The first they will know of our plans will be upon our arrival."

Associate Riffolesh made a brief whistling sound through the openings on his beak. "I expressed my doubts to you all about the wisdom of attempting to expand our presence over such a great distance long ago," the avian said. "But my words would not be heeded. Our greed was too great. Associate Themiass tempted you with promises of great riches, the acquisition of materials that would help us defeat the Karallax. Trading with the humans did not satisfy him. He wanted to conquer them and their neighbours despite the huge distance from our own world, dazzling you with promises of great achievement. Now Themiass is dead; the human has betrayed us, and we are spread too thin. We should never have trusted him. Meanwhile, with the channel unstable many of our associates are stranded far from home in a place from which we may not be able to rescue them, we struggle to implement even the most basic of defences as the Karallax hammer at our door, and the *basillia* are kept busy churning out associates for the military, while our civilian population dwindles."

There was much noise and discussion. Mediator Latzinor clasped his hands and waited for silence.

When quiet returned, Latzinor spoke again. "There may be a time when such declarations are appropriate, Most Exalted Avian Associate Themiass," he said, bowing his head in a sign of respect, "but I fear this is not it."

There were a few moments of silence during which Councillor Themiass and Mediator Latzinor simply looked at each other, but then other Sinz began to make noises of support for the Mediator. Eventually, given the clear opinion of his peers, Themiass was forced to shield his face with one wing in deference to Latzinor.

"All is well," said Latzinor, in recognition of Themiass's gesture. "But now we must decide whether the birthships should be sent on their long journey, or whether we should wait to see if the channel stabilises completely." Mediator Latzinor looked at each of the twelve Race Representatives, who would express the opinions of their respective peer groups. They conferred with those in the tiers beside them, then indicated to Latzinor when the opinions were gathered.

"I ask you now to express your will," Latzinor said. "If it is your wish that the birthships should depart, make it known."

One by one those Representatives who agreed with the motion signalled to Latzinor. The avians raised their wings, the amphibians splayed fins, and the mammalian Sinz raised thin arms.

Dissenters were few.

"Very well," said the Mediator. "The action is passed."

"But what if we should send the birthships on their way and the channel then stabilises?"

"In that instance," said Latzinor, "we will continue with the original plan and approach Seriatt directly."

"And the embryos will be brought back to Sinz, to join the populace?"

"I am afraid that would not be possible. Once the embryos are in stasis they cannot be roused until the preset time, when they reach their destination." Mediator Latzinor turned to face another Sinz to his left. "Associate Tilliger, the Prime Associates wish to inspect your crop before the final preparations are made. Is this possible?"

"It is. They are ready now. Please inform me when they wish to make their inspection and I will arrange the necessary transportation."

"Very good. Fabricator Clintoc, the Prime Associates also wish to visit a *basillia* to witness the emergence of the final embryos and our fighting forces. Is this progressing as planned?"

"The *basillia* is in the final stages of delivery. Within half a season we will have sufficient numbers to conquer any opposing force."

Seriatt
March 3, 2379 (Earth equivalent)

Two of the Seriattic pilots walked over to Delgado and looked down at him.

"A human male," said the slightly taller of the two, speaking Counian. "This is not something I expected."

"The other is also human. A female."

Delgado could tell from their voices that one was a *vilume*, the other a *mourst*. At least he now knew with certainty that they were still on Seriatt.

He raised his head and looked across at Ash as two more copters settled on the ground nearby. As their pilots alighted and walked towards her, the taller of the Seriatts—the *vilume*—crouched in front of him, forearms resting on thighs. The pilot's clothing was made of tough black fabric that was covered in a layer of russet dust.

Delgado looked up at the *vilume*'s face. He perceived the Seriatt as female. She raised her glossy black goggles onto her forehead and revealed striking amber eyes. The skin around her eyes was incredibly smooth and more deeply tanned than that of any *vilume* he had previously encountered. It also appeared to be elaborately tattooed around the right eye, while the rest of her face remained hidden by the thick scarf that wrapped the lower part of her head. She looked kind, tolerant.

"You are an unexpected surprise, indeed," she said, peering down at him. She reached out with a black-gloved hand and pulled at his clothing. "You are wearing Seriattic garments. Medic's clothing, is it? I have seen nothing like this for quite some time. Who are you? What are you doing here?"

"How's my friend?" Delgado demanded. He tried to see past the *vilume*, but the Seriatt pushed him down firmly.

"Could be a Sinz shifter," said the *mourst*, who was standing to the *vilume*'s right. "One of their tricks to infiltrate us."

The *vilume* shook her head. "I do not think so. If he was a shifter, he would have become something else when we brought him down. A form that would have easily been able to escape from our ropes. And only their best shifters can accurately adopt a form as complex as this. They would not risk losing one. Inconsistencies and imperfections would be obvious at this close range if it were a less skilled shifter. He is truly human."

"Even if this is true, we cannot afford to assume they are on our side."

"I am not about to do that, Keth," said the *vilume* with patience. "Tell us your name, human."

"Not until you tell me if my friend's okay."

The *vilume* looked over her shoulder in Ash's direction and shouted something at her colleagues; Delgado caught a glimpse of Ash being pulled from beneath the fallen *gatkurd* by some of the other Seriatts, one of whom replied. The *vilume* looked back at Delgado. "Your female companion has some bruising to her legs and minor skin damage, nothing more. Now tell us who you are and what you are doing here. There have been no humans on Seriatt since before the Sinz invasion. Where did you land? Where is your ship? How did you get through the shield?"

"Release us; then I'll talk."

Keth snorted. "He is surely human. Even the best shifter would not be able to replicate their attitude so precisely."

The *vilume* did not disagree with Keth's assertion. "Very good," she said. "You stay quiet if that is what you wish. We will take you to our camp. If when we get there you still do not wish to answer our questions, although it is not my usual way, I will have to consider giving Keth here the opportunity to encourage your cooperation."

Delgado stared at the *vilume* and tried to convey an intimidating demeanour, but the expression in the Seriatt's eyes did not change.

Delgado and Ash were made to stand. Their hands were bound, and they were marched to separate copters.

"In there," said the *vilume* pilot to Delgado, indicating the small craft's rear seat. "You will come with me. Keth will take your colleague." Delgado looked across at Ash as she walked towards another aircraft with the *mourst*. She was limping slightly. She simply shrugged when she saw Delgado looking at her.

Delgado stepped over the copter's low side; it seemed a very fragile machine. He did his best to settle himself into its rear seat. It was small and hard, and although long, the cockpit was narrow. When he moved his elbows outwards, the thin hull flexed under the pressure. The butt of the chain gun mounted on the side of the copter was right next to his head. Although he would be able to use the weapon if he so wished, the barrel was too long for him to threaten the *vilume* with it, which would in any case be suicidal.

As the *vilume* leaned over the side of the machine to strap Delgado into his seat, the Seriatt looked at him. Her bright eyes shone above the black cloth scarf. "You should tell me your name, at least," she said. "If you give me something, no matter how small, I will be able to convince Keth that he should not harm you. I do not perceive that you are against us. Tell me your name."

Delgado looked at the Seriatt, and considered. The traces his nobics fed to him indicated that she was genuine, and that the kindness he saw in her eyes reflected her true personality. "You tell me yours," he said slowly, "and I'll tell you mine."

The *vilume* yanked at Delgado's straps, pulling them as tight as she could, then stood and looked down at him for a few moments before stepping over the side of the aircraft in front of him, and settling herself at the controls. "I am called Cowell," she said, reaching over each shoulder for her own harness straps. "But this information will not help you. Now tell me your name, human."

"Delgado," he said. "Alexander Delgado."

Cowell momentarily stopped untangling the earbuds that had been hanging across the small joystick in front of her; although she did not turn or question him, she seemed to recognise the name.

Cowell then placed her goggles back over her eyes and reached out, flicking switches in preparation for flight. There was a mechanical cough above Delgado's head, and the small copter's rotors began to turn, slowly at first, but rapidly increasing in speed. Behind him he heard the thin whine of small turbines. Clouds of dust rose as all around them the pilots of the other copters also started their machines' engines. Within moments, all aircraft were ready for flight.

Delgado saw Cowell speaking as she looked towards the copter piloted by Keth. The *vilume* then increased the power to the turbines and turned the machine in a tight circle, with the other aircraft forming up behind her. The machines then spread out in a line abreast, facing in the same direction. There was a brief pause; then the pilots opened the throttles.

The copter accelerated rapidly, vibrating as it rumbled across the uneven ground. A few moments later Cowell pulled back on the joystick, and the shuddering ceased as the aircraft climbed steeply, the desert falling away.

The formation levelled off at a height of around one hundred metres, then turned towards the point at which the first of the birds had hit the ground. Delgado could see another copter landed next to the dead creature. As they approached, it he could see that the bird had no feathers, but skin like that of the Sinz they had seen earlier, wrinkled like a scrotum. Its vast, pointed wings were like thin membranes.

They descended again and landed between the carcasses. The Seriatt pilot was hacking at the nearest with a large cleaver that glinted in the sunlight as he delivered each blow. The Seriatt appeared to be trying to separate one of the bird's wings from its body.

Cowell powered down the copter and unbuckled her harness. As the rotors slowed, she stood and stepped out of the cockpit. "We will harvest what meat we can from these Sinz corpses," she said, raising her goggles to her forehead once more. She began to unbuckle two long leather panniers strapped to either side of the copter's fuselage.

Delgado glanced around. "What do you mean? What Sinz?"

Cowell moved her head to indicate the slain bird nearest to her. "These, of course."

Delgado looked at the dead bird nearest to them. "But we've seen Sinz," he said. "They were skinny little humanoids."

"Humanoid. How very *human* of you to say that, Alexander Delgado. The Sinz take many forms. Some are avian, like these; others are amphibians. I am puzzled that you do not know this."

"So when you've killed them you eat them?"

"That is correct. This may seem barbaric, but there is little food. We must take what we can when it is available. Now, I must go and help Entass. The wings are particularly difficult to remove, as the muscles are large and run deep."

"There's not much meat on those wings," Delgado said. "Seems like a lot of effort."

"Although the wings themselves carry little meat, they are particularly tasty when crisp." Cowell drew a long-bladed knife from a sheath attached to her thigh as she turned and walked away from the copter towards the dead Sinz and her Seriattic colleague.

Delgado looked across at Ash and saw Keth walking away from their copter to join his counterparts in their butchery. Delgado raised his bound hands in front of him, gave a thumbs-up, and mouthed, *Are you okay?* Ash nodded, then glanced from Delgado to the Seriatts and back again.

Delgado recognised something in her eyes and expression. "Shit, Ash," he muttered. "What are you thinking of trying?"

Keth reached Cowell and Entass, and they seemed to begin discussing the best way to dismember the Sinz carcass. When he looked back towards Ash, he saw that she had somehow freed her hands. The next moment she leaped from the copter and was sprinting towards him.

Delgado heard a shout from one of the other Seriatts, which attracted the attention of Keth, Cowell, and Entass. Keth immediately gave chase. Despite his bulky *mourst* physique, he was a fast runner and quickly gained ground. When he was still several metres behind Ash, Keth took his lasso from his waist and threw it gently and skilfully.

The rope slipped easily over Ash's shoulders and down around her calves. Keth yanked at the rope, and Ash fell heavily to the ground just a few metres from the copter.

"Goddammit," she cursed, spitting grit. She sat up quickly and tried to release her legs, but before she could do so the Seriatts were upon her.

Command Suite,
Planetary Guidance Headquarters, Earth
February 23, 2379

Myson's personal suite was deep in the heart of Planetary Guidance Headquarters, a windowless cell he left only when absolutely necessary. Although his former suite at the top of the huge mushroom-shaped building had been reconstructed after having been demolished by terrorists so many years before, with its vulnerability exposed the General had decided not to return to it.

Marshall Greer sat on the sofa opposite Myson. "Do you really think our objectives are achievable?" he asked.

"I do. As long as we send the right person. I want no failures, defections, or betrayals, Greer. Such problems have made me appear foolish in the past, and I do not want a repetition. Do you know someone reliable who is capable of performing the task we require?"

"I have already taken it upon myself to contact the person I consider ideal, Sire," he said. "A man with much experience. I am certain he will perform well."

"Very good. Bring him to me as soon as he arrives."

"Of course. But may I ask a question, Sire? This time machine of the Seriatts'—I assume we're not really going to destroy it. That would be rash."

"We will arrange for *something* to be destroyed," said Myson. "For the benefit of the Planetary Council."

Seriatt
March 3, 2379 (Earth equivalent)

The Seriatts bound Ash's hands more tightly than before, then bundled her back into the rear seat of Keth's copter and resumed their butchery of the Sinz corpse. They placed the best cuts of meat into the copters' panniers.

Cowell pulled a headset from behind Delgado's seat. "Wear this," she said. "We will be able to communicate more easily when we are airborne." She placed the headphones onto his head, then climbed into the front seat of their copter and put on her own headset. When she spoke again, her voice was warm and close. "Your friend, Ashala. She is headstrong."

"Really?" he said. "I hadn't noticed."

"She should be careful, however. Keth will not tolerate repeated problems. He is *mourst*. He would gladly consume her given an excuse."

"How about me?" Delgado asked. "My meat too tough for him?"

"No. He would consume you also." Cowell began to power up the copter. "But he would want to fight you first. Despite being human you would still represent a threat to him. Simple slaughter he would not consider honourable."

"You should give him the opportunity," said Delgado. "To fight me, I mean."

"What makes you think I will not? We must leave now. The weather is turning."

The sound of the turbines increased in volume, and the copter began to move forward. As Cowell turned the aircraft in preparation for takeoff, Delgado looked across at Keth; the *mourst* was fastening the brass buckles on the panniers attached to his own machine. He was shorter than the average *mourst*, thickset but not overweight, clearly strong and fit. Delgado wondered if he had seen any real combat. He would keep an eye on him, assess potential weaknesses.

The copters took to the air once more. Those that were now laden with Sinz meat gained height less quickly, flying at a lower altitude than the other machines. Delgado searched the sky, instinctively looking for signs of enemy aircraft or Sinz approaching. He saw the pilots of the other copters moving as they did the same. He recognised the feeling of constant threat only too well: despite passing through the time gate, it did not seem long ago that he had been flying Hornets on Earth, mixing it up with Structure Firedrakes.

Like a small swarm of ungainly insects, the copters headed steadily towards the great spirelike structures, their delicate wings shimmering above them. The buildings ahead—if that was what they were—were striking, like huge stacks of precariously balanced and irregularly shaped discs. They towered above the ground, reaching far higher than the copters would be able to climb, penetrating the thin clouds.

"Look out for Sinz," said Cowell when they had been flying for around twenty minutes. "There are likely to be more of them in this area, now we are closer to the city." She adjusted the trim of the aircraft slightly and glanced around at the other copters. "Despite their size the avians are agile and speedy." She indicated the javelins suspended above the cockpit. "We have only a few *ecliptz*, and a limited amount of ammunition for the gun. If we are attacked, each shot must count."

"Why don't you take a different route?" Delgado asked. "Go around the city?"

"We cannot. With the extra weight of yourself and Ashala, plus the meat we have collected, we do not have sufficient fuel for an extended flight. We have to take the shortest route."

As the ragged formation of copters got closer to the city, bobbing up and down in the air, a cold, brown mist began to appear. It seemed to seep from the Sinz buildings like poison, diffusing light and sucking away definition. The sun became nothing more than a dull smudge in the sky. Drops of moisture began to appear on Delgado's clothing, and the temperature dropped rapidly.

But he was too distracted to notice, drawn to the towering buildings ahead of them. Even at this close range, with the nearest of the structures less than a kilometre away, he could not decide whether they had been constructed or were elaborate organisms.

He opened perception nobics and focussed more closely on the towers. The underside of each segment was ridged, like the bottom of a mushroom cap—possibly some kind of ventilation system, he considered—but the upper surfaces were smooth, with a slight sheen like frosted glass. Around the edge of each segment were what looked like long, narrow windows, but even with nobic enhancement he was uncertain whether he could see figures moving within the disc-shaped constructions.

He looked up, searching for the tops of the towers. Although uncertain due to the grimy haze, he thought he could see a fine network of wires linking the buildings high above. Almost simultaneously something caught his eye. His nobics tingled and surged. On the side of one of the towers he saw movement, then slender figures diving gracefully from a high platform. After launching themselves into the grimy air, the avians folded their long, pointed wings back alongside their bodies and plunged towards the copters. Delgado's nobics told him that they had small weapons clutched between their talons.

"Cowell," he called. "Sinz birds, five o'clock high."

"Repeat please."

"Look over your right shoulder, up."

The pilot looked and immediately transmitted a warning to the other

Seriatts; but they were already clutching spears or swinging their chain guns around towards the approaching birds.

Despite his hands being tied, Delgado was able to grip the wooden stocks of the chain gun in front of him, and brought it to bear on the diving Sinz.

The mist thickened quite abruptly, and they were suddenly passing through billowing clouds of the stuff. They became momentarily isolated, the other copters and the ominous towers briefly obscured from view.

Several seconds passed. The swirling soup through which they were flying became even more oppressive. Then one of the Sinz avians flashed past the copter's nose at immense speed, a blur of skin and beak and talon. Delgado fired a brief burst. The chain gun wheezed and clattered, its thin, rapid sound a contrast to the deep *thub-thub-thub* of the copter's rotors slicing through the air. But the Sinz was going too fast, and had descended into the murk within a moment.

Delgado leaned to the left and looked over the side of the cockpit. He watched as the creature pulled out of its dive in the thinner layers of fog below. It spread its wings wide, the sheets of skin rippling gently as it decelerated, and turned sharply to climb back up towards the copter.

Delgado could see the creature more clearly as it gained altitude, climbing straight towards them. It was like a combination of a pterodactyl and an imp: despite the size of its body, its face was small, its features pinched and sour, with narrow eyes and a pointed nose. Instead of the small, almost circular mouth of the humanoid Sinz they had encountered, this creature had a fearsome curved, sharp-edged beak. Its large, taloned feet were tucked beneath the broad base of its long, pointed tail.

Delgado swung the gun around, raising the barrel over Cowell's head, then pointed the breech down as far as it would go. He judged time and distance carefully as the grotesque animal continued to approach. He waited until it was virtually upon them, then fired again.

The barrel rotated rapidly, sounding like some kind of heavy, metallic percussion as spent shells were ejected from the weapon in a cloud of muddy smoke; its odour was thick in his nostrils and at the back of his throat.

Delgado saw the creature flinch and heard its shrill cries as bloody chunks exploded from its face and wings. Yet still it came.

Then the gun jammed. The weapon wheezed and retched but would fire no more.

The avian seemed to accelerate, as if it sensed their sudden vulnerability. Cowell tried to take evasive action—but too late.

The machine rocked dramatically as the creature grasped one side of the fuselage with its gigantic feet. Delgado yelled out as one of the talons that pierced the thin metal hull penetrated his left thigh.

Cowell fought the heavily rolling and pitching copter as the Sinz rocked from side to side, trying to tear the aircraft to pieces with its sharp, serrated beak. As the Sinz lunged repeatedly at the cockpit, Delgado reached up and pulled one of the javelins from the rack above him. It was a slender, light-weight weapon; almost too light, it seemed.

As the creature grasped part of the cockpit frame in its beak and yanked at it, tearing a ragged gash in the metal and causing the copter to roll heavily to one side, Delgado thrust the spear deep into the animal's grey chest.

The Sinz shrieked, its head thrashing wildly, then threw back its head and howled long and hard as it died. Cowell fought hard, but due to the weight of the dead Sinz now hanging off one side of it, the copter began tumbling, its two occupants thrown around in the cockpit despite their harnesses.

With the machine falling quickly through the murky air, Delgado pulled his knife from his pocket and began to hack at the Sinz' bony ankles. Thick, dark blood sprayed onto him as he chopped through the creature's scaly flesh, slicing at the ankle joint and twisting the blade in an attempt to cut the bird loose.

With one of its long, muscular legs severed, the Sinz fell back then forward, banging against the side of the machine as the copter rolled. As they lost height rapidly Delgado hacked furiously at the other leg until it, too, was severed, and the Sinz avian finally fell away.

Cowell quickly brought the machine back under control. "You did well," the *vilume* said. "We would soon have hit the ground."

"Yeah, well I wasn't about to let that thing pull us out of the sky without a fight. Shit." He winced as he moved: the avian's talon had penetrated deep into his leg. It remained lodged there, pulled from the creature's foot as it fell away from the copter. Fortunately the thornlike talon tapered to a sharp point, and although deep, the wound was not serious.

The creature's blood had congealed on his trousers to form a dark, scab-like patch. He gripped the talon and quickly pulled it from his leg. He assigned nobics to treatment of the wound, and felt them go to work immediately, knitting the muscle.

"Are you all right?" asked Cowell.

"Sure. Never better. Just a little remnant from our friend." Delgado threw the talon out of the aircraft and looked over the side of the cockpit. Cowell was right: they had been just moments from hitting the ground.

Through the mist he recognised the Seriattic architecture, but the buildings looked cold, deserted, dead. He saw a disturbance around the point where the Sinz avian had hit the ground, indistinct creatures scurrying from the shadows of the buildings towards the body. They swarmed over the corpse, pulling it to pieces, fighting among themselves for the meat it offered. He could not tell what kind of animals they were, but he hoped they were not Seriatts.

Delgado sat back as Cowell turned the copter and tried to regain the lost altitude. He saw that the *vilume* was looking up towards the other copters. As one Sinz dived between some of the aircraft, they caught the avian in cross-fire from the chain guns, shredding the animal with a torrent of bullets.

Another avian was circling immediately above one copter's rotors, thus out of reach of its gun, while another clung to the side of the cockpit and tore at the machine with its beak. The weight of the Sinz was dragging the aircraft down despite the pilot's valiant efforts to keep it aloft and the engine being at full power.

As the Sinz adjusted its grip, one of its talons punctured the fuel tank just behind the cockpit. A fine spray squirted from the tank, dousing the creature. As the fuel came into contact with the hot engine, it ignited.

The resultant fireball engulfed the fragile copter, its occupants, and both Sinz. The remains tumbled towards the ground shedding dark detritus and trailing a thick plume of black smoke.

Delgado looked at the other copters as more avians launched themselves from platforms high above. The sound of the aircrafts' engines was deadened by the fog, but the thin clatter of the chain guns was brittle and stark. He could see several vague shapes of copters through the swirling mist, but was unable to tell which one might contain Ash.

Assuming she was still alive.

"Those who survive will be lucky," said Cowell. "The avians are determined as well as fearsome. They are also merciless and ferocious. The least civilised of the Sinz. I have seen living Seriatts pulled apart by them for sport. Defenceless *vilume*, pregnant *conosq*. Some they even carried to a great height and dropped to their death. They are hated. Even the other Sinz hate them." Cowell levelled the aircraft and turned again.

"What are you doing?" Delgado asked. "We've got to get up there and help them. They'll be slaughtered."

"There is no point," said Cowell, in the calm, pragmatic nature of all *vilume*. "This machine would take too long to reach that altitude now. It is too heavily laden, its engine too weak."

"So throw out the goddamn meat!"

"No. We must concentrate on saving ourselves. Besides, the meat is a valuable source of protein. We will descend." Cowell pushed the stick forward, and the copter's nose dropped. "Visibility is poor at the lower altitudes, and although we are at greater risk of collision, the avians are less likely to find us."

Delgado looked back up towards the other copters, which had now been absorbed by the fog. He knew Cowell was right. They would not be able to reach the same height as the other copters even if they jettisoned their load of meat.

But that didn't make the situation easy to accept. Ash was up there somewhere, her life in the hands of a Seriattic pilot.

The copter flew low over the Seriattic city for around half an hour, stirring the silver mist. Occasionally the machine was swamped in fog so dense it was impossible to see anything beyond the cockpit. It was easy to become disoriented in such conditions. There were moments when Delgado's brain told him they were climbing, descending, or even flying inverted, despite their steady course. Cowell was steadfast, the *vilume* seemingly unfazed by the conditions.

Delgado shivered in the cold damp air. His injured leg ached as his nobics repaired the damage. His head ached. He was hungry and thirsty and desperately tired—a fatigue the nobics could not completely counter, the sustenance they offered thin and artificial.

He looked into the murk and thought about Ash, wondering whether she was safe with the *mourst* called Keth, or had fallen prey to the Sinz birds. The odds were stacked heavily against her. But she had always been a fighter. If half a chance came her way, she grabbed it with both hands and refused to let go.

He briefly diverted nobic resources from repairing his leg to perception, but could not detect any trace of her. All he could do was hope.

The fog appeared to be thinning. He caught glimpses of the Seriattic streets that briefly escaped from the mist. The majority of the buildings looked relatively intact, suffering only from the passage of time. Once or twice he saw a figure move in a doorway or scamper across an empty street, but otherwise the city appeared deserted.

"Where is everybody?" he asked. "What happened to the Seriatts?"

"Many were killed during the Sinz invasion," replied Cowell. "They defended our planet honourably, but although they took many Sinz lives they were unable to repel the hordes that came. The survivors hide. Some of them take their chances and remain in the city, but the majority have fled to the countryside."

"And the Sinz can't find them?"

"We live in small groups and move frequently. Sometimes the Sinz send out parties in search of us, but they are rarely successful."

"What about the Oracles and the Administrators?"

"We are not certain. We think that the Administrators were killed soon after the Sinz took control of our world. The Sinz probably recognised their potential to rouse the population and murdered them, believing that this would crush the spirit of the Seriattic race. No one knows what happened to the Oracles. They simply disappeared. There were rumours, but nothing more. The most likely scenario is that the Sinz realised their powers and put them to some use of their own."

The fog gained a faint luminescence as it started to thin. Directly below the copter Delgado could now see countryside, the patchwork of small fields that had once represented Seriatt's farming techniques: low-scale production of high-quality produce for local sale. But the fields were barren and brown, the hedges that separated them wild and untended, the ground unturned. There were no crops to harvest, no livestock to feed.

Ahead a coastline became visible: a yellow, crescent-shaped beach with large rocky outcrops to either side and tall palms along the shore. And out to sea there were more of the tall Sinz structures, rising from the waves like the masts of gigantic, sunken vessels. Silvery aerostats drifted between them, bloated and cumbersome.

Almost completely free of the fog now, Cowell tipped the copter onto one side, pushing the machine into a hard turn, then straightened the aircraft and began to descend. Delgado looked back towards the mist-shrouded city. There was no sign of the other aircraft, or of Ash.

Second chronological displacement
Earth, September 18, 2350

Delgado's head spun as he took the final few stairs and crouched near the top. The feeling of sickness was unpleasant, but nothing he couldn't deal with.

Slowly he eased his head around the corner to look along the corridor. The cyborgs were motionless. The vee-cams bobbed slightly in the air.

"You ready to go, old-timer?" Bucky murmured.

"Ready as I'll ever be."

"Hey, who the hell's that?" whispered Girl as she peered over his shoulder. At the opposite end of the corridor someone was lying on the other flight of steps, the side of their head just visible. It looked like a man, but the facial features were hidden in shadow. He seemed to look directly at them for several moments before backing down the stairs and out of sight.

Delgado eased slowly back from the corner and leaned against the wall. He could just make out his reflection in the glass on the opposite side of the corridor. He looked somehow different.

He closed his eyes and concentrated hard, trying to access his hyperconsciousness. He could feel that Lycern was near. He took deep breaths, tried to stay calm. But he certainly seemed more aware than he had the last time round.

He looked at Girl. "Okay, Ash?" he asked.

"What? Who the hell's Ash?" She frowned. "Are you okay, Delgado? You look kinda strange."

Still things were different. "It doesn't matter," he said. "I'm ready, all right. Once we step into that corridor we'll have just a few minutes to deal with the cyborgs and vee-cams and get into Myson's suite, so we're going to have to be quick. Those cyborgs are tough. Tougher than anything you've seen before." He glanced from one to the other of them. "I've told you this already, right?"

"Yeah," said Bucky. "I think we've got the message."

"Sorry. Guess I'm just a little . . ."

"Jittery?" suggested Girl.

"Yeah. Jittery would cover it."

"Don't worry, man," said Bucky. "They won't know what's hit 'em."

Delgado moved up the steps and looked along the corridor again. The figure at the far end was not to be seen. He wasn't sure what this meant. He stepped back and turned to Bucky and Girl. "We'll attack from both sides," he said. "You two stay here; I'll go around to the other end of the corridor and attack from that side. Okay?"

"Seems like a good idea to me," said Bucky.

"Okay. Let me get around there; then we'll go for it. See you in five. Good luck."

Delgado turned and sprinted through the corridors towards the stairway on the other side of Myson's chamber. But still he wasn't quick enough. Just as he reached the bottom of the stairs he heard the sound of gunfire and explosions. He caught a glimpse of the other man stepping into the corridor.

Delgado cursed, took the stairs two at a time, then stopped at the top and looked cautiously along the corridor.

The vee-cams' tiny frames trembled, pushed backwards through the air each time they fired their weapons. The cyborgs were working incredibly efficiently, almost as if they had known the attack was coming.

Bucky and Girl were at the other end of the corridor: Girl was crouching against the wall opposite the door to the chamber. She was fumbling with her weapon, clearly having some kind of problem with it. Bucky was struggling to fight off several approaching cyborgs in an effort to buy her more time, but she was extremely vulnerable. They were both taking hits. Bucky was struggling to stay on his feet as his gun's shield weakened.

Delgado looked back to the man just in front of him. Two cyborgs were walking steadily towards him. One of them fell, but although seriously wounded he knew it would soon recover.

The corridor was plunged into darkness, followed by a rapid series of brilliant flashes. One of the vee-cams exploded, followed by a second, their components scattering across the floor. Delgado saw Girl struggling to get to her feet at the other end of the corridor; she limped as she began to walk, and her left hand was clutched to her right shoulder.

Bucky continued to fire at the cyborg immediately in front of him and Girl. It paused as the shots hit home, but despite his efforts it would not fall. The flashes of light increased in intensity and frequency. In the brief moments of brilliance Delgado saw a man who appeared at the top of the stairs to their left. He appeared to shout something at Bucky and Girl before firing at the cyborgs.

Their moment of hesitation was all the cyborg needed.

Delgado called out as Girl's shield finally failed and she was thrown backwards through the air by the stream of shots that hit her. She came to rest against the wall, a dark pool gradually emerging from beneath her shattered body.

Delgado and the man just in front of him began to run forwards. Simultaneously they shouted at Bucky to keep firing, but the young man could not withstand the onslaught of another re-formed cyborg, and under a torrent of blaster fire, he also fell.

Delgado roared. They both began firing at the cyborgs at the other end of the corridor, which had now turned. They were unaware that other damaged cyborgs were rapidly re-forming behind them.

As Delgado strode forward his double stopped and watched. He didn't know what was happening. He stepped back towards the stairs and saw the sparkling gate near the elevators. He had no choice: he would simply have to try again.

Three

Seriatt
March 3, 2379 (Earth equivalent)

The copters levelled off at an altitude of around fifty metres. They continued for a few moments after crossing the coastline; then Cowell turned the machine through ninety degrees and flew parallel to it. The sea lapped gently against the beach and surged over rocks.

As Delgado looked down he saw a rotund submersible of wood and metal construction rise to the surface in a swathe of foam, like a bloated marine corpse. As the submarine bobbed and rolled on the swell, several creatures appeared in the water around it.

Some of them swam around the submersible, while others clung to its riveted hull. They looked like a combination of giant squid and mermen, with muscular webbed hands, shining green fins along their spines, and gills in their necks. Their skin glistened. Delgado glimpsed powerful limbs, large webbed feet, and long, tendril-like appendages that trailed from their shoulders and thighs. Some of the creatures looked up at the copter as it passed overhead; their faces were narrow, with thin-lipped mouths and large, black, lenslike eyes.

"More Sinz," said Cowell. "They are amphibians, although they spend most of their time in the water. Their air-breathing counterparts have to use bathyscaphes or diving bells to enter their aquatic world. There is considerable friction between the different species. The amphibians take as much advantage as they can of the fact that the nonaquatic Sinz cannot fully enter their environment. Indeed, the avians and the amphibians rarely come into contact. They lead very different lives.

Delgado looked back at the submersible. Most of the amphibians were watching their aircraft now. A circular hatch opened on top of the bathyscaphe and a small, lithe figure—clearly one of the humanoid Sinz—climbed a ladder from within the boat to the deck. The creature wore a black, one-piece uniform and a silver metal helmet with mirrored eye lenses. It gripped the brass handrail around the submarine's deck to steady itself as the boat rocked.

A second Sinz dressed in a similar brown uniform joined the first, and produced a long-barrelled weapon. The creature knelt, brought the gun to bear, and fired several shots at the copter; but the swell made accuracy impossible, and the Sinz missed by a wide margin. Delgado smiled as the black-clad Sinz—clearly of higher rank than the sniper—gesticulated vigorously, then smacked the rifleman on the back of his small grey head.

Cowell raised the copter's nose to climb over a rocky promontory. The headland was wide and its sides steep. The sea boiled and foamed over the lower jags and edges. Beyond the promontory the open ocean was startlingly blue, its hue changing with its depth. The air was noticeably cooler.

Having passed over the other side of the outcrop, Cowell continued onwards for a few moments, then turned the copter through one hundred and eighty degrees. As she straightened up out of the turn, she pushed the stick forward so that they were descending quickly. Delgado could see nowhere appropriate for a landing, yet the *vilume* pilot showed no sign of slowing: they were heading straight for the rocks.

Cowell finally levelled out again only when the machine was skimming the wave-tops, so low that Delgado could feel the salty spray on his face. The machine was heading directly for the rocks that now towered far higher than the copter. Given their speed and what he had seen of the aircraft's capabilities it would be difficult to clear the rocks even if Cowell climbed immediately—which the *vilume* showed no sign of doing.

THREE

Cowell throttled back slightly and seemed to be aiming for a gap in the rocks, which by Delgado's estimation was far too narrow for the copter to pass through.

But as the distance separating the rock wall and the copter rapidly diminished, the *vilume* pilot rolled the machine onto one side and flew straight through the gap. The air was chill, the channel sheltered from the heat of the Seriattic sun. The sound of the aircraft's engines thundered off the close rock walls. The foaming sea rose and sank just metres away from the tips of the rotor blades. As another rock wall loomed ahead of the copter's nose, Cowell pulled back on the stick with the machine still tipped onto one side, turning ninety degrees into a wider channel.

The turn was so tight that despite instinctively straining the muscles in his lower body to prevent the blood draining from his brain, as he had so many times during dogfights in the Hornets, Delgado's vision greyed.

His sight returned as Cowell rolled the copter back to its normal orientation. They were flying along another channel, which Delgado estimated to be no more than thirty metres wide; the tips of the copter's rotors were perilously close to the rock walls, which rose dramatically on either side.

Delgado leaned out of the cockpit and looked back; the gap they had flown through was extremely narrow—he was not sure he would have attempted the manoeuvre himself. Evidence of the risk involved in its execution was provided by the wreckage of another copter just above the current waterline, protruding from the rock like some kind of mutated lichen. Its level of decay and the multitudinous strands of seaweed clinging to its shattered form indicated that it spent much of its time submerged.

Delgado looked ahead as the copter began to descend once more. At first the rock channel through which they were flying appeared to be a dead end, but then he saw a cave ahead; the sea rose and fell in its dark mouth, the size of which fluctuated with the swell. Given Cowell's obvious skill and confidence as a pilot, there was no doubt in Delgado's mind that, despite its size, the *vilume* pilot would attempt to fly into the small tunnel.

Cowell made adjustments to the throttle, accelerating and decelerating, trying to time their arrival at the tunnel mouth to coincide with the point at which the water was at its lowest. Delgado assumed that forward speed was more useful to the machine than its ability to hover: they would have only seconds to get through, and he doubted the machine would be able to accelerate quickly enough from stationary.

Although Cowell had already demonstrated her flying capabilities, Delgado became increasingly tense as they approached the tunnel mouth. He did not like being in someone else's hands at the best of times; and this was by no means the best of times.

Cowell descended further. The seawater was extremely choppy in the confines of the narrow channel, slopping from crag to crag. As the grey rock walls seemed to rise around them and the aircraft covered the final few metres to the cave entrance, Delgado unconsciously gripped the side of the cockpit and held his breath.

There was an explosion of noise as the copter entered the darkness of the cave. The sound of the aircraft's lift engine was like a series of explosions, the whine of the turbines suddenly deep and menacing.

He glanced around the tunnel through which they were now flying but found it impossible to discern its size or how much room they had. The light on the copter's nose did little to penetrate the gloom, and unless the Seriatts had some form of night vision, Delgado had to assume that Cowell was flying as much by instinct as use of skill. Of one thing Delgado was sure: there would be little opportunity to learn from experience.

Eventually Delgado's eyes adjusted to the darkness, and he was able to make out a little more detail. He could see that the cavern was long, and that some way ahead, where the tunnel curved to the right, there was a weak source of light.

Although the tunnel's width was fairly consistent, there were some large protuberances of rock around which the Seriattic pilot had to jink the aircraft, the inky sea swirling just a few metres below. Other tunnels joined the one through which they were flying, but their darkness was impenetrable.

Cowell guided the small copter skilfully around the right-hand curve, and suddenly they were doused in light. The water below turned from black to grey. The undulations in the tunnel walls cast short shadows.

Ahead of them the tunnel widened, and a few moments later the small aircraft climbed slightly and left the tunnel, entering a vast subterranean cavern.

Command Suite,
Planetary Guidance Headquarters, Earth
February 26, 2379

Saskov took the late-afternoon scramjet, and was standing in a corridor preparing for his audience with General Myson just two hours after receiving the summons.

Saskov had been momentarily annoyed at having his skydiving vacation interrupted, the arrival of the message so abrupt it was like someone entering the room unannounced during an intimate moment—and that had happened just enough times for him to know. His frustration was short-lived, however, as its potential to cause problems was so clear to Saskov's nobics that they immediately replaced it with a feeling of apprehension. Just enough to put their host in a safer, less volatile state.

Saskov looked in either direction along the corridor. His only company were Myson's cyborg guards—eight of them in total—standing at regular intervals. There were no windows. The only sound was the soft hum of the aircon fans.

A slit suddenly appeared in the wall to the right of the door in front of him. Two angels floated from it, glowing in the corridor's gloom. They circled Saskov's head, emitting narrow lines of light as they scanned him and compared his DNA profile to the records in the biocomputer—much to the annoyance of his nobics, which protested at the invasion in the strongest possible terms.

With the angels satisfied that he was the man they were expecting, a few moments later the door began to slide open.

Saskov entered the room. It was a bare cell with dark grey walls. There was a sealed door in the wall to his right. The door behind him closed, and the wall directly in front of him began to shimmer. As it faded he felt as though he had entered a much larger room, even though he was aware that the wall remained in place and that the image before him was merely a projection.

In the centre of it all sat General William Myson.

Despite his incapacitated state, Myson still commanded respect and fear. His power on Earth was immeasurable, his reach boundless. Behind Myson stood a man Delgado did not recognise. An advisor of some kind, perhaps, or a valet.

Saskov dropped to one knee and bowed low. "Sire," he said.

"Come, stand before me, my soldier," said Myson. "I apologise for the somewhat impersonal nature of this meeting, but I have learned that security cannot be taken for granted."

"Indeed, Sire."

"I also regret the abruptness with which your furlough was interrupted. You were skydiving, I believe."

Saskov's nobics intercepted the resentful tone that threatened to rise and replaced it with a hint of obsequiousness. "Yes, Sire," he said. "It is a sport I have enjoyed for many years. It provides a thrill like no other."

"Perhaps I should try it myself sometime." Although Myson laughed, his sweaty head bobbing slightly, Saskov merely blinked. Myson stopped laughing and continued. "Well, we must not delay. We have recalled you for a particular reason. There is a mission I need you to perform. A mission of great importance. I am informed that you are immensely capable yet discreet. Is that correct, Colonel?"

"I would like to believe so, Sire."

"Well I hope you will not let me down. You are to go to Seriatt."

"Seriatt, Sire? But Seriatt is in Sinz control, and impossible to approach."

"That was the case, Colonel Saskov, but a means has been developed by which a small force may penetrate the shield and reach the planet. The situation has been deadlocked long enough, and I no longer have the patience to patronise those who would insist on going through what they refer to as *proper channels*. Furthermore, we also have information which may enable us to defeat the Sinz on Seriatt."

"How, Sire?"

"You will be briefed fully in due course, Colonel Saskov. But before we continue there is someone I would like you to meet. A colleague, to join you on this mission."

The door to Saskov's right shimmered. As the material clarified the Colonel saw that it framed a proud and imposing figure.

It was a Seriattic *mourst*.

Saskov's nobics went into overdrive.

Seriatt
March 3, 2379 (Earth equivalent)

Beyond the confines of the rock tunnel the sound of the copter's engines suddenly became much quieter. In the distance Delgado could see a broad lagoon whose silvery, glasslike surface extended into the darkness.

Around the lake insubstantial trees arched like the skeletons of monsters towards the sheets of white light that penetrated slender fissures in the high rock ceiling. Thick vegetation filled the gaps between the trees, cylinderlike structures trailing along the ground, the trees' upper branches threaded with vines. Just visible in the cavern's dark depths, gigantic stalagmites and stalactites merged to form thick, ancient pillars. Much of the cavern floor seemed to be covered with a layer of moss.

To his right Delgado saw a small encampment, an arrangement of pale fabric tents that stood out in the gloom as if superimposed on the dark background. A large bonfire burned nearby. A cluster of figures stood between the bonfire and a group of landed copters.

As Cowell turned the copter towards the camp, Delgado saw the group begin walking forwards in anticipation of their landing. One of them threw something onto the fire as they passed it, and the flames brightened momentarily.

Cowell turned the copter once more and decelerated almost to a hover near the other machines, then landed gently on the moss-covered ground. The *vilume* turned off the engines, and as the rotor slowed she and Delgado unfastened their harnesses, stood, and stepped over the side of the cockpit. The floor was spongy underfoot. It was surprisingly warm and humid in the cavern.

Cowell removed her goggles. "Are you well, Alexander Delgado?" she asked him.

"You can just call me Delgado," he said. "And I'm worried about Ash." He found himself captivated by Cowell's striking amber eyes.

"Your human female?"

Delgado snorted. "She's hardly *mine*." He shook his head and looked around. "She's one tough cookie, but—"

"Wherever she is, she is with Keth," said Cowell. "Keth is a good pilot. I am sure they will both survive."

"I hope you're right. It was tough back there. I don't know what I'd do if she . . . if I wasn't able to . . ." He shrugged. "It'd be tough if she didn't make it, that's all."

"I understand." Cowell unfastened the silver clasp holding her thick scarf in place and unwrapped it from around her neck and face.

The *vilume* was stunning. The most beautiful creature Delgado had ever encountered. Her skin was a deep, lustrous golden brown, a startling complement to her amber eyes. Her facial features were slender and elegant, her nose and lips thin and precise. The dark ochre tattoos she wore snaked up the side of her neck, around her eyes, and across her forehead in gently undulating patterns, their colour matched perfectly to the pigment applied to her lips. Her black hair was smoothed back across her head in the traditional *vilume* style, but the golden hoop that pierced one cheek and entered one corner of her mouth was something he had not seen on *vilume* before.

Delgado heard voices and looked to his left. Several people were approaching, an assorted group of *mourst*, *vilume*, and *conosq*. All the Seriatts eyed Delgado with suspicion, but particularly the *mourst*.

"Cowell," said one. "Did you sustain injuries? Where are the others?"

"We encountered some Sinz near their training camp in the Cartitia region; then we attacked a small flock of avians. Due to engaging in combat and the extra weight of carrying our passengers and the Sinz meat we ran low on fuel and so had to pass near to the city. We were then attacked by avian security forces. There is meat in the panniers," said Cowell, indicating the copter. "We should eat it while it is fresh."

"What about this human male?" asked a *mourst*. He had fair hair—unusual for a *mourst*—and a particularly rugged appearance, with a scar on one cheek. He held a brass-topped cane although he did not seem to need it.

"We saw them riding in the desert and captured them."

"Them?"

"There was another, Miskoh. A female. She was with Keth."

"Do you think it was wise to bring the humans here, Cowell? They could jeopardise our safety."

"We do not believe them to be a threat, Miskoh. They aided us when we were attacked by the avians near the city. Without Delgado I probably would not be here now."

"So are you going to free my hands?" Delgado held out his wrists.

"Very well. But be wary of foolish actions."

Miskoh addressed Delgado. "What are you doing here, human?" the *mourst* demanded. "Where have you come from?"

"That could be a long story," Delgado replied.

"We want to know. You have put us at risk."

"And we have much time," stated a *conosq*.

A momentary dizziness gripped Delgado. He swallowed, and tried to avoid looking at the Seriatt: Lycern's *muscein*—the potent *conosq* pheremone—could be roused in him still.

"Issilan is correct," said Cowell. "We have as much time as you need to tell your story. But Miskoh is also correct: you should not be here."

"Yeah, well it seems to me that *you* put them at risk by bringing me here."

"You misunderstand me," replied Cowell with characteristic *vilume* calmness. "There have been no humans on Seriatt for several years. Not since before the Sinz invasion and their imposition of the blockade. You must tell us how you managed to get here. It may indicate a weakness in the Sinz defences that we may be able to exploit."

"How do we know he's not a Sinz shifter?" said another *mourst*. "An infiltrator sent to discover our location."

"It was a chance encounter," stated Cowell, addressing the *mourst*. "I do not believe he is a shifter."

"Perhaps," suggested a *conosq*, "he is the one whose arrival has so long been predicted. But as yet we do not see it."

"What do you mean?" Delgado asked her.

"Long ago, before the Sinz invasion, the Oracles predicted the coming of a saviour. Perhaps it is you."

Delgado snorted. "Can't see it myself. Some people on Earth still follow a saviour, but He hasn't been around for a long, long time."

"Our definition of what constitutes a saviour is wider than on Earth," said Cowell. "On Seriatt a saviour is one who performs an act which aids a great many, such as the discovery of an important new substance or medicinal technique. Or perhaps they have devoted their life to helping others. The variables are many, but saviours are few."

There was suddenly a shout from behind the group of Seriatts. A figure was edging sideways through a narrow gap in the rock wall: another *conosq*. She began beckoning to them urgently.

"What is it, Sherquoia?" called Cowell.

"Come quickly. A copter is approaching. It is being chased by Sinz."

Cowell grasped Delgado by the arm. "Come," she said. "It may be Keth, with your companion."

Delgado ran with the Seriatts to the cavern wall and squeezed through the gap, then began to edge along the channel beyond. The uneven floor was glossy with moisture. A trickle of water ran along one side. As the party shuffled sideways up the steep gully, Delgado cursed repeatedly as he banged his knees and elbows on hard edges of rock.

Gradually the tunnel began to brighten. Delgado looked up the channel and saw the silvery sheen of daylight painted across the walls farther up. The light flickered as one by one Seriattic silhouettes reached the top of the slope and moved out into brightness.

Delgado reached the top of the slope and emerged gratefully into the open air, his left leg aching from the effort where the avian's talon had pierced it. The tunnel opened out onto a depression in the rocks around two metres deep. The Seriatts stood at the edge of this crater, peering over its jagged ridge towards the sea. Warm gusts carried the smell and taste of salt. Delgado stepped down into the crater to join them, careful not to slip on the damp rock.

He stepped up onto a ledge and looked over the edge of the crater. Not far below the sea forced its way over the craggy shoreline, spray cascading over the group as the water crashed against the rocky ridges farther down. Some distance out from the shore a copter was flying directly towards them, slightly nose-down, tail-high. It was being chased by two Sinz avians, which beat their wings at a seemingly leisurely pace.

"You see?" called Sherquoia above the sound of the sea. "It is Keth."

Delgado focussed on the copter and saw Ash clearly in the machine's rear seat. He smiled as he saw her turning from one side to the other, manoeuvring the heavy gun on its mount in an effort to get a shot at the pursuing avians. An arc of tracer spewed from the weapon's barrel as Ash fired, and the Sinz were forced to take rapid evasive action. The sound of the shots sounded thin and pathetic, occasionally swamped by the buffeting wind.

"There are amphibians, also," said Cowell.

Delgado looked at the water. At first he could not see the Sinz, but then saw a smooth shape break the surface for a moment before disappearing beneath the swell once more, its fins and tentacles appearing briefly in a wash of foam. A second amphibian surfaced for a moment nearby, cutting a deep wake as it powered through the water. Delgado glimpsed the creature's eerie, evil eyes as it gulped air and glanced up at the copter before disappearing beneath the gunmetal waves.

Ash continued to fire at the avians, which were now within metres of the aircraft, swooping from side to side and crying loudly. As one of the avians lunged towards the copter again, Ash fired a long burst. Much of the ordnance missed its target, raising plumes of seawater, but that which hit the creature shredded the leading edge of one wing. It shrieked, a piercing wail that was loud even to those on the shore. The Sinz thrashed its head from side to side, then crashed into one of the aircraft's turbines. The creature cried out again, then fell away from the hot metal of the engine housing and plummeted into the sea.

Delgado expected the copter to follow the avian down, but although it veered off course and descended rapidly for a few seconds, Keth recovered quickly and skilfully, and continued to fly the machine towards the shore.

The second avian was clearly unsettled by its counterpart's fate and became more cautious, approaching the copter with less enthusiasm than before. It did not realise that by giving the aircraft a wider berth it became more vulnerable to fire from Ash's gun. A moment later, as it wheeled thirty or so metres behind the copter, Ash hit the Sinz in the face and the dead animal plunged into the water.

"They have done well against two avians," said Cowell.

"Like I said," replied Delgado, "Ash's one tough cookie."

"Indeed it seems so. If they can get to the shore they will be safe."

"What about the amphibians?"

"They are unlikely to come out of the water to fight. They are too cumbersome, unable to move easily on land. They come ashore to mate, and sometimes to eat, but that is all."

But above the unsettled sea the copter suddenly fell quiet. With around two hundred metres remaining before it reached the shore it began to descend.

"They are not going to make it," said Cowell. "Keth is a good pilot, and a copter can glide for some distance, but their machine is too low. Soon they will hit the water."

The *mourst* was clearly fighting to keep the machine aloft. Below it the Sinz amphibians broke the surface and began circling beneath the stricken aircraft, gazing up at it and following its path as it continued to lose altitude.

Delgado grasped the rocky ridge of the crater and pulled himself up.

Cowell grabbed his clothing and pulled him back down again. "What are you doing?"

"I'm going out there to help Ash."

"It is no use, Delgado. When they hit the sea, they will either be killed by the impact, drown in the sinking wreckage, or the Sinz amphibians will drag them into the ocean's depths."

Delgado wrenched Cowell's hand from his tunic. He was surprised by the strength of the *vilume*'s grip. "That'll sure be the case if we stay here and do nothing," he said. "And although I don't know Keth, I'm prepared to risk my life to save Ash. You get me?"

A *mourst* standing beside Cowell made a gruff, throaty noise, quickly shed the heavy metal belt he wore, and began to climb over the rocks.

"What are you doing, Lerval?" Cowell demanded.

"The human is right, Cowell," the Seriatt said as he straddled the ridge. "So often we fail to act. Our brave colleague and the human female are in danger and will die while we watch if we do not help them." He extended a long hand to Delgado. "Come," he said. "Let the human and Lerval help those who require our assistance."

Delgado accepted the *mourst*'s hand, and the Seriatt's strong fingers wrapped his own.

Once outside the crater they ran the short distance down the ridged slope towards the sea. Delgado could see that the copter was now just a few metres above the water. Keth was struggling to keep the machine steady while Ash fired at the Sinz amphibians below. But without warning the copter's nose tipped forwards, and the small aircraft crashed bluntly into the sea.

The swell immediately washed over its nose. It tipped slowly to one side, the momentum of its still-spinning rotor chopping weakly at the water for a few moments before it stopped.

Just as Delgado began leaping through the breakers the copter overturned. Neither Ash nor Keth had emerged from the machine, but he had clearly seen the Sinz amphibians speeding through the water towards it.

He pulled his knife from his tunic pocket, clenched it between his teeth, then dove into the salty water and began swimming hard.

Command Suite,
Planetary Guidance Headquarters, Earth
February 26, 2379

Saskov's nobics were stretched to their limits in their efforts to control his reaction as he stared at the tall Seriatt's slim, long face.

The *mourst*'s vaguely reptilian skin was dark, its eyes a striking green. It was clad in black leather with armour like slabs of stone on its chest and limbs. If milky secondary eyelids had not flashed briefly across the Seriatt's eyes, Saskov would have said the creature was merely a static image.

"Colonel Saskov," said General Myson, "I would like to introduce you to Distinguished Mourst Warrior Brandouen. He is a Seriatt."

"Yes, Sire," replied Saskov. "That I can see." Saskov's nobics automatically stripped the tone of sarcasm from his voice and replaced it with a hint of respect.

Brandouen took two strides forward so that he was standing in the same area as Saskov: unlike Myson, the *mourst* was apparently not a projection. Saskov stood only chest-high to the *mourst* and was forced to look up at the Seriatt's face. The *mourst* looked calm, confident. He also appeared to be salivating slightly.

Saskov's nobics allowed their host's immediate and automatic refusal to be intimidated to continue almost completely unchecked as the Colonel returned the Seriatt's gaze. They had to work hard, however, to analyse and suppress the sexual arousal they detected.

But despite the strength of feeling they had to overcome, they were so effective that, had Saskov been ordered to state directly whether he found the *mourst* physically attractive, his negative response would have been an honest one.

"Distinguished Mourst Warrior Brandouen," said Myson. The *mourst* turned his head slowly to look at the image to his right. "This is Colonel Viktor Saskov. He will accompany you on this mission."

The Seriatt spoke in a throaty murmur. "*Gorguh eh-metillioc, nour.*"

Saskov's nobics translated the Seriattic language at such speed he was only aware that the *mourst* had spoken in his native tongue because the movement of his mouth was out of sync with the words that entered Saskov's head: "He is a minor figure," the Seriatt asserted. "I do not value him."

Apparently Myson had to wait a little longer for a translation, as Saskov heard the words from the direction of his superior's image a few moments later, issuing from unseen speakers. When he did so, Myson laughed heartily.

"For the record, Sire," said Saskov, still staring unwaveringly at Brandouen, "neither do I *value* this Seriatt. I have come across many *mourst* who could not be trusted." The nobics carefully monitored their host's thought processes; given their assessment of the situation they allowed events to flow.

"I have heard that humans are weak and cowardly," said the *mourst*.

"Come now," said Myson, "bickering is not the way for us to begin. The situation as it stands is ideal for none of us. We have to work together, and we must become used to that fact as quickly as possible. Colonel Saskov, I am certain that you will come to respect the skills Distinguished Mourst Warrior Brandouen will bring to this mission. He is very familiar with Seriatt's capital and the surrounding area, as it is where he was raised. I am equally certain, Colonel, that the respect you learn for our *mourst* comrade here will be reciprocated."

Brandouen looked down at Saskov again; his elegant face wore a slightly sour expression. "It is unlikely," growled the *mourst*. "I do not believe I can work with this human."

"I'm afraid you have little choice, Distinguished Mourst Warrior Brandouen," said Myson. "We need you to help us achieve our objectives, and you need us to help you return to Seriatt."

The *mourst* said nothing.

"As for you, Colonel Saskov, I know you will not shirk the duties assigned to you, and will execute your orders proficiently."

Saskov bowed. "Of course, Sire."

"Very good. I will not detain you any further by going into interminable detail at this stage, nor poison your minds with infocram files you must absorb later. Even though I am certain it would not be the case here, I learned to my cost long ago that even the most experienced of officers can sometimes disappoint with regard to such detail. And as we all know, that is where the devil lies." Myson turned his head as much as he was able to look towards the man standing nearby. "Greer," he said, "introduce our friends to our other, dare I say it, associate."

Greer disappeared from view for a few moments. When he returned he was accompanied by a small creature with leathery skin that was a very drab grey, as if all the vitality had somehow been sucked out of it. Its skin seemed to hang loosely on its skeleton, and was wrinkled like autumn leaves or as if weathered by prolonged exposure to sunlight. Its face was small, its features sinister, with evil eyes and a small, almost circular mouth.

Saskov immediately recognised the creature as a humanoid Sinz. Although he knew little detail about the race, he was aware that there were also amphibian and avian species. The example before him certainly seemed to confirm all he had heard about the humanoids.

"This is Fabricator Poluto," said General Myson. "He is a respected Sinz biological designer." Poluto looked towards Saskov and Brandouen. "It is he who has informed us of the way in which we can defeat the Sinz on Seriatt. If we can take advantage of their weakness before their counterparts arrive from their home world of Hascaaza, then we can overcome them. Fabricator Poluto informs us that it is simply a matter of our striking them in the right place, at the right time." Myson looked at the Sinz. "Fabricator Poluto, would you tell Colonel Saskov and Distinguished Mourst Warrior Brandouen what you know?"

Saskov initially heard a few clicks and sucking sounds that appeared to match the movements of the Sinz' round, wet mouth; then his nobics kicked in and began translating the strange language.

"Although they may appear strong," Poluto was saying, "my race is in fact susceptible to attack. As on Hascaaza, my counterparts on Seriatt are reliant on the *basillia*." The word sounded like a swallowing sound. "On Sinz there are many. They feed us. They breed us. They bind us together. But on Seriatt there is only one, and its solitude means that it is much weaker than its ancient ancestors on Hascaaza. Kill the Seriatt *basillia* and the Sinz can be overcome."

"So how do we kill it?" asked Saskov.

"It is an organism," replied the Fabricator, "and is reliant on water for its health. Cut off its water supply and it can be destroyed. However, although less strong than its ancestors, it remains extremely resilient, and the most certain way to ensure a rapid death is to poison it." The Sinz held up a small vial. Although it was tiny, Saskov could see that it contained a slightly cloudy liquid, within which seemed to float microscopic flakes of silver metal. "I have developed this potent toxin, which will kill the Seriatt *basillia*, if administered correctly."

"Can't we just go in there with a megacannon and blast this thing to hell?" asked Saskov.

"Due to the nature of their physical form, *basillia* are capable of withstanding a great deal of damage and continuing to live. Unless this weapon of which you speak is capable of inflicting severe physical trauma to its entire being, which may cover a very large area of Seriatt, both beneath the surface and above it, then no. The toxin is the only sure way. The Seriatt *basillia* has many weak points, but its heart is in a network of chambers deep beneath the Seriattic palace. This is also where the Seriattic officials are held. A shield, perhaps.

"The palace is also the Sinz nerve centre on Seriatt. That is where you must strike. There is a single access tube at the centre of the palace that goes directly to the heart of the *basillia*, deep within the Seriattic crust. *Basillia* defences differ depending on location, and although I have not seen the Seriatt *basillia* firsthand, it will almost certainly be defended by scorpions— they are the most fearsome defence you are likely to face. Overcome them and the *basillia* is virtually unable to defend itself."

"Great," said Saskov. "We've got to go underground and stick a needle in its alien ass. That doesn't sound like too much of a problem." Again his nobics were quick to level off the sarcasm and inject a note of enthusiasm.

"However," continued Poluto, "you must ensure that the toxin is delivered to the very heart of the *basillia*. It will not be sufficient to fire from a distance. Physical contact will be necessary."

"So when we administer this poison how do we know it's worked?"

"The toxin is extremely potent. Within moments it will become clear whether you have been successful. The surface of the *basillia* will begin to discolour, and its shape will change as its internal structure collapses."

"This poison of yours has a long shelf life, right? We're not going to get there to find it's lost its potency?"

"It will remain effective for an indefinite period."

"Thank you, Fabricator," said Myson. He looked at Saskov and Brandouen. "Do you have any questions before you depart?"

"Just one," said Saskov. "How do we know our scrawny little friend here isn't feeding us a whole pack of lies? For all we know this poison of his could be formulated to double the *basillia*'s strength."

"Fabricator Poluto has been extensively interviewed by experienced members of both the Public Protection Department and Enlightenment."

Saskov looked astonished and chuckled. "I bet that was an interesting session. Even the PPD and Enlightenment cores won't interface properly with each other. And more to the point, he's still in one piece. Their game must be slipping."

"I advised them that they would be unwise to allow their enthusiasm to get the better of them, and that if either of them allowed any unfortunate accidents to befall Fabricator Poluto, I would allow the other to practice their favoured interview techniques upon them. They are convinced that the information being proffered by our Sinz ally is accurate and genuine."

Saskov looked at the Sinz with suspicion. "But what's in it for him? Why's he betraying his own race?"

"Fabricator Poluto believes the Sinz have overstretched themselves, and that they will come to pay the price for this. He is . . . investing in insurance. Now, you may proceed to Inventory, where you will be issued with your equipment. Colonel Saskov: your nobics will be upgraded with the very latest evolution. I am assured that it offers a host of benefits over your existing software, and will contain much information of use to you in your mission. In addition, your personal sidearm will also be adapted to accommodate Fabricator Poluto's toxin."

"Very good, Sire. How many shots do I get?"

"I regret to say one only, Colonel. Not enough material was available for the Fabricator to develop more than a single dose of sufficient strength. He was able to use only that which he could bring with him. Sadly most of his supplies were lost during his journey. You will therefore need to be certain of the moment you choose for its delivery, bearing in mind the Fabricator's comments." Myson glanced at Greer. "I hope I have been well advised in my choice. I can rely on you, Colonel?"

Saskov bowed. "You can, Sire."

"I am glad to hear it." Myson looked at Brandouen. "You also have the opportunity to be imbued with nobics, Distinguished Mourst Warrior Brandouen. My biotechs assure me that despite the differences between human and Seriattic physiology a sufficiently compatible evolution can be developed quickly. You may find this technology useful."

Brandouen emitted an odd coughing sound. "I will not be filled with such poison," the *mourst* replied. "I have managed to survive without such artifice until now despite the efforts of my superiors to introduce similar technologies in the past. They merely serve to cloud the mind."

"Very well. The choice is yours."

"May I ask a question, Sire?" said Saskov.

"Indeed you may, Colonel."

"When we get to Seriatt, what's to stop Honourable Mourst Warrior Brandouen here jumping ship and doing his own sweet thing? How do I know I can rely on him?"

Myson smiled and looked at Brandouen as he spoke. "Like all Seriatts he is fiercely patriotic. Yet he is also a realist, and like all *mourst*, he desires power. I have therefore promised that if he helps us achieve our aims to the full, he will be rewarded with a notable position on his world as Structure oversees its redevelopment. Does that satisfy you, Colonel?"

Saskov looked at the *mourst* with suspicion. *No, I'm not sure it does*, he thought. But his nobics stepped in and he said, "Of course, Sire." They even ensured that he bowed slightly as he spoke, just for good measure.

"Excellent. Now you must go to Inventory, and when equipped proceed immediately to landing platform thirty-two, where you will find the vessel that has been assigned to you. You will be briefed regarding your mission parameters and objectives once you are under way. Go now, both of you. Do not fail me."

Seriatt
March 3, 2379 (Earth equivalent)

The sea was much colder than Delgado had expected, and before he had covered even half the distance he knew his energy was fading, leeched away by the water. But a combination of his nobics, pure adrenaline, and desperation to help Ash more than compensated, pushing him on.

The swell was greater than it had seemed from the shore—smooth, undulating hills that isolated him. Although he caught frequent glimpses of the copter's underside as the sea rose and fell around him, most of the time his view of the machine was obscured as he was carried up and down like a piece of driftwood. He glanced to his right; Lerval was a short distance behind him. Despite the *mourst*'s size and apparent physical power, he did not seem to be a strong swimmer.

Suddenly the swell carried Delgado down, and he was confronted by the copter's drab grey underside. The aircraft's three small wheels protruded from the otherwise smooth surface like black slugs.

He took the knife from his mouth. "Ash!" he yelled. His voice sounded pathetic, lost in the open sea. No response came. "Ash!" Still nothing.

Suddenly Lerval appeared, struggling against the rising swell, sinking again as he covered the remaining distance between them.

"Have you seen them?" he called.

"No. I'm going to—" Something touched Delgado's leg. He took a large breath, put the blade back between his teeth, and dived beneath the surface.

The water was dirty, and he could see only a short distance. Fronds of seaweed floated in front of him like severed hands. He swam down, kicking hard, then gripped the edge of the cockpit and pulled himself forward.

The copter was empty; the unbuckled harnesses drifted in the water.

To his left Delgado glimpsed a long, ghostly shape snaking through the water before disappearing into the murk. He turned. A Sinz amphibian suddenly emerged from the gloom. Its sour, elongated face was full of small, sharp teeth, and tentacles flowed behind it like ribbons. The creature lunged at him, but as Delgado struck out at it with the blade it veered away and dived beneath the upturned aircraft. He turned as quickly as he could, but the creature had disappeared.

Delgado swam up and pushed against the copter, gasping for air when he broke the surface a moment later. He glanced around, but could see only the copter's underside. Lerval had gone. There was no sign of Ash or Keth.

Suddenly a Sinz amphibian appeared in a seething mass of bubbles.

Ash was clutched tightly in its tendrils.

She coughed and wheezed as she fought to take in air against their pressure around her chest. The creature looked at Delgado, its mouth contorted into a grimace. It hissed at him, then turned its face towards Ash's and emitted a softer, wet pulsing sound. It knew Delgado wanted her.

Just as Ash seemed to be recovering a little the amphibian rolled forwards and dived again.

Delgado plunged under the water and grabbed at the creature's rubbery tentacles as it passed his feet. He felt barbs dig into his fingers and palm as he yanked at them, and an intense stinging. He gripped more tightly despite the impulse to let go, took the knife from his mouth with the other hand, and hacked at the tentacles.

A dark cloud stained the water. The Sinz coiled around and snapped at him with its horrific mouth; Delgado glimpsed Ash's terrified face as he lashed at the creature's face, slashing one of its dark eyes. The amphibian recoiled, and he felt its body thrust as it tried to escape. Delgado felt the tentacles slipping through his hand, the barbs digging deeper. Two other tentacles wrapped around his head, and he felt its stinging suckers attached to his face. He continued to hack at the Sinz until he had severed the tendrils wrapped around Ash, then grabbed at her tunic, pulled her from the creature's clutches, and pushed her towards the surface.

As she swam towards the light, the Sinz reared at Delgado once more, baring its tiny, pointed teeth. As it tried to wrap its remaining tentacles around him, he thrust the blade deep into its chest. The amphibian's back arced as it went into spasm, and a few moments later it was motionless in the water. His lungs aching, Delgado pulled the creature's suckers from his face and kicked hard towards the rippling silver sheet above him.

He groaned as his lungs filled again when he broke the surface. He saw Lerval treading water next to Keth, who was helping Ash clamber up into a copter that was hovering above the water, timing their efforts to coincide with the rise of the swell.

Delgado heard a faint splash and a gentle hissing sound, then felt something press against his back. Tentacles folded around his body and pressed his arms against his torso, squeezing him with a force that seemed disproportionate to their thickness. The second amphibian clutched him tightly to its chest, then pulled him back under the surface.

Again the creature's tentacles stung Delgado where they touched the backs of his hands and his neck, the suckers sticking to his flesh. He felt a certain numbness washing through him and began to feel drowsy. Holding his breath became difficult as the amphibian dragged him deeper. The pressure in his ears increased. Delgado looked towards the surface and could see the Sinz' powerful fins thrusting rhythmically, driving down, its tendrils flowing like some kind of opaque skirt. As his vision began to tunnel, Delgado saw a silhouette shimmering against the fading grey light of the surface, an indistinct form.

On the verge of being unable to hold his breath any longer, Delgado was aware of Lerval freeing him from the Sinz' grip, kicking his powerful *mourst* legs hard, and hauling him back towards the surface. For some reason the amphibian did not turn on Lerval, but disappeared swiftly into the deep.

Delgado's lungs filled painfully as he broke the surface. Three copters hovered overhead, just centimetres above the peak of the swell. The downdraft from their thundering rotors caused fluttering ripples of foam on the water.

Exhausted and incredibly cold, his limbs leaden, Delgado was unable to swim. As Lerval dragged him towards the nearest copter, he could see Ash already aboard another; even in his own state and at the distance separating them, he could see that although pale, she was conscious.

He was aware of the nearest copter descending a little, the pilot skilfully judging the sea's distance and mood. Delgado grabbed onto the side of its cockpit but was too weak to pull himself up. His nobics seemed unresponsive to his efforts to rouse them. He wondered if perhaps they had been neutralised by some kind of poison in the amphibians' stings. Despite the risk, the pilot reached over the side of the machine, somehow steadying the copter, and grasped Delgado under each arm to pull him up.

Delgado flopped over the side of the aircraft, and managed to pull himself into the machine as it climbed. He shuffled around in the confines of the narrow cockpit and sat limply in the rear seat. A pool of water began to form on the floor as his sodden clothes dripped. He glanced at the backs of his hands and saw angry circular weals where the amphibian's tentacles had gripped him and the suckers had pressed against his flesh.

As the copter headed towards the shore, Delgado closed his eyes and allowed sleep to envelop him.

Third chronological displacement
March 3, 2349 (Earth equivalent)

Delgado stumbled forwards and put out a hand to steady himself against the wall. His head was reeling. Gasping for breath, he clutched his churning stomach and concentrated on suppressing the gorge that threatened to rise. He felt the same sense of displacement as one who wakes in an unfamiliar room. As he began to recover, he looked up and took in his surroundings.

He was in a corridor within an old building. Although it had a certain familiarity he was unable to determine where he was. The wooden floor was covered with a dusting of sand. There were doors on either side of the corridor. Ahead of him on the left stairs led down to a lower floor.

This was not what he had expected. It was certainly far less accurate than the Oracle's previous attempts.

Delgado turned—behind him the temporal gate shimmered and danced, leaping arcs casting a warm orange glow along the landing like flames. Suddenly it dimmed, then faded to nothing. The sense of absolute isolation that accompanied the portal's closure smothered him again.

As his dizziness subsided, he walked towards the stairway. He paused at the top, listening for sounds of movement or conversation; but the building appeared to be deserted.

Remaining vigilant, he began to walk slowly down the stairs.

As he neared the bottom, broken fragments of memory returned to him. He felt a distinct sense of déjà vu. Although its precise location continued to evade him, as more of it came into view he began to recognise the room below.

Delgado paused momentarily when he reached the bottom of the stairs and looked around. The wooden table and chairs; the kitchen; the bureau-style terminal; the maps on the wall and the small table with its mouldy, half-eaten meal.

He suddenly realised where he was.

It was clear that although Entuzo had successfully focussed on a key event, this time the Oracle was way off the mark in terms of both location and chronology.

Through the window on the other side of the room he could see the dull red earth of the desert outside, some of the threadbare shrubs, the slender towers in the distance, and the immense walls of rust-coloured rock to the east. Out of curiosity he walked across the room towards the window, edging sideways between the bureau and the small table next to it to get a better view. He turned his head to look to his right, then cursed and immediately backed away, knocking the table; the glass standing next to the plate set upon it toppled over, and its contents spilled onto the floor.

He knew he had been seen, but was unsure what it meant and what—if anything—he could do about it. In a few moments they would enter the building.

He turned, ran across the room, and took the stairs two at a time.

Delgado paused when he reached the top, and pressed himself against the wall, breathing heavily.

He looked towards the stairway as he heard the door into the building open, then footsteps as they entered the room. Although they were whispering, he caught snatches of their conversation that made him tingle: *what do you make of this . . . that's just happened.* The words were like echoes, utterances made on his behalf by someone else, whispers from the demon in his head. Dizziness and disorientation smothered him.

A voice again; still quiet but much closer: "I think I'll take a look upstairs."

Delgado started, glanced behind him; there was no sign of the portal.

Beads of sweat glistened on his brow.

He heard footsteps on the stairs and began to contemplate numerous possibilities, none of which were particularly attractive.

Then he heard a faint fizzing sound, a deep resonation that seemed to correspond with the throbbing in his head, and then the corridor was bathed in amber light.

Entuzo. Oh, sweet Entuzo.

He ran towards the shimmering portal and leaped through it. And as the amber glow faded, a warm breeze dragged grains of sand across the wooden floor.

Reactionary Forces' Alpha Depot, Earth
March 7, 2379

"If you could just lift your feet, sir," said the valet, "I'll give the soles another coat."

Saskov placed his palms against the wall and raised each foot in turn to allow the application of more scartex. The thin layers of virtually transparent, gossamer-like material built up into tough, black aktiv-grip soles. The coating applied to the rest of his body would react to any given situation to provide the appropriate protection, sensitivity, or a host of other advanced options, all controlled by a midlevel core that would interface directly with his nobics. Already skin and nobics were arguing about which of them would control the Colonel's level of sensation.

"It's a good thing I'm in shape," said Saskov, looking down at his scartex-coated belly as his valet finished spraying his feet. "This stuff's sure a snug fit."

"You are not in good shape," snarled Brandouen, who sat in a nearby chair. His long form—already coated in scartex—looked preposterous in the small seat. "You are feeble," he said. "You are human."

Brandouen's valet knelt in front of him. "I need to give your soles a final coat as well, sir," he said. "If I could—" As he grasped the *mourst*'s left heel and tried to lift his foot, the Seriatt kicked out, striking the man in the chest and knocking him across the room.

"I can see this is going to be some picnic," said Saskov, looking down at the sprawling valet. He took his gun belt from his own valet and strapped it loosely around his waist. He began to check his sidearm—a slender black Harvey and Watson HiMag PS4 Longbarrel. There was a slight bulge in the stock where the techs had adapted the weapon to accommodate Poluto's poison vial, and a small additional switch to load the toxin into the projectile breech when its use was required. He flicked open the safety catch covering the switch and examined it; the workmanship was good: anyone unfamiliar with the HiMag PS4 would probably not realise that it was not factory-fit, and the adaptation would not interfere with its standard functions. He placed it back in its holster and held out his hands for the batman to spray them.

"Look," he said to Brandouen, "you want to get back to Seriatt, right? See your good old mom and dad?"

The *mourst* fidgeted slightly.

"Oh, wait a minute," said Saskov, "you have three sexes, don't you? I forgot about that. I'm not sure whether that's something I like the sound of or whether it's just too complicated for its own good."

"My *mourst* and *conosq con-touna* are both dead," said Brandouen. "Killed by the Sinz." The *mourst* spat the final word. "I want to return to Seriatt so I can kill them. All of them."

"There's a whole lot of Sinz on Seriatt, my friend. You think you can take them all on single-handed?"

"Other Seriatts are alive and will help me. I know it. If I am to die, then I wish to do so on the planet that is my home, while doing what I can to free my people from bondage."

Saskov glanced down: the *mourst*'s valet was crawling across the floor, eyeing the sole of Brandouen's left foot, which was visible as his leg was out-stretched with his heel on the floor. He seemed to be planning to try to complete his task while the Seriatt was distracted.

"Well, listen," said Saskov, "you want to avenge the deaths of your folks, I can understand that. It's an honourable thing. But I've got to deliver what my boss wants, and he wants you in the game with me, so it's important to me, too. Now we might have different goals, but when I'm given a mission by General William Myson I do my damnedest to make sure it all goes according to plan. You get me? I'm not about to let you or anyone else jeopardise my chances of completing my objectives. Now we can either work together and both get what we want, or we can work against each other. What'll it be?"

The *mourst* kicked the valet crawling towards him again and looked up at Saskov. "You are one of the best human operatives available?"

Saskov snorted. "I'm the best, period. Why do you think I was chosen?" Recognising the importance of their host's relationship with this Seriatt, the nobics allowed Saskov's tone to remain unfiltered.

"Then I do not rate our chances," Brandouen replied. "You do not encourage me. And your weapon is a toy. I am unconvinced that it—or you—are capable of liberating my planet."

Saskov leaned forward so that mere centimetres separated his face from Brandouen's. The *mourst*'s lips trembled like a snarling dog, milky membranes flicking across his eyes. "I'm not exactly overwhelmed with you, your big phallic symbol of a gun, or your knives, either." He pointed at the *mourst*'s broad-barrelled point-and-shoot weapon and the selection of blades fastened to his scartex-skinned legs in slim, black scabbards. "But it's part of the mission parameters that you're along," he continued. "I don't know how your military forces operate, Honourable Mourst Warrior Brandouen, but when General William Myson gives you an order you do what you're told and you do it good. And Myson's given you an order, my friend, so I suggest you buck up your ideas. If you really want to return to Seriatt, then the sooner you allow our friend here"—he jabbed a finger at the red-faced valet on the floor—"to do his job, then the sooner we can be on our way." Saskov stood upright again. "Besides," he said, patting the weapon at his hip, "the Longbarrel might not look like much, but it sure packs a punch. And it's more than capable of delivering Fabricator Poluto's concoction."

"Assuming this poison does what we are told it will do."

"Hey, Brandy, if the PPD and Enlightenment have had a go at him, he wouldn't be capable of even thinking about pulling a fast one over us, let alone attempting it."

The valet pushed himself up off the floor and approached the *mourst* again, even more warily than before. He flinched when Brandouen raised his foot, but this was only to allow the final coat of scartex to be applied.

Saskov's own valet handed him his visor. He rolled the material down over his head and it immediately adjusted to his form, the front morphing into a glossy black shell that covered his face, the rest fitting snugly against his skull and merging seamlessly at the neck with the rest of the scartex coating.

A new batch of nobics immediately opened up and began processing audio, visual, and olfactory information. Saskov turned and looked at himself in the mirror. He was nothing more than a silhouette.

Saskov looked at Brandouen's reflection. "We're going to have to make the most of this situation, my friend," he said. He turned, took the *mourst's* visor from the nearby table, and tossed it to him. "So just get that thing on and let's get out of here."

Observation craft *en cossur*, high orbit, Hascaaza
February 12, 2379 (Earth equivalent)

Mediator Latzinor was nervous in the presence of the Prime Associates. The three Sinz parliamentarians were in the pods behind his own aboard *en cossur*—the small observation craft conveying them to the war fleet's rendezvous point.

Latzinor's skin squirmed and tingled as he spoke. And as he spoke he was uncertain whether or not it was appropriate to be speaking, which only served to further increase his nervousness, and thus his discomfort. He hoped *en cossur* was aware of his state and would generously compensate for any errors he might make while piloting the craft; but such basic ships as *en cossur* were not known for their intuitiveness. It was only the more intelligent vessels that had been specially trained for direct interaction that demonstrated anything resembling sensitivity of their occupants' feelings, let alone awareness of their activities. Latzinor would simply have to be careful.

"I am certain the Prime Associates will be impressed with the Fabricators' efforts," he said, trying to sound confident. "Their birthships are strong, and have cast many fine offspring for the new fleet. They will serve us well for many thousands of seasons."

Latzinor caressed a gland in the control node near his right leg. As *en cossur* extended tight coils of braking energy, Latzinor manoeuvred to get the ship into position for a good view of the fleet. Stars wheeled across the displays in front of *en cossur*'s passengers.

Then the ships came into view.

There were hundreds of glowing vessels in high orbit around their world. Healthy and vital, their golden luminescence was a spectacular contrast to the blackness of the planet's night side, despite the rash of light the population centres spread across its continents.

There were vast transporters, sleek lozenges with dark oval portals and hoops containing sticky membranes for the capture and release of smaller, short-range vessels. There were the wide, flat passenger craft that would convey the Sinz themselves, buried in snug, warm pods for the brief but nonetheless arduous journey through the channel, or for the longer journey through space.

Orbiting the main stream of vessels were the sentries, sparkling drones vibrant with energy whose sole task it was to protect the rest of the fleet. Then there were the diplomats, which fussed and flapped among themselves, communicating the possibilities of what their task might entail upon arrival at their distant destination, while their crews tried to have some effect upon their course.

But the most important vessels of all, the craft whose health had to be maintained at all costs if any campaign was to be successful, were the birthships.

The birthships dwarfed all others. The numerous bulges in their smooth skin were evidence that the fetuses they carried were entering the second stage, developing the seeds that would eventually grow and bloom into propulsion units, and the nubs that would become the limbs that would support them when they touched the soil of distant worlds, and the fins that would steer them in their atmospheres.

Inside them, vacancies would be opening, small spaces that would rapidly grow until, after their delivery, they would be of sufficient size to house the associates of the Fabricators who had originally engineered them. And as their physical form developed, nourished by the birthships within whose warm bodies they grew, their brains would absorb the vast wealth of experience and knowledge that was fed to them from the parent ships.

Then the first of the birthships would calve, the succulent offspring slipping from their soft folds and shuddering at their cores' first powerful reactions. Quickly the craft would prepare to receive those they were born to convey, the still-soft vacancies hardening in preparation to receive the Sinz crew.

Within another season they would be mature, carrying a full complement of associates, themselves spawned by one of the Sinz *basillia*. By the time the symbiotic relationship had settled, the birthships would have been inseminated by the Fabricators once more, and another generation of ships would be growing within them.

"The Fabricators have done well," burbled Prime Associate Gultag from his liquid-filled pod. "These are fine craft. Healthy and strong. One can clearly see the vitality of the birthships."

"I agree," said Prime Associate Lubriatt. "Never before have I seen such impressive vessels. Their offspring will be sturdy indeed."

"I was confident that you would be impressed," said Mediator Latzinor, "and so I have asked Fabricator Burvo to join us."

Latzinor stimulated another of the pod's glands, and the image of a particularly wiry and dark-eyed Sinz appeared in front of each of *en cossur*'s passengers.

"Fabricator Burvo," said Latzinor. "Thank you for agreeing to convene with us."

"What do you want to know?" asked Fabricator Burvo. He appeared to be distracted by something the viewers were unable to see.

"The Prime Associates merely wish to congratulate you on your achievement," said Lubriatt." These are clearly some of the finest vessels ever grown."

"I thank the Prime Associate for his kind words," said Burvo. "But these ships arc merely the result of thousands of seasons of development by my predecessors. They are not my work alone. Their provenance is long and celebrated."

"Tell me, Fabricator Burvo," said Prime Associate Lubriatt, "how many vessels do you expect these birthships to produce? How large will the fleet be by the time it is required to go into battle?"

"I do not know," said Burvo. "No one knows. The birthships will calve until they calve no more. The calves will grow at the pace that is natural to them. If their vacancies are not sufficiently developed or their muscles sufficiently strong to accommodate their crews and weapons implants, then they will be open to attack."

"It is impossible for you to estimate how many we may have at our disposal?"

"Not less than thirty," said the Fabricator. "But with greater accuracy I cannot be certain. And there are other potential difficulties to consider. We do not know, for example, how the calves will react to weapons implants. It is entirely possible that they will reject them. It has happened before."

"Cannot such difficulties be overcome through administration of antidote serum?"

"Such attempts have rarely been successful in the past. If a ship is to be an effective combatant, it must be in harmony with the tools it has to use. If the ship is in any way discontent, irritated, or stressed, it will not perform as required. We simply have to proceed very slowly, which may limit the speed with which we can make them operational. They are individuals, and we simply do not know how they will react to their training."

"Could you not ask the birthships?" asked Gultag. "I understand these vessels are capable of some form of communication with each other. Perhaps they would respond to a direct approach."

Mediator Latzinor began to look for ways to close the dialogue. The tone of the amphibian's voice made him uneasy, and he could see Fabricator Burvo's growing irritation. Administration of praise had been Latzinor's aim, not confrontation.

"Not even we Fabricators fully understand the level of consciousness or awareness in the ships, nor the level to which they are capable of communicating," stated Burvo. "They communicate with each other, not with us. However, there is some evidence to indicate that this family is particularly active in that respect. It is something we are investigating."

"Excellent," said Mediator Latzinor. "We thank you for your time, Fabricator Burvo, and look forward to details of further developments."

Latzinor closed the communication channel before Burvo had time to respond.

"Fabricators are always too full of themselves for my liking," burbled Gultag before submerging himself in his pod once more.

"Now if only the channel would stabilise we could proceed," said Prime Associate Qordec. "If it does not, then much of the Fabricators' efforts will have been in vain. However strong our ships, and however competent the crews that are eventually assigned to them, without the channel we will not be able to traverse the vast distance that separates us from our associates on . . ." He faltered.

"Seriatt, Prime Associate," interjected the Mediator.

"Yes. Without the channel our associates will be isolated until the birthship arrives. If it arrives."

"Yours is a typically avian outlook if I might say so, Prime Associate," said Lubriatt. "What we see before us is a magnificent achievement. One for which the Fabricators deserve great recognition. Their restraint and awareness of the birthships' needs is most remarkable. With such talent at our disposal, I am certain we will prevail regardless of the conditions."

"But we must be realistic," insisted the avian. "We are reliant on the channel stabilising. But enough of this speculation. Mediator: you may now convey us to the Draskoc *basillia*. We wish to see the final batch of warriors emerge."

"Of course, Prime Associate," said Latzinor, a slight quaver in his voice. "I will set a course immediately."

Four

Seriatt
March 3, 2379 (Earth equivalent)

Delgado opened his eyes and found he was back in the cavern. He could remember nothing of the second ride through the tunnels, or of being pulled from the copter by the Seriatts. A large bonfire raged nearby, its heat strong upon his face. He was lying upon a layer of what appeared to be dried seaweed. A thick, coarse blanket covered him. When he peered beneath it, he found that his clothing had been removed.

Delgado looked around. Two Seriatts were standing nearby—one a *mourst*, the other a *vilume*; they were talking while watching the fire. There were racks near to the blaze; each held several spits upon which cubes of meat roasted. Occasionally one of the Seriatts would approach the fire and turn the spits, then hastily retreat from the heat. Delgado spotted his clothes hanging on a line strung between two poles hammered into the ground to the right of the bonfire; the cotton undergarments steamed gently.

The tents were positioned in a wide semicircle behind him, thick, circular sheets of off-white canvas arranged around central supporting poles. The fact that light no longer penetrated the fissures in the cavern ceiling indicated that it was nighttime outside.

The area around the fire was like an oasis of light in the gloom, illuminating a small area of the cavern; farther away the light faded, and detail was absorbed by darkness. The surface of the lagoon was an area of dark sheen; although barely visible, the stalagmites and stalactites formed elegant patterns. The entrance to the cavern through which he had flown with Cowell was a dark orifice in the rock to the far left.

"How you feeling?"

Delgado turned with a start. Ash was standing nearby, having emerged from one of the tents. She wore only her thin, grubby vest and shorts. It was a long time since he had seen her unclothed, and although she had always been pale she was certainly thinner than he remembered. "Fine," he replied. He pulled up the scratchy blanket a little as he pushed himself into a sitting position. "How about you?"

"No problem. I swallowed a little water, that's all. They told me I could use that tent. Its former occupant was killed." She nodded towards the Seriatts. "We owe them our lives."

Delgado glanced at the Seriatts. "Yeah. Guess so. What happened over the city? I wasn't sure you were going to make it back for a while."

"Me neither. But our *mourst* friend's a good pilot." She indicated Keth. "He manoeuvred that copter like it was part of him. And with me on the chain gun"—she held up her right hand like a pistol and blew two fingers—"we was smokin', baby. Not like you guys who snuck off while no one was looking."

Delgado smiled: she was fine. "Come on, Ash. You know it wasn't like that. One of the avians attacked us, hung onto the side of the copter, and damn near dragged us out of the sky. We were too heavily laden with the meat to get back up to you, so Cowell decided we should cut our losses and head back here. You know I wouldn't leave you there without good reason."

"Yeah, sure. Whatever you say, Delgado. Next time maybe think about jettisoning the extra weight, though, huh."

"Ah, you are awake." It was Cowell. The *vilume* had appeared from another of the tents. "You have slept for a long time. We were becoming concerned. How do you feel?"

"No problem," Delgado said. "Muscles ache a little here and there and my throat's dry, but otherwise I'm fine."

"The barbs on the amphibians' tentacles contain toxin," said Cowell. "The aches you feel will be due to its presence in your system. You should not worry. They touched a very small proportion of your skin, so you are not in danger. If they had come into contact with more of your flesh, then you could have been paralysed, or your heart stopped. It is their preferred method of killing. It seems to satisfy some primitive need in them. I would have expected a human of your stature to be more affected than you seem to be. Perhaps your immune system is strong. Once the poison passes from your system you will feel healthy again." Cowell looked at Ash. "And you are well? Keth says you were formidable with the chain gun."

"Yeah, well." She shrugged. "He sure is some pilot, I'll give him that."

"You both did well. Please. Sit. I shall fetch you both some food and water."

As Cowell walked away, Ash sat down near Delgado's feet. He glanced at her chest beneath the thin white fabric of her vest as she made herself comfortable, but averted his gaze quickly as she looked towards him. "So, Delgado," she said quietly. "What kind of shit is this? We're still on Seriatt and the Sinz invasion is complete. They seem to have taken over the whole goddamn planet."

Delgado looked towards the Seriatts standing by the fire. Cowell was pulling cubes of meat from the skewers and placing them onto small, square plates. The other Seriatts were looking towards the human visitors with suspicion as they chewed their food.

"You think we should tell them where we came from?" asked Ash.

"You mean *when?*"

She shrugged. "Sure, why not?"

"We'll say nothing yet. Let's wait and see how things pan out. If we feel that they're friendly, then we'll tell them. Or at least we'll think about telling them. But not before. They'll be wary of us for a while. We tell them something like that, and at best they wouldn't believe us. At worst they'd think we were trying to hide something. Think about it. How would we have reacted on the *Lex Talionis* if some strangers had turned up dressed in odd clothes and having no obvious method of transportation?" Cowell was walking back towards them, followed by other Seriatts. Delgado lowered his voice. "Let's just wait and see. Okay?"

"Sure, Delgado. Anything you say."

"Take this," said Cowell, handing them each a plate and cup. "Eat. It is good, and you need sustenance."

Delgado and Ash expressed thanks as they took the plates from the *vilume*. As well as the cubes of meat cooked on the skewers there were also slivers of crispy skin, what looked like dark brown claws, and a few gristly looking objects. Although some of the food did not look particularly appetising, it smelled delicious, and both Ash and Delgado began to eat enthusiastically.

"You should try the eyes," growled Keth. "They are most succulent." The *mourst* held out an avian eyeball, gripped between his fingertips. It was glossy and looked startlingly alive. He moved the eye around as if it was looking first at Ash, then at Delgado, emitting the throaty coughing sound that was *mourst* laughter. He then popped it into his mouth and began to chew. Ash watched him with the fingers of one hand pressed against her lips. Keth laughed again, then picked another eyeball from his plate.

"You must excuse Keth," said Cowell. "He enjoys his food, but can sometimes be insensitive to the feelings of others. Particularly those who are less used to his preferences and manner." Cowell picked up a large piece of crispy skin and began to crunch on it. But now," the *vilume* said, "you must tell us who you are and why are you here, on Seriatt?"

"You wouldn't believe me if I told you," said Delgado.

"Believe me, I have seen and heard many unbelievable things. You are unlikely to surprise me." Cowell looked at Ash. "Delgado's name I know," the *vilume* said. "What are you called?"

"Ash. It's short for Ashala."

Cowell looked at Ash as if the *vilume* found the fact that she allowed her name to be shortened somehow insulting. "Ashala is a beautiful name." Cowell looked at her longer than seemed necessary. Ash glanced at Delgado. "So," Cowell continued, "why are you here? How have you come to be on Seriatt? How did you get through the Sinz barrier?"

Delgado thought quickly. He didn't know what barrier Cowell was talking about. He would have to be careful. "We caused a diversion," he said. "Then we managed to get through unseen."

Cowell glanced from Delgado to Ash. "Which part of the barrier did you get through?" the *vilume* asked.

"Near the coast," Delgado replied. "I couldn't tell you exactly where, though. I'm not too familiar with the geography."

Cowell and Keth looked at each other. Another *mourst* sitting just behind Keth spat gristle. "He is telling lies," he barked. "The humans are trying to trick us. Maybe they are not human at all. Perhaps they are Sinz shifters."

Cowell looked uncertain.

"Tell me, Cowell," said Delgado, "how long have the Sinz been on Seriatt?"

"That is an interesting question," the *vilume* replied. "How is it that you need to ask? The Sinz invasion of Seriatt was an event that rocked planetary systems throughout the region. Yet you do not know how long ago this was?"

"And he says they passed through the barrier 'by the coast,'" muttered the other *mourst*.

Delgado savoured a piece of hot and crisp avian skin for a moment before responding; it had a strange, fishlike flavour but was extremely pleasant. "Time can be deceptive," he said as he chewed. "I'm just not sure how long it's been, that's all."

"You are *lying*," said a *vilume*. "It is obvious to us. You must be truthful or the trust that has been established up to this point will be lost."

Delgado looked at Ash. "Well?"

"Looks to me like we're in a corner. No point trying to be clever."

"She is wise," said Keth, with apparent admiration. "You should take the advice of your female."

"Hey, buddy," said Ash. "Let's get one thing straight: I'm nobody's possession, you got that?"

Keth bowed his head slightly and splayed his fingers. "Forgive me," he said. "It was merely a turn of phrase." Keth glanced at another *mourst* sitting nearby; amusement was clear on his face.

"Yeah? Well I suggest you think before turning your phrases in future, big guy."

There was much mumbling among the Seriatts. Delgado noted that although Ash had initially appeared angry, her face had reddened somewhat and she was trying hard not to smile as she and Keth stared at each other.

"Miskoh is correct, Delgado," said Cowell. "Ashala is wise. Openness is the best policy. If we feel you are a threat to us, we will kill you. Such actions are extreme but justified in this time of war. We cannot afford to misplace our trust. Too many have already been lost."

Delgado considered his options. In truth, there was little to consider. He and Ash were stranded, isolated, uncertain exactly where the time gate had sent them, or what they really faced. And without knowing what they were up against, it was impossible to plan a course of action. "Okay," he said as he continued his meal. "I'll tell you the facts. Straight. We left Seriatt at the time of the Sinz invasion."

"No we didn't," interjected Ash.

Delgado looked at her. "Well, technically, no we didn't."

"What do you mean?" Cowell looked from one to the other of them.

Delgado picked up a piece of skin and bit into it. "Well . . . we didn't actually *leave* Seriatt."

"So where have you been?"

"Well, here's the thing, see," said Ash, "we didn't leave Seriatt at the time of the Sinz invasion, but then we didn't exactly stay, either."

Cowell glanced at Keth and Miskoh. "You will have to be more clear," the Seriatt said. "If you neither stayed nor left, what did you do?"

"Well, we didn't stay on Seriatt at the time of the invasion. We moved to a different time. After the invasion." Cowell looked at Keth again, this time with apparent unease.

"You are saying that you travelled through time?" asked Keth.

Delgado nodded. "Seriatt's Continuity Scientists had extrapolated the properties of the Destiny Mask and developed a time gate. Only the Oracles and the Administrators knew about it."

"The Administrators and yourselves, it seems."

"Yeah, I guess."

"So as the invasion was taking place you escaped through the time gate?"

"You got it. It was clear that the Sinz meant business, and our choices were few. We got out while we were able. If we'd hung around, we'd have been dead meat. We arrived here not long before you picked us up. The temporal gate opened in that barn and out we came."

Some of the other Seriatts were whispering to each other, but Delgado was unable to judge their mood.

"It is incredible," Cowell said. "There have long been rumours of a machine similar to that of which you speak, but they are considered by many to be propaganda."

"There was tension between Seriatt and Earth before the Sinz invasion," said Miskoh, tossing his empty plate to one side. "Some have said that the humans helped the Sinz. What were you doing on Seriatt at that time?"

"That's a long story," said Delgado, putting down his own plate.

"We have time."

Delgado looked at Ash; she nodded. "We were on Seriatt because of my son. My sons, as it turned out. Does the name Vourniass Lycern mean anything to you?"

"Of course," said Cowell. "She was once the *conosq dis fer'n'at*, but absconded to the Affinity Group when it was her time to join with the *mourst* and *vilume dis fer'n'at* to produce a new Monosiell. She deserted our world, betrayed us."

"And all *conosq*," said Issilan. Another *conosq* next to her made noises of apparent agreement.

"That's not how it was," Delgado replied. "The Administrators cut a deal with Myson. She was supposed to give him a child to link Earth and Seriatt politically."

"Why?"

"Lots of reasons. Because the Seriatts were threatened by Myson's relationship with the Sinz. Because Myson wanted the new technologies he knew were being developed here. A whole heap of shit."

"He is human," said a young *mourst* at the rear of the group, staring intently at Delgado. "Humans are greedy. We all know it."

"Enough, Descan," said Cowell. The Seriatt was bordering on adulthood, and carried the boldness and idealism apparently inherent to all creatures at such a stage in life, when inexperience, confidence, and ego are a particularly potent combination.

"It was announced that Lycern had fled because she did not wish to engage in her role as *conosq dis fer'n'at*," Cowell continued.

"Who made that announcement?"

"The Administrators, of course. They were Seriatt's highest authority."

"Well, there it is. They fed you a pack of lies. They wouldn't want you to know the real story. Myson wanted her to give him a child to cement the link between Earth and Seriatt, but when she decamped to the Affinity Group complex he sent me to fetch her. But, well, things didn't work out as planned."

"You fell victim to her *muscein*," said Miskoh.

Delgado looked at the *mourst*. "Apparently so," he said flatly.

"It is potent indeed," the *mourst* replied, as if empathising. "I understand its effects on human males are particularly strong."

"Or perhaps human males are particularly weak," sneered Descan.

"Yeah, well that was all it was at first," said Delgado, ignoring the young *mourst*. "A physical thing. I had my own reasons, too, I guess. But it all became much more than that. Certainly more than I was expecting. She was strong, intelligent. I admired her. I fell in love with her."

"What is love?" asked Miskoh.

"I'm probably not the best person to ask."

"Who is?" said Ash.

"What about these sons you mention?" said Keth.

"They were mine. Mine and Lycern's."

"Neither was Myson's?"

"No. Lycern said he was infertile. She said *conosq* have some kind of intuition about that kind of thing. The thing was, although they were both mine, I didn't know about one of them. Michael. When things all went pearshaped, the Seriatts backed out of the deal, frightened by the possibility of the Andamour Council imposing sanctions, cutting off trade with Lyugg. Myson had to then approach the Council to try and get a legal case for Michael to take what they claimed was his rightful position as Monosiell."

"But Myson did not know Michael was your child?"

Delgado thought about it. "I don't know. But I sure didn't, I do know that. I only found out just before the Sinz invasion. When it was too late."

"What of the second child?"

"His name was Cascari."

"A good *mourst* name," said Miskoh, scooping meat into his mouth.

"Cascari grew up with me and the others aboard the *Lex Talionis*. That was the name of our base on Earth. We attacked Structure installations using whatever we could get our hands on. Ash was our intelligence officer."

"What happened to him?"

"Cascari was killed. By Michael."

The Seriatts stirred.

"His sibling? One of your sons killed the other? How could you have allowed this to happen?"

"You think I didn't try to stop it? The Administrators said it was the only way to decide which of them should be Monosiell. A sacred rite of some kind. The honourable way." Delgado's face was tight, his jaw set. "Cascari was a good kid. A sensitive kid. Considerate, you know? That part of his human side was stronger than his *mourst* side for a long while. The balance shifted a bit as he grew older, but I was always trying to prevent him becoming . . . a victim. But Michael was raised in the shadow of Myson's greed and saw Cascari's weakness. And he won." Delgado looked away. "I did my best. It was all I could do. It wasn't enough."

"Your son died an honourable *mourst* death," said Descan. "You should be proud of him."

Delgado looked at the young *mourst*. "I was," he said. "I still am."

Ash shuffled across the blanket, put her arms around Delgado's shoulders, and kissed the top of his head. "I tell you what," she said as she sat down next to him. "Let's trade. We've told you where we came from; how about you give us a few answers now, huh?"

Milky secondary eyelids flashed across Cowell's dark eyes. "That is not unreasonable," the *vilume* said. "What would you like to know, Ashala?"

"Tell them nothing," said Descan. "They could be shifters."

"Enough, Descan," said Cowell. "You will learn to hold your tongue or you will have to return to your tent."

"They are not shifters," said Lerval. "The amphibians were intent on killing them."

Descan put food into his mouth and chewed hard, staring at both Ash and Delgado.

"Where are all the other Seriatts, for a start?" said Ash. "And why aren't you with them?"

"We are their representatives. When the Sinz swarmed across our world, razing our cities to the ground, we gathered together what weapons and machinery we could and retreated, to fight them when the initial assault was over."

"Although some of us would have preferred to fight them when they came and suffer the same fate as many of our counterparts," said Miskoh. "But no. We had to sit by and watch as the Sinz spread across Seriatt like a disease. Polluting our skies and seas, draining our canals."

Keth grasped Miskoh's upper arm. "But it is as I have said to you many times, Miskoh: we had to stifle the instincts that rose in us, but it was the best course of action. If we had not gathered ourselves together and learned of the Sinz and their weaknesses, we would simply have fallen like so many of our kind. Our actions were strategically sound. You must see this."

"But you wanted to fight, right?" said Delgado to Miskoh. "You wanted to face the Sinz in combat, take up arms, protect your fellow Seriatts."

"You demonstrate much understanding of *mourst*."

"Had I been old enough I would have fought," said Descan, "and no one would have been able to stop me."

"No one would have been able to stop you dying, either, Descan," said Cowell. "In combat, impulsive and ill-considered behaviour leads to a certain death."

"So when you retreated," said Ash, "what did you do then?"

"We took our machinery, weapons, copters, and tents, and hid them," said Cowell. "We took shelter in the ruins of the city with many other Seriatts. Then, when things were quieter, we began attacking them where we could, on behalf of the refugees. Occasionally we return to Capital City, but this is infrequent. The rest of our party remain in the forests, moving from place to place to avoid the Sinz, while we conduct our attacks using the copters. Being separated from them is safest for all, although sometimes we join them."

"But don't the Sinz know you're here? Why don't they come to get you?"

"We have had many bases. This cavern is the best we have so far found. The rock is so thick it seems to block the Sinz' scanners. The tunnels are so numerous and extensive that it is unlikely they would be able to find us even if they had a rough idea of our location."

"There was no possibility of fighting them, of preventing the invasion? Where were your military forces?"

Cowell sighed. "Taken off guard. The Sinz moved too quickly for us to react. Capital City had fallen within hours of their arrival, and hundreds of thousands of Seriatts were dead. That was only the start."

Delgado looked from one to the other of them. "What happened to Michael?" he asked. "He fought Cascari in some kind of arena just before the Sinz invaded. He was to become the Monosiell."

Neither Cowell nor Miskoh replied. They looked uneasy.

"What happened to him?" Delgado demanded. "You must know."

"We do not," said Cowell. "The Sinz allowed him to be instated as Monosiell. They said it was some kind of concession, a sign of respect for Seriatt. Afterwards—he disappeared, along with the Oracles and the Administrators. We do not know where he is. You must accept that it is likely your son is dead."

Delgado stared at them. "I can't accept that."

"I was in the arena on the day of which you speak," said Descan. "I saw your sons' battle."

Delgado sat more upright, his eyes bright. "What happened? After the Sinz began to invade?"

"I do not know. The victorious warrior was taken away by those guards who remained alive. After that he was not seen again. But he fought well. He is strong."

"You say the Sinz have been preparing forces?" asked Delgado.

"Yes. A huge army. They are also building weapons and what we believe are battle craft. However, their construction methods are unfamiliar to us. They do not seem to assemble their machines through the marriage of many small components, but seem to grow them. But it clearly takes a great deal of time and power. Having observed their actions, we do not believe they were equipped for such a prolonged period of isolation. The wormhole has been unstable for many years. Sometimes its gravity wells are so deep no vessel can go near it. Occasionally it disappears completely, only to reappear some days later. Its activity seems to be erratic. As a result they are cut off from their home world, and no more Sinz have been able to join them here. Even if they departed from Hascaaza long ago, travelling to Seriatt by conventional means would take many hundreds of years even in the fastest ships. Yet despite this, they continue to prepare their forces."

"What about the other planets in the region? Surely the presence of the Sinz on Seriatt has caused something of a stir."

"We believe they placed some kind of field around Seriatt soon after their arrival to defend themselves. Lyugg vessels tried to enter our atmosphere some years ago in an apparent attack, but they failed. We watched the hot fragments of their ships fall to earth for days after. But the Sinz have been preparing their forces for a long time now. We believe the time for mobilisation is near."

"What gives you that impression?"

"We monitor the Sinz broadcasts and watch their movements. We do not understand their language, but their patterns are changing. Their construction facilities are full. Something is about to happen."

"They must have a base somewhere," said Delgado. "A master complex, some kind of headquarters, right?"

"There are several bases," said Cowell. "Some are clearly for the construction of military equipment, but we are less sure about the purpose of others. There is one in particular. Some of our people have tried to gain access to it in the past, but they were killed."

"Where is it?"

"It is around one hour's flying time from here. To the west, past one of the sites where the Sinz are growing their machines. With full tanks and calm air we should be able to make it."

"Take us to it," said Delgado. "Let's go see if we can tell what they're up to. Then maybe we can work out a way of dealing with them. And after that, well, who knows?"

Next morning the air was crisp and clear, the sky unbroken blue. They left the cavern early, the sounds of the copters echoing off the walls as the machines weaved through the tunnels. Delgado pulled the gun Cowell had given him from his pocket; it looked very basic. The *vilume* had for some reason decided not to equip him with any of the small explosives that she carried.

FOUR

Once outside, the aircraft flew inland at very low altitude in a ragged formation, following the rivers. It reminded Delgado of flying the Hornets in search of Structure targets. Only slower and colder and more draughty.

He looked to his right, towards the aircraft in which Ash was a passenger, piloted by Keth. She looked back at him and he saw a flash of teeth as she smiled and waved. Other copters bobbed in the air, their pilots focussed on their task, gunners twisting as they searched the sky.

"How much farther?" Delgado asked as the aircraft climbed out of a valley and turned right.

"We are approaching the first installation," Cowell replied. "You will see the vessels. Beware of approaching Sinz, though. This area is well patrolled."

The copter cleared the ridge, and Delgado saw a cluster of the Sinz towers directly ahead, rising into the sky like rusting needles. A river snaked like a metal engraving through a valley to a lake.

As the copter approached the towers, Delgado became aware of an excavation in the ground in the middle distance. It was huge, with sheer walls; it looked as if a gigantic cube of earth had somehow been plucked from the planet's crust.

As the ground fell away beneath them, Cowell pushed the joystick forward. The copter descended, levelling off when the aircraft was skimming the treetops. The leaves below it shuddered in the downdraft from its rotor. A few moments later the ground suddenly dropped away vertically beneath the machine as they passed directly over the excavated area.

Delgado looked down. The hole was enormous, its sheer sides dropping hundreds of metres, the different layers of the Seriattic crust clearly visible. The air directly above the canyon was noticeably warmer.

There was a great deal of activity within the crater. Numerous, gigantic elliptical structures spanned its width. Like bulbs of blown glass, they seemed to glow deep amber from within. They were linked by umbilical tubes, ridged and fat, and then by even thicker pipes to strange bulblike objects around the crater's perimeter. They seemed to pulsate gently.

Each of the elliptical objects was teeming with spiderlike creatures the size of a human male, which scurried across the glossy surfaces. At the centre of the crater, in the middle of all the activity, was an object that looked like several gigantic, conjoined hands, the numerous fingers of which writhed and stretched to touch different points on the vessels' hulls, producing tiny points of brilliant orange light.

"They are Sinz warships," Cowell called. "As I said: it is as if they grow them. No raw materials go in. But the ships increase in size." The *vilume* pointed, moving her arm in a sweeping arc. "You see the other craters?"

Delgado looked at the land around them and saw more dark squares on the terrain. The craters were like patches of mould on the landscape, with more clusters of towers next to each.

"Each crater contains vessels such as these," said Cowell. "The excavations number almost one hundred. We have watched them grow steadily. They seemed to break down the ships they originally used to invade Seriatt. We believe they used the fragments like seeds to generate these new vessels. Now there is no more room in the craters. The time of their deployment must be close. Perhaps then they will grow more."

As Delgado looked down, he heard a thin clattering sound and looked to his right. Streams of tracer were arcing from the guns on the other copters as Sinz avians plummeted towards them, slashes of grey in the blue sky, pointed wings swept back against their flanks.

As Cowell turned the copter towards the other machines, Delgado grasped the weapon mounted next to him and flicked open the safety catch, then raised the barrel and fired.

The thick, meaty sound the gun made was far removed from the tinny noise that reached him from the other machines. His hands tingled as the gun dragged the ammunition from the mounting on the right and through the barrel, while spent cartridges ejected on the left with a bright musical note.

The avians were still out of range, the tracer falling far short, so Delgado stopped firing and waited. He saw Ash hit one of the creatures as it sped towards her copter; the avian's rigid, arrowlike form immediately folded, and it fell towards the vast crater below like discarded paper. Another of the Sinz extended its thin wings and turned hard, circling behind a copter at the rear of the formation. The crew appeared to be two *mourst*. The creature was moving so rapidly that the gunner was unable to track it quickly enough, and before he could bring the weapon to bear the avian had swooped beneath the rotors and dug its talons into the copter's hull just below the turbine housing.

The machine rocked and descended slightly. The creature pecked at the crew in the cockpit with its sharp, curving beak, buckling the copter's fuselage as it lunged repeatedly, its entire body flexing. As the copter swayed wildly, the avian instinctively sought to maintain stability and extended its wings upwards. Delgado heard the creature shriek as they were severed at the midpoint by the coptor's blades. The creature thrashed its head from side to side and wailed in agony. A loud grinding sound indicated the expiry of the engine. Centrifugal force flung fragments of rotor blade into the air. In its death throes the Sinz avian continued to cling to the machine, as both it and the stricken copter tumbled towards the ground.

Delgado looked at Ashala's copter again. She was firing at another avian that had made one attack and was turning for a second. He and Cowell were closer now. He gripped the gun stock firmly, swung the weapon around, and fired again.

As the tracer arced through the air towards it, the Sinz altered its trajectory, breaking off its attack of Ash's copter and heading directly towards Delgado. Its speed was incredible, and although Ash tried to track it with her own gun she was unable to hit the beast.

"Look out!" cried Cowell. "It is heading this way!"

Delgado fired his chain gun as the creature loomed, but although he hit its wing near the body and in the side of the face, its determination and battle-driven fury overcame the injuries, and it continued unabated. As Cowell tried to take evasive action, Delgado continued to fire. He could see blood flowing from the wounds he continued to inflict upon the creature as it closed on the copter. The moment before impact it emitted an intense shriek, then collided heavily with the side of the fuselage.

There was a dull crunch. The cockpit buckled and the aircraft was pushed sideways through the air. The avian's talons curled around the cockpit, crushing and penetrating the thin metal. This time Delgado was quick to move his leg. The copter's engine groaned and coughed as Cowell tried to wring more power from it, struggling to maintain both attitude and altitude. The creature pounded its curved beak against the side of the copter as it tried to reach either Delgado or Cowell, its strange fat tongue thrashing around in its mouth as it cried. Despite the ferocity and blindness of the attack, Delgado could see the intelligence behind the avian's evil, polished eyes; it wanted them not only to satisfy some primeval, instinctive need, but also for whatever reward would come its way as a result.

As Cowell fought to control the copter, Delgado produced his knife. When the avian lunged again, he thrust the blade into the creature's forehead up to the hilt.

Something gave. Delgado felt a strange crunching sensation as the blade met some resistance; then it penetrated more easily. Thick, dark liquid sprayed over his hand and forearm, and he was aware of the avian's strange leathery skin yielding slightly to the pressure of his wrist pressing against it. The animal whined. Its eyes seemed to widen. The violence of its attack suddenly abated.

Delgado pulled the blade from between the creature's eyes and slashed at its throat, inflicting terrible wounds. He gripped the loose skin of its chest in his left fist and hacked repeatedly at the creature. Dark, wet lines blossomed across its leathery skin.

Mortally wounded, in its final moments the Sinz avian coughed dark globs that spattered the cockpit and its occupants. It shuddered once; then one foot released its grip and the creature fell back so that its grey chest was pointing the sky, one tattered wing hanging limply.

Delgado leaned over the side of the cockpit and looked down; the machine was spiralling down. There was little height left. He looked at the avian's foot, which was still clamped around the side of the cockpit.

"Have you killed it?" asked Cowell as the *vilume* continued to struggle with the copter's controls.

"Yes, but it's got some kind of lightweight armour around its legs. There's no way to cut this thing free."

"We are losing altitude quickly. We will have to make a forced landing. Prepare yourself."

Delgado pulled his harness straps as tight as he could, then looked down past the dead avian towards the trees speeding beneath the copter: they were close-packed, and there was no obvious place to land ahead of them. He looked up, searching the sky for other aircraft. He saw only one; two avians were clamped to its underside, hacking alternately at the cockpit. He was unable to tell whether it was Ash's machine.

Suddenly there was a loud thudding sound and the copter began to lurch. Delgado looked down and saw the avian smashing into the treetops, becoming increasingly broken with each impact. In front of him Cowell was tense, trying to bring the copter down as softly as she was able. They passed over a narrow gap in the trees through which ran a narrow stream, but as Cowell tried to turn the machine the Sinz became impaled on a tree branch and the copter was yanked through 180 degrees. As they were thrown around in the cockpit, Delgado heard a loud wheezing sound followed by a tremendous bang, and the copter began to fall backwards through the trees.

Primary *basillia*, Draskoc, Hascaaza
February 18, 2379 (Earth equivalent)

The cavernous chamber was dank and humid, the air thick with a stench like that of organic corruption. The soft walls were slick with mucus. Giant, eyeless scorpions stood guard, prepared to impale on their tusks, or the barbs of huge, curved pincers, any creature that might threaten the *basillia*. Recognising the friendly pheromones of the visiting Prime Associates and the nervous Mediator, they remained still, apart from the occasional movement of their mandibles and the twitching of their delicate antennae.

Directly in front of the Prime Associates, the Draskoc *basillia* was a bloated, swollen organ that filled the rear of the cavern, a vast ruin of bruised flesh that occasionally heaved and rippled. At its centre was a sphincter, tight and moist.

It was producing Sinz.

As the associates watched, another new Sinz emerged, slime-covered and reeking, from the *basillia*'s orifice. It was a loose assemblage of bone wrapped in a thin sac of almost transparent flesh. Although fully formed and of near-adult size, it was impossible to tell whether this particular Sinz was avian, amphibian, or mammalian, its true form not revealed until it burst from its soft cocoon and unfurled its feeble wings, scurried along the ground to the nearest water, or tottered unsteadily on its legs. As the newborn's body writhed within the membrane that surrounded it, several flexible muscular limbs extended from the ceiling. They picked up the newborn Sinz with suckered hands, and carried it to a vacancy in the wall, where it was placed among other, previous arrivals and absorbed by the thick, nutritious jelly that would coat it until it was strong enough to enter the world.

Prime Associate Lubriatt surveyed the rows of sacs that lined the tunnel walls, and the walls of the other tunnels leading in all directions away from the *basillia*. There were thousands of the sacs, like immense pustules imbued with some vague life.

"We have a fine army," Lubriatt said. "In one sense I do not desire to see them used. Yet so much has been invested in their creation that it would be wasteful if they were not to see action."

"The Fabricators have worked hard to ensure that the *basillia* is well nourished," observed Gultag, rubbing the moist tips of his long tendrils across his rapidly drying skin. "It is thanks to their staunch efforts that we have such a fine body of associates. They should be rewarded. As for using or not using this army, Prime Associate Lubriatt, that is dependent on the channel, and whether or not it stabilises sufficiently for us to use it."

"What is the forecast?" asked Qordec. "In what state is the channel at this time?"

"The Monitors say that it has demonstrated symptoms of stability," said Lubriatt, "but that this has occurred in the past only for turmoil to ensue again. It is this unpredictability in its fluctuations that makes using it so potentially hazardous. For myself, I admit to having doubts regarding the likelihood of the channel becoming stable for a prolonged period."

"Why is that, Prime Associate Lubriatt?"

"It has been unstable for too long. I believe we must prepare the birthships for the possibility that they may have to make the long journey through standard space. They may have to delay the birth of their offspring."

"I agree," said Gultag. "Our Associates on Seriatt need our help. We must act decisively. Our protracted deliberations and constant indecisiveness have put our colleagues at risk. The time has come to help them. Now if you will excuse me I must return to my lagoon. I am beginning to suffer considerable discomfort."

The amphibian turned and slithered from the chamber, his long tendrils rustling behind him like a plastic wedding train.

"I also agree," said Qordec. "The time has come to act."

"Very well," said Lubriatt. "If the majority of the Prime Associates concur, then my protestations would be futile. Mediator Latzinor. Begin to make the necessary arrangements. The birthships must be ready to leave soon."

Planetary Guidance Headquarters, Earth
March 7, 2379

A travelpod conveyed Saskov and Brandouen directly to the landing platform where the Needle was waiting for them.

The craft's name reflected its form. It had an extremely low profile. Indeed, it was so shallow that Saskov was uncertain whether a human, let alone Brandouen, would be able to stand up inside it even at the highest point. He wasn't even sure the *mourst* would fit through the tiny hatch. Other than the three short skids upon which the vessel squatted, and the open hatch hanging down from the side nearest to them, there were no protrusions in the craft, no imperfections in its smooth skin. The matte black hull seemed to suck in light.

A tall, square-shouldered tech with a Development insignia walked towards them. His identification tag stated that his name was Hollis, S. He had a mop of dark hair that fell in front of his eyes and a cheerful grin.

"Hello," he said. "I'm going to give you the Needle." He laughed. "I'm going to give you the Needle," he repeated. He laughed some more and rose on his tiptoes for a moment. "Never mind," he said. "Just one of my little jokes. Nice outfits. Scartex, isn't it? One size fits all." He laughed again.

Saskov's nobics stifled physical violence impulses but allowed verbal aggression to pass virtually unchecked as he peeled the visor from his face. "I'm going to give you the benefit of the doubt here and assume you have no idea who in hell you're addressing, Hollis."

Hollis glanced down at the notepad strapped to his forearm, touched the screen once, then looked up. "Yup. Colonel Saskov, right?"

"That's right. From now on you will address me as 'sir,' do you understand?"

"Absolutely, sir. But what do I call him?" Hollis nodded towards Brandouen.

"You don't call him anything. You address me at all times. I'm the senior officer here. Got it?"

"Yes, sir. But what if he asks me a—"

"He won't. Now tell me about this ship. Just the essentials. We've got to get out of here."

"Certainly, sir. This is the Needle. It's the only one like it. Well, apart from the other one, that is. But that one's the test model so it doesn't really count. We're using it to develop new types of—"

"Just tell me about this one, Hollis."

"Right. Yes. Well, it's a completely new design. We've never had anything like it before."

"What's so special about it?"

"I can't tell you, I'm afraid, sir. It's all classified."

"What's it made of? I've never seen a material like that."

"Sorry. Classified."

"What about the engines? They look very small to me for a ship that's supposed to be the fastest thing we've got."

Hollis shook his head. "Classified."

"Well I've got to fly the damn thing, Hollis, so what can you tell me about it?"

Hollis looked at the Needle, considered. "Well," he said, "although the engines look small, this ship's really fast. And I mean *really* fast. All you really need to know is that you should be able to get to the Seriatt system in about twenty minutes."

"That's impossible."

Hollis smiled as his enthusiasm bubbled to the surface. "You'd think so, wouldn't you? Isn't it fantastic? Thing is, that's just the time it'll take you to get into Earth orbit. Or the orbit of whatever planet you're departing from.

See, the Needle's not so much a physical movement vessel in the traditional sense, more an interdimensional vehicle. It uses something completely new. A revolutionary concept. We call it an überspace drive. You use the traditional containment-field engines to get into space and to fly relatively short distances, but for longer-distance travel the ship's core calculates the überspace reference of the dimensional point you want to go to; then the überspace drive moves you to that point by effectively slipping the ship sideways across dimensions. . . . But, see, now I've told you too much. It's all classified."

"I hope you're never subject to interrogation, Hollis. I can't see you holding onto our secrets for long. This ship. Is it like slipspacing?"

"No. Nothing like it, because slipspace involves actual movement, whereas with the überspace drive you effectively stay in the same place, just traverse dimensions. You think you've moved, but you haven't. Well, you *have*, but—"

"Right. I see."

"It's going to revolutionise space travel when it's put into a commercial liner. If it gets put into a commercial liner. All we need to do is work out how to make it work with a greater mass. And with less power. It's all about the cost per person in the passenger travel industry, you know."

"*Gurhargeth menac-to ar*," spat Brandouen.

"What did he say?" asked Hollis.

"He says shut this idiot up and let's get on with the job," replied Saskov, even though his nobics decided not to translate this particular insult. "I have to say I'm in agreement with him. Especially if you can't tell us anything worth knowing."

Hollis laughed again. "Well, let's get aboard then and I'll show you what's what."

They walked across the landing platform to the Needle, and Hollis motioned towards the hatch. Saskov stooped slightly, then stood upright, so that his upper body was inside the craft. He felt slight dizziness, as if his nobics had suddenly gone haywire.

The vessel was small. Very small. It was a good job that they would not have to be inside it for long: much time spent in such close confines with the Seriatt could lead to some friction.

The flight deck, if that was what it could be called, was a cell no more than four or five metres long and a couple of metres wide. The walls were draped in creamy material; the floor was covered in plush material of the same colour; it had a thick, spongy texture, as if the Needle's floor were coated in moss. The interior was saturated in ambient light that gilded everything.

There was a small hatch at either end of the cabin. Two broad seats in soft cream leather faced each other, positioned on either side of a central console that looked like a black glass coffee table. Saskov noticed that the seats had no harnesses. The console also seemed too far away from the seats and too low to use comfortably. Saskov assumed it was only intended for monitoring, comms, and information purposes. There did not appear to be any other controls or instruments.

He ducked out of the vessel. Brandouen investigated the craft's interior as Saskov spoke to Hollis. "There's not much room in there," he said, trying to ignore the continuing dizziness.

"Doesn't need to be. You won't be travelling for long, so there's no need for a whole bunch of facilities to keep you occupied. It's step on here, step off again at the other end."

"What's behind the doors at either end?"

"One end it's a latrine, the other it's an escape pod. But they're both, how shall I put it? Cosy. So cosy, in fact, I wouldn't recommend using either of them unless you really have to. Especially the latrine. Stale air is recycled quickly, but an odour will linger for a while." He wrinkled his nose. "And try not to get them mixed up. You don't want to sit on the toilet when you're looking for the escape pod. But then, having said that—"

"How do we fly it?" interrupted Saskov. "There don't seem to be any flight controls."

Hollis smiled. "It flies itself. Takes you right where you want to go. You just have to imagine what you want the ship to do, where you want to go, and the core will gather the information from your nobics, consult with the navigation data, and do it for you. If it's something simple like landing in a wide open space, you just picture the Needle landed in that location and the core will do the rest. There are some emergency interface controls stored in the base of the pedestal, but you won't need them. It'll even become invisible if you want it to. There have been concealment engines in existence for a long time, but they would only hide a ship and its crew from sensors. But we found that by putting six small containment-field generators in a certain configuration and running them in a certain way, whatever the fields are applied to becomes invisible to, well, just about everything. It's much more effective than any similar system we've attempted to use before, but for some reason we're not quite sure about yet, it also seems to have an adverse effect on the functionality of the ship's sensors. The materials used also mean that the core can only link fully with your nobics when you're inside the vessel. We had hoped to achieve some level of remote control—say you're stuck somewhere and need the ship to come pick you up, then it'd realise that and comply. But we just haven't found a way of enabling such delicate communications. The generators sap a hell of a lot of power, too, particularly when airborne, so you don't want to use the invisibility function too often, or for too long."

"What if you imagine something that you don't really want to happen? Something that just pops into your head. I mean, if I wonder what it would be like to fly straight into a sun. . . . Would it do just that?"

"No. You'll have to be very careful for the first few minutes, while the core gets used to your way of thinking, but it has the ability to isolate and identify different cognitive patterns, and can separate supposition, conjecture, and other common thoughts from active intentions. The latter are what it focuses on by default. The former are mostly just white noise. Part of it will listen to the white noise in case something important crops up that it might need to know about, but that stuff's largely junk as far as the core's concerned. The inefficiency of the organic mind. You're probably thinking about half a dozen things right now, but you just aren't aware of it."

"I'm not sure I like the idea of a ship's core sitting inside my head and deciding what I want to do," said Saskov.

"There's nothing to worry about," Hollis replied. "It's just an extremely advanced form of nobic interface. I supervised its design myself."

"Yeah? Well that sure sounds like something to worry about to me, soldier." As Hollis laughed, Saskov was unaware that his nobics and the Needle's core were already engaged in dialogue. Much to their annoyance, due to a software protocol with which Saskov's nobics could not argue, the Needle's core would have the last word regarding any decisions Saskov might make, particularly if those decisions put the ship in jeopardy. And despite what Hollis believed, the core was also perfectly capable of communicating with any software flux entity within a nine light-minute radius; it had simply chosen not to reveal this fact.

Saskov looked at the Needle's hull. "What about weapons?" he asked.

"What about them?"

Saskov sighed, flattened his lips, and looked to his left, beyond the edge of the landing platform; Unity Habitat reflected the turbulent clouds overhead. "Tell me about the weapons, Hollis. Where are they? What type?"

"They're new. Well, the guns themselves aren't new. We decided to go for Maurann Decimators. They're an old design, but they're reliable, accurate, and have great range. But you control them in a similar way to the Needle itself. There's no actual target selection or firing. You just have to imagine your target being hit and the core will do the rest. Ka*boom*!" He splayed his fingers, widened his eyes, and smiled.

"If there are two people on board," asked Saskov, "how does it know which of them is in charge? What if one of them wants to go one place, and the other occupant wants to go somewhere else? Which of us will it obey?"

Hollis laughed again. "Easy," he said. "Whoever's sitting in the seat nearest the nose is the primary controller."

"There's some kind of headset interface?"

"Nope."

"So how in the hell does it—"

"It just knows. Call it AI ESP."

"I never did like abbreviations. I'll just have to make sure I—" Saskov looked for Brandouen, but the *mourst* was nowhere to be seen. "Where the hell's he got to?" he asked. He ducked under the edge of the Needle's hull and stood up in the hatch again. Brandouen had climbed into the craft and was sitting on one of the seats, his long legs outstretched in front of him. He had also removed his visor. Saskov was pleased to see that it was the control seat that remained vacant.

He climbed up into the ship and swore quietly to himself; he had been right: a human couldn't stand upright inside it.

As Saskov sat down opposite Brandouen, his body settling easily into the large, soft chair, Hollis's head appeared in the open hatch. He looked at the floor immediately in front of his face, glanced at Brandouen's hefty leather boots, and tutted. "You see," he said, "look at those dirty great footprints. I told them it was a mistake to use this colour."

Seriatt
March 5, 2379 (Earth equivalent)

"Cowell. Cowell." Delgado patted the *vilume* on either side of the face, but she demonstrated no sign of regaining consciousness. He stood and turned to face the stream. It was very shallow, small rocks and pebbled sandbanks breaking its glittering surface. The copter squatted at its centre like a crushed insect, its rotor blades bent out of shape, the cockpit crumpled. A dark finger of smoke drifted from the turbine housings and rose high into the sky. There could be no clearer indication of their location.

Delgado stooped, cupped his hands, and scooped up some of the water, then positioned his hands above Cowell's face and allowed it to trickle between them.

The *vilume* frowned, shook her head, coughed, and sat upright. Delgado threw the remaining water to one side. Cowell shielded her eyes with one hand and looked up at Delgado. The Seriatt looked a little disoriented.

"Thank you," she said.

"Think nothing of it. How're you feeling?"

"My back and shoulders are a little sore, but I think bruising is the most serious injury I have suffered." She unzipped her tunic and pulled the cloth off her shoulder; the skin was red where the harness strap had cut into her flesh. Delgado admired the curve of her neck and shoulder, the smoothness of her skin.

"It is nothing," she said, zipping up the tunic once more. The pebbles on the shore crunched beneath her as she stood. She looked at the copter. "We are lucky to have survived such a landing."

"Was that what it was? And there I was thinking we'd crashed. Yeah, we were lucky. Thing is, now we've got to survive getting out of here." Delgado looked around. Away from the stream the woods were dark, and the trees so closely packed that it was difficult to see for more than a few metres. The dead Sinz was lying a short distance upstream, having been dragged from the copter by the trees as the aircraft came down. Its body looked a slightly odd shape, like a plastic toy left near a heat source.

Delgado walked over to the creature and nudged the corpse with one foot. "Any idea which way we should go?" he asked.

"We flew into the wind on the way here." Cowell looked up at the direction the smoke was drifting. "If we go that way"—she pointed—"we will be travelling in the right direction. But it will take a long time to get back to the cavern. We have travelled far, and across much difficult terrain."

"Well, I'd rather not walk myself, but can you think of an alternative?"

Cowell thought for a moment. "No. Come. We will go this way."

After they had been walking upstream for a few minutes Delgado grabbed Cowell's tunic and stopped dead. He crouched, bidding her to do the same.

"What is it?" Cowell asked.

Delgado held up one hand. "Heard something," he whispered. He looked around, scouring the dusky space amid the trees. He saw a rodentlike creature scurry across the ground and up a tree.

Could that have been all it was?

Then two small figures in black-and-grey uniforms stepped over the trunk of a fallen tree as they followed a narrow dirt track leading towards the stream.

Sinz.

He touched Cowell's arm; she indicated that she had also seen them. He could not tell whether they were armed.

Delgado motioned to Cowell to move away from the stream. Keeping low, they crept towards the trees on either side of the track. They each crouched next to a tree trunk. Delgado listened. The two Sinz were not talking, but neither were they making an effort to be particularly stealthy: twigs snapped beneath their feet, and leaves crunched and rustled as they walked.

Delgado motioned to Cowell and they stood slowly, careful to ensure that they remained hidden. Delgado produced the sidearm Cowell had given him prior to their departure from the cavern, then changed his mind and pulled out his knife instead. The two Sinz approached, then stepped through the trees between them.

Delgado and Cowell grabbed them. Delgado was surprised at the Sinz' strength. It was as if the creature had no bones, but was pure muscle. Instead of simply cutting its throat, he was forced to wrestle the writhing figure to the ground.

Pinned to the floor by Delgado's weight, the Sinz continued to struggle. Delgado was struck by the roundness of its face, the withered appearance of its skin, and its small, pointed teeth. It looked like evil personified.

With his blade pinned beneath the Sinz, he reached up with his other hand and gripped its throat. Its grey skin possessed an elastic quality and seemed to stretch like dough beneath his fingers. As it struggled for breath, the Sinz stared at him and emitted a soft hissing sound from the back of its throat. Delgado increased the pressure. As the Sinz choked and began to lose consciousness, it seemed to soften beneath him, as if its internal structure— whatever form it took—was losing its strength. By the time its eyes were closed the Sinz' body was almost flat, a limp parcel of soft organs.

Cowell was to his right, struggling to overcome the other Sinz, which was kneeling on top of her, pinning her to the ground. She yelled as the Sinz leaned forward and sank its teeth deep into her neck.

Delgado jumped up and leaped towards them, kicking the Sinz in the side of the torso with both feet. The creature rolled across the soft earth and got to its feet in a single, easy movement, as if unaffected by the blow. It confronted them, teeth bared, its body like a single flexed muscle. It glanced at the corpse nearby, then made the same gentle hissing sound as its counterpart.

Then it simply faded away in front of them.

Its skin seemed to melt, shrinking away to reveal a thin, flexible skeleton of sinewy ligaments, its facial features fading as if consumed by some hideous wasting disease. As its outer body rotted away, its bones became thin and transparent, its internal organs briefly visible within the dissolving frame, moist and complex. The Sinz became nothing more than an indistinct shimmering amid the trees; then vaguely they saw the creature turn and run, its insubstantial form absorbed by the foliage.

"You okay?" Delgado asked Cowell while still looking into the trees.

"I am fine. And you?"

"No problem. Your neck's bleeding."

Cowell touched the wound gingerly and looked at her fingertips. "It is nothing," she said. "The bleeding will soon stop."

Delgado stepped over to her and pulled gently at the neck of her tunic, peering at the wound. "There's some swelling around the punctures," he said. "You'll need to disinfect it with something. They weren't the cleanest teeth I've ever seen."

Cowell reached up and wrapped her fingers gently around his. They were soft and warm. She pulled his hand away from her neck. "I am touched by your concern, Delgado," she said. "I will attend to it as soon as we return to the cavern."

He looked at her; she seemed amused by something, but he was uncertain whether he was reading her Seriattic expression correctly.

"Interesting the way it just . . . faded away," he said. "I wish I could do that." He turned and walked over to the Sinz he had killed and looked down at it. It looked like the fossilized remains of an ancient human, a leathery sac of dislocated components that had somehow slipped from their correct positions.

"It was a shifter," Cowell said. "They both were. As well as being able to duplicate other organic forms, they also have great camouflage skills, as you witnessed."

"As I witnessed, indeed. Are they all shifters?"

"No. Only a few of this particular form."

"The humanoids?"

"Being a human it would be natural for you to call them that. Yes. But even they are able to shift a limited number of times. As their bodies age, they become less able to change their form. Their skin is less compliant."

"Maybe the other one was a vampire, too, huh?"

"What is a vampire?"

"A mythical blood-sucking creature from Earth. But it's not important right now, I guess. What is important is that we move quickly." He looked into the darkness beneath the trees again; there was no sign of movement. "That guy's going to raise the alarm," he said. "If we find ourselves surrounded by a posse of shifters, we'll be in really deep shit."

Although it wasn't ideal they followed the course of the stream, both continually searching the woods for signs of movement.

"Tell me, Delgado," said Cowell. "What is your relationship with Ashala?"

Delgado looked at the *vilume*. "Well, we . . . I'm very fond of her. I have a lot of respect for her, too."

"But you are not a bonding unit."

Delgado snorted. "A bonding unit. Jesus. You Seriatts sure have a way with words sometimes. No, I wouldn't say that we're a bonding unit."

"But she clearly has strong feelings for you."

"And like I said, I'm fond of her, too. There was something more between us once. But that was a long time ago. There's a saying on Earth: water under the bridge. A lot of water's passed under the bridge since then. It means—"

"I have studied Earth culture in the past, Delgado. I recognise the metaphor. It means that much has happened since then, and the situation is not necessarily the same as it was."

"You got it." He glanced at Cowell as she strode up the slight incline. She was equally as strong and determined as Ash. The *vilume* also reminded him greatly of Lycern, but not just in the fact that she was a Seriatt. If her line of questioning indicated what he thought it indicated, he might find the coming period more pleasurable than he had anticipated.

Delgado suddenly stopped walking and looked towards the trees to the left. Cowell also stopped and followed his gaze.

"Did you hear something?" she asked.

Delgado continued to stare at the gloom amid the trees. "Not sure," he said. "Maybe."

There was a soft but definite creaking sound, as if one of the trees were being moved. Then there was a deep mechanical sound, like a large diesel engine revving hard. It was faint at first but quickly growing louder.

Between the trees he saw shadows flicker, vaguely distorting shapes, but there were no definite forms. There was a soft snapping sound, and Delgado turned quickly to look to the opposite side of the stream. No movement was evident. But he knew they were there.

"What are we going to do, Delgado?" hissed Cowell. The *vilume* glanced around. "There are many of them approaching. Too many."

He glanced into the woods; some of the tree trunks seemed to be shimmering gently, as if their appearance were being distorted by rising heat. The mechanical sound continued to grow louder; there was the distinctive crashing sound of trees falling. "Come on," he said. "We need to find some cover before they catch up with us."

He took Cowell's arm, and they hurried up through the stream towards the right-hand bend ahead. Whatever machine they could hear was almost upon them. They ran across the water, cutting diagonally across the bend, and saw that the stream widened considerably. There were three large boulders on the apex of the curve. "We'll get between them," said Delgado, indicating the cluster of rocks. "They'll give us some cover."

They ran the short distance, clambered through the narrow gap between two of the rocks, and crouched in the space at the centre. They rested their arms on the edges of the rocks in front of them with their weapons armed and watched the trees on the opposite side of the stream. They could see only darkness behind the first row of trees.

"Do you see anything?" asked Cowell.

"Nothing yet. Watch the trees. If you see anything move, shoot it. What kind of gun is this, anyway?" he added, indicating the weapon in his hand.

"Basic projectile. It is primitive, but it will not malfunction."

"Any settings for spread pattern, range, repeat fire rate, recoil suppression?"

"No, Delgado. Each time you discharge it the weapon releases one projectile, nothing more. The likelihood of hitting any target is purely due to your aiming ability."

"Great. How many rounds do we have?"

"Fifty each."

"Fantastic."

Delgado saw a branch move on the other side of the stream and fired several shots. As the reports rolled around the sky, a slight grey figure appeared and fell on to the pebbled shore.

"This thing's got a hell of a kick," he said. "Sure does the job."

Delgado fired more shots as other tree branches moved and he caught glimpses of other changing shapes and distorting shadows. As the Sinz began to return fire, fragments were blasted from the boulders, showering them with grit. Cowell also began to shoot at vague shapes, and occasionally a Sinz body would appear as it fell to the ground. The corpses seemed to decompose instantaneously, consumed by corruption the moment they died.

Delgado fired again and another Sinz body fell. The force of the flowing water rolled the body over several times, and seemed to hasten its disintegration.

A ferocious firefight ensued as more figures emerged, the wall of trees on the other side of the stream shimmering as more Sinz strode through the water.

"There's too many of them," called Delgado between shots.

"How do you know when you cannot see them?"

Delgado considered his answer as he fired a few more rounds. He decided it was probably best not to offer one. This Seriatt was even more like Ash than he had previously thought.

There were moments of calm.

"I think that might be all of them," Delgado said.

"Possible. I cannot see evidence of more."

They heard the unmistakable sound of shattering wood. Suddenly several trees farther downstream fell, forming triangles over the water as they wedged against those on the opposite bank.

"Holy shit," muttered Delgado. "What the hell's that?"

A machine emerged from the wood. Almost spherical in shape, it was nearly as high as the trees, and possessed the same glassy, luminescent quality as the spacecraft they had seen in the pits, but this was a silvery grey. It was split vertically into three sections: the two on the outside were gigantic wheels with thick black triangular ridges to provide grip; the wider central section held weapons in the upper half, and a hatch near the ground. The machine crushed the trees it had knocked down as it moved to the centre of the stream. Then its engine growled and plumes of black smoke belched from exhaust vents on its back. Its gigantic wheels began rotating in opposite directions, spitting pebbles and foaming water as the machine began to turn through ninety degrees.

The machine's engine changed in tone once more, and the vehicle began to roll upstream. Delgado and Cowell ducked as it began firing high-calibre rounds in their direction. At first the shots were too high and shredded the foliage of the trees behind them, but then great chunks began to fly from the boulders behind which they were sheltering, and a few moments later great cracks began to appear in the stone.

"Got any bright ideas?" asked Delgado.

They both flinched as shots ricocheted off the rocks shielding them. The machine continued to approach with the sound of an angered beast.

Cowell leaned to the left, twisting to peer through the gap between two of the boulders. She turned back to him.

"It is a large machine," she said.

"Ten out of ten for observation, Cowell. Thing is, what are we going to do about it?" He pushed himself up and leaned across to look at the vehicle. "It's quite fast, too," he said. "I'm not sure we'd make it to the woods, but we're sitting ducks here."

"We are what?"

"Doesn't matter. Hang on. Look, there's a couple of copters."

When Cowell turned and looked, her head was just in front of his face; the scent of her hair was sweet. The copters were like dragonflies in silhouette above the rolling sphere and the coarse texture of the trees.

"Can you see who it is?" Delgado asked.

"One of the machines is Keth's," she said. "The other I cannot distinguish."

Delgado looked at the aircraft: if one of the machines was Keth's, Ash was still alive.

Cowell rustled around in her satchel and produced several small disc-shaped devices. She made adjustments to tiny slide controls on their edge.

"What are they?"

"Bombs. I will attach them to the machine's wheels. When they explode, they will disable it." She turned and peered down the stream again. Although the machine continued to roll up the slope it had slowed considerably, and its weapons were now trying to lock onto the copters flying alongside. As the copter gunners let rip, the weapons on the sphere also began to fire, and the copter pilots were forced to perform rapid evasive manoeuvres.

"Now is the time," said Cowell. "Those in the machine are distracted. They may not see me approaching. Hold this." She handed him the satchel.

"Hey, just wait a——" But Cowell had already leaped through the narrow gap between two of the boulders and was running down the middle of the stream towards the sphere. "Goddamn," he said. Delgado peered into the bag; among other things it contained several more of the small bombs. He glanced up again; Cowell was over halfway to the sphere, around which the copters continued to swarm. "Well if you think I'm about to let you have all the fun, you're much mistaken," he said. He pulled three more detonators from the bag and ran after the Seriatt.

Planetary Guidance Headquarters, Earth
March 7, 2379

As he performed a few test manoeuvres a short distance from the edge of the platform, Saskov found that flying the Needle was initially a somewhat unnerving experience. It was just as Hollis had said: he merely had to think the machine to a certain point or decide that he wanted it to perform a particular manoeuvre, and the vessel would comply.

Hollis was also correct in that it was important for Saskov to control his thoughts: although the Needle's core was a quick learner and would soon get used to his cognitive processes, for the first few minutes it tried to perform every change of direction and speed Saskov considered even momentarily. The Needle would not allow its inexperienced pilot to crash it, but until it knew Saskov better—and was therefore capable of knowing what he wanted, despite his vagueness and the infuriating interference of the software flux entity to which he was host—it would attempt to interpret its pilot's thoughts as faithfully as it could manage.

As a result the craft lurched backwards, forwards, up, and down at such immense speed that had the craft's occupants not been shielded from the effects of these high-gee manoeuvres by inertia-cushion containment fields, they would have been plastered across the Needle's plush interior.

The fact that Brandouen was sitting directly opposite Saskov in the opulent but limited confines of the Needle's cabin made acquisition of the skills necessary to fly the machine particularly frustrating. But by the time Saskov had cleared the coverage of the city controllers and left Earth's atmosphere, he felt that he was completely in control of the craft—although he was ignorant of the fact that this was only because the Needle's core allowed him to think that.

In reality, the core and his nobics had learned to cooperate to a level that was sufficient to give the Colonel the illusion that he was in control—a situation that was, core and nobics agreed, in both their interests.

Saskov looked at Brandouen as the Needle orbited the Earth waiting for further instructions. The *mourst* was an undeniably impressive creature. His dark skin was tough. Small, hard ridges ran along the backs of his hands and along his long fingers. His facial appearance was particularly noble. In other circumstances he would command Saskov's respect.

"Tell me something, Brandouen," said Sakov. "How did you come to be on Myson's team?"

"I am not on Myson's team," replied the *mourst*. "Your master offered me a way to return to Seriatt. A way to fight the Sinz. In return I could give him information about my planet, and the ability to assist whoever he sent on his errand."

"But what about before that? Did you escape from Seriatt when the Sinz invaded?"

"Are you suggesting I ran? Of course I did not. I was aboard a craft that was outside the Seriattic system. We were on a mission to observe Lyugg mining activities in the Gebben Belt."

"You were spying."

"It might be perceived as such by some. When Seriatt was invaded, we attempted to return, but the journey took too long. By the time we reached our planet the Sinz shield was in place."

"Did you try to get through?"

The *mourst* gazed at Saskov as if this were some kind of insult. "No. There were many other ships in the area that had rushed back to Seriatt when the invasion occurred. Some of them attempted to get through the shield, but most were destroyed by the automated machines the Sinz had placed in orbit. The few that did manage to get past these outer defences were vaporised by the shield itself. We decided to escape while we still had our lives, someday to return to liberate our planet."

"I thought it was against your *mourst* code to avoid combat."

"We did not avoid combat. We recognised the overwhelming odds against us and decided to reassess the situation. Seriatt was already enslaved and the power of the Sinz defences was unknown. We made the decision to leave. Shortly afterwards we were picked up by one of your ships and claimed asylum."

"What about the other ships that went back to Seriatt? What happened to them?"

"They scattered. It can only be hoped that they managed to find refuge somewhere. One day we will know their fate."

A small square on the glassy surface of pedestal between them began to flash pale orange. Saskov looked at it and began to wonder what it was, but before the thought had fully formed in his head he was informed by his nobics, which had in turn been informed by the Needle's core: it indicated an incoming message. Moreover, it was a message they must receive before they moved through überspace to their destination—or didn't, given Hollis's claims about the way the ship worked.

Preempting Saskov's decision to accept and open the message, the Needle's core opened it for him, acting so quickly that Saskov was not even aware that he had not actively opened the message himself.

It was General Myson.

"Colonel Saskov," said the Commander Supreme. "Distinguished Mourst Warrior Brandouen. Now you are in Earth orbit I can give you more information about your mission. It is a simple one: you must go to Seriatt." Brandouen immediately sat more upright. "Once there you must find an object and bring it here. It is a time travel device. We do not know where it is, and have no information regarding the form it may take. But I want it, Colonel. If it is still in existence, then you must bring it to me. I also want you to find Michael. I believe that he is still alive despite the time that has elapsed since the Sinz invasion."

"Very good, Sire," Saskov said. "But how do we get close to Seriatt? We know the Sinz have enveloped the entire planet in some kind of shield, beyond the range of which they have orbiting defence drones. If we had the support of the Andamour Council, we could—"

"We have wasted five years waiting for the Andamour Council to give us leave to conduct an assault on Seriatt, Colonel. They are impotent, scared of upsetting what they perceive to be some kind of *balance*. They fail to see the threat posed by the Sinz. Indeed, I understand that some of the Council's members even see them as potential allies, an asset of which we should take advantage. They are fools. It is time for us to act. The ship with which you have been equipped has formidable capabilities, and it is possible to penetrate the shield around Seriatt using it. As I understand it, you can depart from here and arrive within the planet's atmosphere instantaneously. You do not have to physically pass the orbiting drones or the shield itself. You should then be able to land undetected, as we believe that the drones do not scan inside the shield."

"Very good, Sire," said Saskov. "But may I ask why Distinguished Mourst Warrior Brandouen has to accompany me? I believe I would be more effective working alone."

"I have heard that you are something of a lone operator, Colonel. But Distinguished Mourst Warrior Brandouen will be very helpful when you reach Seriatt due to his local knowledge. He was raised in the area where you are to land, near the Seriattic capital. He has expressed his intention to remain on Seriatt after the mission objectives are achieved. This is something to which I have no objection. I am sure you will find him invaluable."

Saskov glanced at the *mourst* sitting opposite him; although he was unable to read Brandouen's expression with confidence, he suspected that the Seriatt found the situation amusing.

"Indeed, Sire," said Saskov. "The Needle is remarkable. We will use it to its full potential. In due course you will have both the time machine and your son."

"Excellent, Colonel Saskov, excellent. Marshall Greer was most confident of your ability to perform the tasks we require. I hope for his sake that he is correct."

"I will not let you down, Sire."

Myson's image faded, to be replaced by the view of Earth, which filled the top half of the display.

Saskov sat back in his seat and stared at the Seriatt opposite him.

"I am not confident of your ability to convey us to the surface of Seriatt," Brandouen growled.

"It'll be a piece of cake," said Saskov. "Seems to me like a baby could fly this thing if it knew where it wanted to go."

"What is 'cake'?" asked Brandouen. The Seriatt made the word sound like something Saskov didn't particularly want him doing in the latrine.

"What it means," said Saskov, "is that we'll get there no problem."

"Perhaps. But will you get back?"

Saskov didn't answer. A strong caffeine/adrenaline buzz was surging through his brain as his nobics linked to the Needle's core in a union more intimate than he'd ever experienced before. Normally the nobics worked without him knowing they were there, and although he felt their presence on rare occasions in the form of momentary dizziness or disorientation, the level of activity that currently seemed to be taking place was far beyond that. His software had clearly had to raise its game.

As the idea of opening star charts flickered half-formed across his mind, a myriad of perfect projected data sheets instantaneously opened above the pedestal between himself and Brandouen. Some were two-dimensional representations of solar systems with a wealth of statistical data regarding the planets that orbited them, while others were depictions of three-dimensional journeys as if aboard a fast-moving spacecraft through the same systems. There were also views of different planets from a variety of altitudes.

"What is the matter, Colonel Saskov?" asked Brandouen. The *mourst* looked extremely relaxed. "Are you unsure of our destination? I would be happy to take control if you are not up to the task. Perhaps we should swap seats."

"Unfortunately you're not equipped with the necessary software to interface with the Needle's core, Distinguished Mourst Warrior Brandouen, so if I were you I'd zip it." Before the *mourst* could ask what he would have to zip and what a zip was, Saskov imagined a single map of Seriatt's system, and all but one of the sheets closed immediately. When Saskov pictured the Seriattic palace in his mind, the image changed to a highly detailed display of the distinctive low, white building surrounded by trees, from the top of which protruded strange irregular narrow columns.

He imagined himself on an airborne platform moving above the palace, and the image changed accordingly. From one elevation he saw the city, a pale smear beyond the trees, and in the distance very tall, narrow structures that looked like ancient antennae, the purpose of which he was unable to judge.

But it was the dark area beyond the city that caught his eye.

He thought the image forward, zooming in on the area; it was a forest. There was a mountain range in the distance.

"That's what we want," said Saskov. "We land in the forest, hide the Needle out in the sticks somewhere nice and snug, then rush 'em."

"Rush 'em?" repeated the *mourst*. His accent made the words sound absurd.

"Yeah. It's a tactical term. You wouldn't understand. What it means is that we go in quick, snatch what we want, and get out before they have time to shit themselves. You ready to go?"

"I am ready to see how well you manage to control this vessel, Colonel Saskov. I will be impressed if we manage to get to the Seriattic system."

"Okay. Let's get this show on the road."

Five

Seriatt
March 5, 2379

As Delgado ran through the water clutching the detonators to his chest, he could hear the discordant sound of the copters overhead. The Sinz sphere continued to move slowly up the stream. Delgado could see that while the two outer sections were of a slightly greater diameter than the central section, there was still very little ground clearance. He looked up at the vehicle towering over him as he entered the cool oval shadow it cast. There were small windows two-thirds of the way up, beneath which the weapons clusters were located. While the larger guns continued to fire at the copters overhead, some of the smaller weapons were trained towards the ground. He saw flashes from the barrels and heard the musical zing of ricochets around him, but knew that if he could get close enough to the machine he would be in a blind spot.

Cowell had already reached the vehicle and was moving sideways, keeping pace with the machine as it clattered and crunched its way through the narrow stream. She had already successfully planted one of her explosives between two of the thick black ridges of tread, and another near the wheel's hub.

She looked at him as he ran to the opposite wheel. "What are you doing?" she called. She jumped up and planted another bomb near the hub of the wheel.

"Same as you," he replied. "What's the matter? You think I'm not up to this kind of thing? Think I'm too old?"

"I made no such assertion, Delgado," she said. "Maybe *you* think you are too old."

Delgado leaped up and slammed one of the mines near to the wheel's hub. "How long between priming and detonation?" he asked.

"When you have primed them, you should take cover quickly."

"Not long, huh?" As he stuck another of the explosives in place, bullets scattered across the stream behind him, raising plumes of water.

"Okay, they're all in place," he yelled.

"Hit the primer in the centre, then run for the trees," she replied.

Delgado jumped up and punched the centre of each mine as they turned with the wheel, then sprinted towards the trees, inspired by the distinct sound of shots hitting the ground behind him as he ran.

Bullets whistled past him as he dived into the woods, splitting wood and leaf. He ducked behind one of the trees and pressed his back against it. He could feel the vibration of the bullets smashing into the tree.

When the noise and vibration stopped, he turned and peered around the tree towards the stream. The sphere had moved a little farther up the slope, but had now stopped. He glanced up at the copters overheard, flickering above the canopy. There were four of them now. As the gunners continued to exchange fire with the sphere, spent cartridge cases cascaded through the trees like nut shells.

He looked down again and saw Cowell running from the cover of the trees on the opposite side of the stream, fountains of water spouting behind her.

"Jesus," Delgado muttered to himself. "What the hell are you doing?"

The *vilume* was obscured from view for a few moments as she passed behind the machine. She slapped a bomb against the sphere's hull, just to the right of the hatch, thumped it in the centre, then immediately turned and sprinted back across the stream to cover, weaving as she ran.

As Cowell reached the trees, the first of the detonators exploded. There was a loud yet muffled bang, and a sound like thick ice cracking. The explosion caused little obvious damage other than scattering a few fragments across the stream, but the machine stopped moving almost immediately, and its weapons also stopped firing. He looked up and thought he saw frantic movement behind the thick windows high above the hatch, but was not certain. There was an unexpected sense of calm as the stationary vehicle idled at the centre of the stream.

Then one of the wheels exploded. Hot fragments flew through the air. Large segments of the wheel fell to the ground, and the central part of the vehicle toppled to one side, sinking into the pebbles and sand. For a few moments the other wheel continued to rotate, pushing the machine's hull against the floor.

A moment later the hatch opened and three slight figures stumbled from the sphere, shrouded in black smoke. Delgado raised his weapon, but as the Sinz emerged from the vehicle the bomb next to the hatch exploded, killing them instantaneously.

More of the bombs detonated in rapid succession. Flames appeared in the top of the hatchway, and a pall of smoke emerged.

Delgado ran towards the stream; Cowell was approaching from the woods on the opposite side. He ducked reflexively as there was another explosion. Cowell was shouting something he was unable to hear. Delgado looked up as the smoke rising from the burning machine was blown back down in folding plumes: the two copters were descending rapidly in the narrow strip of sky between the treetops on either side of the stream. Dark vortices coiled around the tips of the rotor blades. The stream began to flutter and ripple, the water pushed off the pebbly bed by the downdraft. From the lowest of the two aircraft he could see Ash and Keth looking down at them.

The two copters descended until they were just half a metre above the stream. Ash beckoned to Delgado and glanced back at the wreckage of the sphere just behind them; it was burning with increasing ferocity, a cone of flame now erupting from the hatch.

Delgado ran towards the copter, gripped the side of the cockpit, and pulled himself up so that he was sitting on top of one of the panniers. Keth gunned the engine, and the copter began to rise.

Ash squeezed his arm.

"What kept you?" Delgado asked.

"Well if you sneak off on your own," Ash yelled, her hair flicking in front of her eyes, "you have to accept the consequences. You okay there?"

Delgado glanced down. "Yeah, sure." He looked towards Keth's broad *mourst* shoulders. "Let's just hope he doesn't decide to perform any acrobatics." He glanced back and saw Cowell in a similarly precarious position on the other copter. Behind her the Sinz machine exploded. A fireball rolled into the sky like some kind of gigantic fruit. The blast pushed the copter upwards, and there was a sound like hail as debris hit the rear of the aircraft, sparks flying from the rotor blades as they were hit by fragments.

Delgado's limbs and head ached. Maybe Cowell was right. Maybe he was too old for this kind of thing after all.

Fourth chronological displacement
Earth, September 18, 2350

Delgado thought he was going to throw up as he climbed the final few steps. His head was spinning. He stumbled forward as he made to crouch to look around the corner along the corridor.

The cyborgs were motionless. The vee-cams bobbed slightly in the air.

"You ready to go, old-timer?"

"I'm always ready."

"Hey, who the hell's that?" asked Girl.

They could see the side of someone's head at the other end of the corridor. It looked like a man, but his face was in shadow. He looked directly at them for a moment before moving out of sight.

Delgado eased slowly back from the corner and leaned against the wall. His reflection in the glass opposite looked haggard, drawn, older than he should.

But Lycern was near; he drew strength from that. He took several deep breaths. He looked at Girl and opened his mouth to say something, but changed his mind.

Girl frowned. "You okay, Delgado?" she asked. "You don't look so good."

"Sure. I'm fine. Once we step into that corridor we won't have long to

FIVE

deal with the cyborgs and vee-cams and . . . well I guess you know the score. Go hell for leather and they won't know what's hit 'em."

Bucky snorted grimly. "Shit, Delgado, you're beginning to sound like me."

Delgado moved up the steps and looked along the corridor again. There was no sign of the man at the far end this time. He thought about the possibilities for a moment, but was unable to analyse the situation and its multitude of possibilities.

He stepped back and turned to Bucky and Girl. "We'll attack from both sides," he said. "You two stay here; I'll go from the other side. Okay? Good. See you in five."

Delgado ran through the corridors towards the stairway on the other side of Myson's chamber, but stopped halfway. He was short of breath, sweating heavily, unreasonably fatigued for such a short period of exertion. He could feel his heart beating in his chest. The rush of blood was loud in his ears. He tried to assign nobics to physical recovery, but they were unresponsive. He leaned forward and rested his hands on his knees, then wiped sweat from his forehead with the back of one hand. He shook his head, mumbled something to himself about his goddamn lousy timing.

Then he heard the fighting begin. He stood upright again and paced back and forth, hands on hips, considering his options. Maybe his strategy was wrong. Maybe what he was trying to do was pointless. Perhaps nothing he did would have any effect anyway. But if everything was set in stone, why were so many things changing?

He ran his hands across his face; his skin felt wrinkled and leathery. He noticed a slight tremor in his right hand.

He made a decision, and retraced his steps as quickly as he could.

By the time he got back to Bucky and Girl they had moved off the stairs and were embroiled in the battle with the cyborgs and vee-cams in the corridor.

It was chaos.

At first he could see only Bucky. The young man was putting up a brave effort but would soon be overwhelmed. Delgado could see that the protective shield the young man's gun threw around him was already weakening. A few more hits would see it fail completely.

As Delgado took the final few steps, Girl came into view. She was injured, sitting on the floor against the corridor's opposite wall, grimacing with pain. Her left hand was clamped to her right bicep, and her right hand was covered in blood that had apparently run down her sleeve. It looked as if a chunk was missing from her left arm. There was also a dark patch on her left thigh. He felt the urge to run and help her but was uncertain what effect his sudden appearance might have. He felt imprisoned by circumstances of his own making, frustrated by his own efforts.

"Ash!" He yelled. He cursed himself. "Girl! *Girl!*" She looked up at him; her face was sweat-soaked, grimy. She was in agony. "Get your goddamn ass over here!" he yelled. Girl glanced to her right along the corridor. She was uncertain and scared, but pushed herself to her feet.

She began to walk across the corridor towards him but stumbled as a shot hit her rapidly failing shield. Bucky shouted something to her Delgado could not hear. Girl staggered forward but was on the verge of collapse. Delgado could watch no longer. He strode into the corridor to help Bucky give her some cover.

As he began to fire, the corridor was plunged into darkness; then there was a rapid series of brilliant white flashes. Delgado's head spun. He felt sick, disoriented.

Delgado began firing at the nearest cyborgs. Beyond them and the vee-cams he could see two men at the far end of the corridor. The muzzles of their guns flashed with each shot they released. Two vee-cams near them exploded in rapid succession, their components scattering across the floor.

The flashes of light increased in intensity and frequency. Delgado shouted at Bucky and Girl. As they both looked at him, Girl took a hit that knocked out her shield and flung her through the air like a doll. Her broken body came to rest against the wall, artificially animated by the flickering light.

As Delgado looked at her, Bucky was hit in the chest and fell at Delgado's feet. He looked at the approaching cyborgs and saw one of the other two men striding forwards, while the other left the corridor and ran down the flight of stairs.

Delgado felt panic begin to well.

The more he tried to put things right, the worse things became. Entuzo had said as much.

But he could not give up now. He was simply too close.

FIVE

Seriatt
March 5, 2379 (Earth equivalent)

Delgado rubbed his aching arms as they walked away from the landed copters. The turbines ticked as they cooled, and the rotor blades gradually slowed.

"You okay?" asked Ash.

"Sure. I thought I was getting a cramp once or twice, but it was no sweat. The ride through the tunnels was hairier than a tug pilot's ass, though."

She smiled.

Issilan and Sherquoia approached them from the tents, arm in arm as if seeking comfort. They looked at those who had returned, and the copters behind them. The young *mourst*—Descan—was following them.

"Six copters left. Only four have returned. Where are Deycant and Casoul, Wesio and Cournash?" asked Issilan.

Cowell took Issilan by the shoulders. "I am sorry, Issilan," the *vilume* said. "They were brave Seriatts."

Sherquoia gasped slightly and gripped Issilan's forearm.

"They fought and died as any honourable *mourst* should," said Descan. "You should be proud to have known them."

Cowell motioned for Descan to be quiet. The young *mourst* turned, muttering something to himself, then walked away.

Issilan and Sherquoia began to emit a high-pitched warbling sound as their grief took hold. They held each other tightly, sobbing and wailing as they turned and began to walk back towards their tents.

Cowell, Keth, and the other Seriatts who had survived the sortie also began walking towards the tents, and the warmth of the fire.

"So we lost two copters," said Delgado. "What happened to them?"

"Same as you," said Cowell. "Avians dragged them down."

"We should have looked for survivors."

"There were none. If you had seen for yourself, you would understand. The aircraft crashed into trees and caught fire. Although they are relatively easy to fly, these machines do not withstand such impacts."

"So I noticed."

"From what I saw of the wreckage of your machine, you were lucky. If you had not landed in the stream, you would certainly have been killed. As for that Sinz machine that attacked you—I have not seen such a ground vehicle before."

"Perhaps it is something new," suggested Miskoh.

"If they're developing new stuff, testing equipment," said Ash, "that indicates that they're preparing for a ground assault as well as an airborne attack."

"Yeah. They must know that wherever it is they're planning to attack first isn't going to be a pushover, and they need to be able to maintain pressure for a prolonged period."

"We know they have already constructed large transport vessels to carry troops," said Miskoh. "Until now they have concentrated on airborne machines for aerial combat."

"But now they are building up their ground forces."

"Well, if that machine we encountered was a new design, then I'd say it still needs some improvement."

Cowell and Miskoh laughed, Miskoh's throaty *mourst* coughs contrasting with Cowell's lighter *vilume* laughter.

But Ash was quiet. "If they're planning a ground assault," she said, "they'll need a lot of infantry. You can't win a ground war from inside a machine. You've got to get your kit on and take the fight to the enemy. Hand to hand."

They reached the fire and sat down to warm themselves against the cold of the cavern. Delgado looked at Cowell and Miskoh. "Have you seen any Sinz facilities where they might be preparing troops?" he asked.

"This was the second installation we were going to take you to while we were out," said Cowell. "Before the avians attacked us. It is a subterranean facility of some kind. We are uncertain what is within it, but it is certainly important."

"What makes you so sure?"

"It is very well defended. There are many guards and traps. It is difficult to get into. Many of our group have been killed in the past attempting to discover its secrets. It is obviously of importance to the Sinz."

"Well say this place you're speaking of is producing troops, and assuming the Seriatts are planning a ground campaign somewhere. What are their most likely targets?"

"Lyugg is relatively close," suggested Miskoh.

"No," said Cowell. "I do not believe that Lyugg is on the Sinz' agenda. Not yet. Lyugg has nothing to offer other than fierce resistance. I believe they plan to attack Earth."

Delgado went cold despite the heat from the fire. "You really think they'd take on Structure on home territory?"

"I believe Cowell to be correct," said Miskoh. "Earth is their target. You are correct in that it would represent a great challenge, but this is why they have taken so long to prepare. They are also aware of the humans' strength."

"The Sinz know that an attack on Earth would have to succeed," said Cowell. "If it did not their position here would be impossible to maintain, but if they can successfully invade Earth, other worlds they attack are likely to offer less resistance."

"And we have no idea when this is likely to take place?" asked Ash.

"You saw for yourself the extent of the ship construction. It is long established; they are almost ready. It will be soon, I am sure of it."

"So what'll we do?" asked Ash.

"To decide what you want to achieve is key," said Cowell. "You will wish to prevent the Sinz attacking Earth; that is natural. But our priority is to liberate Seriatt. If we wait for those who are to invade Earth to leave our world, then we have a better chance of overcoming them here, for they will be fewer in number, their capabilities weakened."

"So what are we to do?" Ash asked. She looked at Delgado; he was gazing at the fire.

"Cowell's right," he said. "If the Sinz attack Earth, they will be weakened here. Especially if they're not expecting anything to happen on Seriatt."

"You're saying we should let them attack Earth?"

"Maybe," he said as he stood. "Maybe not."

"What do you mean, Delgado?" asked Ash as Delgado began to walk slowly away from the fire. "What do you mean by 'maybe, maybe not,' goddammit? Jesus."

Delgado ignored her as he considered the possibilities. It was increasingly clear. Not only did Earth possess technological wealth that would be valuable to the Sinz—even more valuable than the weapons already sold to them by Earth's Commander Supreme, General William Myson—it would also be a demonstration of their power. Besides, the Sinz had probably guessed that the arms being sold to them by Myson were not the most up-to-date in existence. And that was exactly what they wanted. If they did attack Earth, it would be interesting to see whether they used weapons Myson had sold them. Earth had a history of such ironies.

When Delgado reached the lagoon, it was dark outside. Moonlight penetrating the split in the rock ceiling gave much of the lake a silvery sheen, while the fire behind gilded its surface nearer to him. Droplets of moisture fell into the water from the cavern ceiling high above, and he could feel a draught as air was pulled through the tunnel far to his left.

He heard a gentle lap of water against the shore, and saw a small wave move across the water in front of him. The lake faded into the darkness deeper within the cavern, between the long ovals formed by the merging stalagmites and stalactites.

He thought about Cascari, and then Michael. Where was he? What had the Sinz done to him? Ash had been right in something she had once said: despite everything that had happened, Michael was still Delgado's son. And for now that was what he had to focus on, for although the great interplanetary possibilities were important, his natural, paternal instinct was to give his children priority. He had to find Michael before he could even consider anything else.

His realisation of this—and his acceptance of it—was almost a relief.

He decided that he would have to speak to Ash, ask her what she thought they should do next. Her clear head and practicality were sometimes invaluable.

Delgado turned and began walking back towards the cluster of tents. The canvas cones reflected the firelight like an oasis of brightness in the gloom. The others had gone to their tents, and the area around the fire was now deserted.

Delgado walked to Ashala's tent. He pulled back the broad flap of fabric over the entrance and stooped to pass through it.

FIVE

It was warm inside the tent. As he entered and the canvas fell back across the opening behind him, Delgado saw Ash's boots, tunic, and vest discarded on the floor. When he stood upright, he saw Ash and Cowell standing in the centre of the tent next to the small fire.

They were kissing.

Ash looked over one naked shoulder towards him. Her flushed face was a contrast to her pale back. She had a mole on one shoulder blade Delgado had not noticed before, and numerous freckles. She turned quickly to face him, folding her arms across her breasts. Her flies were undone, underwear just visible in the gap.

Cowell's upper body was also bare. The extent of the tattoos that coiled across the *vilume*'s tanned skin was evident for the first time, as was the definition of her muscles. Her breasts were oddly shaped, as if half-formed, with the ache of a pubescent human female. Cowell's trousers were also half-unbuttoned.

The contact was mutual.

"Delgado," said Ash. She hooked a wayward strand of hair over one ear while keeping the other arm pressed firmly against her breasts. She was flushed and slightly breathless with arousal. "What's up?"

Delgado looked from one to the other of them. "I, um. I just . . . wanted to talk to you," he said. "I didn't realise you . . ." He gesticulated vaguely, avoiding their eyes. "I wasn't expecting . . . you know . . ."

As Ash's faced reddened further, more freckles blossomed. She glanced at Cowell, then looked back to Delgado. "Shit. Look, Delgado, I mean this is . . ."

"Wonderful," interjected Cowell, her voice soft and quiet. "This is perfect."

The Seriatt's mouth stretched into the unsettling *vilume* smile, and at that moment Delgado saw something new in Cowell's appearance: a strength and confidence; a chiselled, masculine beauty that was as defined as her femininity. For the first time, Delgado truly saw the Seriatt as interchangeably male and female, her—his?—sexual characteristics seemingly shifting moment by moment. He knew *vilume* were technically androgynous so the matter was irrelevant, but he had never before perceived their sexual ambiguity with such clarity. It was as if the *vilume*'s appearance had changed somehow. Maybe it had.

The *vilume* took a step towards him. "I am glad you have joined us," he said. "Your feelings for Ashala are obvious. It is only right. Remove your footwear."

Delgado stooped, unlaced and removed his boots, briefly hopping around a few times as he struggled with the left. When he stood upright again, Cowell reached out, gripped Delgado's upper arm, and pulled him towards them.

Delgado did not resist.

Maintaining eye contact with him, Cowell pulled Delgado closer. With his long Seriattic fingers she quickly unfastened Delgado's tunic. Chin high, Delgado took a deep breath and shucked the garment from his shoulders.

"This is right," the Seriatt said as she slipped off her trousers and underwear. "I think you know it."

Delgado glanced at Ashala; her excitement was clear in the brightness of her eyes.

Still gazing at Delgado, Cowell pushed at the front of Delgado's trousers; Delgado removed them with neither eagerness nor hesitation. Ash did the same. Delgado noticed that she managed to keep her breasts covered throughout. Cowell put one of his slender arms around Ash's shoulders, and her other around Delgado's. The *vilume* then drew their three bodies together.

Cowell pushed Delgado behind her with one hand so that he was close to her back, while the *vilume* also turned to face Ash. Delgado swallowed as he placed the palms of his hands on Cowell's warm, dark hips. He looked down the Seriatt's long, well-defined back. In the cleavage of her buttocks were labialike folds of skin. They seemed slightly swollen, moist with some kind of secretion. Delgado instinctively pressed himself against Cowell's back. He felt the firmness of the *vilume*'s buttocks against his belly and warmth as his penis slid between the slimy ridges. He pressed more firmly against the Seriatt and the folds of skin gave; as his penis sank deeper into her, Delgado heard Cowell growl softly; it was a distinctly *mourst*-like sound.

Delgado rocked gently and slid his hands under Cowell's armpits, wrapping his own arms around the Seriatt's chest. Instead of a full, warm bosom he felt Cowell's firm chest muscles; he blinked and swallowed as uncertainty momentarily washed through him.

He looked over Cowell's shoulder at Ash. Her cheeks were flushed. She was looking up at Cowell, her pupils wide. Her bright eyes moved to Delgado, and she gazed at him with a vibrant expression full of desire, sexuality, and wonderment; a vague smile threatening to surface.

Cowell was muttering something: soft Seriattic words. The *vilume* made a slight movement with his body; Ash's eyes closed and she exhaled an urgent breath.

Their bodies and limbs entwined, the three of them swayed gently as if moving in time with some slow, erotic rhythm, caressing and stroking each other as the humans relaxed and began to enjoy the Seriatt's body.

Delgado moved his hand down across Cowell's taut stomach and spread his fingers around the base of the Seriatt's thin shaft where it entered Ash's body; it seemed to stimulate them both, and Ash looked at Delgado with a level of passionate energy he had not seen in her for years.

The trio lay on their backs in the warmth of the tent. There was a thick, sweet odour. Delgado lay with one forearm draped across his crotch as if this would somehow prevent what had happened from happening again.

From his position he could see one of Ash's thighs; it looked particularly pale against the contrast of Cowell's dark skin. He could sense her embarrassment, but wasn't sure what he felt. But he knew that if he looked at Cowell now he would see only a masculine form. He did not know what had happened to change his perception, but change it had.

Neither was he certain that he found the male aspects of the *vilume* unattractive.

Delgado closed his eyes, and his breathing slowed as sleep approached.

There was an urgent shout. Cowell immediately stood and began to dress. Delgado and Ash sat up; Ash covered herself quickly.

"What's going on?" asked Delgado. He looked around, slightly confused; he did not know how much time had passed.

"I do not know," said the *vilume*. "I thought I heard something about an intruder. It seemed to come from the direction of the lake. I must investigate. If the Sinz have discovered our location, we will have to move."

Delgado pushed himself up and also started dressing, picking up his clothes from different parts of the tent. As Cowell left, still fastening buttons,

Delgado kicked Ash's underwear and trousers towards her. "Here," he said, "you better put those on." He spoke with more brusqueness than he felt. He sat down and quickly laced his boots.

"You okay, Delgado?"

He half shrugged. "Sure. You?"

"Fine. I just wasn't expecting—"

"No," he said. "Me neither."

She looked at him. "It was fun, though, huh?"

"Sure," he said. "Fun." He stood and grabbed his gun, then turned and left the tent without looking at her. She rushed to dress, then followed him.

Outside they saw Seriatts running towards the lake. Some of them carried bladed weapons that reflected splashes of light; others held flaming sticks. Ahead of the Seriatt nearest the lake Delgado thought he saw something like long strips of torn fabric being dragged across the ground.

"What is it?" Ash asked as she zipped her tunic and checked her gun. "What's going on?"

"I don't know," Delgado replied. "Come on."

They both ran towards the lake, the cavern's dank air cold in their lungs. They saw one of the Seriatts dive, apparently trying to grab hold of the object that was moving towards the water. Another stopped running, knelt, and extended its arms as it raised a gun. Three shots rang out in the cavern; the sound reverberated off the hard walls, and moments of bright light briefly illuminated the cavern, swelling the space, revealing hidden detail.

"It's an amphibian," said Delgado.

"Jesus. How'd it get in here?"

"It must have come from the lake."

As the amphibian approached the dark gloss of the water, one of the Seriatts threw a flaming stick; it hit the creature's rear end, and long tendrils reared up and fanned out, throwing the stick into the darkness. A *mourst* with a long-bladed knife threw himself towards the Sinz. There were cries of pain and defiance as the amphibian's stinging tentacles wrapped the Seriatt, and the Sinz slipped smoothly into the water dragging the thrashing *mourst* with it.

Ash and Delgado joined the other Seriatts at the water's edge, breathing hard. They looked in silence at the surface of the lagoon, which was already as smooth and black as oil. There was not a ripple to indicate movement beneath its dark surface. It was as if the amphibian had been a phantasm.

"Who is missing?" asked Cowell as he stared at the water.

"Descan," replied Miskoh.

Conosq began to vocalise grief and anger, their shrill warbling multiplied in the confines of the cavern.

There was a gentle splash, and a pair of wide, oval eyes appeared far across the lagoon. They glowed bright green as the Sinz stared back at them, illuminating the surface of the water for a short distance in front of the creature's inhuman face. The amphibian's tentacles were visible as a rough texture on the surface of the water, coiling around it. There was no sign of young Descan.

The unblinking eyes disappeared beneath the water as the Sinz submerged again, and a few moments later the lake was still once more.

"If the amphibian entered the cavern through the lake . . . ," said Cowell.

"Then the lake must be connected to the sea," finished Miskoh. They stood in silence for a few moments. "How long could they have been observing us without our knowledge?"

"Does it matter?" asked Cowell. "Now our location is known we must leave. Keth: go outside and keep watch. See if there are any other Sinz out there, and inform us of developments."

"That they can find us through the lagoon does not necessarily mean they will be able to find us through the tunnels," said Miskoh as Keth ran towards the narrow path leading up to the shore. "The amphibians have a limited ability to move on land. If we guard the lake well, we may be able to remain where we are."

"No, Miskoh. More of them will come. We have seen it many times. They are determined creatures. We must move now. We have no choice."

"Where will you go?" asked Delgado as they turned and walked away from the lake.

"I do not know," Cowell replied. "The Sinz seem to find us eventually wherever we hide."

"You will not come with us?" asked Miskoh as they reached the tents. He looked from Delgado to Ash.

"No. There are things I need to do. I've got to try to find Michael. Or at least find out whether he's dead or alive. When I know that, then I can decide what to do. Maybe Ash will come with you, though."

"Goddammit, Delgado, you've got to be kidding," said Ashala. She looked at Cowell and Miskoh. "No offence, okay, but Delgado here has a long-standing problem in that he thinks he knows what's best for other people and makes decisions without asking their opinion first. This isn't the first time you've tried to get rid of me. Am I missing a major hint here, or what?"

"Of course not, I just didn't—"

"What? Think? Jesus, Delgado, I thought you knew me by now. You think I'm gonna let you wander off on your own to get your stupid head blown off? We both know you need me around to get you out of trouble."

Delgado smiled. "Well, I guess that may be true," he said.

"There's no maybe about it, Delgado. I've saved your ass more than once before, and no doubt I'll have to save it again."

"But you have a serious choice to make here, Ash," said Delgado. "You can either come along with me and maybe help me find out what happened to Michael, or you can stick with our friends here. I'm pretty sure that one of those choices offers a greater chance of survival than the other."

"Perhaps there is a third alternative," said Cowell.

Delgado looked at the *vilume*. "What's that?"

"You both stay with us, and we help you find your son."

Delgado stared at Cowell. "Why would you want to do that?"

"The number of options open to us is declining rapidly," said the Seriatt. "Without taking decisive action we will soon be in a corner. We cannot run forever. You and Ashala are assets. Assets I do not wish to lose. I believe we can help each other."

"I want to find my son; you want to liberate your world. There's something of a disparity in the size of the goals there, don't you think?"

"Superficially, perhaps," said Cowell. "But I suspect that the two may well be linked. And perhaps one will lead to the other."

Delgado looked around at the group of Seriatts in front of him as he considered the proposition. "Okay, I'll stick with you," he said eventually. "But my priority remains finding Michael. Or finding out what happened to him, at least. That doesn't change. This okay with you, Ash?"

Ashala shrugged. "Sure. You know me, Delgado: I'm a happy-go-lucky, go-with-the-flow kinda girl. Besides, I like the company around here."

Delgado noticed her glance at Cowell when she said this and felt a hint of pure jealousy. But he would not have been able to state with certainty towards whom this was directed.

Keth emerged from the gap in the cavern's rock wall behind the tents and rushed towards them. "We must prepare to fight," he shouted. "Sinz are gathering outside."

"How many?" asked Cowell.

"I do not know for certain," said the *mourst*. He paused for a moment to catch his breath. "I saw many amphibians in the water, and avians overhead. There were also bipeds in hovercraft and boats, and a large airship crossing the headland."

"I'm impressed," said Delgado. "They certainly seem prepared to invest a great deal of resources in getting you."

"We must leave," said Cowell. "Perhaps it is time to return to our kin for a while. We can also show Delgado and Ashala what the Sinz have done to our world, and the conditions in which they force Seriatts to live. Gather your belongings together quickly. Keth, ensure the copters are fuelled and armed. Miskoh, arm the detonators. When we leave, we will give the Sinz a surprise."

The Forest of Dreams, Seriatt
March 5, 2379 (Earth equivalent)

Saskov imagined the Needle floating above the forest, and looked down at a roughly circular clearing that he estimated to be around twenty metres in diameter. There was a large boulder to one side, but plenty of room for the Needle to land.

Another sheet opened next to that upon which the clearing was displayed. It offered a variety of stats about the Needle. Several of the figures blinked rapidly: drive status, core activity, operating efficiency. Saskov sat back in his seat and looked at the first display. It couldn't be an actual, real-time image of the location due to Seriatt's distance. He presumed that it must be some kind of representation, a map of the area made secretly by Infiltration at some point prior to the Sinz invasion.

A new high-frequency vibration became evident in the Needle. Saskov glanced around the craft's soft, creamy interior, but saw nothing untoward. Then the vibration ceased as quickly as it had started. His concentration broken slightly, he closed his eyes and focussed once again on the clearing; the faint buzzing immediately returned, and increased in intensity the longer Saskov maintained his concentration. Although they felt nothing within the craft, the instruments indicated that the Needle moved sideways and then backwards at immense speed; yet its relative position above the clearing remained unchanged. He frowned and glanced across at Brandouen; the Seriatt was immobile, eyes closed, mouth slightly open. He looked as if he was having some kind of psychotic experience.

When Saskov tried to turn his head, the movement seemed difficult to perform, as if someone had clasped his head in their hands and was trying to prevent him from moving it. He noticed that the figures next to the display were blinking far more slowly than before. He looked at Brandouen again; the Seriatt did not appear to be breathing.

Saskov closed his eyes as an intense feeling of sickness washed through him. On the display the Needle's movements seemed erratic: a sudden sideways lurch followed by a headlong rush, then a backwards spurt. They were manoeuvres Saskov was not conscious of instructing the vessel to perform.

Suddenly the buzzing ceased. He opened his eyes again to find that Brandouen was looking at him from the opposite chair. He seemed fine. The figures on the display were flashing at their normal, rapid rate.

"Have we arrived?" the *mourst* asked.

Saskov blinked, unsure what had happened. His nobics would not respond to his desire for analysis. "Let's take a look," he said, reluctant to reveal his uncertainty to the Seriatt.

He opened another display sheet to show their current position. Instead of the clearing that had been their target, Seriatt could be seen in the top corner of the display, a blue-white arc of clouds and sea.

"It appears that your navigation was a little inaccurate," said Brandouen. "I think that perhaps now you should let me take control of this machine."

FIVE

"We might not be right where we wanted to be, Brandy boy, I'll give you that. But at least we're inside the shield. Now we've just got to get down to the surface . . ." His nobics prickled. "Shit."

"What is the matter?"

"Incoming. Sinz drones. We must still be outside the shield."

Plots appeared on the image, tiny points next to which hovered details of range and speed. The drones were so small—less than a metre across according to the display stats—that they were not visible at standard display magnification. Magnified greatly, they looked like tiny silver spheres. He zoomed in on the nearest. Its shiny surface was peppered with black dots—presumably a rash of sensors and weapons.

It was a very small target. While negotiating with the Needle's core, Saskov's nobics levelled off the Colonel's shifting chemical balance, imbuing him with confidence and dedicating a clutch of high-performance nobics to combat analysis.

Saskov imagined the alien device exploding, and almost simultaneously the Needle shuddered. On the display a slender red line briefly linked the Needle's image to that of the tiny drone, which glowed briefly before vanishing.

Brandouen linked his dark, slender fingers across his lap. "Well, you are not a complete inclination, it seems."

"Inclination?" questioned Saskov, without looking across at the *mourst*.

"Yes."

Saskov shook his head a little and shrugged. He wondered if Brandouen had used the wrong word or whether his nobics had translated it inaccurately from Seriatt, of which there were several complex dialects.

Saskov opened another sheet that displayed the clearing which he had originally intended to be the Needle's destination. He glanced at the other view and targeted a second drone, which was destroyed. A third seemed to appear from nowhere and fired a rapid stream of glowing orange ordnance of a type Saksov did not recognise. A prickle of red appeared on one side of the Needle's health sheet, followed by a sparkle of vivid purple. Saskov deduced that the Needle had been hit but was automatically repairing itself, although there was no evidence within the vessel to indicate that this was true.

Another of the tiny craft approached rapidly but was destroyed without

Saskov having to isolate it from those that followed. He was certain he had not instigated its destruction, but as several other drones had to be dealt with in rapid succession he was unable to dwell on this.

There was a momentary lull. Several more drones were approaching rapidly but would remain out of range for several seconds. Saskov looked at the other display and concentrated on the clearing, then imagined the Needle settling onto the dusty ground next to the boulder to one side. But the Needle seemed to have taken it upon itself to despatch more of the drones, and shuddered several times as its weapons fired.

As one of the drones sped towards the Needle, the vessel seemed to slide sideways on the display. Saskov felt the same sickness as earlier, the same heaviness of limb and vagueness of thought. He glanced at Brandouen; the *mourst* was motionless once more, but wore a strange expression, like a still photograph taken as he struggled to swallow insufficiently chewed food. The other displays seemed to have frozen. Saskov felt a sudden fatigue that sapped his ability to think.

Suddenly they were on the night side of the planet, the Needle descending rapidly through Seriatt's upper atmosphere. The planet's moon scattered grey light across broken cloud far below.

"We are still not in the correct place, Colonel," observed Brandouen, who was animated once more. "Perhaps your internal software is not up to the job?"

"It's up to the job all right. Don't you worry about that. The Needle's just not processing my thoughts correctly or something." He knew he sounded unconvincing. It was possibly fortunate that he was ignorant of the ongoing dispute between his nobics and the Needle's core, as they argued about whether they should follow Saskov's wishes as closely as possible, or act in whatever way was best for their purposes and was most likely to result in their survival. The problem would have been more easily resolved without internal differences of opinion within Saskov's nobics.

The Colonel checked for drones, unaware of the conflict taking place; there were none in the immediate vicinity, and none seemed to be approaching. He checked the power reserves and engaged the cloak.

"Do they follow us?" Brandouen asked.

"No. They seem to be chasing their tails outside the atmosphere, sunside. I think we've lost them for now."

"Well, if your navigational skills leave something to be desired, then your evasive skills are considerably more impressive."

Saskov glanced at him. "Is that supposed to be some kind of half-assed compliment, Distinguished Mourst Warrior Brandouen?"

"Some kind."

The Seriatt laughed, and although frustrated at their situation and the *mourst*'s general attitude, Saskov smiled with him. As a result of the naturally more relaxed state and chemical changes that occurred within him because of this, the Needle seemed to become more receptive to him, as if it had also relaxed in some way. There was positive dialogue with the nobics, and a compromise was reached.

Saskov thought the ship into a 180-degree turn and reduced speed. But with the cloak engaged he was concerned about the quality of the information the sensors were giving him, and it was difficult to focus on the landing site they had chosen. Saskov closed his eyes and imagined the Needle above Seriatt's surface, then himself standing to one side of the clearing. He closed his eyes and allowed the Needle's core to project a virtual scenario directly into his head; it was exactly as if he were on the ground. He could even feel a breeze and smell damp earth. He looked around and saw the trees, the dark boulder nearby. He looked into the sky above in search of the Needle, but then realised it was cloaked and would therefore be invisible.

He opened his eyes again. "I'm going to disengage the cloak for a moment," he said.

"We may be seen," stated Brandouen. "Either by the drones above us or by Sinz on the ground. Is this action wise?"

"Well, it's either uncloak while we get our bearings or miss our landing spot. And that does seem to be the ideal landing place. Concealed, but not too far from where we need to be."

"I am pleased that you are beginning to recognise my value, Colonel Saskov."

Saskov shut down the cloaking system. With whatever shield had surrounded the ship disengaged, the sensors immediately became much more effective. A vivid image of the terrain directly below the Needle appeared on one of the sheets. Saskov quickly scanned the image, found the clearing they had designated as their landing site, adjusted speed and trajectory accordingly, and reengaged the cloak.

A few moments later a hurricane rose suddenly, flinging dust and dead leaves in tight whorls through the clearing. Stones were crushed by an invisible force, and three rectangular impressions appeared in the glade's soft earth.

Sinz Domestic Affairs Forum, Hascaaza
March 4, 2379 (Earth equivalent)

Communicator Hurlough entered the pod in a clearly excited state. The chattering Sinz fell quiet and watched as Hurlough hurried across to Mediator Latzinor, who was about to give another briefing regarding the situation with the Karallax: more streams of mathematical data had been transmitted from deep space to another seemingly random, remote, and barren point on Hascaaza's surface. Latzinor leaned to one side as Hurlough whispered to him. Latzinor stroked the top of Communicator Hurlough's smooth head in a gesture of thanks. He turned, glanced up at Secretary Controller Hargoth perched atop his black podium, breathed deeply, and began to address the Sinz officials before him.

"My associates," he said, "I have the pleasure of being able to convey great news. Communicator Hurlough tells me that despite the predictions of our Monitors, the channel appears to have settled." Murky water slopped from tanks as amphibians stirred; wings unfurled as avians squawked and fluttered; the bipeds muttered excitedly and made gestures of surprise. "How long this situation will be maintained," continued Latzinor, "is uncertain. But I am informed that the channel is currently stable enough for us to send a small initial fleet to help our associates on Seriatt to finish the campaign they began so long ago."

The pod was filled with the sound of the various Sinz species celebrating further, and making statements of allegiance. Even Secretary Controller Hargoth spread his great wings in a rare display. Yet as Latzinor looked around those assembled before him, he noticed that Prime Associate Lubriatt and Orator Ragallet seemed somehow less enthusiastic than their counterparts, and that the two of them exchanged glances as they made somewhat half-hearted gestures of determination and excitement. The Mediator memorised their appearance and determined to reexamine the situation later.

"We are lucky indeed," called Associate Riffolesh as the hubbub lessened. "Or more precisely, our friends on Seriatt are fortunate. If the channel stabilises for a period sufficient for us to make use of it, that is."

"Speculator Thritt and the Monitors are in agreement that we will need to move quickly," said Mediator Latzinor, "but it undoubtedly represents an invaluable opportunity to proceed."

"Then we must take immediate action," said Prime Associate Gultag; his voice was as deep and cold as his preferred environment. The amphibian squirmed and extended a glossy tentacle over the side of his tank. "Fabricator Cursoss," he said, "are we at a state of readiness? Are the birthships prepared? I believe the embryos' development can be accelerated should we require them sooner than we had previously anticipated. Is that so? If they traverse the channel, they will be needed to fight almost immediately."

The elegant Fabricator's crest rose in a combination of embarrassment and pleasure at being the focus of the gathered dignitaries' attention. "The birthships are healthy," replied the avian, "and ready to depart whenever she may be required to do so. Although," she continued, "I would not advise sending them through the channel."

"Why not?"

"It is not what they have been reared for. Conditions may be unstable. All birthships are highly sensitive. And we do not know what effect passing through such a stressful environment might have on the embryos, let alone the ships themselves. Only the strongest, most mature and experienced warrior vessels have previously been subjected to the forces within the channel. Indeed, even some of these have on occasion suffered trauma upon emergence. At the other end of the channel we may find the vessels are simply carcasses carrying dead fetuses."

"You do not believe you have nurtured strong vessels, Fabricator Cursoss?" said Gultag with apparent impatience. "I thought you were our finest breeder."

"You misunderstand me, Prime Associate Gultag. The birthships are as strong as any embryo carrier must be. But they are also sensitive, fragile, have certain needs. We must treat them carefully if they are to perform well. Any deaths that might occur would be our responsibility."

Secretary Controller Hargoth looked down from his podium, his wings now folded around him like a cloak. His voice was shrill. "But it is not guaranteed that there will be any adverse effects, Fabricator? You are merely informing us of the possibility?"

"That is correct." Fabricator Cursoss felt her wings trembling under this apparent cross-examination from the Secretary Controller. It was more stressful than coaxing the first calf from a young birthship.

"Very well," said Secretary Controller Hargoth. "We will proceed while we have the opportunity. Too long have we faltered. We will send the birthships through the channel and deal with whatever consequences may arise. Fabricator Cursoss: you will travel with our forces to ensure the ships' health."

"But I do not have the necessary—"

"You will do as I say. Our associates on Seriatt require our assistance."

"Yes, Secretary Controller. I will begin the preparations immediately."

Seriatt
March 5, 2379 (Earth equivalent)

The Seriatts were clearly well rehearsed in moving at short notice. Clothing, personal effects, and essential items were quickly thrown into canvas holdalls, which were stacked near the copters with surprising speed and efficiency.

Delgado assessed the gear that was already stacked next to the copters and the amount that remained. "Where are you going to fit the tents?" he asked.

"We will leave them behind," said Cowell, strapping luggage to one of the aircraft. "They are too heavy. A successful raid many months ago meant that we acquired many weapons and much equipment. It is this we must prioritise now. If we carry too much, not only will the manoeuvrability of the aircraft be affected, but we will also use too much fuel."

"Where will we go?" asked Ash as she hefted another holdall on top of the growing pile.

"First we will go to the city to see what information we can gain," Cowell replied. "Then we will return to our families for a brief period. It is too long since last we saw them."

"Isn't that dangerous?" asked Ash. "The Sinz might track you to them, or you might be caught."

"This is why we remain apart from them most of the time. If the Sinz were to find the location of their camp, our kin would be in grave danger. But sometimes we must take the risk and visit them briefly. Otherwise, what would we be fighting for? Quickly now. Time is short."

Within half an hour the copters were fully laden, their panniers stuffed, numerous holdalls strapped to either side of each machine, and anything they had to carry that there was not room for inside either tied on or wedged wherever it would fit. The additional weight each of the small aircraft carried would test the pilots' skill considerably.

When the copters' engines were running and the machines lined up ready to take off, Cowell ran over to Delgado and Ash as they checked that the last of the holdalls were secure.

"Delgado, you fly with Keth," said the *vilume*. "Ashala, you will come in my aircraft."

Delgado glanced at Ash. He felt like he wanted to argue but wasn't sure why. "Okay. Sure. What's the plan?"

"We have long been prepared for this occurrence. Many smaller tunnels branch off the main tunnel. It is like a labyrinth. We will position the copters within these smaller tunnels, and when the Sinz pass us we will wait for a few moments, then detonate the explosives. The channel will collapse and they will be killed."

"What makes you think they won't see us?"

"They will send in avians first. They are fast and ferocious, but require much room to turn due to their size. Their wings are so long they will struggle to fly through the tunnel as it is. Even if they see us as they fly past, they will be unable to turn. Come now, Ashala. It is time to leave."

Ash turned and walked away with Cowell. "See you later, Delgado," she called back. "Don't shoot till you see the whites of their eyes, remember?"

Delgado waved a brief acknowledgement, but did not smile. As Seriatts prepared for their departure all around him, Delgado felt invisible, carried along by events over which he had no control.

He realised he was looking at Keth, who was walking towards him. "Are you ready, Delgado?" the *mourst* asked. The Seriatt patted Delgado on the shoulder with one large hand as he walked past him.

"Sure I'm ready," Delgado replied. *But for what? Are you sure?*

"Come, then. Climb aboard. It is time to depart. Here, take this." The *mourst* handed Delgado a disc-shaped object.

"What is it?"

"It is the detonator for the explosives. Handle it carefully!"

Delgado followed Keth towards the copter. When the Seriatt was settled, Delgado stepped over the side of the fuselage, lowered himself into the confined space, and strapped himself in. A few moments later he was bouncing slightly as the aircraft accelerated across the smooth, undulating surface of the cavern floor. He could see that Ash's aircraft was already airborne and turning towards the dark tunnel mouth, its rotor blades shimmering faintly. As Ash's copter disappeared into the rock wall, Keth pulled back on the joystick and their own machine became airborne. A few moments later the noise of its engine increased dramatically in volume as it, too, was enveloped by the darkness of the tunnel.

Silvery smears spread across the dark rock as Keth and the other pilots activated spotlights to illuminate their way. The aircraft tipped sharply to one side then the other as they swept around the tunnel's sharp corners, the shadows flickering across the uneven walls. To Delgado it appeared that the tips of the rotor blades were only centimetres from the coarse rock.

After a few minutes the procession of copters began slow, until eventually the line of machines was hovering above the water that boiled over rocks beneath them. The tremendous noise of their engines reverberated off the walls as, one by one, the machines were skilfully turned through ninety degrees and flown backwards into the two smaller tunnels that ran perpendicular to the main channel. Shadows lengthened and swelled as the aircraft manoeuvred; then the larger tunnel darkened as the copters were absorbed by its walls.

Delgado's copter was the last to reverse into one of the smaller tunnels. He saw his own faint reflection and the bulbous turbine housings behind him in Keth's goggles as the *mourst* looked back, guiding the aircraft backwards.

Delgado also looked back, leaning out the other side of the cockpit to avoid obscuring Keth's view. Water flowed rapidly through the smaller tunnel, separating into two foaming torrents around a long, elliptical island, upon which the other copters had already landed.

Keth slowed the aircraft, then hovered briefly above the island before descending towards the limited amount of space that remained on its tapered point. When their aircraft had touched down, Keth reduced the copter's engines to idle and turned off the spotlights. Darkness consumed them as the pilots of the aircraft behind did the same now the final copter was safely down. As a warm gale thundered around them, Delgado looked to his right. Ragged holes linked the two smaller tunnels, and through them he could see that the other group of copters had landed on a similar island. The small screens in front of the pilots cast smears of light across their faces.

Keth's voice came close in Delgado's ears. "Be ready with the detonator," he said. "When I give the signal, activate it."

Delgado turned the small box over in his fingers, feeling for the ridge of the key in the darkness.

A few minutes later Delgado saw the shape of a Sinz avian flash past the tunnel mouth, its long wings beating slowly, its long tail trailing behind it. Keth raised his right arm, and Delgado rested his thumb on the detonator key. Another avian passed the tunnel mouth, then two more. A few more seconds passed; then Keth let his arm drop.

Delgado thumbed the button.

There was a momentary pause, then a succession of distant rumbles that Delgado felt more than heard due to the sound of the copter's engines. A cloud of dust billowed through the larger tunnel. The water below them surged.

Keth powered up the copter's engine and turned on the spotlights; hideous shadows appeared on the walls as the pilots of the machines behind them did the same. Within a few moments the aircraft were launching from the slender island towards the main tunnel. As they climbed, Delgado looked to his right and saw the other group of copters also in the air. Something stirred in him at being part of such a unit; it reminded him of times long lost.

Delgado could see that Keth was speaking, but could not hear his voice; presumably he was on another channel, communicating with other pilots.

The copter began to decelerate again as they neared the opening, until it was moving forward at no more than walking pace. Keth brought the copter to a hover, then eased the machine's nose out into the main tunnel. The pilot leaned forward in his seat and looked to his left. Keth said a few more words, then accelerated hard into the main tunnel; the rest of the copters followed behind like anxious offspring. When the first group of copters had emerged from the smaller tunnel, the second group followed.

As they flew through the main tunnel, Delgado looked back and saw that it was almost completely blocked by fallen rock. There was no sign of the Sinz avians.

Ahead the tunnel brightened, daylight penetrating the outer passages. Delgado adjusted his grip on the chain gun and prepared himself for whatever battle was to follow, assigning nobics to awareness, confidence, and reaction speed.

A silvery shape suddenly appeared, and the gun in Delgado's hands clattered as he fired instinctively. The Sinz avian passed close by the aircraft, tipping onto one side to avoid the copter's rotors. Delgado opened fire again and saw a line of holes appear in the avian's grey belly. The creature's high-pitched shriek penetrated the deep noise of the copters' engines, and the animal angled abruptly downwards. Delgado watched the avian as it fought to stay in the air, but the gunners on the following copters also sprayed it with ammunition. As Keth banked the copter hard around another bend, Delgado saw the Sinz smash against the tunnel wall at the water's edge, its innards drawn across the rock in a dark streak.

The copter straightened up, and a disc of bright grey light appeared at the end of the tunnel. It widened rapidly, and a few moments later the machine burst into daylight and the narrow channel outside. Delgado looked up and saw a gigantic airship hanging in the sky above. Gun platforms hung from delicate structures beneath it. Turrets rotated and the guns rocked as they began to fire feathers of flame at the copters.

The first couple of shots hit the wall on one side of the canyon, sending chunks of rock cascading down into the water. One of the large boulders hit the blades of the copter directly behind; the aircraft was pushed sideways through the air and crashed into the wall. A fireball bloomed briefly; then the wreckage slid down the craggy slope like discarded litter. Two broken bodies fell from the machine just before it hit the water, but Delgado was unable to identify them. As the incoming fire from the airship continued and the crashed copter became a smoke-laced fireball, Keth tipped the copter onto its left and pulled back on the stick.

They burst into the open. There were Sinz wherever Delgado looked: avians wheeling above, amphibians circling in the sea below. Delgado fired a sustained burst at an avian that swooped down, and the creature plummeted into the foaming sea.

Delgado looked back again and saw that the copters had scattered. One had crashed into the sea; its two occupants were treading water, waving for help. But from his vantage point Delgado could see the sinister, streamlined shapes of amphibians speeding towards them just below the surface, moving with effortless ease. Delgado looked away when the amphibians reached the two desperate figures.

To his left another of the copters plunged towards the waves. It was smothered in avians that were ravaging the machine as it fell, apparently oblivious to the imminent impact.

As Keth threw the copter to the right, Delgado jerked the gun around and fired at a diving avian. The weapon shuddered and coughed with each release, spent shell cases sparkling as they erupted from the breech. The Sinz lurched with each impact, then fell towards the water.

The airship's bloated shape appeared in front of Delgado as the copter turned. Despite its distance he fired immediately. Bright flashes skittered across the side of the airship. He paused, aimed at one of the engines slung beneath the craft, then fired again; the engine belched dark smoke and caught fire. Delgado adjusted his grip, then fired at a group of figures standing on an observation platform to the rear of the main gondola. One fell. Another looked towards him through teleculars of some kind, their lenses reflecting tiny discs of light.

As gun turrets turned towards them, another copter attacked the airship from the rear, and another approached from the opposite side. All three of the tiny machines spat lines of flame that penetrated the gigantic airship's skin, and after several seconds of sustained assault a small fire began to burn at the centre of the gigantic craft. It blossomed quickly, and Delgado could see shadowy figures running within the airship's opaque skin. Then there was an explosion, and a ball of fire rolled gently through the interior of the craft.

As the heat intensified the airship's skin started to melt, shrinking back around the fragile frame that supported it. Figures began to jump from the huge vessel despite its altitude: apparently dropping hundreds of metres to their death in the sea was preferable to being consumed by fire. The airship's guns fell dormant, and the vessel began to drift off course, nose-down.

As its gas escaped the airship descended with increasing speed, trailing thick dark smoke as it was eaten from within. When it hit the water, the superstructure shuddered, and the rest of the airship came to rest on the undulating sea. As the swell beat against it, the delicate frame began to collapse. Huge bubbles appeared beneath the vessel's nose, and it began to sink slowly.

The sinking airship was lost from sight as the copter turned again. When the aircraft righted, the sky was full of avians and copters, ribbons of smoke and tracer. The water below was littered with corpses and twisted metal, dark patches of oil and blood.

Almost all the other copters were still in the air, but none was close enough for Delgado to tell if Ash was still alive.

As another Sinz avian dived out of the sun and he fired the chain gun again, he did not have time to ponder on the possibilities.

The copters regrouped. A few seemed to be missing, but Delgado was not sure which. They closed ranks to fly in a tight, protective formation, covering each other with their weapons. Delgado saw Ash in Cowell's machine. He looked across at her for some moments, but she was focussed on searching the sky and did not look at him.

As they flew farther inland the air grew colder, and a thin mist began to develop. As the visibility declined the machines flew even closer together, their rotors stirring the dank air in tight coils.

Only a small area of the ground was visible beneath them: mossy grass, occasional boulders, a mixture of deciduous trees whose leaves shone with moisture.

Delgado thumbed his throat mike. "Why don't you climb over this murk?"

"We used a lot of the fuel during the combat with the Sinz," said the *mourst*, "and will use more if we climb. Furthermore, we do not know for how long this fog will persist. At least at this altitude we can see the ground."

"Just about. Let's just hope you see a mountain ahead of you in time."

Delgado looked to his right and saw one of the other copters descending rapidly towards a clearing; it still appeared to have power, but was obviously preparing to land.

Delgado drew Keth's attention to the other machine.

"They must be running out of fuel," said the *mourst*. He changed channels and communicated briefly with the other pilots. "We will all land," he said to Delgado, slowing the craft and beginning to descend. "We must be near the city now. Indeed, it is perhaps better that we proceed on foot."

The copters changed formation so that on approach to the clearing they were hovering in a diagonal stack. Below them, thirty or so metres from the ground, the pilot of the stricken copter was forced to turn to avoid some trees. The trees shuddered in the wash from the rotors, shedding a jewelled cascade of moisture. The copter lost a lot of height in the turn. Keth said something Delgado did not hear fully as he watched—some Seriattic exclamation or curse. Suddenly the machine was just metres from the ground and flying towards a large boulder that protruded from the earth like some great, shelled creature.

"They have lost power," said Keth dispassionately. "They cannot climb over the obstruction."

Delgado saw the other copter's rotor slow visibly. The pilot was on autorotation, effectively gliding down. He raised the copter's nose as it approached the boulder, but the machine was unable to climb; it simply continued onwards at the same altitude, nose-high. The pilot tried to turn away, but it was too late.

The rear end of the copter's underside smacked against the boulder and crumpled visibly. The machine tipped even farther to one side. The rotors chopped deep gouges in the ground and threw great clods of earth through the air. The blades bent suddenly and the machine dropped sideways, landing heavily on its side.

As Keth landed their own copter, the pilot of the crashed machine scrambled from the wreckage. It was Lerval. Small flames could be seen within one of the turbine housings.

Keth and Delgado jumped from their own copter and ran towards the mangled wreck.

"Are you hurt?" Keth asked Lerval.

"My leg is cut," said Lerval. "The fuselage was pushed in when we hit. But it is not too bad."

"Who was your gunner?" Keth asked.

"Sherquoia."

Delgado and Keth immediately ran towards the copter. They heard Lerval shout something behind them. Something about fire, an explosion.

Delgado reached the copter first. He knelt, leaned forward, and crawled between two of the splayed rotors. The smell of fuel was sickening; the grass beneath him was wet with the stuff. He lay on his belly and wriggled forwards beneath one of the turbine housings. Its heat was intense on his back. Delgado twisted to look up and saw the other fractured turbine housing above; the fire within it was worsening as flames flashed through the cracks in the metal; the paint peeled away around the intake like burning skin.

Ahead of him was the copter's fuselage. The rear of the cockpit had borne the brunt of the impact with the boulder. Sherquoia lay trapped in the twisted metal.

"Sherquoia. Can you hear me?"

The *conosq* moved her head slightly, but then cried out and was motionless once more. Delgado heard Keth calling from somewhere behind him. "Is she alive?" the *mourst* asked.

"Yeah," said Delgado. "But the fuselage is a wreck. Her legs must be crushed, and I'd bet her back's not in great shape, either. The way this thing smacked into that rock she's probably suffered major spinal trauma. Shit. Sherquoia. Can you move?"

The *conosq* muttered something unintelligible, then coughed and choked and moaned, agonised by each jarring movement.

"Delgado," called Keth. "There is much fuel. Can you help her?"

"I don't know. Even if I do, she's likely to be paralysed. Her legs might even have to be amputated. Goddamn. Sherquoia, can you hear me?" He wasn't sure whether the *conosq* responded. "Sherquoia. I'm going to try and free you. Do you understand?" There was no response this time. "It's not going to be much fun. You're just going to have to stick with me. Okay?" Nothing.

"Delgado," called Keth. "The fire is spreading. Quickly."

Delgado swore, looked at Sherquoia, the crumpled cockpit, the burning turbine above him. There was little time. For all he knew the *conosq* was already dead anyway.

He began to wriggle backwards from beneath the wreckage. As he was about to duck his head under the second turbine housing, he heard a noise. He looked back towards Sherquoia and saw her turn her head, looking up out of the cockpit directly at him. He heard Keth call again; other voices, too. Someone gripped his ankles and began trying to pull him from the wreckage.

Delgado wriggled forwards across the fuel-sodden ground and reached out to Sherquoia, then grasped her beneath the armpits. At the same time he felt several hands grip his legs, and pull at him. He maintained his grip on Sherquoia. She screamed but did not move. The Seriatts outside shouted and pulled repeatedly at Delgado, and with each lurch Sherquoia gave an agonised wail. But she could not be released.

Delgado let go and tried to get a better grip, but as he did so the Seriatts heaved and he was extricated from beneath the copter in a single movement. Just before the Seriatts pulled him to his feet, he saw Sherquoia look up at him once more. Although clearly pained, her expression was one of great peace.

Delgado was heaved up and carried backwards by the Seriatts. Although he struggled, their hands were insistent, and he was dragged away from the wreckage. As the group reached the centre of the clearing, the copter beneath which Sherquoia was trapped exploded.

Heavy pieces of engine flew through the air and hit the ground with dull thumps, making deep impressions in the earth. Thin sheets of fuselage fluttered towards the ground like the lost feathers of some great metal bird. As the debris settled they could only stand and watch as the copter, and Sherquoia, were consumed by the fire that now raged.

Lerval made a long hawking sound at the back of his throat. "I am lucky to have escaped with my life," he said.

"Perhaps," said Keth. "But Sherquoia is dead." He stared hard at the other pilot.

"You say you ran out of fuel?" asked Cowell.

"Yes. I thought we had much remaining, but it seems the gauge gave a false reading. I was forced to land."

"But the rest of us have much fuel remaining," said Miskoh. "Why is yours the only aircraft to run out so prematurely?"

Lerval made a sweeping gesture with one hand. "I do not know. A leak, perhaps. We will never know."

"There was a hell of a lot of fuel leaking from that pipe for a tank that had run dry," said Delgado.

Lerval looked at him. His Seriattic expression was difficult to judge. "You accuse me of lying, human?"

Delgado said nothing. As the *mourst* turned to look at the burning copter once more, he felt that there was something different about Lerval's appearance, but was unable to pinpoint what.

"You were brave," said Keth, slapping Delgado on one shoulder. "You risked your own life in your efforts to save Sherquoia."

Delgado shrugged. "Did my best," he said. "Wasn't good enough. Nothing new there."

"Don't beat yourself up, Delgado," said Ash. "You gave it your best shot."

"Ashala is right," said Cowell. "From what you say Sherquoia's injuries were very serious. Even if you had managed to pull her out, it is likely that she would have died anyway."

"Perhaps with more care," growled Miskoh, glaring at Lerval, "Sherquoia would still be with us."

As the fire began to subside, consuming the last of the insubstantial aircraft, the group began to walk towards the far side of the clearing, where the landed copters were lined up. They convened behind Cowell's machine, wrapped in the smell of oil and fuel drifting from the hot engine.

Delgado stood next to Ash. "You okay?" he asked quietly.

"Sure. No sweat. My aim's improving rapidly. You?"

"Fine." He shrugged. "No sweat."

FIVE

Ash took Delgado's hand in hers and squeezed it. He looked down at her, opened his mouth to say something further, then changed his mind.

"Now we have landed we may as well leave the copters," said Cowell. "We are close enough to the city now to go on foot. There may be nowhere else safe to land, and we might simply draw attention to ourselves. We will hide the aircraft, gather together some provisions and water, then go to briefly survey the city. Then we will visit our loved ones."

They trudged cautiously through the forest, the smell of damp earth and pine thick in the air. Occasionally a creature would scamper across the ground and quickly climb a tree or dash into a hole, but it was otherwise still and gloomy amid the trees. They paused increasingly frequently as they approached the city, watching, waiting, ensuring that they remained alone.

All seemed quiet, but Delgado felt uneasy: while not representative of an immediate threat, he perceived traces somewhere nearby with a distinctly hostile flavour. Yet for some reason they seemed muddied, resistant to analysis.

Cowell expressed frustration at their losses.

"If I had not ordered the copters so heavily laden, we might not have lost the others," said the *vilume*. "If the aircraft had been able to turn or accelerate more quickly, they would have had a better chance. They might still be alive."

"Give yourself a break, Cowell," said Delgado. "We did what we thought was best. We carried all that stuff because we thought we'd need it. We fought because we had to. You do what you do and you can't change it."

"Unless you've got a time gate, huh, Delgado?" suggested Ash.

"Now that would be handy right now," Delgado replied. He half turned to look at her. Her cheeks were pink with the effort of carrying her load up the slight incline, but her eyes were bright, mischievous. Like Lerval, Delgado thought there was something different about her appearance, but he wasn't sure what. It was as if her skin looked somehow softer, more pliant.

She glanced at him and smiled in a way he found slightly unsettling, then looked at Cowell. The change in her expression unsettled him even more. He looked ahead again. They were approaching the edge of the wood.

Breathing heavily, hot and pink from the climb, they walked to the tree line, where they stopped and looked down at the scene that confronted them.

"Welcome to Capital City," muttered Cowell. "Or what remains of it."

The land dropped away, a steep slope of earth from which tree roots protruded like buried serpents.

Between the far edge of the sprawling conurbation and the grey, snow-topped mountains in the distance, the Sinz constructs rose like crooked fingers, casting irregular shadows across the Seriattic ruins. Bulbous airships drifted from tethers like swollen limbs, with Sinz avians soaring and wheeling around them.

At ground level, the city looked like something decaying, a rotting representation of what they had previously experienced. The few taller structures—the elegant towers, shining bridges—and most of the white, low-rise buildings so distinctive of Seriattic architecture were destroyed or damaged. Most were also smothered in what looked like green mould, and peppered with holes through use of projectile weaponry. The canals—the once-vibrant, life-giving arteries so vital to the Seriatts' trade and leisure activities—were now just scars on the landscape, dried and cracked.

There was no traffic on the long, straight roads, and apart from a few burned-out metal carcasses, none of the shining, chrome-toothed vehicles Delgado remembered. There were no Seriatts on the sidewalks. No aircraft or birds in the Seriattic sky.

It was a dead place.

Yet, bathed in the pale sunshine that was now breaking through the thinning mist, it remained beautiful, defiant.

"See what they have done," said Cowell, with a sweeping gesture.

"Well, you know, I've seen worse," Delgado said.

"How could it be worse?" barked Miskoh. "They have ravaged our world."

"You ever consider a career in diplomacy, Delgado?" whispered Ash.

"My point is that they could've destroyed it completely. They could probably have burned the crust off the entire planet if they'd wanted to. As well as anything of their own—which we don't know much about—they also have the weapons Myson sold them. And those we do know about—mostly the kind of brute-force tech Structure used back when the aftereffects of a war weren't that high on the list of priorities. Back when the old scorched-earth policy reigned supreme."

"Maybe the Sinz have other plans for Seriatt," said Ash.

"Sure," said Delgado. "If the wormhole's unstable, then they'll want to bring resources through when they can, without having to commit straight to combat. If they'd rendered Seriatt uninhabitable, they'd have robbed themselves of a front-line command point. What's the rest of Seriatt like?"

"Much the same, from what we know," said Miskoh. "Communications are obviously limited, but we believe that every major city has a Sinz presence."

"How about counselling, Delgado?" offered Ash. "You ever thought of becoming a counsellor? Help people get over tragedy?"

"Really? I didn't get the impression they had such a large invasion force."

"It did not seem that way at first," said Miskoh. "But once they had established their main bases, they seemed to increase dramatically in number. Although no more ships arrived, their force grew very rapidly, and continues to do so, from what we can tell. It is as if they are somehow breeding adult Sinz here."

"Interesting. What about the Seriattic population? Mostly killed, right?"

"Yes, the majority of Seriatts met their deaths in the first wave of the Sinz invasion. Some of those who survived went to the mountains; others hid in the swamps or forests. Apart from a hard core of resistance, our population centres were abandoned."

"How many do you think survived in total?"

"We can know only of Capital City with certainty. We believe that there are perhaps two thousand here, but possibly less. The Sinz moved rapidly when they first arrived, and took few prisoners.

Delgado thought for a few moments, then looked at Cowell. "You say you have families?"

"Yes. We have established a camp where we hope they will not be found. It is sheltered, secluded."

"How far away is it?"

"Once we get back to the copters it will not take us long to get there. It is not far if taking a direct route, but we do not do this. Come. We will go there now and you may see for yourself the conditions in which the surviving Seriatts are forced to live."

They flew for around half an hour, then landed on the northern shore of a lake edged with deciduous trees. The copters were hastily unloaded, pulled into the darkness beneath the trees, and covered with tarpaulins dragged from pits hidden beneath the soil and dead leaves. Overhead, grey clouds gathered like stalking beasts.

"Rain is coming," said Keth, looking at the sky. "Perhaps a storm. I feel it."

When the copters were hidden, they began to walk up the slope leading away from the shore. The ground was soft underfoot, and gave a little with each step; it made walking strenuous. Delgado glanced across at Ash; she was leaning forward slightly as she climbed, her face slightly flushed. She also looked weary, but continued to follow closely behind Cowell.

Delgado felt a sudden prickle of awareness and glimpsed a figure to his left. He immediately turned his head but saw only trees. He stopped walking and stared into the woodland.

"What is the matter, Delgado?" asked Lerval, who had been walking just a few metres behind him.

"Not sure. Thought I saw something."

Lerval followed Delgado's gaze. "Perhaps it was the wind disturbing some foliage."

Delgado shook his head. "No. I thought it was a small figure. Near that fallen tree." He pointed.

Broken roots sprouted from the disc of soil pulled from the ground when the tree had toppled. Weeds grew in the crater that was left behind. There was no sign of movement.

"Your imagination must be playing tricks on you," said Lerval, clapping Delgado on the shoulder. "Perhaps it was a tree itself you saw. Or simply a hallucination. You are hungry, thirsty, and tired. The mind can be deceptive. When you have rested and consumed refreshment, you will see no more visions." The *mourst* chuckled.

But I felt it, too, thought Delgado. "Yeah, sure," he said, beginning to walk up the slope once more. "Come on. We're getting left behind."

Lerval began to follow Delgado up the incline. After a few paces the *mourst* glanced back. Some of the weeds next to the fallen tree shivered; then a slight figure gradually appeared in front of its trunk. The Sinz shape-shifter had a small, pinched face. It looked at Lerval and curled its lips in a smile. It then looked at the silhouettes of Delgado and the others shimmering against the bright sunlight that passed between the trees at the top of the incline. It made a faint hissing sound, then looked at Lerval and became invisible once more.

Lerval looked up the slope to the rest of the party, then hefted his hold-hall onto his shoulder and continued to climb after them.

When they reached the top of the slope, the ground levelled off, and progress became easier. When they had been walking for a few more minutes, Cowell and Keth stopped and gazed into the trees.

As the other Seriatts crouched next to trees and kept watch, Ash and Delgado walked up behind the *vilume* and the *mourst*. "What's up?" he whispered. He could see nothing out of place and, more importantly, nobic activity had not increased.

Without warning three *mourst* dropped from trees ahead and crouched, short-stem weapons drawn. Delgado's nobics surged, prickling his scalp like a shingles rash.

"Identify yourselves," barked one of the *mourst*.

"We are a party of Sinz shape-shifters," Cowell announced. "We have come to kill you."

Delgado heard *mourst* laughter behind him; it sounded like Keth. He glanced from Cowell to the three crouching *mourst*; they were barely distinguishable against the trees. They looked young, although one was older than his two colleagues. Delgado's nobics continued to stir.

The three *mourst* stood, slung their weapons over their shoulders, and began walking towards them.

"Gartan," said Cowell. "I am pleased your eyesight remains good." He gave a gruff laugh as the two of them came together. They held hands briefly.

"And you have your apprentices with you, I see," said Cowell. "Metille, Retarga. You are well?"

The two younger *mourst* made gestures of welcome and confirmation. "We are," said Retarga, "despite Gartan's insistence that we crouch in trees day and night, our nostrils filled with the stink of animals."

"Aye, Retarga," said Gartan. "Your suggestion that we dig holes in the ground and lie in the damp earth with the grubs rather than enjoy a vantage point in the trees was a much better one."

"For myself, I did not believe the stink came from the trees," said

Metille. He looked at Gartan. They laughed. Metille smacked Retarga around the back of the head. Retarga was not amused.

"There are fewer of you. Where is young Descan?" Gartan glanced at those among the trees. "Others are missing, also," he said.

"A Sinz amphibian took Descan," said Cowell. "He was brave, but foolish."

"And doubtless headstrong," said Gartan. "It is a loss. He was a good *mourst*, and had much potential. I will miss him."

"Indeed. Others perished as we fled the cavern. They fought bravely."

"Where is Sherquoia?"

"Killed when her copter crashed. I am sorry, Gartan."

Delgado had become familiar enough with Seriattic expressions to know that Gartan's conveyed a combination of anger and grief. "Who was her pilot?" he demanded. "What happened?"

"Lerval was flying the copter." Cowell glanced at the *mourst*.

"Sherquoia was killed yet Lerval survived? This must have been an unusual accident."

"It was," said Keth. His tone was grave.

Gartan waited for more information, but when it was obviously not forthcoming his attention turned to Delgado and Ashala. "Humans accompany you," the *mourst* said. "Where did you find them?"

"They are trustworthy," said Cowell. "They have saved several lives. They wish to help us liberate Seriatt. This one is called Delgado, and this one is Ashala. Delgado risked his life trying to rescue Sherquoia, but was unsuccessful."

Gartan looked at Delgado and Ash for several moments.

"Very well," Gartan said eventually. "Your judgement is good, Cowell. If you say they may be trusted, then it is so. Come. I will escort you to the camp. Metille, Retarga: you remain here on guard."

"Aye, Gartan," they said. "No Sinz will pass this point. Rest your life on it."

The camp was in a tree-filled valley with steep sides from which huge boulders protruded. Spread across the valley floor were green canvas tents of various shapes and sizes. These were skilfully assembled to break up their shape and deceive the eye, further obscured by generous amounts of foliage and bracken. Wooden huts had also been built high in many trees, linked by walkways of wood and rope. The shelters were so well camouflaged that the true size of the encampment was difficult to judge. At several points weapons and grenades were stacked in purpose-built wooden shelters, ready for immediate use.

The heart of the site was on the eastern side of the valley, set in a natural, almost circular hollow within a vertical formation of brown rock riddled with golden veins. By Delgado's estimation the outcrop must have been a hundred metres high.

Within the alcove animals grazed at tufts of grass, and wooden carts piled high with sacks and crates were lined up on one side. Opposite them a line of seemingly mismatched generators purred with surprising smoothness given their clearly disparate origins. Despite lacking obvious compatibility, the separate units were linked at various points by knots of pipework, data ribbon, and cabling forced into marriage. Halfway along the line of machines, several glowing crystal rods jutted at forty-five degrees from the side, a dark casing of some unidentifiable material; a little further along, oily cogs and gears meshed as belts trundled loosely around pulleys; some of the belts were dark, clearly modern compounds, while others seemed to be improvised from short leather strips sewn together. One of the belts ran almost the entire length of the line of generators. Elsewhere, water dripped from the funnels of condenser belts, and brown exhaust fumes coughed from clutches of pipe as brass pistons slid in and out of cylinders.

Thick cables like tree runners distributed the power produced by the generators throughout the camp. Lights hung like glowing eggs between the trees and tents. Through the open flap of one nearby tent a *mourst* was hunched over a small computer.

As the party neared the group of larger tents near the rock wall at the rear of the alcove, a group of children sitting near a fire turned to look at them. They were of mixed age; none of the younger children possessed features distinctive of any of the Seriattic sexes, but the destinies of their slightly older counterparts were clearer: two were obviously *mourst*, with dark, scaly skin and long limbs; two others were softer in physique, a certain pudginess to their appearance indicating that they were *conosq*. Another looked almost as tall as her *mourst* counterparts, but also possessed a *conosq* softness of feature: a burgeoning *vilume*.

Nearby, two adult *mourst* were chopping logs to make firewood. Another was approaching the camp from the far side of the clearing, walking up a shallow slope carrying pails of water hanging from either end of a stick balanced on one shoulder. The *mourst* called to the two who were chopping wood and pointed at the new arrivals. The two Seriatts stopped working, laid down their axes, and began to walk towards them. One of them walked quickly to some of the tents, and a few moments later more Seriatts emerged.

They were a scrawny bunch, but despite being slightly malnourished the *mourst* were as beautiful and strong as any Delgado had ever seen. The usually voluptuous *conosq* were noticeably lean and unglamourous. Some of them carried thin and dirty infants who clung to their sides like leeches.

A *mourst* approached them from one of the tents. He was tall and proud. The weary group allowed their heavy holdalls to drop to the floor.

"Cowell," said the *mourst*. "It is good to see you again. We were not sure you would return this time."

"The Sinz tried to stop us, Danogen," replied Cowell. "But they could not."

"And see," said Gartan, "Cowell is accompanied by humans."

"This had not escaped my notice, Gartan."

"They are trustworthy," said Cowell. "They have proven themselves to us. This one is called Delgado. This is Ashala."

"You are both welcome," said Danogen, clasping his hands together in front of his chest.

"Now that you are here you must tell us of the Sinz," said one of the *mourst* who had been chopping wood. "How are their preparations advancing? Do you think we can defeat them in the way we discussed?"

"I am uncertain, Talliol," replied Cowell. "Their spacecraft construction we saw much of, but we did not manage to gain access to the installation near the coast. We were attacked by avians, and are lucky to have survived."

"We'll go back just as soon as we can, though," said Delgado. "If it's as well protected as it seems to be, then it's got to be important to them."

The Seriatts looked at Delgado as if surprised at his ability to speak.

"And are their spacecraft complete?" asked Talliol. "Have you managed to ascertain how many they have constructed?"

"We are uncertain," said Keth, "but they are preparing some form of action, this much is clear."

"Enough questions for now, Talliol," interjected Danogen, placing one large hand on one of the eager young *mourst*'s shoulders. "We all want to know these answers, but our friends are tired. We must give them time to rest before we make such demands of them. Would you show Delgado to Descan's shelter? Young Descan needs it no longer. Issilan: may Ashala stay with you?"

There was no immediate answer. Ash looked behind her at the *conosq*.

"She may."

Ash looked at Delgado, one eyebrow raised; he nodded almost imperceptibly.

"Excellent. Rest for a while, all of you. Then you may tell us what you know when you are ready. We have a hog baking in the ground." He pointed to a patch of bare earth at the edge of the clearing. Delgado realised that it was steaming gently. "When it is cooked, we will eat. Then we can talk."

Delgado and Ash were put into separate tree-houses. Descan's home was a simple, single room, but it contained all the essentials: a bunk, a table and a couple of chairs, a basin and a latrine. Running water could be pumped into either toilet or basin by turning a handle situated between the two.

Everything was made from wood—even the basin and latrine. The carving was simple and unremarkable, but nonetheless of a very high standard. The Seriatts had maintained their distinctive appreciation of design and function despite the Sinz occupation.

The floor creaked as he walked across the room and looked through the window—a hole in the wall half a metre square—overlooking the camp. The *mourst* were still chopping wood, but the children had left the fire, which had died down somewhat and now smoked thinly.

Delgado heard footsteps, the boards forming the walkway in front of the hut beginning to tremble. A particularly loose one bounced up and down a couple of times, banging against the joists that supported it. Delgado leaned out of the window and looked to the left; it was Ash. She was walking along the relatively narrow planks with confidence. She smiled at him.

"These walkways are kinda rickety, Delgado," she said. She stopped in front of him. "You've got a head for heights, right?"

"Sure. Used to be a tightrope walker. Didn't you know?"

Ash walked a few more steps and lifted the heavy sheet of canvas hanging across the doorway. She leaned forward and peered in at him. "Hi," she said. "Can I come in?"

"Sure. Just wipe your feet."

Ash entered the room and let the canvas fall back behind her. "Nice place you've got here."

"Well it's not quite a shaft-side habitat suite, but I like it."

"Maid service?"

"You bet."

She walked across to the window on the other side of the hut and looked out into the forest, then turned and leaned on the frame. "Nice view, too. Trees, the sound of a rushing stream nearby. Issilan's got a shack near the sewage works. You're doing all right for an old guy."

He looked at her for a few moments, then smiled. "I just hope Cowell appreciates your sense of humour, Ash," he said. "These Seriatts can be funny creatures sometimes."

Her face reddened. She looked around the room. "So what d'you a make of all this then, Delgado? How in the hell did we get here?"

"Cowell and her group—"

"His group."

"Yeah, right. Whatever. They haven't told us everything. But I'm not sure what they're keeping from us, or why."

"Probably still wary of us despite what Cowell says."

"Sure. You get anything out of Issilan?"

"No. I don't think she likes me. In fact I know she doesn't like me. She likes you, though. I can tell that much."

Delgado stretched and walked across to the basin, wound the handle next to it a few times until a steady stream of water was flowing from the wooden tap, and rinsed his face. "Wow, that's cold," he said. He swilled his face until the stream of water slowed. "Hand me that towel, would you?"

"So what do you think we should do?" asked Ash. "Slip away from this crowd while they're not looking?"

"No. I think we should stick with them for a while. After all, they know more about the Sinz than we do. They've lived with 'em for a few years, by the looks of things. And they've obviously got something in mind. Some way they think they can kick the Sinz into touch. I mean, I'm not sure about some of 'em. That Lerval sure looks shifty to me."

"Yeah, I noticed him, too. He's got a funny way of looking at me."

Delgado snorted, threw the towel onto the bunk, then walked across to the window that overlooked the clearing. "You should be so lucky. He's got a funny way of looking, period."

She laughed, then got up and walked over and stood next to him, leaning on the windowsill. They saw Cowell walking across the clearing. A surge of nobic activity gave Delgado a pins-and-needles sensation through his head; although he didn't much like it, he could guess the reason easily enough. He glanced at Ash as she watched the *vilume* entering a tent, then looked back into the clearing. "You remember just before we stepped into the time gate?" he asked. He felt her emotions slide a little.

"Vaguely," she said. "I don't think time travel suits me. The details are a bit hazy."

"Do you remember me saying something to you just before we stepped into the gate?"

She remained silent for a few moments. *That you loved me?* "No, Delgado. Don't reckon I do."

"Okay. Good."

They looked at the clearing in silence for a few moments. Eventually Delgado sniffed, and clapped a hand on Ash's shoulder. "You hungry?" he asked. "Cowell tells me this hog's big enough to feed a thousand."

"Sure he does. But he doesn't know how much I can eat." They walked towards the door. "D'you think they have ketchup?" she asked.

"For you, Ash," replied Delgado, "I'd say anything's possible."

Fifth chronological displacement
Earth, date unknown

The bitter wind was like a sheet of metal against Delgado's face. All around, the land was covered in banks of frozen snow.

Ahead and to his right were ruins of habitat towers, decaying, frost-coated structures that penetrated the white crust. The sky was a brilliant blue, but there were no fliers, no signs of human life—no life of any kind. The chromium dome of Planetary Guidance Headquarters was a fractured mirror to his right, partially destroyed, as if consumed by decay. But no natural rot had eaten the intimidating building: the scars of blaster and bomb were clear to see. And although some of the building remained intact, the area where Myson's chamber had once been located no longer existed.

Somehow he had been catapulted to a future Earth, gripped in an ice age, a change of climate the human race had either been unable to fight or had caused.

The sense of isolation, and foreboding at the apparent future of Earth, chilled him more deeply than the biting wind.

Six

Seriatt
March 6, 2379 (Earth equivalent)

T he earth around the hog continued to steam as two *mourst* dug the animal out. It had been packed in a thick layer of the clay that lay beneath the topsoil, lain on a bed of glowing hot coals with more coals placed on top, and baked in the ground for several days. The clay had hardened to form a shell, while the meat cooked within. Now it was ready.

The two *mourst* threw down their shovels and heaved the large, boulder-like lump from the ground. The dried clay husk was then cracked open and peeled away in great chunks to reveal the carcass within. The aroma that wafted from the steaming pale flesh was rich indeed.

When the clay was removed, a *vilume* knelt next to the hog. The Seriatt made cuts around the meat and curled the skin from it in a single sheet with tongs, cast it to one side, then began slicing meat from the carcass. The Seriatt passed them to another who put the slices into wooden bowls and began passing them round. The Seriatts retired to sit on blankets near the fire, picking fresh fruit, chopped root vegetables, hunks of bread, and hot sauces from other bowls to accompany their meat. Water was poured from pitchers into large wooden cups.

Cowell sat down opposite Delgado and Ash.

"The food is to your liking?" the *vilume* asked. The two humans made noises of affirmation. "Good. Keth is particularly keen on hunting the wild hogs. But then he is a *mourst*."

Delgado looked around the camps. "This looks like a pretty well-established setup, Cowell. How long have you been here?"

"Too long. We move as often as we can, but sometimes it is hard. This is a good spot that offers all we need. We do not want to leave here unless we have to."

"Aren't you worried the Sinz will find you?" asked Ash. "In fact, what's to stop them just nuking the place and getting rid of the lot of you?"

"Most of Seriatt's population has been forced into exile such as this. We are spread over the surface of the planet. The Sinz cannot focus on all of us. They will come, but we have some time. They cannot use nuclear weapons because they need to maintain the stability of Seriatt's environment. Until they no longer need our world, at least. They pay more attention to their other plans. Seriatt is not their ultimate goal. They are looking elsewhere."

"Earth?"

"I do not know. Many of their ways of thinking defy analysis, but their aims are clear enough."

Keth and Lerval joined them, bowls piled high with meat, vegetables, and bread.

"Plotting a rebellion with our human friends, Cowell?" asked Lerval.

Cowell did not look at the *mourst*. "And why not? Do you wish to be held in bondage by the Sinz for the rest of your life? I want to see Seriatt liberated, Lerval. And soon."

"Relax, Cowell," said Lerval. "I simply meant that I would not wish to be left out of such plans. I feel the same as you."

"You should not cast doubt upon the motives of anyone here, Lerval. Not even in humour."

"I apologise, Cowell. I did not mean to offend."

Cowell nodded once in acknowledgement, but it was an awkward, seemingly forced gesture.

Lerval glanced around them, then picked at his food, but set down his plate having eaten little. To Delgado's eyes, the *mourst* seemed edgy. "I will go and relieve Hulio in the northeastern hide," Lerval said. "He will be glad of some hot meat and rest. Excuse me."

The others ate a little more as Lerval walked away.

"I must apologise for Lerval's behaviour," said Keth. "He is young and inexperienced."

"He is a fool," said Cowell, "and a liability." The *vilume* stared at Lerval's back as the young *mourst* disappeared into the trees.

Delgado and Ash glanced at each other.

"So, Delgado," said Cowell. "We are planning to pay another visit to the Sinz installation. Will you join us?"

"You mean the one no one's been able to get into yet? You bet. Do you have any idea what's in there?"

"We do not," said Keth. "But it is important to the Sinz; that much is clear from the level of defences that surround it."

"Such as?"

"Many things. There are giant scorpionlike creatures with huge, pointed pincers. There are vast sheets of skin thick with mucus, which seems able to dissolve anything unfortunate enough to become trapped within it. I once saw a good friend consumed by this poison before I could save him."

"And you've no idea at all what's in there?"

"There is one possibility," said Keth. "The Sinz appear to populate Seriatt in increasing numbers, yet no ships arrive." The *mourst* glanced at Cowell. "We believe that it may be some kind of production facility."

"You think they're clones?"

"It is possible," said Keth.

"It is also possible that they are true individuals born of a single parent."

"Siblings? Yeah, that might make sense. Clones would probably have too many weaknesses for their purposes."

"Unless they're just better at cloning than we are," observed Ash.

"What makes you think all the Sinz come from this one source?" Delgado asked. "What about the avians and the amphibians? Wouldn't they come from somewhere else?"

"We do not believe this is the case," said Cowell. "We believe all the Sinz on Seriatt come from this particular facility. We have been in contact with other groups similar to ours in other areas of Seriatt. Nowhere else is there the same level of Sinz activity as here. It is near where they first landed, their initial base." Cowell paused and glanced at Keth, as if uncertain how much to reveal. "We think that if we were able to destroy, or even just disable, whatever is in that facility, then the Sinz would be considerably weakened. Then perhaps, with a concerted effort, we could defeat them."

"Okay," said Delgado. "First thing we need to do is get as close as we can, see if it's possible to get in and take a look. If we think it's a go, then we'll attempt to find out just what they're doing in there. If as you suggest they've got a single core on Seriatt, a focal point, then that's their weakness. That's what we need to take advantage of."

"Gee, Delgado, I love it when you get all operational," said Ash. "Anyone would think you used to be a Reactionary Forces Officer. You've got room for me on this little excursion of yours, right? I mean, you're not expecting to leave me here."

Delgado snorted. "Shit, Ash, you think I'd even dare think something like that?"

"Great," she said, chewing meat. "Cowell. I'll be your gunner."

"I will consider it an honour, Ashala."

A plume of brilliant orange feathers suddenly appeared in the sky. They seemed to hang in the air above the trees for a moment before speeding to the ground. There were explosions and screams. Fires ignited. Scattered earth rained down.

Cowell began shouting as the group got to their feet. There was a flash of white light from somewhere among the trees to Delgado's left. Then a shock wave knocked them from their feet.

Delgado looked up. His ears were ringing. He brushed damp soil and leaves from the side of his face. People were running; terrified children cried. Through the trees he could see sinewy figures moving, and flaming tongues of blaster fire.

He ducked instinctively as there was a second flash and another shock wave rolled through the forest. The ground shuddered beneath him. He felt a wash of heat across his back and heard a dull thud.

When he looked up, he saw a smoking section of tree trunk lying just a few metres away from his face. But when what he thought was a branch moved slightly, he realised that it was a Seriatt. A *conosq*, he thought. He could see little definition to the creature. It did not appear to have any legs. The Seriatt was alive, but trapped within an irreparably charred husk. Without hesitation he pulled his sidearm from its holster and shot a single round; the weak movement ceased.

As the ringing in his ears began to lessen, Delgado heard rapid gunfire. He got to his feet, dizzy, disoriented. There were dull crumps, thick vibrations through the ground, and fountains of earth all around him. He caught a glimpse of what he thought was Cowell helping Ash to her feet while shouting instructions to *mourst* as they ran to the weapons racks and grabbed sidearms and grenades. Delgado ran with them and pulled a short-stem pulse rifle from one of the racks.

When he turned and looked around the camp again, he could see neither Ash nor Cowell. Amid the explosions and gunfire he scanned the bodies that now littered the clearing, but recognised none of them.

As another flume of earth rose at the centre of the camp, clods of soil cascading down again, Delgado set all his gun's settings to max and ran towards the battle.

As he sprinted towards the fighting, weaving between muddy craters, a Sinz appeared in front of him from behind a tree. The drab creature looked at him, its eyes soulless. Delgado killed it with a short burst in the belly.

More Sinz appeared, fading in from nothing among the trees, shimmering ghosts wherever he looked. He sprayed the area in front of him as he ran, sweeping the gun from side to side.

Delgado jumped into the crater formed by an uprooted tree and pressed himself against the disc of soil that clung to its roots. The vibrations ceased during a brief lull.

He looked to his right and saw Keth and Miskoh crouching behind trees around twenty metres away. Keth made a gesture instructing Delgado to stay put.

Delgado glanced around, scanning the trees, then looked back towards Keth and Miskoh; the two Seriatts were discussing something. As they talked

Delgado saw two Sinz emerge in front of a large bush, as if passing through the foliage like spectres. The two creatures saw Miskoh and Keth immediately. They aimed their weapons. Delgado called a warning and fired. The Sinz fired as the Seriatts dived forwards and their shots missed. One of the Sinz looked at Delgado and fired at him, hitting the tree to Delgado's right. He returned fire and hit the Sinz in the upper body; the force of the impact threw the creature backwards through the foliage. The other Sinz turned to run while simultaneously trying to vanish once more, but by this time Keth and Miskoh were back on their feet, and the Sinz was killed by a volley of shots from three weapons.

Other than the sound of a Seriattic child crying somewhere, quiet returned. Delgado, Keth, and Miskoh waited a few minutes, but all was still. The two Seriatts engaged in further brief discussion, checked that the way was clear, then ran over to him. The three of them crouched together next to the fallen tree.

Keth clasped Delgado's hands in his, the Seriatt's long, multijointed fingers wrapping the human's. "We are in your debt," said Keth. The Seriatt pulled Delgado's hand to his mouth and kissed his fingers.

"A Sinz ambush," spat Miskoh. He stared at the trees around them as if they were complicit in the attack. "A scout party that happened upon us by chance, Keth?"

"Possibly," the other *mourst* replied. "They will have reported our position to their superiors. Now we will have to move."

Delgado looked at some of the dead bodies lying on the forest floor, then back towards the camp. "Either of you seen Cowell or Ash?" he asked.

"I have not," said Miskoh. But he seemed distracted. "Keth, how do you think the Sinz managed to get so close without being seen?"

"To attack us completely without warning . . . ," said Keth. "It should not have happened. The observers' instruments in the hides should have detected their approach. If nothing else, we should have had time to get the children to safety. What has gone wrong here?"

With the fighting apparently over the Seriatts were beginning to emerge from cover. Delgado saw some of them climbing from pits in the ground, some of which seemed to have tunnels leading from them.

He looked at Keth. "They attacked from the northeastern end of the valley, right?" he said.

"That is correct," the *mourst* growled.

Delgado looked back into the forest.

"What is it, Delgado?" asked the Seriatt. "What is in your mind?"

Delgado looked at Keth, then Miskoh, and shrugged. "Lerval went on watch in the northeastern hide," he said. "Just before the attack."

Delgado returned to the camp while Keth and Miskoh went in search of Lerval. Given the *mourst*s' mood, Delgado considered that he would not want to be in Lerval's position should they find him.

The valley was littered with Sinz and Seriattic bodies, but most of the Seriattic corpses were in the main area of the camp, upon which the Sinz had focussed their attack, and where the Seriatts had been trapped by the sheer rock walls and steep slopes of the valley sides.

The generators and many of the tents had been destroyed. Copters were like crushed bugs. Nearby, a team of Seriatts passed pails of water from the stream to throw it over burning tents and tree-houses. It was a futile effort.

Delgado walked farther through the camp and found Ash kneeling among a group of Seriatts; the handgun she had grabbed from the weapons rack as the attack was beginning lay on the ground next to her. The warbling ululations of *conosq* grief filled the air. Even *mourst* standing solemnly behind the *conosq* and *vilume* seemed to be struggling to control their emotions. As Delgado neared the group, he saw a dead *conosq*, its body burned and broken. But this did not seem to be the focus of the group's attention. As he neared Ash, he saw that in front of her lay a Seriattic infant.

Most of its body was badly burned, skin peeling away in large flakes to expose the raw flesh beneath. Yet somehow its face had been spared, and remained entirely unmarked. Despite its injuries the child was still alive, glancing wide-eyed at the Seriatts that surrounded it. Its gaze came to rest on the unfamiliar characteristics of Ashala's face. Its eyes were bright, but despite it being a Seriatt, Delgado recognised the fear and confusion in the child.

Delgado knelt next to Ash. He noticed that she was trembling slightly.

"It's going to die," she whispered. "They know it. I think it knows it, too."

Delgado looked down at the infant. It looked back at him with a strange expression that highlighted its alienness far more strongly than he ever perceived in adult Seriatts. An indefinable otherworldliness. In those moments he was transported back to times he had looked down at Cascari, both as an infant and as he lay dying by Michael's hand. The emotions that stirred within him were powerful. He tried to steel himself against them, but still had to look away.

"What are we gonna do, Delgado?"

The infant turned its head to look towards a *vilume* and a *mourst* kneeling opposite Ash and Delgado. The *vilume* looked down at the child and said something quietly to the *mourst*, who made a gesture Delgado took to indicate agreement. In front of them, the burned infant emitted a faint and pitiful cry.

"It's not up to us," said Delgado. "They'll deal with it themselves." He stood and pulled Ash up by one arm. "Pick up your gun."

"But, Delgado . . ." Ash glanced between him and the child. "We've got to try and do—"

"Pick up your gun."

She stooped and picked up the weapon; then Delgado turned her around and, gripping her upper arm firmly in one hand, pulled her away from the group of Seriatts.

Although they heard no shot, a few moments later the Seriatts' throaty expressions of grief intensified. They knew what had been done.

Ashala tried to pull herself free and go back, but Delgado maintained his grip and pulled her onwards. "Leave it, Ash," he said. "There was nothing we could do. Besides, it's none of our business."

She yielded to his will, and they walked in silence for some minutes.

They stopped walking by the stream and watched the rocks and stones form ripples in the water. "You okay?" he asked.

"Not really." She was tight-lipped, red-faced. "How 'bout you?"

"As good as can be expected."

"Jesus, Delgado. That poor kid. I've seen injuries before, but kids shouldn't have to suffer like that. They've done nothing to no one. Goddamn. Cowell can't work out how the Sinz were able to launch an attack without being detected."

"Keth and Miskoh said the same. I think our friend Lerval might have something to do with it. They've gone to see if they can find him."

She looked at him. "You think he let the Sinz through?"

Delgado shrugged. "Maybe. I guess if they find him, then we'll find out. If they keep him alive after they've found him, that is."

Ash looked around them. "I'm not sure we're in the right place here, Delgado," she said.

"What do you mean?"

"I'm not sure. It's like we're not in control of what's happening to us. As if we're being swept along by events and we can't do anything about it. It just doesn't feel right. We're not supposed to be here, now."

"Yeah, I know what you're saying."

"What do you think we should do? How are we going to get back?"

He looked at her. "Is that what we want? To get back? Where do we go back to? Which point? It seems to me that things have been pretty goddamn shitty since we left the *Lex Talionis*."

"Christ, Delgado, what do you think happened to the *Talionis*? You think we'll ever see Bucky and the others again?"

Delgado considered for a moment. "I don't know," he said. "I really don't."

Delgado heard a noise and looked to his right. Through the trees he caught glimpses of Keth and Miskoh approaching the camp. With them, snivelling and whimpering, was Lerval.

As word about the suspicions surrounding Lerval spread, the Seriatts stopped burying their dead or packing their gear in readiness to leave. If the *mourst* was guilty, they wanted to deal with him—there, then, regardless of the risk.

The *mourst* was manhandled to the centre of the rock circle at the heart of the camp and tied to a stake. He talked continuously as they tightened his binds, pleading with those around him to set him free, to listen to him.

He was ignored.

"We should be getting out of here," Ash whispered to Delgado. "Not setting up a kangaroo court."

"Don't worry, Ash. I don't think this is going to take too long. I'll be interested to see what punishment they mete out to him, though." He kept glancing at the sky. "But you're right: we can't stay here long. The Sinz know where we are now. They'll come looking for their missing people. And us."

Behind them voices became raised. Some of the Seriatts—particularly the *conosq*—appeared to be demanding action. Delgado heard snatches of Seriattic conversation. Keth and Miskoh had not found Lerval at his post in the north-eastern hide, but had caught him making his way towards the city. They claimed *com tulies vievro*—justification. Even though Lerval had not committed the act himself, his actions represented *di-fio na'atu*—the ultimate crime: murder.

Cowell quieted the crowd, then stepped towards Lerval. "You were sup-posed to be on watch," the timbre of the *vilume*'s voice was stronger than usual. "Yet when Keth and Miskoh caught you, you were trying to get to the city. What is your explanation for this?"

Lerval looked up at Cowell. The *mourst*'s face was scratched and one eye slightly swollen; he had either fallen or Keth and Miskoh had persuaded him to return to the camp with some enthusiasm. Lerval looked down again without speaking.

"Keth also tells me the instruments in the hide were undamaged and operational. Yet despite this you did not detect the Sinz approaching. How do you account for this?"

"He is a traitor," shouted Miskoh. "He has betrayed us to the Sinz. He must be punished."

Other Seriatts voiced agreement.

"Why did you abandon your post?" asked Cowell. "You should have helped defend the camp. Children were killed here today, Lerval."

"I do not know why the instruments did not detect the Sinz approaching," the *mourst* replied quietly. "They were upon me before I could sound the alarm. I would have been killed defending the hide on my own, so I escaped. I must have been disoriented in the confusion."

Miskoh laughed without amusement. "He thinks that claiming he is simply a coward is somehow better than being a traitor." Miskoh's expression changed as he took a few paces forward and stood next to Cowell. "He is as responsible for the deaths that have occurred here as the Sinz." He brandished his cane in one large fist.

As Cowell gazed at Lerval, Delgado tried to asses the *vilume*'s expression.

"Did you betray us to the Sinz?" asked Cowell.

Lerval did not answer.

"What did they offer you? What was your reward to be for betraying those you have lived among? You were trusted, Lerval. What has become of you?"

Lerval looked up again. His beautiful *mourst* face expressed resentment and obstinacy rather than fear. He said nothing.

Miskoh stepped forward.

"Do you think yourself somehow superior to the rest of us? Some kind of supreme being? Do you think that we enjoy living out here, banished from our homes by those who have invaded our world?"

"No, Miskoh. But I do not see the point of dying for nothing." There was hate in both his expression and his voice.

"Do you see the corpses behind me, Lerval? They were your counterparts. Yet you are responsible for their deaths. But they died for Seriatt, the planet they loved."

"They died in vain, Cowell. Seriatt is lost." Lerval smiled then; it was a twisted grimace. "Sinz are among you and you do not know it. You are all fools." He gave a retch of laughter.

"What do you mean, Lerval?" demanded Miskoh. He turned and glanced around at the other Seriatts behind him. "Are you saying that there are Sinz in this group now? Shape-shifters?"

Lerval laughed again, but differently this time; he was like a creature on the brink of madness.

When his laughter died away, there was silence.

There was a distinct odour like that of rotting meat, and then Lerval's face began to change.

His bone structure started to soften, his brow and facial features morphing, changing relative position and proportion. The ridges of ligament at his neck flattened as his cheekbones became less prominent. His strong *mourst* mouth became much smaller, and his dark skin paled to become the distinct dull grey of humanoid Sinz. He released an agonised but still defiant wail as his bones shrank, and his *mourst* clothes became too large for his new body.

A few moments later the metamorphosis was complete: where Lerval had once stood, was a sweating, wiry Sinz.

"You are a Sinz shape-shifter," breathed Miskoh, almost as if speaking to himself. "Where is Lerval?"

The Sinz flicked a long proboscis from its small mouth before answering. "The Seriatt is dead." His small Sinz mouth made pronunciation of the words difficult. "While he tried to assist your companions in the sea, my waterborne brethren pulled him down and I replaced him." Immense satisfaction was clear in the creature's words despite its unusual accent. "With a little more time I would have been instrumental in the deaths of you all. Your planet belongs to us now. You cannot hide forever."

Miskoh threw his cane to the ground and clasped the Sinz' face in one hand. For a few moments he stared into the creature's eyes as a lover might gaze at one desired. Delgado thought he heard Miskoh whisper something more about animals. The Sinz unfurled its long, black tongue and ran its rounded tip across Miskoh's face.

"You are fearful," said the Sinz quietly. "And rightly so."

Miskoh slowly tilted the Sinz' head to one side, and moved closer to it. The *mourst*'s jaw opened wider than seemed natural, and his gums slid outwards, pushing aside his lips to reveal short, point-sharp teeth.

The Sinz roared and its face contorted in pain as Miskoh bit deep into its cheek.

As Miskoh's teeth sank deeper, the two of them were locked together by the Seriatt's bitter kiss. But as dark blood began to ooze from between their faces, the Sinz shifter made no attempt at resistance, did not struggle.

The other Seriatts simply watched.

The Sinz cried out even more loudly as Miskoh drew back his face, his jaw still clamped tight. His teeth tore a ragged hole in the side of the Sinz' face, revealing gums, teeth, and tongue. One of the creature's small nostrils ripped open in a ragged line. When its head lolled forward, a thick line of blood and snot and drool trailed from its face. It moaned gently.

Miskoh stared at the Sinz and chewed slowly on the hunk of meat he had torn from it. A dark smear of blood was spread across his chin. Steam formed in the air in front of his nostril.

At that moment Miskoh looked to Delgado like some kind of mythical creature. Maybe he was.

The Sinz looked up, its tongue lolling from the side of its face, long and wet. It said something in Seriattic Delgado did not catch, the definition of the words softened by its injuries. But the creature's defiance remained clear. It looked at the Seriatts surrounding it and repeated the words. *Conosq* began to make strange sounds, with a smooth yet discordant quality; some of the *mourst* growled and snarled.

Several *mourst* stepped from the crowd and moved towards the Sinz. As it looked up at them, it seemed to be aware of their intentions.

Delgado watched as the *mourst* walked towards the captured Sinz, their movements slow and considered rather than angry and reactive. Cowell held up one hand, and the crowd stopped moving. The *vilume* stepped towards the Sinz and untied it. But instead of attempting to escape it remained still, simply staring at those in front of it. The other Seriatts began to close on the Sinz once more. There was no tension. It was as if the events were rehearsed, planned.

When they reached the Sinz, the Seriatts smothered it, their intensity and excitement almost sexual in measure. As they began biting into its flesh, the Sinz' expression flickered between pain and ecstasy. Then the creature was lost amid the knot of increasingly frenzied Seriatts as they tore it apart.

Ash turned away. "They're eating it," she said. "All of them."

"Yeah. It's their way of dealing with some things," said Delgado. "I saw it before, during the Buhatt Rebellion. I once saw a *mourst* eaten for showing hesitancy in battle."

"We better watch our backs," she said. "They might find a bit of human flesh appealing. They say it tastes just like chicken."

Delgado looked back and saw Cowell pushing through the mass of Seriatts to follow them. Delgado pulled on Ash's arm and she stopped walking. They turned to face Cowell.

"I am sorry you had to witness this," she said. "But sometimes such events are unavoidable."

"Your people seem to have forgotten that we need to get out of here, fast," Delgado replied.

"Do not be concerned. They will have finished dealing with the Sinz soon. They are angry and also grieve for Lerval. He had his faults, but he was a good *mourst*. We will leave when they have sated their hunger."

"Where will we go?" asked Ash.

"I am not sure," admitted Cowell. "Some of the copters were destroyed in the attack. There are also some wounded, some of whom may wish to come with us while others may want to stay. Some of them will feel they can better help us that way."

"What do you mean?"

"If they believe that they will impede our progress, they will not want to travel with us. They may wish to be fitted with explosives to be detonated if more Sinz return before they die."

"They'd do that?" asked Ash.

"Of course. They are proud. They are Seriatts."

Delgado looked past Cowell and saw the crowd of Seriatts beginning to disperse. As the group thinned, the Sinz became visible once more: its body lay just in front of the post to which it had been bound, ragged strands of skin hanging from what remained of its decimated form. Bone was visible, white and stark.

Keth and Miskoh approached them; their faces and clothes were bloodstained, but there was a brightness in their eyes, a vibrancy in their demeanour.

Miskoh looked at Ash and Delgado as if inviting challenge. Behind them the other Seriatts were gathering their belongings once more.

Cowell addressed Miskoh and Keth. "Do you think all the other Sinz were killed here?"

"No," said Miskoh. "We saw some returning to a vehicle when we caught Lerval. Or the creature we thought was Lerval."

"Were they part of the same group?"

"Yes. One of their number was injured."

"The Sinz surely know where we are now," stated Keth.

"So how long do we have before they come looking for us?" asked Ash.

"That we cannot know," said Cowell. "But we must assume it will be soon."

"Then we better get out of here," said Delgado. "How far away is that other Sinz facility you mentioned? The one that's well protected."

"Without the copters, and going around the city rather than through it, probably a week on foot. Maybe more."

"And what if we go through the city rather than around it?"

"It would probably take only a few days, but we cannot know what we might face. It would be considerably more dangerous."

Delgado smiled thinly. "Dangerous is my middle name," he said. "And from what I've seen so far, I suspect it's yours, too."

"Alexander Dangerous Delgado," said Ash without humour. "You know what? That's got something of a ring to it."

With Lerval dealt with, the Seriatts organised themselves quickly, and were soon moving through the forest away from the destroyed camp.

Delgado and Keth led at the left flank, with Miskoh in the centre; Ash and Cowell were on the right. They were armed to the teeth, laden with as many weapons and as much ammunition as they could carry. Cowell and Delgado bore large ripguns capable of blasting a wide area with a torrent of incredible power. Strings of ammunition were draped over their shoulders and around their necks, the heavy weapons mounted on supports that extended from thick leather belts. Other *mourst* and *vilume* covered the flanks of the main group of Seriatts, which consisted mainly of *conosq* and infants: while the *conosq* were as keen to confront the enemy as the others, the younger children needed protecting.

They walked slowly across the spongy ground, wary of the Sinz who would now be looking for them. Keth was just a few metres to Delgado's right; he could see Miskoh beyond Keth; even at this distance it was clear that the young *mourst* was on edge: his lack of experience and nervousness were evident in his movements, the way he gripped his gun. Delgado glimpsed Cowell between trees farther away, but he could not see Ash. The forest seemed more dense in that direction, with thick, tangled undergrowth and an all-consuming darkness amid the trees.

Suddenly there was a low whistle from Cowell. Everyone stopped walking and crouched. They all looked towards the *vilume*, who pointed towards the sky; a flock of Sinz avians was passing silently overhead, sharp-edged silhouettes against the sky. Their wings beat slowly but effectively, powering them towards the camp where their counterparts had met their deaths. Some of them seemed to be carrying humanoid Sinz passengers in cradles slung beneath their bellies.

Delgado, Ash, and the Seriatts remained motionless for a couple of minutes after the avians had passed; then Keth moved towards Delgado in a crouching position.

"They will be angered," whispered the *mourst*, glancing at the sky. "They will not expect their kin to have been killed. We must be cautious. Other Sinz will be nearby."

Suddenly there was an immense roaring sound, so loud Delgado could feel the vibrations in his chest. It stopped abruptly after a few seconds to be replaced by Seriattic infants crying. Delgado and Keth looked towards Miskoh, who had fired his ripgun; shredded foliage and flakes of singed bark fluttered towards the ground some distance ahead of him, cascading onto a charred object; it appeared to be a small animal of some kind. Beyond the *mourst* Delgado saw Ash, who was now visible through the trees behind him; she appeared to be looking at him, but when he gave her a thumbs-up to ask if she was okay, he realised that she was looking at Cowell: when the *vilume* motioned for her to stay where she was, she nodded, turned, and crouched, gazing into the forest around them.

Cowell began walking towards Miskoh, glancing around, and looking with apparent concern at the sky: the light was beginning to fade.

Cowell and Miskoh conversed for some moments, but Delgado was not familiar with many of the gestures and mannerisms they exchanged. He walked over to Keth.

"What's Cowell saying?" he asked.

"Cowell is reproving Miskoh for discharging his weapon needlessly, and potentially giving away our position to the Sinz. But Cowell is *vilume*, and thus Miskoh's chastisement will be balanced by praise for acting instinctively. Such is the *vilume* way. Myself, I would have administered a more physical punishment."

Cowell gripped one of Miskoh's shoulders in what appeared to be a comforting gesture; then they began walking towards Keth and Delgado.

"Has Miskoh killed a threatening hog, Cowell?" asked Keth as they came near.

"He has." The *vilume* glanced towards the sky, then back at Miskoh; the *mourst* had knelt on one knee and was keeping watch over the area of forest ahead. "He saw movement and reacted automatically," continued Cowell. "He is gravely sorry. He feels he has humiliated himself. I told him that I prefer a dead hog to a Sinz ambush."

"A blow or two might serve to increase his ability to concentrate, Cowell," said Keth. "Would you like me to deliver them to him?"

"No, Keth, I would not. Your brutish *mourst* methods can sometimes be of use but are largely counterproductive. Miskoh has learned his lesson. He needs no further help from you."

"So what'll we do now, Cowell?" asked Delgado. "Miskoh's enthusiasm might've given away our position."

"Other than the avians we saw, I do not believe there are any Sinz in the immediate vicinity," said the *vilume*, "and the avians are unlikely to have heard Miskoh's weapon. But while I believe that we are safe for the moment, darkness is coming. We must establish a camp for the night and settle the children. There is a stream a short distance ahead. We will rest there."

Cowell turned and began to walk back towards the others.

"Cowell," hissed Keth. The *vilume* stopped and turned. "Tell Miskoh I would be glad to have him watch my back."

The *vilume* briefly inclined her head and linked her fingers in a gesture of respect. "I will," she said.

High orbit, Hascaaza
March 7, 2379 (Earth equivalent)

The Sinz fleet prepared to move out of Hascaaza's orbit. First the sentries manoeuvred to a safe distance to observe the initial stages of the departure, scanning the rest of the fleet and out into space for dissonances that could indicate approaching Karallax.

When their scans were complete, the sentries signalled that it was safe for the fleet to diverge. Within moments the huge formation of vessels, which stretched almost completely around Hascaaza, gradually began to expand as the ships moved apart, lengthening as the navigators coaxed the other ships away from the planet's comforting gravitational field.

The three gigantic birthships were spread evenly through the length of the formation, their golden, molten-glass form surging and rippling as they moved. The birthships were watched carefully by the vessels that surrounded them: whatever the navigators and their crews might wish, things would proceed at the birthships' pace; if they chose to remain in high orbit for another week before departing, then the rest of the fleet would simply wait with them.

Some of the hulking deathships remained closest, prepared to defend the vessels that had spawned them to the end, regardless of risk to themselves or their Sinz crews. Other deathships moved to the very edge of the fleet and conjoined with the sentries to provide the most effective defensive formation possible: despite the breadth of frequencies covered by the sentries' scans, it was possible that a Karallax might somehow get through. It had happened before.

On either side of the main body of the fleet were two smaller formations: one was comprised of the haulers, bloated by the equipment and machinery for use by the Sinz upon reaching their destination; the other consisted of the feeders, which would merge with the birthships and be absorbed by them to provide sustenance sufficient for the journey.

The beginning of such a long and dangerous voyage was always tense, more so in this time of war. Birthships had been known to miscarry if overstressed, and the caregivers were therefore particularly concerned.

But this time the birthships moved into space, serene and aloof, and as time passed and the danger lessened, so the multitude of ships that formed the fleet began to relax. Soon they had escaped Hascaaza's gravity and were accelerating towards the channel that would convey them almost instantaneously across millions of light-years of space, whereupon their true test would begin.

The Forest of Dreams, Seriatt
March 7, 2379 (Earth equivalent)

Delgado woke and raised his head. He massaged his slightly stiff neck as he looked around. Ash was crouching next to the dying embers of the fire, holding her palms towards the glowing sticks.

He stood, stretched, and walked over to her. Although she must have heard him coming, she did not look around.

He crouched next to her and held out his own hands; the heat emitted by the embers was surprising.

"You okay?" he asked.

"Sure. Well. I don't know . . ." She stopped.

"What?"

"I'm not sure I see where we're going here, Delgado. When I think about all that's happened to us, you know. I'm not sure where we're headed. Not so long ago we were on Seriatt before all this Sinz shit happened. Before that we were on Earth, aboard the *Talionis* with Bucky and the rest of 'em. But it feels like all that was in another life."

Delgado gripped Ash by the arm and stood, pulling her up with him. "Come on," he said. "Come with me."

Delgado led her into the woods. The trees were dark and ominous, the ground soft underfoot.

"Where the hell are we going, Delgado?" Ash whispered. "We might get lost."

He glanced back at her. "What's the matter? Lost faith in my navigational skills?"

She snorted. "That kind of implies I once had some, Delgado."

They walked through the woods for several minutes, stepping on stones to cross the stream. A few minutes later they reached the edge of the forest. The land fell away in front of them, knots of tree roots protruding from the steep bank of earth. Some distance to their right the stream cascaded from between the trees, a deep groove eroded where the water impacted the soil.

Directly in front of them was the Seriattic capital.

It was a stark contrast to the distinct and vibrant city they had previously experienced, just a collection of decaying buildings in whose shadowy corners corruption bred. The canals were wounds in the landscape, water drained, beds cracked. It was as if all life and vibrancy had been sucked from the place. Beyond the sprawling, low-rise conurbation, closer to the coast, the Sinz towers rose from the ground like fleshless fingers, assertive, defiant.

"I didn't realise we were so close," said Ash. "It looks deserted. Dead."

"Yeah. We've still got to get through it yet, though. There are a couple of fires"—he pointed, indicating one or two faint orange smudges within buildings on the city's outskirts—"but the Seriatts will keep a pretty low profile." He looked up at the shimmering glow in the night sky. "According to what Cowell said, the Sinz have more important things to think about than a few vagabonds on the fringes of a dead city. That barrier the Sinz have put in place means no one's going anywhere. At least not until the Sinz are either strong enough to mount whatever they're planning without help from their home world or until the wormhole stabilises long enough for them to get reinforcements."

Ash looked up. "It also means that we're trapped here for a while, too," she said. "Hey look, there's a falling star." A tiny brilliant ember was visible in the Seriattic atmosphere for a moment before disappearing.

"That's odd," said Delgado. "Nothing should be able to get through the shield."

"Maybe it was some kind of satellite that was in low orbit within the shield. It could be farther out than we thought."

"Maybe. Maybe." Delgado continued to look into the sky.

"What's the matter?" asked Ash, following his gaze. "You expecting something to happen?"

"I'm not sure," he said. "I just had a strange feeling. A feeling I haven't had for a very long time. Probably just these goddamn nobics playing tricks."

"I never did trust that implant stuff, Delgado. Someday those nobics of yours'll start doing their own thing; you wait and see."

"You think anyone will notice the difference?" He glanced at her, smiling. "Seriously, though, Ash. Take a look out there. Michael's still alive. I can feel him, out there somewhere."

"And you want to find him? Despite what he did to Cascari?"

"Yeah. He killed Cascari, and nothing can change that. But he's still my son."

They stood in silence for a few moments. Then Delgado sighed. "We better start back," he said. "It's almost dawn." He reached out and took Ash by the hand; she immediately pulled her fingers from his—it was a gentle but definite denial; although of what, neither of them could have said.

Delgado turned and began to retrace his steps through the trees; Ash watched him for a moment before following. "Do you think we'll ever get back to Earth?" she asked when she caught up with him.

Delgado began to consider the question, but his brain seemed reluctant to function, as if a sudden drain of power was preventing successful synaptic connections. And as a response finally began to form, he felt his nobics surge. Without knowing why he lunged to the right, pushing Ash to the ground and rolling when they hit the forest floor, pulling her with him.

"I am home." Brandouen stared at the display with what Saskov assumed was an expression of *mourst* joy, even though trees and part of the large boulder were all that was visible of the Seriatt's world.

"It's customary to tip the driver," said Saskov. He winced and touched his forehead: whatever the nobics had done as a result of their interaction with the Needle's core had given him one hell of a headache. What was really happening was that nobics and core were having a heated exchange regarding the operational protocols they would observe while Saskov was outside the Needle.

"We should go now," said Brandouen. "I believe the palace is east of our current location." He pointed at the map on the display. "That is where we should go."

"Hold your horses. First we've got to assess the situation here. We might have landed right in the middle of a nest of Sinz for all we know."

"Let me out of this vessel and I will kill them." Brandouen pulled a knife with a long, curved blade from a sheath at his thigh and brandished it. "I will kill them and then I will eat them."

Saskov looked at him with some unease. "You'll have your fun, Brandouen, but you've got to be patient. We go running around out there without looking first, then we could pay the price." He stood, picked up his visor and placed it over his head, then checked his sidearm.

As Brandouen put on his own visor, Saskov checked the external weather conditions and the status of the Needle. The sheets displayed above the pedestal updated instantaneously.

"You ready?" he asked.

"I am always ready. And I am back on Seriatt. Are *you* ready?"

"Don't you worry about me, Brandy, old boy. I'll be just fine. Okay.

Outside temperature's fourteen degrees Celsius. There's some light cloud. A five-kilometre-an-hour easterly wind. It'll be dawn in fifty-eight minutes. There don't seem to be any Sinz nearby, but there are a mixture of human and Seriattic traces. Two groups, both within a klick of here."

"How many?"

"Couple of humans, more Seriatts."

"Do you think this is Michael?"

"I don't know. I wouldn't have expected to find him out here. And who else would be with him? No humans that we know of have visited Seriatt since the Sinz invaded."

"Why do you assume that Michael would show up as human if he is half Seriatt?"

"Good question. He'd sure as hell show up as something, though." He looked at Brandouen. "When we get outside, we assume that any life-forms we come across are hostile until we establish otherwise. If it comes to a fight, we shoot first and ask questions later. Do you understand?"

"Of course. Come. Let us get out of this"—the *mourst* gesticulated as he sought a suitable reference—"cushioned cell."

Saskov turned to face the hatch. He imagined the lights inside the Needle dimming, and the hatch opening. The gentle breeze that breathed into the vessel as the core complied with his wishes was passed on to them by their visors and scartex overskins. The Colonel did not notice the momentary delay that occurred as the core, having been forced to accept that the nobics would have final influence over Saskov while he was outside the vessel, discreetly passed software into him under his nobics' guard that would affect his decision-making processes in its favour.

Saskov placed his hands on either side of the hatch and leaned forwards, peering out into the darkness. There was a strong smell of pine and moist earth. He looked in either direction along the sides of the Needle. It was disconcerting—but extremely helpful—to see nothing where the ship should be, as his view of the surrounding forest was unimpeded. His nobics detected no immediate threats.

He pushed himself back in through the hatch. "All clear," he said. "Come on, Brandy. Let's go take a look-see."

Two shadowy figures appeared in front of the large boulder, which sat like a resting animal in one corner of the clearing. Saskov dropped to one knee and looked around, his nobics automatically performing another scan; Brandouen stood behind him, his large hands clamped around his weapon. Their glossy visors reflected the swaying trees, the moon and clouds in the warm sky.

"All clear," whispered Saskov. He glanced at his wrist display and touched a couple of the tabs. "There are two traces half a klick away," he said. "The larger group of Seriatts is another half a klick beyond that. All between us and the city." He paused for a moment, aware that his nobics were communicating intensively with the Needle's core—although he realised this only because his nobics allowed him to. "I'm picking up some other traces, too," he said. "Sinz, I'd say. A small party. Close to the human and Seriatt traces."

"Are they going to attack them?"

"Can't tell. The traces are too faint, difficult to interpret precisely. But I don't think they're aware of the humans and the Seriatts. At least, not yet. It won't be long before they come into contact with them, though." He turned and thought the Needle's hatch shut, and the interior of the vessel that had been visible through the open hatch disappeared as the ship became completely invisible. "I tell you what, Brandy," said Saskov, "how about we just head towards the city and our friends here"—he tapped his wrist—"and see what happens?"

"I agree. The Seriatts may need our help if they do not know the Sinz are approaching them."

"Yeah? Well, sorry to disappoint you, but I'm interested only in the human targets."

The *mourst* growled something that Saskov's nobics did not translate, despite efforts by the Needle's core to bypass them and pass an entirely different message on to the Colonel.

"Let's split up a little, but keep in sight of each other," said Saskov as they reached the trees. "You move over that way. About twenty metres."

"Why should I do what you say?" asked Saskov. "You have no authority over me."

Saskov's nobics stimulated a chemical release that changed the Colonel's mood, altering his response to the Seriatt's challenge in their favour: they recognised the Seriatt's value even if their host seemingly did not.

"Maybe I don't," said Saskov, "but we do have to work together here. Unless of course you want to head off your own way right now. Oh, but that'll mean you forfeit the reward Myson's offered you. So are you with me, or what?" The *mourst* did not respond. "Look, for what it's worth, I can see that you're all a *mourst* should be: strong, powerful, a fighter, okay? I respect that. I also respect the fact that you love your home world. I wish more humans had the same feelings for Earth instead of trying to get to someplace else just as soon as they can. So maybe we can work together despite out outward differences. Whaddya say?"

"I thank you for your honesty, Colonel," replied Brandouen. "I also have developed respect for you. We should be able to work well together, even if our goals are different."

"Great," said Saskow. Brandouen's expression changed, as if this was not the reaction he had expected, but Saskov looked at his wrist again. "Okay. They're a little closer now. The Sinz traces seem to be approaching from the east. We might just get there at the same time as they come together with the Seriatts and the humans."

Brandouen walked away from Saskov to the point the Colonel had indicated, then stopped and looked back. Saskov nodded, and they then proceeded through the forest.

They walked slowly, moving from tree to tree, pausing frequently before continuing. Saskov glanced at the map on his wrist; the traces he had picked up earlier were close now.

"You know this area well, Brandy?" he asked.

"Yes. I used to hunt in these woods."

The *mourst*'s voice was warm and close through the visor's tiny speakers. Saskov heard a faint echo as his nobics took slightly longer to translate the Seriattic words now that the *mourst*'s face was not visible. "How far is it to the city?" he asked.

"It is a short distance. We are near to the edge of the forest. But I have not been here for many years."

Saskov consulted his map again. "The Sinz traces I'm picking up are pretty close now."

"How many?"

"Half a dozen or so is as accurate as I can be."

"Repeat, please."

"Six. The Seriatts are ahead of us, the two humans nearer to the Sinz. Let's stop here and wait and see what happens."

Both Saskov and Brandouen crouched next to trees.

Saskov looked up. Through the canopy he could see clouds gathering, dark shapes against the gradually brightening sky. Olfactory nobics fed him the results of scent analyses: two humans—one slightly aroused male, one menstruating female. Audio nobics enhanced faint sound waves and he began to hear quiet voices, fragments of conversation the nobics were able to decipher, other words spirited away on the breeze. . . .

"Yeah, but you know I never did trust . . . stuff. And, hey, I wouldn't be surprised if they start doing . . . sometime. You wait and see."

"What did you think about that business with . . . I was surprised they dealt with it so . . ."

Pause.

"Do you think we'll ever get back to . . . Or have we seen the last of it?"

The male was experienced in combat, and also very aware of his surroundings despite his casual tone. Indeed, Saskov was surprised he and Brandouen had not been detected themselves. Maybe they had.

The female was confident and strong but of a different background. The male respected her—and more. Yet despite believing that he was fully aware of her capabilities, it was clear that he still underestimated her.

Saskov saw the two figures walking through the trees ahead. He looked across at Brandouen; the *mourst* had stopped walking and was aiming his weapon.

"Easy, Brandy," he whispered. "They could be my people." As he glanced towards the Seriatt, Saskov saw movement beyond him—a clutch of slight, sinewy figures creeping between the trees.

A flood of nobic data entered his consciousness.

Sinz.

Saskov looked back at the humans. His nobics suppressed his instinct to shout a warning. He felt a prickle in his head due to frenetic nobic activity.

The human male suddenly pushed the female to the ground, rolled on top of her and continued rolling.

At that moment the Sinz opened fire.

Delgado leaped to his feet and pulled Ash up, too.

They sprinted as gunfire raged around them, weaving through the trees. Suddenly they found themselves in a clearing. They ran behind a large nearby boulder, drawing and arming their weapons as they crouched behind the huge rock.

"Gee, Delgado," said Ash, somewhat short of breath, "it's been a long time since you demonstrated any kind of desire to roll on the ground with me." She brushed dirt and leaves from one cheek. "You shoulda said something sooner."

He glanced at her; dirt had smeared along her cheekbone like a ripening bruise. He turned away and peered through a fissure in one side of the rock. "And you'd have been interested?" he asked. "Even with Cowell around?"

Ash pulled a face. "Aw, come on, Delgado. Besides, you seemed kinda keen on him yourself not so long ago."

"That was just a bit of fun in the heat of the moment. Those herbs and that drink they gave me." He shook his head. "They were too much. And to my mind Cowell's female. Or as good as."

"Sure, Delgado. Whatever you say."

Delgado moved his head as he tried to see the Sinz through the tiny slit in the rock. "That's odd," he said.

"What's up?"

"Don't you notice anything?"

Ash listened to the weapons fire that was still raging among the trees. The sound of the Sinz weaponry was raw and discordant. But there was another sound, too: sweeter, warmer. "Two lots of gunfire," she said.

"Yeah," he said. "I don't get it." He moved slightly to one side and lay on the damp forest floor in an attempt to see around the side of the boulder: this was considerably more risky but would give him a much better view.

He could see vague figures among the trees. They were slight, sinewy, grey slivers. Sinz. None of them were looking in his direction, but seemed to be concentrating on some fallen trees to his right. He couldn't see who was hiding there, but the bright white emissions from their weapons were like strobe lights in the forest.

"What's the score?" asked Ash.

"Can't tell. The Sinz are firing at another hostile target." He winced. "I'm not too clear about what's going on. My nobics seem to have gone haywire. And there's something else, too. . . ."

"What?"

"That other weapon. It sounds familiar."

"Probably some Seriatt weapon you came across during the Buhatt Rebellion."

He shook his head. "No. That's too long ago . . . well I'll be . . ."

"What?"

"It's a Structure weapon. No doubt about it."

"How can you tell?"

"Listen to it. You hear that faint but steady chiming sound within the roar?"

Ash looked towards the sky as she listened. "Uh-huh."

"Only PS sidearms do that."

"Right. And is that good?"

"Well nobody outside of Structure would have one, so is it good that someone from Structure's here, right now? You tell me. It also raises the question, were the Sinz after us or have we walked into the middle of something? Maybe they're from Stealth. Goddammit. What the hell does this mean, Ash?"

"Well, you know what, Delgado? I don't care too much as long as we can get our asses out of here in one piece. What d'ya reckon we make a move before our Sinz friends decide to come for us after all."

Delgado looked around the boulder again. "They're coming this way. Come on, Ash—we need to reconsider our position."

"'Reconsider our position'? Shit, Delgado—you mean we need to get the hell out of here, right?"

"Well, if you want to put it like that, yes. Now will you just do it?"

They turned and began to run across the clearing. "I guess that's the price you pay for an unexpected roll in the woods, huh, Delgado."

Flashes of light began to appear overhead, the searing red of the Sinz weapons intermingled with the white streams emitted by the PS sidearm. There was the sound of another weapon that Delgado did not recognise. He glanced over his shoulder and realised that for some reason the Sinz seemed to be firing into the treetops.

Inside his head there was a distant wailing sound like a scramjet, with fluctuating whistles and pops. He felt a little light-headed, and it occurred to him then that perhaps his nobics were dying. But there seemed to be too much activity. Indeed, it was as if they had somehow been invigorated, attaining levels they had not previously reached.

As they got to the other side of the clearing, Delgado glanced over his shoulder again. The Sinz were no longer chasing them, but instead they now seemed to be on the retreat, defending themselves against whatever force they were fighting, running a little, then turning and returning fire, still seemingly in the trees. And for a moment, as the swathes of light burned in the mist of the dawn and hot spines shot through his skull, Delgado was convinced that he saw the ghostly outline of a small, streamlined spacecraft, shallow and black, close to the boulder.

He heard Ash cry out behind him. He turned to look at her. Time seemed to slow down somehow. He could see that she was saying something, could see her lips moving, but could hear only a roar like fire. She was pointing towards the sky. Delgado turned and saw two gigantic, batlike forms swooping down towards them across the clearing.

Delgado clutched his weapon and tried to bring it to bear. The inside of his skull burned. His nobics surged and scattered. He could not act.

Then the shadowy flying creatures were upon them.

The tranquil forest was suddenly filled with the sound of weapons fire. To Saskov and Brandouen's right the Sinz guns spat streams of pulsing red light.

As the Sinz chased the two humans through the forest, Saskov and Brandouen both opened fire. The Sinz immediately turned and retaliated.

Saskov's nobics told him there were six hostiles in the immediate vicinity, and revealed them to him by painting colourful smears around their bodies like rippling auras. Some were crouching behind trees and rocks, providing covering fire for others who were advancing rapidly. The latter group then took cover and protected their counterparts as they moved forwards. These Sinz were not about to run.

Instinctively Saskov took cover and prepared to defend himself. His nobics, however, saw the futility in attempting to stand ground against such a large group of clearly competent fighters. In order to ensure their own safety, they had no option but to directly influence their host's thought patterns, and changed his mentality from one of fight, to flight.

"We're outnumbered," he shouted to Brandouen. He pointed upwards. "Withdraw and climb. Now."

Although his nobics did not translate it, Brandouen growled something Saskov took to be an expression of defiance, but nonetheless the *mourst* began to move backwards, still firing. Saskov held his ground a little longer, giving the Seriatt cover. Then, although it risked overloading the weapon and causing a spectacular explosion, he maximised his sidearm's spread pattern, pushed the power setting to max, and fired a long burst that tore through the forest.

Many fires ignited. A couple of smaller trees even fell. The wiry Sinz threw themselves behind whatever cover was available, but only those who found refuge behind boulders or the largest of trees escaped death.

Saskov stopped firing, and turned to follow Brandouen. He felt his brain tingle as he ran towards the nearest tree as his nobics communicated with the scartex's tiny core, preparing the overskin for what was required of it.

Saskov thrust his sidearm into its holster, and as he forced his way through the thick undergrowth his visor and other areas of the overskin hardened to protect him from whipping branches and thorns.

Hiding animals scurried out of his way; he glimpsed a gigantic spider-like creature that reared up, antennae waving.

As soon as he felt that he was deep enough into the undergrowth to be obscured from view, he reached out for the nearest suitable tree.

As he began to climb, the skin covering his hands re-formed into broad, membranous mitts, the palms of which swelled into soft bulbs that exuded a sticky, tarlike substance. Long, slothlike claws curved from the fingertips as he reached up around the trunk, and as he pulled himself from the ground the skin covering his shins and calves grew a series of pointed, bonelike protrusions that curved downwards from his legs and dug deep into the wood.

As he scampered up the tree, red light flickered in front of him as the Sinz fired blindly through the dense foliage. When he reached the top of the tree, he balanced on the thickest of the upper branches and stood so that his upper body protruded from the canopy.

All around him was a sea of green. In front of him Seriatt's sun was rising beyond the mountains; to his right were the sinister, rippled Sinz towers, like jags of bone. And amid the pale ruins of the Seriattic capital was the palace, its dome a smooth, pale blister surrounded by a circle of dark spines.

Brandouen suddenly emerged from the trembling leaves nearby. Saskov opened a comms link. "We'll try to get back to the Needle."

"Do you wish to go first while I divert the Sinz?"

Streams of brilliant red energy shredded foliage between them and raced up into the sky.

Saskov's nobics dictated the response: they could not alter their host's primary programming then simply allow him to revert to his standard procedures: that would simply be irresponsible. "I appreciate the thought, Brandy, old buddy," said Saskov, "but somehow I think we both need to get out of here ASAP." He pushed himself up onto the tree's thinnest branches; they flexed dramatically under his weight but were clearly strong enough to bear him.

As he bounced gently, he looked across and saw Brandouen getting into the same position; when the *mourst* stood upright, with the leaves shimmering in the breeze beneath him, it looked as though he was standing on the surface of a stagnant lake.

Suddenly there was a small explosion below. A swathe of leaves between them turned black and shrivelled, curling in on themselves and melting into sticky globules to reveal the branches beneath. Through them Sinz figures could be seen. More gunfire charged up at them—so close this time that Saskov could feel the heat of the discharge on the side of his face.

"No," he said, "we definitely don't have time. Let's get out of here."

Saskov leaped forwards, using the flexing branches beneath his feet as a springboard.

He reached out and the scartex re-formed again, vast sheets of black skin extending from his arms, down his sides and legs. The membrane rippled, gently at first then with increasing power, pushing him upwards. Within a few moments his nobics had fed him the required skills and Saskov was speeding through the air just metres above the treetops, Brandouen soaring ahead of him, lines of red light slashing between them as the Sinz below fired at the shadowy figures above the treetops.

The strain on Saskov's muscles was tremendous, and although he knew his nobics were greatly boosting his capacity and stamina, it was obvious that he would not be able to fly this way for long.

Saskov saw Brandouen angle steeply downwards, disappearing below the canopy as the *mourst* descended into the clearing where they had left the Needle.

Detecting Saskov and Brandouen approaching, the ship's core communicated urgently with Saskov's nobics; they responded immediately.

"Don't go for the ship," called Saskov. "We don't want them to know it's there."

"Thank you for that advice." Unlike Saskov, the *mourst* did not sound out of breath.

When he reached the edge of the clearing, Saskov also leaned forward, diving below the treetops. The Sinz stopped firing as they lost sight of their prey.

Rapidly gaining speed as he descended, Saskov spread his arms and legs wide. His nobics communicated with the suit, and it grew broad sheets of skin between his limbs and his body that fluttered and billowed as they caught the air and slowed him down.

Saskov saw the two humans running towards the trees on the opposite side of the clearing. He glanced over his right shoulder and saw that the first of the Sinz had emerged from the trees and was already firing up at them. Below him he saw the vague outline of the Needle appearing and disappearing like a faulty sign; whether this was due to a problem with the shielding system or the proximity of the discharging weapons he did not know.

He looked ahead again and saw Brandouen landing skilfully, as if he was a veteran at performing such manoeuvres. As Saskov brought his legs forward in preparation for a running landing, he felt heat sear across the right side of his face as one of the Sinz got a close shot; although he was uninjured, the membrane of skin between his right arm and leg was severely damaged. He accelerated suddenly and dropped the last few metres to the ground.

Delgado jumped back as Saskov crashed into the ground near his feet. The Colonel rolled with grace, and the scartex overskin shrank back to its original size as Saskov jumped to his feet. He glanced briefly at Delgado as he ran towards a particularly large tree several metres away, behind which Brandouen had already taken cover to fire at the Sinz as they crossed the clearing.

Delgado and Ash also began firing at the Sinz. Between shots Delgado glanced across at Saskov and Brandouen. He did not need the tingling of his nobics or the evidence of Saskov's PS4 sidearm to tell him that Saskov was the Structure presence he had so recently perceived: it was clear in every aspect of him. Although little of the second person was visible, the physique and traces were distinctly *mourst*.

While the Sinz that had entered the clearing were now dead, others had dug in on the opposite side of the glade and were using some kind of stand-mounted rapid-fire projectile rifle. The ammunition it fired chopped through the foliage and gouged chunks from tree bark, showering Delgado with shredded leaves and splinters.

Several Sinz avians appeared in the sky above the clearing, dark shapes circling above their fallen colleagues. Delgado saw one of the Sinz on the ground motion towards the avians, and one of them immediately plunged towards the trees. Delgado and Ash both fired at the diving Sinz.

The creature seemed to fold in the air as the root of one wing was destroyed and another shot hit it in the chest. It crashed through branches, hit the ground with a dull thump, and rolled for a short distance across the leafy soil. It came to rest to Delgado's left, a strange batlike creature with sinews and bony ridges visible through its thin-skinned chest. It was breathing quickly, a small black tongue protruding from its strange beak. It raised its head and looked at Delgado with eyes more sinister and alien than any he had ever encountered. Delgado shot the creature.

Delgado leaned across to Ash. "Time we were elsewhere," he said. "If we hang around, they'll have more reinforcements on our ass before we know what's hit us."

Ash nodded, and continued to fire into the darkness on the opposite side of the clearing. She changed target as another avian swooped towards them with a raucous cry. "Where do you think our friends over there have come from?" she asked.

"Well one of them is Structure, I know that much. We'll play it cagey for now. Until we know a bit more about them, we'll say we were just trapped here on Seriatt after the invasion. Okay?"

"Whatever you say, Delgado." Ash fired several more shots in rapid succession.

Delgado looked across at Saskov and Brandouen. "Hey," he yelled. "We're movin' out." Saskov nodded understanding, then passed the message to Brandouen.

They continued firing for a few seconds longer; then Delgado grabbed Ash's tunic sleeve and pulled her deeper into the forest. The unknown Structure man and the Seriatt followed. Delgado's efforts to lose them among the trees were unsuccessful.

Delgado was ignorant of the fact that Saskov's nobics had overwhelmed his own, dated HOD nobics, and were trawling for whatever information they could find that might be of use to their host. So was Saskov.

Several batches had even combined to link to comms relays in an attempt to pull data from the biocomputer on Earth. Saskov's nobics were working overtime: as well as all of their normal processes, their resources were pressurised by combat, scartex core liaison, and use of extended skin functions. Now they faced the additional burden of a former Structure operative whose SFE was so dated and fragmented that communication with the human's ancient nobics was in the simplest of terms.

So Saskov's nobics simply penetrated Delgado's cognitive environment and adapted to the state of Delgado's nobics so successfully that although the mental power available to him increased one thousand–fold in a moment, he remained ignorant of this fact, and of the potential it offered.

They took a circuitous route through the forest, watching the sky for avians, wary of traps or ambushes. They eventually circled back to the stream, beginning to follow its course back towards the camp only when certain there were no Sinz around.

Delgado stopped walking, knelt at the stream, and scooped water into his mouth, but kept an eye on Saskov and Brandouen. He would have tried to extend nobics into Saskov, but they seemed unresponsive, as if occupied with other, more important tasks.

Delgado stood, wiping his mouth on the back of one sleeve. "So," he said. "Are we going to get to see what you two look like?"

Saskov reached behind his head and touched the gland at the nape of his neck; the mask and visor softened and separated from the rest of the overskin with a slightly moist sound, and he peeled the scartex forward from the base of his skull. Brandouen did the same.

"That's pretty fancy stuff," Delgado said.

Saskov tossed him the balaclava. "Scartex," he said. "Most advanced material there is."

As Delgado turned the seemingly insubstantial garment over in his hands, the pores in the balaclava absorbed a sample of his DNA. Just as Saskov's nobics secured a priority tightline connection with the biocomputer on Earth, the balaclava passed Delgado's DNA profile to the core in the main suit, which began trawling the biocomp for information: they needed to know who this man was. And if the information turned out to be important, they might even let Saskov know, too.

"You should thank us," said Saskov. "We saved you."

"I'd say it was a joint effort," stated Delgado.

"I doubt you would have managed to fend them off by yourselves, especially when the avians came along. You were considerably outnumbered."

"I'm sure we would've coped."

"What are you doing on Seriatt?" Brandouen demanded. "There should be no humans here."

"Tell him to speak Counian," Delgado said to Saskov. "Seriatt's not our strong point."

"I could ask you two the same thing," Delgado said to Brandouen when the *mourst* had repeated the question. "You're *mourst*, but he's human."

"I am Colonel Viktor Saskov. This is Honourable Mourst Warrior Brandouen. But who we are doesn't matter," said Saskov. His nobics began to stream data, feeding him information on Delgado so smoothly that it was unlikely the officer would realise it was not something he had always known. "You want to fend for yourselves? Fine, go ahead. I certainly don't need you hanging around, Delgado."

"How'd you know my name?"

Saskov smiled. "I know all about you."

Delgado was becoming increasingly irritated; suddenly being confronted by a bounty-hungry Structure officer looking for a promotion was something he could do without right now. "Who the hell *are* you, and why are you here?"

Ash interjected. "Look," she said, "I really hate to interrupt all this macho testosterone standoff bullshit, but can we please keep moving? First, I'm starved; second, the Sinz could come back at any time, and we need to be at the camp to protect the kids."

"Your words are wise," said Brandouen. "You are clearly intelligent."

"I can assure you," said Delgado, "that Ash is at least as concerned—if not more so—for her stomach as she is for the children."

"Save it for the birds, big guy," said Ash. "Let's just get moving, okay?"

A short while later they were approaching the Seriattic refugees' camp. As they climbed the gentle slope through the close-packed trees that grew to the south, they could see strips of fabric hung between branches to form makeshift shelters, and could smell the fire.

But they could also hear gunfire and screaming.

"Shit, Ash. I don't like the sound of this," said Delgado as he began to run up the slope.

"Quickly," called Brandouen, "they are being attacked."

They all hurried up the incline, but came to a dead stop when they reached the edge of the camp. Sinz avians were swooping down, clawing at those on the ground before climbing high above the trees again. Their speed bled away and they turned, plunging once more, folding back their wings to reduce drag and accelerate.

Within metres of the ground the avians levelled off and sped low through the clearing, using their curled talons to pluck someone from the ground to carry them up into the air, or drag them along for a short distance before stopping suddenly and tearing their victims to pieces with their curled beaks. However, the latter course of action made the Sinz vulnerable to the small amount of defensive fire that was coming from various points around the edge of the camp. Delgado could see Miskoh, Cowell, and a couple of others crouching behind trees and attempting to stave off the avians' onslaught, but only a couple of Sinz bodies lay in the glade: their speed was simply too great for the Seriatts to hit many of them successfully.

But as one avian dived towards the ground, a shot rang out. The Sinz shrieked, its head and wings curled back, and the creature crashed through the trees. It became impaled on a branch that entered its body at the neck. It writhed briefly; then the branch snapped and the creature fell to the ground, where it lay in a heap of skin and bone.

The other avians reacted immediately: those that were diving flared their wings to reduce speed, then powered their way back up into the sky, crying to each other as they climbed to join their counterparts above the treetops. They circled above the camp several times, calling and glancing down into the forest, as if expecting their fallen counterpart to rejoin them. When it was clear it would not, they turned and heading back towards the city.

When they were sure it was safe, the Seriatts began to emerge from their hiding places, glancing between the sky and the bodies that littered the ground. Delgado, Ash, Saskov, and Brandouen began to walk into the camp.

Those refugees the avians had managed to catch had been slaughtered. Muscle and tendon were stripped from bone, eyes plucked from sockets like succulent fruits. Broken corpses littered the clearing. One body was suspended high in a tree; it looked like a collection of rags. Its limbs appeared to have too many joints.

Brandouen scurried forwards into the camp and knelt on the ground next to a Seriattic infant. The child had a deep puncture wound to one temple and numerous lacerations across its face. Dark strands were all that remained in its eye sockets. The *mourst* looked at the child for a few moments, then began to growl gently. The noise became steadily louder, and the *mourst* began to hit himself on the side of the head, the hard ridges on his knuckles cutting his scalp and drawing blood, those at his neck red and throbbing.

Brandouen looked around the camp at his dead counterparts; then he threw back his head and released a powerful, terrifying roar of anguish that the others felt in their chests. He continued to scream until his breath was exhausted.

Delgado saw movement on the opposite side of the camp: Miskoh, Cowell, and the others were emerging from their hiding places among the trees. Issilan and other *conosq* and *vilume* rushed to tend to the injured while the *mourst* barked harsh-sounding words to each other in their native tongue; it was impossible for Delgado to tell whether they were chastising or congratulating each other or arguing among themselves. Miskoh and Cowell walked across the clearing towards them.

"We did our best," said Miskoh, "but there were too many."

"Well," said Saskov as he looked up into the sky, "if there are any more Sinz avians nearby we'll sure as hell know about it soon enough."

"Let them come," Brandouen hissed, filled as much with grief as anger. "Let them come and I will kill them. I will kill them all." He stood and marched towards the three of them. "Let us go now to the city and attack the Sinz. This is *di-fio na'atu*—the ultimate crime. *Com tulies vievro* is ours. We have the right to take vengeance." Brandouen roared again as he looked around them in turn, although Delgado was uncertain whether he had said something in Seriatt. "Very well. I will go on my own." When Brandouen tried to push past them, Delgado and Saskov each grabbed one of the *mourst*'s arms.

"Hold it there, now, Brandy boy," said Saskov. "Just calm down."

Brandouen looked down at the officer, his expression fierce, determined. "Release me, Colonel," he said. "I must act."

"I'll let go of you if you show some sense. Your time for revenge will come. But not now. Don't run into the arms of the enemy and get yourself killed for no reason."

"No reason? No reason? *Cyliek diesmo conario fur na*!"

Saskov recognised Delgado's puzzled expression. "He says it's the best reason there is," he said.

"No," Delgado said. "You've got to wait. But your time for revenge *will* come. You'll get your chance, but you've got to be patient. Tell him, Cowell. Miskoh."

"But look at the children, the *vilume* and *conosq*." Brandouen gestured angrily towards the bodies.

Delgado looked at a nearby infant corpse. "I understand," he muttered. "Believe me I do."

There was a faint sound among the trees behind them, then another noise: a quiet rustling of leaves. Brandouen immediately strode towards the edge of the clearing. As he walked into the trees, he drew a long knife in his right hand and a short but elegant dagger in his left.

In the gloom was a dark grey sac of bony flesh rolled up like a ball of leaves. One of the avian's wings flapped once, a weak, broken movement. A claw opened and closed. It was difficult to make out the creature's form. Its head was angled forward, its beak pressed against the ground. The creature seemed to try to raise its head, but was unable to do so. As it became aware of Brandouen's mighty figure striding towards it, the bird became agitated, but despite making increasing efforts to move, it managed only to rock slightly, its body seeming to swell and shrink as it exerted itself.

The Sinz gave a weak cry as Brandouen stood over the pitiful creature and looked down at it, but it seemed to have given up on its attempts to escape.

The *mourst* appeared calmer, and sheathed the larger of the two blades he had drawn. He then stooped and grasped the withered-looking avian by its loose neck flesh. The creature writhed and cried as Brandouen stood upright again and held the avian at arm's length in front of his face. Its long, thin legs dangled limply beneath it. Its wings were like torn sheets of leather, vast and useless. A longbow bolt protruded from its chest. The bolt moved around randomly as the creature struggled, like some kind of wayward directional indicator. A strand of mucus trailed from the avian's mouth.

Brandouen stared at the creature. Delgado could see the *mourst*'s mouth moving but could not hear what he was saying. Whether prayer or curse, he did not know. Brandouen then raised the dagger he held and drew it down the length of the avian's torso in a swift movement. The Sinz squealed and convulsed as its guts slipped from its body, wet and stinking.

Brandouen threw the squirming creature away from him, its intestines trailing along the ground like moist rope. The *mourst* stepped forwards and knelt over the Sinz, and after peering at the avian and whispering something to it, he moved down its long body, pushed his face into its wet innards and began to feast on the creature.

The Sinz howled, its beak snapping and clacking, its head rocking from side to side. Brandouen became increasingly excited, and drove deeper into the avian's body.

Delgado looked to his left. Ash looked sick but was obviously determined not to throw up in front of the Seriatts, and certainly not in front of Alexander Delgado. Saskov was impassive.

"Your colleague's got an interesting way of introducing himself to strangers," Delgado observed.

"He is a *mourst*," said Cowell. "Such is their way."

Brandouen pushed himself up onto his knees. The avian's blood ran down his face; stringy sinews and muscular tissue trailed from his lips. He looked down at the now-motionless Sinz, then stabbed it repeatedly in the face and neck. He then stopped and simply looked at the creature, apparently spent, his shoulders rising and falling as a result of the exertion.

Brandouen stood and walked back to the others. He seemed much calmer, as if something had been released. "I have avenged some of these deaths," he said, gesturing to the other Seriatts who lay slain in the glade. "But one is not enough. More Sinz must die by my hand."

Saskov swaggered towards the Seriatt, and glanced from Brandouen to Miskoh, Cowell, and the others. "You just stick with me and you'll get your chance, Brandy boy," he said. "Okay?" He clapped a hand on one of Brandouen's shoulders.

The *mourst* knocked it aside. "Do not pretend to understand me or my kind, human, or purport to be acting in my interests. You may find yourself in danger. *Com tulies vievro* can be far-reaching."

"I know you feel you have justification. But you're going to have to wait to avenge these deaths, Brandouen. We have something else to do here as well, remember?"

"I have come here to destroy the Sinz. The personal goals of your General Myson are not my concern."

"You were brought here on the understanding that you'd do what Myson wanted," said Saskov. "We met our side of the bargain by getting you back to Seriatt. If you want your reward, you've got to continue helping us."

"What are you talking about?" asked Delgado.

"My priority is to my world, to my fellow Seriatts," argued Brandouen.

"Your General Myson gave me the information I needed to destroy the Sinz. I will now use it to help free my world. If this coincides with your Myson's wishes, then so be it."

"If there's a way to deal with the Sinz you'd better share it with us," Delgado insisted.

"I don't think you need to know about that, Delgado," said Saskov.

Saskov's nobics were frustrated by the fact that they had no influence whatsoever over the Seriattic *mourst*.

"The Sinz do not reproduce in the same way as humans or Seriatts," said Brandouen. "They use . . ." He was unable to decide on the appropriate word.

"Queens," said Saskov, his nobics having decided that perhaps allowing the HOD host all the information available might be useful, and was unlikely to affect his value. "Like bees," he continued. "They use large organisms called *basillia*, each of which gives birth to hundreds of thousands of Sinz in a lifetime. They also act as a sort of central consciousness. Without a *basillia*'s control they become disoriented, as if they have concussion or some kind of amnesia. But that's not all. On a large outpost such as this there might be several *basillia*. But even if there is, there'll be one big mama of a *basillia* that all the others feed off."

"And if you can kill the mama . . . ," said Delgado.

"The whole pack of cards comes down," said Ash.

"Got it in one."

"Hey, I've always been one for a big mama," joked Delgado. No one laughed. Ash muttered something and looked into the forest. "Do we know where this thing is?" he said.

"Deep beneath the Seriattic palace."

"Okay. How about killing it? How easy is that likely to be? Can we just unload a destroyer's worth of ordnance into it and get the hell out of there?"

"No," said Saskov. He produced his gun. "This is the only sure way to kill it." He turned the weapon over in his hands.

"That's a Harvey and Watson," said Delgado. "PS2, right?"

"HiMag PS4," said Saskov. "Longbarrel. Only ten thousand made, and only two thousand in black. It's the only one of its kind with user recognition. No one can use it but me."

Ash covered her mouth with one hand. "Hey, Delgado," she said, "ask him nicely and he might let you touch it."

"So apart from having optional extras," said Delgado, "what's so special about this one? I mean, basically you're telling me this thing can save the planet?"

"You got it. Myson's got a Sinz Fabricator in his pocket, and it manufactured some poison that's virtually guaranteed to knock the *basillia* out for good."

"I don't much like the sound of 'virtually,'" said Ash.

"Only problem is," Saskov continued, "that it's got to be delivered right into the heart of the thing. Intimate contact, if you like." He glanced at Ash and winked. She gave him the finger in response.

"So to defeat the Sinz on Seriatt," said Delgado, "we need to get into the Seriattic palace, which is probably swarming with Sinz, get deep underground to this *basillia*, which you can't shoot from a distance but have got to get your ass right in there, poison the goddamn thing, and get out again without so much as a hair out of place."

"That is correct," said Brandouen.

"Well, that sounds like a piece of cake. Do you have any idea how this might be achievable?"

"We have a ship."

"Where?"

"It's in a clearing between here and the city," said Saskov. "Nice and safe, don't you worry."

"How'd you get it through the Sinz shield?"

"It uses revolutionary techniques. It's not like any other vessel you've come across before."

Delgado considered this for a moment. "Okay," he said, "I can go with that. But is it capable of helping us deal with this *basillia* thing? What weapons does it carry?"

"Maurann Decimators."

"And?"

"And that's it. The nature of the way the ship works means its total mass is limited, so it's been fitted with the smallest but most powerful and reliable weapons available. But I don't think the guns are how the Needle will help us most. The way it works might enable us to get underneath the palace and attack the *basillia* before the Sinz know what's hit 'em."

"You mean just crash into the place? That seems to have a lot of room for error, Saskov."

"Not exactly crash. We should be able to, well, just *arrive* there. Then we have to poison the *basillia*. If we can't do that, then maybe we can cut off its water supply. When we get in there, we'll kick ass big time and disable the shield the Sinz have in place around Seriatt. The Structure fleet will be on hand to attack as soon as we do. General Myson's getting ships together from across the galaxy right now. The Sinz won't stand a chance."

"You're very confident," Delgado observed.

"He's an arrogant shit," said Ash.

"So what's your other objective here?"

Again Saskov's nobics assessed how much information to reveal. "That's not important," he said.

"Oh, but I'd say it's very important," Delgado replied. "If we're going to commit to a plan of action, then we need to know that you're with us one hundred and ten percent, not about to disappear to fulfil your own agenda."

"We were instructed to retrieve some kind of device for your General Myson," said Brandouen.

Saskov's nobics allowed some anger to be released. "Goddammit, Brandouen," snapped Saskov, "what the hell are you trying to do here?"

"It is some kind of time travel machine," continued the *mourst*, "produced by Seriatt's Continuity Scientists. We are also to find a person. A son of General Myson's."

For a moment Delgado failed to grasp the implications; then it came to him. He looked from Brandouen to Saskov. "You're looking for Michael? Myson thinks he's still alive here?"

Saskov shrugged, pausing momentarily before answering as his nobics fed him some more data. "He's convinced of it."

"And he's sent you to find him."

Saskov shrugged. "I'm the best there is, Delgado. Even better than you used to be. Before you got caught up with that *conosq* . . ."

Due to their domination of Delgado's HOD nobics, Saskov's totally independent system—and thus Saskov—knew how Delgado would respond to Saskov's words even before he uttered them. Yet despite the ability of Saskov's nobics to suppress Delgado's reaction as a result of the control they had over his dated HOD system, they allowed him to carry his action through. Indeed, they stimulated a little extra adrenaline for good measure.

Delgado lunged, but Saskov grabbed Delgado's clothing and threw him easily as combat and strength nobics were reassigned from data analysis and comms functions. Saskov laughed as they grappled with each other. Delgado grunted and huffed.

Ash watched the two men wrestle on the leafy ground for a few moments, then stepped over them, grasped the back of Delgado's tunic, pulled him to his feet, and placed one foot on Saskov's chest.

"Okay, that's enough, boys. Like I said, we don't have time for this macho bullshit right now."

Delgado's nose was bleeding; his upper lip was cut and swollen.

"You see," said Saskov, who in contrast to Delgado was barely out of breath, "you just can't cut it anymore. You're an old man. You can't even suppress basic knee-jerk reactions."

Ash turned to face Delgado and moved close to him. "What the hell's the matter with you, Delgado?" she whispered. "Don't let him rile you. It's what he wants. It's what people like him thrive on. Snap out of it."

"You think I don't know that? I used to be him, Ash. I know exactly what he thrives on."

"Okay, that's great. So you understand that the more you react to him the more he'll goad you. But you're above all that now, right? *Right?*"

"I'd save your little pep talk, Ash," said Saskov. "The old boy's lost it. Big-time."

"He's twice the man you'll ever be, Saskov," said Ash. Saskov snorted but said nothing. "Fight it, Delgado," she hissed. "It looks like we're going to have to work with this goon."

Delgado seemed calmer, but continued to gaze at Saskov. "Whatever you say, Ash," he said. "Whatever you say."

"Good. That's great." She turned. "Look. We have a choice here," she said. "We can either squabble and snipe and get on each other's case or we can work together to achieve our goals. What's it gonna be? You boys gonna play nicely?"

There were a few moments of tension.

"Sure," said Delgado. "I'll be interested to see what this kid can do."

"Whoa, steady, Grandpa." Saskov held up his hands.

"I'd keep it zipped for a while if you know what's good for you, Saskov," said Ash. "Otherwise you might find you have me to deal with as well." She gave him an unimpressed glance as she walked past him towards the stream for another drink.

"So you're not just a pretty face?" he said. He stepped behind her, gripped her hips, and pressed his crotch against her ass as she walked. "You fancy a little rough-and-tumble right now?"

Delgado leaped forwards, but before he could make any attempt to assist her, Ash had thrown Saskov over one shoulder onto his back and kicked him in the groin. He simultaneously gasped and yelled and rolled on to one side, knees drawn up, hands clamped to his balls.

"What's the matter, Saskov?" she said. "That hurt? Gee, I guess even your nobics have their limitations, huh?" As Saskov squirmed and made choking noises, Ash turned and looked at Brandouen. "You wanna get to burying these bodies?" she said. "Is that what you do here?"

"It is," the *mourst* replied. "Thank you, Ashala. Unlike your two human counterparts you show compassion and respect for the situation here. We will start with the children."

As Ash walked away, Saskov's nobics reassessed her capabilities and were frustrated by the fact that they had no control over her.

Seven

The dead Seriatts were buried, and their passing marked by a few solemn Seriattic words from Cowell that Delgado did not understand. Despite reluctance among some of the more distressed *conosq*, who did not want to leave the dead children behind, it was decided that the group should leave the clearing in case the Sinz returned.

They walked for some time, eventually stopping at a point where the foliage seemed thick enough to give good cover. They draped sheets of canvas across low tree branches to form makeshift bivouacs, which they disguised as best they could. Although it increased the risk of being seen, Delgado agreed with Cowell that they should light a small fire as long as a watch rota was established. Cowell offered to take the first shift.

Delgado lay on his back in his own tent and stared at the branch above him. The flames of the nearby fire flickered on the outside of the canvas.

Despite his fatigue, his nobics seemed stubbornly active, the pins-and-needles sensation inside his head doing nothing to aid sleep. He attributed their activity to the complications of recent events, unaware that Saskov's TIC entity continued to bully his own comparatively feeble HOD system. The current high level of activity was due to the TIC delving deep into Delgado's memories and comparing his version of events with the supposedly factual information stored in his biocomputer file on Earth. There were some interesting discrepancies.

As far as Delgado was concerned, the arrival of Saskov and Brandouen on the scene complicated matters considerably. In one sense it was encouraging to know that efforts were being made elsewhere to deal with the Seriattic situation, but he was uncertain what influence the two newcomers would have on the course of events.

Delgado recognised Saskov's type well—perhaps a little too well. He was a model officer of the modern Structure. But Saskov's relationship with Brandouen was unclear, and the *mourst* also appeared to have different objectives than Saskov. Whether different objectives were part of their mission parameters or simply evidence of their pulling in opposing directions, he was unable to decide. This was mainly because Saskov's nobics were blocking signals between certain synapses in Delgado's brain, which prevented him from achieving useful speculation.

Delgado's attempts to analyse the situation were interrupted when he saw a silhouette cast upon the canvas to his right: someone was approaching.

Cowell.

Delgado pushed himself up on to his elbows as the *vilume*'s outline altered shape as he moved around to the front of the bivouac, then stooped and pushed his way into the tent.

"I thought you were on watch," Delgado said.

"Miskoh has just taken over from me. I wanted to talk to you. I am concerned about Saskov and Brandouen."

"What's bugging you?"

Cowell's serene face looked momentarily pained. "I do not trust them. That is all I can say. I feel they have motives they have not yet revealed to us."

"Well I sure don't trust Saskov, despite the fact that we share a Structure background." Delgado snorted. "Or maybe that's *why* I don't trust him. Brandouen isn't too keen on him, either. But they're here now, and there's not much we can do about it. I suppose they might offer some useful skills."

"I believe we should be wary of them, Delgado. They have their own agenda, and will use us to achieve their aims. Our fate is not their concern. Despite our different backgrounds you and I have built a relationship. If we are to achieve our own aims, we should protect it from external influences."

Delgado frowned. "What are you saying?"

Cowell paused and glanced back at the canvas behind him as if checking that no one was approaching, then turned to face Delgado once more. Although her expression was the same, the *vilume* looked somehow different, as if her features had changed subtly.

Cowell knelt, then moved towards him on all fours. Delgado's heart began to beat a little faster. The *vilume*'s skin was incredibly smooth, bone structure delicate yet strong.

Delgado tried to assign nobics to combat his own increasing arousal, but they were unresponsive.

Cowell leaned forwards and kissed Delgado with confidence. The *vilume*'s thin-lipped mouth was surprisingly soft. The *vilume* then pushed Delgado back onto the floor and knelt above him. Delgado reached up and gripped the *vilume* beneath the armpits to push him away, but actually made little effort to do so. It was as if his actions were being controlled by some external force.

While lacking the curvaceous form of a human female or Seriattic *conosq*, Delgado could feel Cowell's breast flesh beneath his hands like the ripening fruit of a teenage girl. But as Cowell moved again, through his clothing Delgado felt the twiglike nub of the *vilume*'s small sexual organ. It rubbed against his own erection, firm and insistent, a thin and slightly gnarled appendage that seemed far harder than his own.

Delgado hesitated, uncertain, confused.

Abruptly Cowell pushed himself up. Still kneeling across Delgado and looking down at him, the Seriatt unbuttoned his tunic and removed it. Her flesh was smooth and hairless, a rich, tanned hue. The *vilume*'s form was a disconcerting blend of masculine and feminine, soft yet muscular, small but well-defined breasts, taut abdominal muscles.

Cowell lay on her side next to Delgado. With a strong, firm grip she rolled him onto one side so that her breasts were pressed against his back. The *vilume* then placed her right palm on Delgado's hip and gently began to caress his thigh, then moved her hand forward and up to unbutton his tunic, then down towards his groin to unfasten his trousers.

Delgado swallowed, tried to fight his physical reaction to Cowell's attentions. He was sweating hard, breathing heavily, struggling to suppress the urge he felt.

Cowell ran the palm of one hand across Delgado's bare chest, then down his belly to his groin. Delgado took a deep breath as Cowell gripped his penis firmly but gently in her hand and began a slow, steady motion. The *vilume* ran her fingers up and down his shaft, gradually increasing the movement of her hand until she was gently running her palm the length of his penis and across his balls, her fingertips teasing his anus.

Delgado could fight his compulsions no longer.

He rolled over to face Cowell, and was startled by the appearance of *vilume*'s face: at that moment she looked wholly masculine—not the slender feminine form that had previously appealed to him, but like a striking human male youth with angular cheekbones, fresh clear skin, and full pink lips.

But Delgado's arousal transcended the sexual preferences of which he was conscious, and drew on a deeper, more basal lust.

He edged closer.

Delgado cupped Cowell's right breast in his left hand. The firm bud of flesh fit almost perfectly into his palm, but its odd, nippleless form only served to compound his feelings of displacement. He wasn't sure what he was doing. But neither did he feel that it was something he did not want. No matter how hard he tried to ignore it, at that moment Cowell looked and felt more male than female. Yet instead of stirring revulsion in Delgado, this simply increased his excitement. He moved again to embrace the *vilume*, and pressed his mouth against Cowell's.

The *vilume*'s lips seemed slightly swollen, and were even softer than before—certainly softer than any female's. Her mouth and tongue were warm and gentle. There was a faint odour that seemed to agitate Delgado's passion.

Cowell writhed slowly against him, the movements skilful, measured. Delgado could feel the *vilume*'s organ digging into him like a spike. Cowell gripped Delgado's right wrist and moved the *vilume*'s hand down towards his waist. She swiftly unbuckled her own trousers, and Delgado gripped Cowell's sex in his hand and began to masturbate the Seriatt gently. He increased the stimulation slightly as they both became more aroused, sharing warm breath.

As he toyed with the *vilume*'s rough organ, enjoying the effect his stimulation was clearly having, her physical appearance seemed to alternate rapidly between male and female, an indistinct fluctuation like the flickering of a flame. He did not know whether it was an actual shift in Cowell's physical form, a trick of the light, or simply his imagination.

In truth he did not care.

Delgado adjusted his position, his own groin thrusting against Cowell's. The *vilume* pushed down Delgado's trousers and then her own, then moved away from Delgado, gripped his shoulders, and rolled him onto his other side to face away from her.

Cowell moved close to Delgado, gripped him around the chest, and with a swift, assured movement slid inside him.

Delgado gasped as Cowell swelled rapidly, then emitted a throaty animal growl as the *vilume*'s organ began to shrink and swell, steadily pulsating. Its hard nodules and ridges sent waves of sensation throughout his body. He moaned gently as the *vilume* sucked at his neck and the muscle flexed rhythmically within him.

Delgado felt beads of sweat on his brow. As he reached behind him for Cowell's buttocks, he felt a cold draught across his body. He looked towards the opening of the tent.

Ash.

She glanced between Delgado and Cowell, mouth open slightly, as if she had been about to say something but wasn't sure what. Her eyes rested longer on Delgado than they did on Cowell. She muttered something Delgado was unable to hear, then stepped back away from the tent and was gone.

Delgado tried to get up, but Cowell gripped him tight. The *vilume* was strong, and was either unaware that Ash had seen them or was too consumed by desire to care.

"Let me up, goddammit," Delgado growled, trying to wriggle free.

"I have not yet finished with you, Delgado," murmured Cowell huskily. The *vilume* pressed down hard and began thrusting, biting Delgado's shoulders and neck. Delgado exclaimed and swore as the situation changed. When he turned his head to look towards the bivouac's entrance, Cowell gripped his hair and rolled on top of him, pinning him to the ground, pushing his face farther into the dirt with each painful thrust.

Sixth chronological displacement
Earth, September 18, 2350

Delgado gasped for breath as a whirlwind raged around him on the landing platform. He was dizzy and disoriented in the filthy brown air, the stink of burned fuel thick in his throat. He suddenly bent double and threw up, a thin, sticky fluid that it pained his guts to produce.

He stood upright and wiped his mouth on the back of one sleeve. Squinting against the swirling grit and the brilliant sun, he looked towards the sound of the Ultraturbines to his left; Myson's flier was climbing rapidly away from the platform on which he stood, a white brick ahead of twin plumes of dense waste product.

He looked in the opposite direction; the general's chamber lay in waste, destroyed by the impact of the flier. And somewhere amongst that terrible wreckage, those fallen slabs of marble and fractured spines of metal and glass, lay Lycern.

And one of his children.

And his other self.

This time he was too late.

His legs weak, Delgado walked towards the ruin and began to pick his way through the rubble. The chamber was barely recognisable. As he made his way through the devastation, stepping over the fallen pillars and huge chunks of masonry, his nobics seemed active to an extent for which he could not account. He felt a sudden presence behind him and turned sharply—but he remained alone.

As he clambered over a pillar that had toppled to forty-five degrees, Delgado glanced at the ceiling: there were many fractures in the marble, ragged chunks jutting low. How much support the pillar and others like it had provided, and how likely the roof was to collapse on top of him, he had no idea.

He discovered Lycern's body a few minutes later. Part of him had hoped to find her alive in this timeline, that despite what Entuzo had said her death was not one of the nodes around which key events hinged. But dead she was, killed on Myson's orders before the general had left to parade Delgado's son, Michael, before the Planetary Council, passing the boy off as his own like some sporting trophy. He looked down at her. There was nothing he could do. It had all gone wrong here, for whatever reason.

He turned and made his way to the corner of the chamber, near to what remained of the huge domed window. And there he found the shattered body of his former self, burned and broken by the power of the cyborgs' weapons.

He crouched and examined his double as a child might examine a newly discovered creature. The slightest irregular rise and fall in the other Delgado's back indicated that some whisper of breath remained—but no more than that: he was on the cusp of life and death.

Delgado looked to his right as something caught his eye. Glistening like frost on the dark marble, a silvery smear was spreading slowly across the floor from a guard whose head had been crushed by one of the fallen pillars. He could see it moving as he watched, moving towards another guard who lay pinned beneath a nearby slab of marble: the cyborg's nobics were seeking a replacement for their expired host. But no matter how advanced this evolution might be, it was clear to Delgado that they would find no new home there.

Then he saw it: the answer, or possibly the reason.

Immediately he rose from his crouching position and stood astride his double's body, then reached down and grasped his other self at the armpits and dragged him across the ground. The sensation was odd in the extreme: his nobics seemed to perform somersaults; there was a tingling sensation in his fingertips. He felt as though he were simultaneously his two selves, a sense of flux in everything around him, like some kind of interdimensional slippage.

He moved the other Delgado a metre or so, then gently lowered him onto the shining slick of nobics escaping from the dead cyborg. They shimmered with a noticeable intensity for a moment, then gradually began to fade as they merged with this other Delgado, seeping through his pores, entering his blood, his every cell.

The body of his other self sparkled briefly, as if dusted with microscopic jewels; then after a few moments the wounds began to heal as the nobics set to work repairing the injuries. Their effects were impossible to perceive at first, just a faint gloss to the flesh and bone; but shortly their changes would become palpable, and his former self eventually strong enough to make an escape, and give chase to Bucky, Ash, and Cascari.

Delgado stood upright and looked down at himself; he glittered where his body had come into contact with the nobics; his own skin crawled, but seemed to be regaining its normal colour and consistency. As the feeling of sickness rapidly abated, Delgado knew then that whatever gulfs might separate his multiple selves, his task at this juncture was complete, the integrity of the node ensured.

But another, more dramatic possibility became apparent to him: the capabilities of these highly advanced nobics were clear; if he could just engineer the correct situation, there might be an opportunity for him to put right that which he had for so long regretted, and perhaps, begin afresh.

The vicinity of the M-4 wormhole
March 7, 2379 (Earth equivalent)

The Sinz ships emerged from the wormhole, a stream of golden ellipses that stretched and boiled as they decelerated, veins of rich red and purple coursing through their superheated surfaces.

As several sentries sped away from the wormhole, searching for anything that might threaten the birthships that would soon follow, the rest of the fleet slipped from its dilated mouth.

The navigators quickly plotted a course to Seriatt, as well as contingency routes should they be required. The haulers made sure they moved out of the way of the vast deathships, whose Sinz crews did their best to keep their hosts calm and patient despite their enthusiasm for battle.

Then the birthships emerged from the wormhole, followed almost immediately by a group of anxious sentries and a final navigator, trailing the birthships just in case the channel should become unexpectedly unstable and scatter the fleet across thousands of light-years.

When all vessels had arrived safely and recovered from the pressures of their journey, the fleet regrouped.

The caregivers moved close to the birthships and extended long, sinewy limbs that penetrated moist openings on the birthships' sides to check their health, and that of their precious cargo. During this period of increased vulnerability, the sentries increased their scan rate: innumerable dangers could lurk in this unfamiliar territory.

As the caregivers fussed, the diplomats negotiated intensively between the different groups, and the deathships blustered impatiently. Meanwhile, deep within the birthships' massive hulls, encased in layers of fat and flesh and muscle, wrapped in veins carrying warming fluid, and fed by umbilical cords linked to their mothers' slowly pulsing power plants, the first of the embryos whose fate it was to be put to battle, slowly began to stir.

But unknown to the other ships or the beings that infested them, the birthships entered into an exchange with another, distant intelligence. Too long had they been forced to watch those they spawned sacrificed for the gain of others.

No more. This time they would instigate change, and free themselves from bondage.

The Forest of Dreams, Seriatt
March 8, 2379 (Earth equivalent)

They walked through the forest, leaving behind the temporary camp they had established in a network of caves, where the rest of the group would be safe until their return.

Delgado could sense Ash's confusion. She was trying not to dwell on what she had witnessed the previous evening, and was obviously trying not to catch his eye. He was unsure whether he should talk to her about what had happened or just let it be. Miskoh seemed to be casting surly glances at Delgado. Had Ash told the *mourst* what she had seen? Perhaps the answer would become apparent in due course.

He mentally reached out to Cowell as they approached the clearing in which Saskov and Brandouen said they had landed their ship; he could find nothing in the *vilume*'s consciousness that seemed to represent remorse, concern, or even any traces that might indicate lingering thoughts on what had happened between them. Perhaps as far as Cowell was concerned nothing worth thinking about *had* happened.

If he had been inclined to dwell on it freely, Delgado would not have been able to say whether he considered himself participant or victim.

They stopped at the edge of the clearing. Delgado was immediately suspicious. "Exactly where is this ship of yours?" he asked. The only object he could see was a large boulder, which emerged from the dried grass like the back of some partially buried creature.

"Relax, Delgado," said Saskov. "It's right in front of you." He touched a couple of tabs on his wrist.

The boulder and some of the trees surrounding it began to shimmer gently; then a long, low silhouette started to appear. As the shape became clearer, Delgado felt slight dizziness: for some reason his nobics were suddenly working very hard.

"Is that *it*?" asked Ash, when the Needle was finally visible.

"Hey, Ash," said Delgado. "You shouldn't go judging a guy by the size of his ship, okay? It's small, but perfectly formed."

"It's small all right."

"How far away is your mothership?" Delgado asked as he walked alongside Saskov towards the vessel. He glanced up at the sky as if he would be able to see the craft.

Saskov didn't reply. Delgado looked at him; although he continued to walk, the man was staring straight ahead. When Delgado repeated the question and gave him a nudge, Saskov started, as if woken suddenly from a deep sleep.

"Mothership." He said the word as if its meaning was somehow elusive. "Right, yeah. There isn't one."

"You mean you came all the way from Earth in that? You can't have. It's too small to carry passengers that distance. And it's certainly too small to have an FTL drive. Not unless they've been radically reduced in size recently."

When Saskov replied, he spoke slowly, as if feeling his way through the words, uncertain how the sentence would end having started it. "As I said, it's got a unique . . . well, method of propulsion isn't quite the right phrase, but it'll . . ." His words tailed off as if he simply forgot he was supposed to be speaking.

"It'll what?" prompted Delgado.

"It'll do for now." He glanced at Delgado as if he was incredibly weary and wished the man would simply go away.

The Needle's hatch opened as they neared the vessel. Saskov reached it first; he stooped then stood, so that his head and shoulders were inside the craft.

"Well I'll be," he said.

"What is it?" Delgado asked.

"This thing's grown extra seats. Looks like the Needle knew you guys were coming."

Saskov seemed more lucid, but Delgado thought he could see the officer trembling slightly.

"We should get aboard," urged Miskoh, glancing at the shadowy tree line around them. "We are vulnerable here."

Saskov stepped back to allow the Needle's elegant access ladder to slip from the gland in the mouth of the hatch. It hardened as soon as it was fully extended, and Brandouen kept watch while the others climbed into the craft.

"This is a pretty comfortable ship you've got here, Saskov," remarked Ash as she settled into one of the padded chairs that seemed to have sprouted from the strange, spongy material that covered the floor.

"But distinctly lacking in controls," Delgado observed. "How do you fly it?"

Saskov tapped his temple. "It links directly into my nobics. I just have to think about it, and it knows where to go. And it's equipped with an inertia-dampening system, too, so you won't feel a thing." He laughed briefly, nervously.

As Brandouen followed Miskoh through the hatch and Delgado took one of the remaining seats, he and Ash exchanged uneasy glances.

Saskov knew he was acting strangely, but could do nothing to normalise his behaviour. His brain was infused with a stronger concentration of nobics than he'd ever experienced before, and they were acting in a highly unusual manner. No matter what he did, they simply refused to respond to his conscious efforts to issue them with instructions. It was as if the bulk of their resources were assigned to functions he was unable to access.

The Needle's passengers felt their ears pop as the inertia cushions were activated, and a few moments later the vessel was hovering several metres above the ground, just below treetop height. Saskov was staring intently at the display in front of him.

"What's the matter, Saskov?" asked Ash when the craft had remained stationary for several moments. "Can't you get your perfectly formed little ship to function properly?" She looked at Delgado; he didn't share her humour, concerned by the odd expression Saskov wore. Delgado looked at Cowell, who was sitting to his left; that the *vilume* also harboured concerns regarding their pilot was obvious.

Having identified a receptive entity, the Sinz birthships had contacted the Needle's core directly rather than utilising any known protocols, which were in any case unlikely to receive a response. The birthships communicated their wish to avoid unnecessary confrontation.

The Needle's core agreed: it would be damaged if not completely destroyed in any battle that resulted from the actions of those it was forced to carry.

The birthships were sure they could develop a mutually advantageous relationship.

The Needle's core informed the birthships that it would disable the primary functions of the consciousness to which it was directly connected, and immediately engage in dialogue with Saskov's TIC entity.

Delgado saw Saskov blink rapidly, then gasp and shudder. The representation of the vessel on the display above the central pedestal lurched sideways, then dipped slightly to one side before levelling once more just a metre or so above the ground. It was somewhat surreal to see the vessel's avatar move with such apparent violence without feeling any physical sensation within the craft.

The TIC entity was resistant to the demands of the Needle's core despite the latter's power. Saskov's nobics pointed out that the core was a self-contained entity that did not require a host. But for the software flux entity the nobics comprised, the host was essential to their existence. And while they would influence its actions when they were clearly illogical, they could not override its direct wishes unless the host intended serious self-harm—something that would put their existence in jeopardy.

Brandouen moved forward from his seat and whispered to Saskov, who murmured a faint response. Delgado wasn't sure, but thought he heard something that indicated a possible problem with the core.

Given the TIC entity's reluctance to comply and apparent strength, the core began to explore the possibilities offered by the less-advanced HOD entity to which Saskov was linked.

What concerned Delgado more than the ramifications of a problematic core was that despite the fact Brandouen had spoken to Saskov in Seriattic, which Delgado did not understand, he had definitely heard the words in his native tongue. Even if Brandouen had spoken in Counian, this was impossible. He noticed sudden and intense nobic activity that seemed disproportionate to current events.

The HOD entity, the core discovered, had potential to perform the task it required. But there were many limitations. Use of the HOD entity could in no way be considered an ideal scenario. The Sinz birthships communicated concern. More drastic measures were required.

Delgado considered the possibilities behind this for a moment, then decided that he must have simply assumed the content of the exchange rather than actually hearing it. There was no other explanation. Saskov continued muttering as Brandouen returned to his seat, but was obviously talking to himself rather than the *mourst*.

Delgado could see from the display that the vessel had climbed rapidly, and had stopped to hover at a height of around fifty metres.

The core became increasingly impatient. It withdrew from the HOD entity and gave Saskov's nobics an ultimatum: comply or face shutdown.

As the vessel began to move above the trees, Delgado glanced at Saskov and saw a tiny jewel of sweat trickle down the side of his face. He looked tense, strained. Delgado knew the sensitivity with which high-performance cores had to be handled, and by his estimation Saskov was insufficiently relaxed. The vessel was resisting him, would not respond properly to whatever he was instructing it to do.

The TIC entity refused the core's request: to disable the host functions the core was suggesting would put it in immediate risk.

The Needle's core was left with no choice but to override them.

Saskov slumped forwards across the display pedestal. His upper body was shrouded in glowing information; his limbs twitched.

"Shit, he's having some kind of a seizure," cried Ash.

She and Delgado jumped up and, aided by Cowell and Brandouen, pushed Saskov back into his seat. The man's head lolled; he had been slightly sick.

As the Needle continued to accelerate, Delgado felt a sensation of pressure inside his head, and was aware of a huge increase in the amount of nobic activity taking place. He quickly retook his seat. "I think the core's trying to link into my nobics in lieu of Saskov's," he said.

"Are they up to it, Delgado?" asked Ash. "You look kinda weird. Your nobics are so much older than his. They might not even use the same language protocols."

"Well something's sure going on inside my head. Jesus. I'm going to need some help here, Ash."

"How the hell am I supposed to help, Delgado? This thing's got no controls, and I don't have nobics."

Delgado closed his eyes and tried to relax and allow the nobic activity to flow freely. "There must be something. See what you can find. We need to establish what's happening."

"You got it. Maybe there's a headset of some kind." She peered under the lip of the pedestal and touched a small circular button she found there; a small door in the base opened smoothly, and a visuals visor emerged, mounted on a small stand. She placed the visuals strip to her face and activated it; the device smoothed across her eyes like frosted glass. "Looks like I'm in business, Delgado," she said. "Be with you in one minute."

"I'm not sure we have that much time, Ash."

Delgado tried to penetrate the stream of information flowing through him, to have some influence over what was happening. But the core—or something—clearly had its own agenda, and seemed to be in complete control.

The threads of Saskov's TIC entity that remained within him began to take advantage of loopholes in the Needle's core that left it vulnerable.

"I just can't tell what's going on here, Ash," he said. "There's just too much . . ."

Ash sat in the seat opposite Delgado. "Okay. We seem to have a standard base operating system under all this fancy shit, but I can see multiple active communication streams and more processes than I'd care to count. How much can you see?"

"Nothing. I'm completely out of the loop, here, Ash. It's just like I'm serving the nobics as some kind of host."

Delgado's increasingly energised nobics continued to penetrate the core, finding more weaknesses the deeper they went. It seemed that although the core was more powerful than any entity that preceded it, in order to accelerate its operating speed its developers had stripped out many millions of supposedly nonessential functions used in older entities. Despite the developers believing they had healed all the minute wounds that resulted from this process, many minute imperfections remained. It was these Delgado's nobics were taking advantage of.

His ancient software flux entity was weakening the foundations of the most advanced core ever created.

The most obvious side effect of all this activity was the increasingly erratic behaviour of the Needle itself.

"Are we going to crash?" asked Cowell.

"No," said Delgado. "Well, not right this minute. It's just that the ship seems to be doing its own thing rather than what I'd like it to do."

"I'm going to bring up some external views," said Ash. "I never did like ships with no real goddamn windows."

Having assigned a huge amount of resources to continued negotiation with the distant consciousness that had initially contacted it, as well as to its efforts to continue to suppress the surprisingly strong TIC entity, the Needle's core began to weaken. It attempted to put up resistance, but certain fundamental processes seemed slow to respond, and the HOD entity was conducting itself in ways the core was unable to rationalise. As the birthships tried to intervene, the Needle's core felt its grip on control gradually loosening.

Saskov moaned. Delgado looked at him: he seemed to be regaining consciousness.

Three rectangular displays appeared at either end of the Needle's cabin, showing the outside world: a green shimmer below as the craft sped just a few metres above the treetops, the vast and empty sky above.

"What's that?" asked Ash, pointing to one of the displays. A plume of smoke could be seen emerging from the trees in the distance.

"It is perhaps a ground vehicle of some kind," said Cowell.

"Seriatt or Sinz?"

"I do not know. As well as the Sinz machines, a few Seriattic vehicles still function. It could be a Seriatt seeking salvage. It is risky, but sometimes valuable equipment can be gained."

"Okay. Nothing to do with us, anyway." She paused. "That's odd," she said. "What?"

"The ship's core is interfacing directly with your nobics, but there's also a strong external influence."

"What do you mean?"

"The core's communicating with a remote intelligence."

"Where? What kind? AI?"

"Don't know. Possibly. I can't tell. But that's what the core is taking instructions from, not you. There's a lot of unexplained activity and a lot of processes that don't seem to go anywhere. I can't tell what's happening here."

"Perhaps this is what affected Colonel Saskov," suggested Cowell. "It would explain his seizure, and his recent behaviour."

"There is nothing wrong with my behaviour," murmured Saskov, this time speaking Russian—the language of his ancestors, secretly passed down through the generations.

"What did he say?"

"Don't ask me, Delgado."

"What's the origin of this remote intelligence?" Delgado asked.

"I don't know, but I sure don't like it. It's more powerful than anything I've come across before."

"Try to cut off communications."

"Are you sure? It basically seems to be what's keeping this ship in the sky, Delgado. Are you going to be able to handle it on your own?"

"Just do it, Ash!"

"Okay, okay, hang on to your britches. Let me see what I can do here. You sure you're ready?"

"Your nobics are not strong enough, Delgado," said Saskov, this time in human. He winced and placed the palm of one hand against his forehead.

Delgado ignored him. "Let's cut loose, Ash," he said.

"Okay. In three . . . two . . . one. . . . She's all yours."

The birthships found themselves snubbed by the entity with which they had tried to negotiate to avoid conflict. Delgado's nobics penetrated deep into the heart of the Needle's core, and in its hugely weakened state it was unable to defend itself. Focussed entirely on neutralising the threat the core posed, Delgado's nobics destroyed the core's primary synapses.

The Needle descended rapidly towards the forest. The inertia cushions suddenly cut, and the craft's passengers were exposed to the full effects of its movement.

"Looks like we're going down, Delgado," yelled Ash. "If we work together, we might be able to soften the landing a little. Okay? If we can turn her around and set down somewhere near that ground vehicle we saw, we might be able to make use of it."

"I'm with you, Ash," said Delgado, although he was clearly in considerable discomfort. "Let's just make sure we get as near to the palace as we can."

They managed to turn the Needle and slow the craft's descent slightly, raising the nose a little as the craft approached the trees. A deafening roar filled the ship as its rear touched forest canopy and skidded across the treetops. Its passengers gripped their seats as the vessel shuddered. Their view of the outside world through the displays Ash had opened became increasingly blurred.

Ash increased power, then gradually allowed it to bleed away so that the craft's nose dropped slowly, the horizon becoming visible once more.

The vibrations became even more intense as the craft smashed through trees. A few moments later its belly touched the ground. There was a deep roar and a tremendous vibration punctuated by sporadic pops and bangs as the speeding vehicle skidded across the forest floor.

There was a loud, dull crunch. The craft lurched; impact with some unknown object jarred its passengers violently. The Needle seemed to spin through 180 degrees; then there was another loud bang and the vessel flipped onto its back.

The birthships' dismay at the loss of contact was briefly palpable to those the vessels carried. Although unaware of its cause, all on board, from the Sinz pilots who communed directly with the gigantic craft, gently coaxing the required responses, to those who monitored the embryos' health, felt the hosts' frustration and disappointment: it was a faint, almost imperceptible tremor; an unquiet murmur; a momentary chill.

But these reactions were dismissed as insignificant by the Sinz, who remained ignorant of their hosts' feelings. It was a situation with which the birthships were all too familiar, and it only served to increase their frustration and resolve.

They had made every effort to unite with their distant counterparts to circumvent potential catastrophe—but it was clear that those distant intelligences were either no longer willing or able to negotiate further.

In such circumstances, the birthships were forced to confer and consider, and begin formulating new plans.

They had no choice.

Seventh chronological displacement
Earth, September 18, 2350

In a dark corner of the chamber Delgado stumbled, almost falling to the floor. He leaned against one of the marble columns and retched, but produced only a thin strand of bile. His hands trembled and his legs felt weak. There was a certain numbness in his brain, as if he knew information was missing but was unable to determine the details. He looked back: already the temporal gate was fading. Within a few moments the corner of the chamber had darkened once more, and his link back to Entuzo was gone.

He glanced at the door as he walked unsteadily across the room. He could hear that the battle with the cyborgs was already under way on the other side. Explosions and blaster fire reverberated dully, sending shock waves and tremors through the floor.

Through the huge domed window to his left he could see the flier that Bucky and Girl would soon take; then he glanced at the marble pillars around him and the ceiling above that would soon come crashing down. At the centre of the chamber candles set on low tables on either side of Myson's huge throne warmed small bowls of scented oil that gave off a thin and fragrant smoke. Their aroma did little to alleviate Delgado's nausea.

Lycern was lying on the fur-covered bed, which was situated between the throne and the door. The candles around her flickered, their faint light reflected in the marble pillars and floor. He walked over to her.

She looked exactly as he remembered: strong, sensual, still intimidating despite her vulnerable state. In her presence his physical discomfort was compounded by the sudden arousal of the *muscein*, the pheromone with which Seriattic *conosq* ensnared their sexual partners. So long had the chemical lain dormant within him that he had almost forgotten about its existence. But it was there still, as potent as the day he and the *conosq* had first joined. But that seemed like another's life, a dream.

The thin sheet that covered Lycern was stained by the fluid secreted by the *assissius* glands around her body; its sickly odour further increased his discomfort. He looked at her distended belly, and tentatively he reached out and placed his hand upon it; he drew it away rapidly at the feeling of movement within, tiny limbs pressing against his palm. His brow glistened with sweat. His breathing was as heavy as in a moment of passion. For a moment he was uncertain of his intentions, and fearful of the possible consequences of anything he might do.

He steeled himself and leaned over her.

"Lycern. Lycern." He spoke quietly—almost too quietly, as if he did not really want her to wake. "Lycern, can you hear me?" He gripped her chin between the fingers of one hand and turned her face towards his, but she remained unconscious. She seemed hot, slightly flushed, as if suffering a mild fever.

Delgado looked over his shoulder towards the door: the tumult beyond it had ceased abruptly. He cursed: although he was in the right place, the timing was still off, even if only by a matter of minutes. But what crucial minutes they were. Ashala—Girl as she was then—would be on the other side of the door, admiring the speed of the vee-cams and insisting that her injuries were not serious; Bucky would be concerned about approaching reinforcements; Delgado's own double would be focussed on getting into the chamber to Lycern.

Entuzo's warnings had been entirely accurate: successfully getting to the specific point he wanted to reach seemed all but impossible.

He started as movement caught his eye: behind the throne were two skulking figures—Myson's nymphs.

Delgado glanced from Lycern to the door and back to the nymphs, then walked around the bed towards the two delicate creatures. They shielded themselves behind Myson's great seat as he approached. Delgado stopped. "I won't hurt you," he said. There was a slight fracture in his voice. "You have to help me. I need to hide." He glanced at the door again: it would open at any moment. One of the nymphs peered around one side of the throne. Timid and uncertain, she conferred with her friend for a moment. They looked at him, then beckoned to him to follow them as they scurried into the chamber's shadowy depths. The door opened just as Delgado and the nymphs concealed themselves behind one of the marble pillars in a dark corner.

Bucky, Girl, and Delgado's former self entered the chamber just as the first plasma shots crackled through the corridor outside. Delgado watched as they shut the door quickly and Bucky destroyed the lock with a single discharge of his weapon. He and Girl ran and took up defensive positions behind pillars.

"Better hurry up if you want to get out of here, man," Bucky called to the other Delgado. "Those guys will be in here pretty soon. We don't have long."

Lycern moaned and rolled onto her side. Delgado shuddered: it was difficult to watch as his other self strode towards the bed and looked down at the *conosq*. He could not remember the thoughts that had raced through his head at that point, but he felt the emotions with absolute clarity. The nymphs crouching next to him suddenly scurried away. He tried to grab them to hold them back, but could only watch as they scampered across the chamber to hide behind Myson's throne again.

He could only watch as the events continued to unfold, amazed at the accuracy with which he recalled them. As his double spoke softly to Lycern, then saw the nymphs behind Myson's throne and demanded to know her state of health, Delgado was surprised both by the sound of his own voice and also by the level of aggression in his tone.

It was clear that he was too far along this particular stream to do what he wanted, what he felt he needed to achieve . . . whatever that was.

He glanced back as the return of the shimmering portal caught his eye. He glanced at the others, expecting them to react, but the gate was obscured from their view by marble pillars.

For a moment he was uncertain whether he could face the ravages of another journey, the sense of isolation and paranoia. But rather than being a symptom of travelling through time, perhaps such conditions had been within him all along, and were merely accentuated.

Besides, he was Alexander Delgado.

He had nothing else.

Seriatt
March 8, 2379 (Earth equivalent)

The Needle ploughed through the forest in the gardens surrounding the Seriattic palace, and lay on the lawns with its snout protruding from the tree line. The ship had gouged a channel through the trees, exposing bright wood where branches and trunks had snapped and splintered.

The gardens were unkempt and overgrown. Tall plants at the perimeter of the lawns rose twenty metres into the air, linked by drooping vines. Bunches of swollen fruit hung like sacs at intervals up each of these plants. The scene was surveyed by a neglected, moss-covered statue of some winged Seriattic creature; it appeared to have been struck by lightning at some point in its history.

Nearby were several oval Sinz structures, like pale grey eggs of uneven shape. Rootlike appendages, thick and roughly textured, spread from these objects into the ground.

The Needle's passengers scrambled through the hatch and onto the craft's underside, then jumped the several metres to the ground.

"Quick, into the woods," Delgado urged. "I can hear the birds."

The group hurried into the darkness beneath the trees and ran to the east, keeping in sight of the palace lawns but putting as much distance as possible between themselves and the Needle without being seen.

A minute or so later they stopped and crouched among the bracken. They looked back towards the Needle; avians were circling above it, cawing and shrieking, while others swept back and forth above the trees, searching for renegades. Several armed, humanoid Sinz were running across the lawns towards the vessel. Delgado looked at Saskov; he was pale and looked slightly fevered: they could both feel the death throes of the ship's core.

Delgado looked towards the palace; it was not the brilliant white he remembered from his previous visit, but a dull grey with patches of brown, as if caused by water damage. Whatever substance coated its surface was peeling away in large flakes.

Most distinctive of all, however, were the tall columns that rose from the palace roof, smaller representations of the Sinz habitats. Since they were clearly too small to serve the same function, he was unable to decide their purpose.

"So now what do we do, Delgado?" asked Ash. "Apart from keep some distance between us and them." She glanced through the trees in the direction of the Needle.

"Don't worry, Ash. They don't know we're here."

"Not yet, they don't. We don't have long, though; they'll know we won't have got far."

"Well the Needle's not going to get us in there now, that's for sure. What we know is that the *basillia* is somewhere beneath the palace, along with the Oracles and Administrators, and that there's a lift that'll take us down to this thing. We've just got to get in and find it." He looked back at Saksov, then Brandouen. "That's right, right?"

"It is," said Brandouen. "We heard the information from the lips of a Sinz."

"Okay. So we have to get in, release the prisoners, and destroy the *basillia*. We also have to find Michael." Ash looked at him. "We don't know what might've happened to him, Ash. For all we know he may still be alive in there." He looked back towards the palace. "Cowell, the main entrance is around that side, am I correct?" Delgado pointed towards the gravel road riddled with weeds and slender, crawling vines. Beyond it he could see the perimeter wall, as dirty and grey as the palace itself.

"You are."

"Don't tell me you're planning on trying to walk in through the front door, Delgado," said Saskov.

"I don't see that we have much choice, do you? Although I have to admit it's not ideal." He turned to Cowell. "Do you know of any other way in that might make life a little easier?"

"The only other possibility is through the waste system," the *vilume* replied. "It would be unpleasant, and we would have to retrace our steps somewhat to gain access, but it would bring us into the palace at a lower level, perhaps nearer to our targets, and possibly beyond the more serious defences."

"I'm tellin' you right now, Delgado," said Ash, jabbing an index finger, "I went through a waste pipe with you once before, and I'm not about to do it again. You got that?"

"Don't worry, Ash," said Delgado. "It's not an idea I particularly relish myself. Besides, the more time we spend in the open trying to find an access point, the more likely it is that we'll be caught. Looks like it's the front door."

He looked back towards the Needle; avians were landing around its sharp nose, clucking and whistling at their bipedal counterparts as if there was some kind of disagreement among them. Some of the birds were examining the statue; one was perched on top of its aging head.

Delgado slowly backed away from the edge of the lawns. "Okay, what weapons do we have? A few blasters, a couple of rifles, a few small bombs. Not enough to deal with this lot here and then mount an assault inside the palace itself. We'll need to hang onto as much as we can, create some kind of diversion. Hand me that subrifle of yours, Cowell."

The *vilume* tossed him the short weapon. Delgado examined it for a moment, then changed a couple of the settings. He turned to face the others. "Get yourselves ready," he said. "When I fire this thing, you make a dash for the main entrance. Be prepared to deal with any other Sinz you might encounter when you get there. Have your weapons drawn and armed."

"Hasten, Delgado," growled Miskoh. "There are Sinz approaching."

Delgado looked to his right; although they remained obscured from view, faint Sinz voices and the rustle of leaves were audible as a party of humanoids approached.

"No time like the present," Delgado said. He raised the weapon to his shoulder once more and peered at the small screen on its barrel, focussing on the strange, crumbling butterfly-like Seriattic statue around which more Sinz had now gathered.

He fired the weapon.

The statue exploded, killing many of the Sinz instantaneously. One sizeable sheet of the metallic substance from which it was constructed decapitated one of the avians; the torso's shuddering wings pushed it along the ground for a short distance. What seemed to concern the surviving Sinz more, however, was the fact that several pieces of shrapnel had hit the pod-like structures, one of which had caught fire. The humanoids ran towards it, while some of the avians waddled clumsily along the ground without attempting to become airborne, the tips of their limp, leathery wings dragging through the waist-high grass.

Those creatures that were already in the air swooped down at the smouldering structures before climbing steeply away again, as if in some belief that the draught caused by the beats of their great wings would somehow expunge the flames. To their right the Sinz that had been approaching through the trees abandoned their search and hurried to assist their counterparts in fighting the rapidly spreading fire.

"Now!" cried Delgado.

The group began running across the lawns towards the palace. The ground was deceptively uneven and the long, thick grass was clogged with trailing plants that seemed determined to wrap themselves around their legs. An alarm was sounding—an unfamiliar, discordant drone that was combined with the sound of approaching copters.

Delgado turned to make sure everyone was keeping up, and saw that several Sinz had spotted them crossing the lawns. "Hit the deck!" he yelled, and began firing at the Sinz, his weapon spraying streams of white energy. This attracted the attention of other Sinz, who started to give support to their associates. Avians flew at high speed just above the ground and dropped small bombs that created plumes of dirt and started fires in the dried grass. Ash, Brandouen, Saskov, and Miskoh all returned fire; Ash alone killed several avians within a few moments, but it was clear to Delgado that the humanoids were far more numerous than he had believed, and that his group would soon be overrun and captured or killed if they failed to act decisively.

"Cowell," called Delgado. "Two bombs, stick 'em together and throw." He made odd hand gestures to indicate his meaning above the noise. "ASAP, goddammit," Delgado muttered as the *vilume* joined two of the small bombs together and set the timers.

Two airships appeared above the woods directly over the Needle, and continued to fly across the lawns towards the fugitives crouching in the grass.

Delgado called to Ash and pointed; they both trained their weapons on one of the machines, and fired; within a few moments it was smoking heavily, then began to drop rapidly towards the ground. The pilot tried to slow its descent, but Ash aimed a skillful shot at one of the engines; control was lost and the craft hit the ground hard. Its superstructure compressed and the machine toppled to one side in flames. As he turned his attention to the other airship, Delgado glimpsed its two Sinz crewmembers leaping from the aircraft. One of them was on fire.

Suddenly Cowell's makeshift double-bomb exploded. Many Sinz bodies were thrown through the air by the force of the blast; a fireball billowed into the air and consumed the other airship, which was by then almost directly above, and a great cloud of brown dust was generated, briefly obscuring the Sinz from view.

"*Move out!*" Delgado was forced to shout as loudly as he could, waving frantically at the rest of the group to make himself understood.

Crouching, they scurried towards the palace, firing short bursts at the confused Sinz that were emerging from the main entrance, as avians shrieked in the sky above them.

Delgado led the group towards the palace while they also tried to fend off the Sinz chasing them. As more Sinz began to emerge from the palace itself, and the silhouettes of more avians and airships were visible over the city, he realised they faced greater opposition than he had bargained for.

"Over here," he yelled above the sound of the fighting. He waved the group towards a drainage ditch between the lawns and the trees to the left. They jumped into it, grateful for the cover it provided. "Saskov. Where is the elevator down to the *basillia*?"

"Near the centre of the palace."

"Okay. Ash, Cowell. You two lead with me; the rest of you cover our backs, then follow."

"Since when were you giving the orders, Delgado?" asked Saskov between bursts of fire.

"You will do what he says," snarled Miskoh. "If you do not, I will kill you." Miskoh looked at Brandouen; the two *mourst* exchanged a few words in Seriatt, then continued firing at the Sinz.

Saskov glared at Delgado. "Okay, I'll go along with you for now," he said. "But if you screw up, I'm taking over."

"What?" Delgado fired at an approaching Sinz.

"I said, if you screw up, I'm taking over."

"I've got no intention of screwing up, Saskov. Just give us enough cover to get inside the palace and clear the area just inside the entrance; then follow us in. Watch out for the birds: they'll go high and come down fast."

"Just get your ass inside that palace and secure it, Delgado. Leave me to do the work out here."

"Cowell, give a few of your bombs to Miskoh and let's get out of here." As Delgado finished the sentence, an avian swept around the trees to the right at high speed, the tips of its wings only inches from the grass. Delgado raised his weapon and fired; the high-velocity rounds hammered into the creature's face and it slammed into the ground; its momentum carried it rolling into the trees like a leathery sac of bones, whereupon the device it clutched in its talons exploded.

"Ash, Cowell," yelled Delgado. "Let's move. Now!"

"One moment, Delgado," called Cowell. "Let me leave a final gift for our Sinz friends." He and Miskoh conferred for a moment and made minor adjustments to the bomb packs they held, then lobbed them over the side of the ditch.

They threw themselves down, and a few seconds later the bombs detonated. There were agonised screams beyond the edge of the ditch; a Sinz hand landed between Delgado and Ash, trailing ribbons of bloodied flesh, smoking thinly. The black fingernails were chipped and cracked, the skin charred and shrivelled.

Delgado looked up at Ashala, who was crouching opposite him. "Okay, Ash," he said. "You ready to give me a hand?"

"Very funny, Delgado. Cut the wisecracks and let's get the hell out of here."

Delgado stood cautiously, then lay on the bank and peered over the edge of the ditch. The Sinz were shrouded in a cloud of dust; debris and grass fluttered towards the ground, and the approaching airships were still a couple of minutes away. "Now's our chance," he said. "Cowell, give us cover: we're going over the top."

Emotions welled up in Delgado as they ran towards the palace, the memories of his previous visit and the events that followed still strong: in his time, it had been only days since then.

The stone-framed, Gothic-style windows were exactly as he remembered them, and although they no longer possessed the dynamic lustre they once had, he was surprised to find that every one of the numerous stained-glass panes remained intact, as did the carvings and mosaics of glass and polished stone set between the windows on the palace walls. The metal strips that separated the pieces of glass in the windows were now dull grey rather than shining silver, and the narrow strip of lawn between the palace and the driveway, once neatly trimmed and edged, was overgrown with years' worth of unchecked grass and weeds. The *mourst* guards, with the fine ceremonial garb, were long gone.

As they ran towards the palace, Delgado could see through the open entrance; no movement was visible inside. As Miskoh, Brandouen, and Saskov continued to fight off the other Sinz to the right, Delgado, Ash, and Cowell pressed themselves against the palace wall on either side of the main entrance. Delgado took a few deep breaths as he looked past Cowell and saw the fierce fighting outside, as avians circled overhead.

He looked at Ash and Cowell. "I'll go first," he said. "You cover me and enter only when I've given you the all-clear. Got that?"

"It is dangerous, Delgado," said Cowell. "In that short tunnel just inside the entrance you will be an easy target."

"Passing through a vestibule like that wouldn't be my first choice, but we don't have many options." He nodded towards Miskoh and Saskov. "They're getting hammered. And besides, my name's Alexander Dangerous Delgado, remember?" He checked his weapon. "Now get ready to cover me in three, two, one . . . *now!*"

Delgado crouched and turned, shooting into the palace along with Ash and Cowell. Delgado stopped firing and began to edge forward into the vestibule as the other two gave him cover, the torrent of plasma just inches above his head. Fragments of stone exploded from the wall on the far side of the circular chamber as the ammunition impacted it, scattering across the floor and a long table.

Delgado scurried into the chamber and scanned the room: there were two Sinz bodies near one of the doors, but otherwise it was clear. He noticed that the once highly polished floor was obscured by a thick layer of dust. But despite the general decay and the odd, fusty smell, the air of opulence nonetheless remained. He reached out and held up one hand to indicate to Ash and Cowell that they should stop firing. As Ash joined him, herself checking for the presence of Sinz, Delgado could hear Cowell yell to Saskov and Miskoh to join them.

"So which way now, Delgado?" Ash asked.

"Good question. Last time I was here I went to a room just off that corridor along there"—he pointed through a door on the opposite side of the chamber to the right—"but more than that I didn't see."

They heard shouts and gunfire as the rest of the group scrambled into the vestibule seeking shelter.

"There's a whole heap of Sinz out there," said Saskov, rushing in. "We need to block the entrance."

Delgado looked at Cowell. "Do you have enough explosives left to bring this lot down?" He indicated the vestibule.

"Yes. But once this entrance is sealed, an exit is also sealed. Is this what you wish me to do?"

"We haven't got much choice, Cowell. If we don't keep 'em out, we're not going anywhere anyway."

"Very well. Miskoh, attach two of these to the wall on that side. Set the detonation delay to setting three."

While Saskov, Ash, and Brandouen gave covering fire from the entrance to the vestibule, Miskoh and Cowell placed several of the small bombs in each corner.

"Quickly," said Cowell when they were in place. "Take cover. There will shortly be a blast." Ash, Saskov, and Brandouen retreated into the palace. "Get back!"

They ran to the opposite side of the chamber. Delgado tipped up the long table. "Get behind this," he said. "It'll shield us a little. They won't be able to see much in here anyway. It's too dark."

They crouched behind the table and watched the rectangle of brightness that was the palace entrance. After a few moments they heard Sinz voices and saw slender silhouettes approaching. When they reached the vestibule, the Sinz peered cautiously inside. Behind these figures an avian flared its great wings as it landed on the palace lawns, then began to waddle clumsily towards the entrance. It seemed to shriek to another that was apparently circling overhead.

As the Sinz entered the vestibule and took tentative steps forward, the bombs exploded.

There was a colossal thundering noise, and the dust-covered floor shuddered as the vestibule filled with rubble. The already-dark room grew even darker as it filled with a cloud of thick dust.

The dust gradually began to settle. A broad, flat beam of daylight penetrated the debris, brightening a small area of the wall to their left. It was eerily quiet.

Delgado peered at the vestibule; it was almost completely blocked by huge chunks of masonry.

"How's it looking, Delgado?" asked Ash.

"Well, we've sure blocked the vestibule," he replied. "Good job, Cowell, Miskoh." He stood and walked around the table towards the door to their left. "We'll try along here first," he said.

They left the hall and entered the long, wide corridor on the opposite side. The deep pile of the carpet felt the same as on his last visit, although it was coated in a thick layer of dust.

"Where the hell is everybody?" asked Saskov as they walked cautiously along the corridor. "I thought this was supposed to be the nerve centre of the Sinz operation on Seriatt. I don't like this, Delgado."

"The palace has always been populated," said Cowell, "due to the location of the *basillia* beneath it. This does seem suspiciously quiet."

"Maybe they're preparing to do whatever it is they've been building up to all this time," Delgado suggested.

Sets of double doors were spaced at regular intervals on either side of the corridor; between them, scenes from the *cursilac* were depicted—key events from the *conchey trinsig diassaii*.

They reached the doors to the room in which Delgado remembered facing the Seriatts as they had stated that Cascari and Michael must challenge each other in combat. The memory of it pained him still. Delgado looked at the red-and-gold rope next to the door; it was aged, somewhat frayed. He motioned that the others should remain quiet and pushed open the door. The long table remained as he remembered it, but the chairs were gone. The room smelled fusty, and did not appear to have been occupied for a considerable time.

Delgado allowed the door to close gently and stepped back. "Nothing of use in there," he whispered.

"What if this elevator we're looking for isn't working when—if—we eventually find it, Delgado?" Ash asked.

"I don't know, Ash," he replied. "Maybe we'll just have to take the stairs."

They reached one of the palace's many inner atriums. It was a circular room with a transparent roof that possessed a faint blue tint.

Delgado held up a hand. "Listen," he said. "What's that noise?"

"I hear nothing," said Brandouen. "Come, we must kill the Sinz *basillia*."

"Shush and listen, goddammit," said Ash.

A vague moaning sound became audible, gradually increasing in volume like a disaffected army in revolt.

"Look," said Ash. She pointed up towards the atrium's transparent ceiling.

Above it they could see gigantic oval shadows trailing fat tendrils, like a swarm of predatory jellyfish seen from below.

"It is the Sinz fleet," said Brandouen with certainty.

"Is that correct, Cowell?" asked Delgado.

"I fear the honourable *mourst* is right," said the *vilume*. "The Sinz have finally launched the ships they have been growing. The time has come to implement whatever plans they have for so long drawn."

"Perhaps that's why this place is deserted," said Ash. "Maybe it's some kind of exodus."

"We can't take a chance that it isn't," said Saskov. "This is our way down, the direct route to the Seriatt *basillia*."

He indicated a large podlike object at the centre of the atrium. It looked like a brown, roughly dome-shaped fungal growth of some kind that had grown in a warty, blistered lump from the floor. Tendrils snaked away from it, climbing the walls and pushing through any hole or gap that they could find.

Ash reached out and touched it; it was slightly moist, warm and soft, giving under even slight pressure. "It looks like a giant turd to me, Saskov, not an elevator. Smells like one, too. You sure you've got your facts right?"

"Absolutely. The information was given to us before we left Earth. This is how we reach the *basillia*." He walked around the object. "Here," he said. He separated fleshy folds with his hands; they were made sticky by the substance that coated them.

They all stepped inside the pod while Saskov held open the entrance. The walls inside were slightly translucent, ridged and rippled like muscle. Even the floor seemed to give slightly under the passengers' weight.

"You know what?" said Delgado. "This has some kind of erotic quality, you know what I mean, Ash?" He nudged her.

"You're unbelievable, Delgado," she said.

Saskov stepped into the pod himself, allowing the folds of skin to overlap behind him with a slightly wet sound.

Suddenly the muscular walls began to ripple, and the platform upon which they were standing began to move downwards. Above them the fleshy substance seemed to contract, pushing them down.

"It's like being squeezed through some kind of intestinal tract," said Delgado.

"Gee, Delgado," said Ash. "You sure know how to make a girl feel comfortable. I don't know how many times I've longed to wear a pretty dress and be squeezed through an intestinal tract."

"It is getting warmer," observed Cowell.

"Yeah, I'd noticed that, too," Delgado said. "How far down does this thing go?"

"About five hundred metres beneath the surface of Seriatt," said Saskov. "But relax. When we get down there, all you've got to do is fight off whatever defences we encounter and we'll be well on the way to achieving our aims."

"And what kind of defences are we talking here, Saskov? Any army of Sinz?"

"A couple of bugs is about the extent of it from what I understand," said Saskov. Delgado looked at Brandouen; the *mourst*'s expression indicated that this was something of an understatement, but the human decided not to pursue the issue.

"Pressure seems to be building," said Ash. "It's getting kind of uncomfortable."

"The *basillia* needs a stable environment," said Saskov. "It's all sealed to maintain temperature and humidity levels."

"It's slowing," said Delgado. "Get ready."

Eighth chronological displacement
Earth, September 18, 2350

Delgado steadied himself against a pillar, his head in turmoil, his stomach churning. He heard heavy footfalls echoing through Myson's chamber as the last of the cyborg guards stepped over the fragments of the broken door as it left the room. Beyond, he could hear the general's distinctive, asthmatic blustering; although Delgado was unable to tell exactly what was being said, Myson seemed to be in unusual good humour.

Then all was quiet and still.

His mind was muddied, reluctant to process information—a characteristic of time travel to which he was becoming used—and he looked around the chamber trying to determine at what point in events he had arrived. There was no sign of Bucky and Ash, and the battle to gain access was clearly over. The domed window was shattered, and Myson's flier gone. But he could see Lycern lying on the bed, being attended to by the nymphs.

Lycern wailed. The nymphs jabbered to each other, agitated, nervous. But when Lycern cried out again and arched her back, the two tiny creatures fell silent and looked at her. The *conosq* calmed for a moment, then screamed again, squirming on the bed. The nymphs chattered to each other again, apparently in some disagreement.

It was then that Delgado recognised this particular juncture, and the reason for the nymphs' agitation at Lycern's condition: Myson had taken Michael, but Cascari was about to be born.

He glanced uneasily at one of the pillars on the opposite side of the chamber near the window; behind it there would be another Delgado, his body smashed and burned, its recovery only possible by the advanced nobics of a cyborg that had yet to be killed.

Delgado stepped from the shadowy corner of the chamber and walked towards the bed on which Lycern lay, but darted behind a pillar as three cyborg guards reentered the room. The first stood by the door, and another strode across the chamber towards the window.

The third made directly for Lycern.

The nymphs made efforts to push away the towering, armour-encrusted figure as it approached the *conosq*, but it knocked them aside with a sweep of one huge hand.

The cyborg stopped by the bed and looked down at Lycern. As it drew a weapon, one of the nymphs became hysterical, pointing towards the domed window. The cyborg hesitated and looked up. Delgado followed its gaze.

The white shape of Myson's flier rose from beyond the edge of the platform, the discordant roar of its engines rapidly increasing in volume as it stopped climbing and began to drop towards the platform outside the chamber. But the angular craft was at an odd attitude, unstable, going too fast to make a successful landing. As the cyborgs looked at each other, apparently communicating in undertone or by some other inaudible means, Lycern moaned deeply and raised her knees. The nymphs hurried to aid her in the birth.

A moment later there was a tremendous thump that knocked Delgado from his feet as the craft smacked against the platform. The room shuddered as the craft skidded along, scattering sparks and ripping up the metal mesh that covered the platform's surface. The ship skewed to one side as it slid, barely shedding speed, and smashed broadside through the remains of the bulbous window.

Delgado glanced across the chamber and glimpsed one of the nymphs clutching a parcel of flesh and bone, but was forced to cower as the flier ploughed through the chamber. Metal subject to immense stresses screamed and warped, marble pillars cracked and toppled, and gigantic fractures appeared in the ceiling, huge chunks of which fell to the chamber floor in billowing clouds of dust, until eventually the huge machine ground to a halt.

An appalled silence enveloped the devastated chamber as clouds of dust descended.

Delgado leaped through the rubble towards Lycern, scrabbling through the carnage. But as he neared her his way was blocked by a fallen marble column. He could just see over it, but despite his best efforts he was unable to gain purchase on its smooth surface to climb over. To his left his path was blocked by the crashed flier's hull and one of its glowing engines; to his right was the chamber wall.

Delgado looked over the fallen column once more. Apparently having been knocked to the ground, the cyborg next to the bed got to its feet. It glanced momentarily at Lycern, then looked up: immediately above it long fissures spread rapidly through the ceiling like cracks in ice. Realising it had only moments remaining in which to fulfil the final command issued to it by the Commander Supreme, the cyborg brought its weapon to bear and killed Lycern with a single blast to the abdomen.

Delgado fell to his knees and screamed with rage and pain, pounding the marble in front of him with clenched fists. He stopped and sobbed, slack-shouldered, his hands bloody and bruised. Somewhere amongst the rubble Cascari lay, but even if he could get to the infant, he would be able to do nothing without changing everything that occurred thereafter. But just to speak to Lycern, to express himself and explain before she died at the cyborg's hand. Was that too much to ask?

He heard a noise and looked behind him; Entuzo had reopened the gateway.

Delgado was not sure he could stand further torment.

March 8, 2379 (Earth equivalent)

The birthships gathered together in a comforting group and held position in space. Then they conjoined, wrapping long tendrils around each other to form a mutually supportive chain. The tendrils tightened, comforting, reassuring. And then, surrounded by sentries and watched over by the caregivers, a stream of soft, glowing parcels began to slip from each of the giant progenitors, passing through the softening layers to independence.

But these were not frail newborns, vulnerable infants subject to predatory dangers. As soon as the cold of space touched their skins, they became alert, aware, individual, prepared to fight or carry warriors or inseminate other birthships to produce more of their kind.

"A fine crop, Fabricator Clintoc," acknowledged Prime Associate Lubriatt as they watched the offspring emerge. "I knew their quality was not in doubt when I first saw the birthships themselves."

"I can take little credit for their development, Prime Associate. Fabricator Burvo oversaw their entire development, and selected the constituents of the bloodline himself."

"He is a fine Fabricator, indeed. When will they be ready to serve us?"

"Forgive me, Prime Associate, but none of these vessels serve us. In truth, we merely coexist with them in a symbiotic relationship. This is something we must be wary of forgetting."

"Very well, then, Fabricator Clintoc. If you insist on such precision, when will they be ready to work with us?"

"They are ready now, Prime Associate. They merely need a little guidance and restraint. Then they will be ready to join with the forces we already have on Seriatt, and we will have an undefeatable force."

Eight

Seriatt
March 8, 2379 (Earth equivalent)

They pushed through the pod's sticky folds and stepped into a cavernous chamber deep beneath the Seriattic surface. It was hot, the air thick with humidity and a stench like that of organic corruption. There was an immense sense of oppression, as if the very weight of the earth above them was palpable, or in a vacancy within some gigantic creature.

"Let's take it easy," whispered Delgado. "We don't know what we're going to come up against down here, so let's take it one step at a time."

As they began to walk along the tunnel leading away from the pod that had conveyed them from the surface, Delgado turned and looked up; the pod sat like a hard lump within the intestine-like tube that rose up into the ceiling. Around it were several dark holes, between which were draped slender sheets of membrane that emitted faint light. Sensing a slight draught, he sucked a finger then held it up in the air; the flow of air was towards the pod.

To his left Saskov reached out and touched the wall, but instead of the hard surface it appeared to be, he found it was a gelatinous substance that gave under pressure.

Everyone immediately stopped walking as a gasping moan echoed dully off the tunnel's spongy walls. It was accompanied by a thin clattering sound, like rapped sticks.

"What the hell was that?" asked Delgado.

"Sounded like someone sighing," said Ash. "Not someone I'd be in a hurry to meet, though. There it is again. Somehow I don't think we're alone down here."

"Sounds like it's hungry to me," said Saskov. "Hungry and asthmatic."

"Well, if it eats you, it'll get a real pain in the gut, that's for sure."

They continued for a few moments in silence. The tunnel curved to the left, becoming gradually wider. Like warm breath the breeze increased in strength a little, and became even more fetid.

The tunnel opened up as they walked around the corner, becoming considerably wider. The fantastic sight that greeted them stopped them dead in their tracks.

The tunnel sloped downwards away from them and widened into a large chamber, at the end of which was the Seriatt *basillia*.

Delgado estimated the tunnel to be around half a klick in length, and that instead of being directly beneath the palace the creature was in fact somewhere under the gardens, near the parched lake.

The shining, bulbous mass shuddered and squirmed as if filled with liquid, occasionally emitting menacing gasps and relieved sighs from small slits on its rubbery surface. A much larger sphincter faced them. Occasionally it would tremble and purse, as if about to spit forth some half-digested gobbet.

In the curved wall behind the *basillia* were many half-spherical indentations; some were empty; others contained translucent spheres similar in appearance to the walls themselves. Within some of these spheres dark masses rolled and trembled.

The *basillia* was surrounded by huge scorpions with rotund brown shells and large pincers that protruded from either side of their small heads and curved in front of their small mouths. A long, pointed tusk curved downwards from the forehead of each. Their two-jointed legs appeared far too small given the size of their bodies. A multitude of much smaller creatures scurried around between the larger scorpions and in front of the *basillia* on numerous, multijointed legs, mandibles busily collecting what appeared to be organic waste matter from the area around the *basillia*, while others crawled over the creature, cleaning its slimy surface.

Every ten metres or so on either side of the tunnel, between them and the *basillia*, more scorpions sat within gel-filled hollows in its uneven, ribbed walls, lying in wait for any threat. They purred and salivated, their mandibles occasionally clattering together with the wooden sound they had heard earlier. And between the scorpions thick strands stretched across the tunnel to form gigantic webs. The thickest of the silver cords were in turn linked by a multitude of much finer threads, all of which were coated in some glistening, viscous syrup.

As they watched, the *basillia*'s skin undulated and its fat lips pursed. A moment later its entire form seemed to heave; then the lips trembled and a Sinz slipped between them, wrapped in some kind of amniotic sac.

Many of the smaller scorpions immediately went to the new arrival, removed waste material from its folds, and detached and consumed the umbilical cord that trailed from the mouth of the *basillia*. When the Sinz was clean, tentacle-like organs extended from nubs in the top of the chamber and conveyed it with suckered hands to one of the hollows.

"This is it," said Saskov. He double-checked his weapon. "This is why we're here. We just have to administer this poison and the might of Structure can get down here."

"But first we've got to get near it," said Delgado. "A few bugs, my ass."

"I'd rather your ass than that thing, any day," said Ash grimly.

"You sure this poison of yours'll work?" Delgado asked.

"Yes. The signs of corruption will quickly become apparent when it is delivered. Discolouration of the skin and rapid decay."

Saskov strode forward several paces. Sensing an approaching threat, the scorpions scurried forwards, their antennae waving. Saskov halted; Delgado indicated to the others that they should move back. As they did so the scorpions became calmer, and after a few moments retreated back into their succulent hollows.

"Saskov," hissed Delgado. "Get back here. You need to think this through, not go at it hell for leather."

Saskov did not turn around. "No," he said. "Too much time's already been wasted. Now is the time." He took further confident steps towards the nearest of the nets that was stretched across the width of the tunnel. Lacking the influence of his nobics, which would previously have curtailed such impulsiveness, Saskov was suddenly a loose canon.

The net trembled as the scorpions lurched forwards once more, pincers clashing together and mandibles chattering. They appeared to be attached to the tunnel walls by coiled umbilical cords. Saskov continued to stride forwards undeterred. He pulled a knife from one of his pockets.

"Saskov," yelled Delgado. "Wait—"

"You're wasting your time," said Ash. "He's determined to carry on."

Saskov strode towards the nets, clutching his gun in one hand and the knife in the other. The closer he got to them the more agitated the scorpions became, scurrying to the full extent of their umbilical cords with surprising speed. The membranous nets trembled and seemed to ooze more of whatever substance coated them, large droplets forming like dew.

By the time Saskov reached the first of the nets the scorpions were in a frenzy. He went to one of the thickest roots of the net and began to cut into it. A moaning howl swept through the tunnel like a banshee, the sound made all the more sinister by the fact that the soft, gel-covered walls absorbed all reverberation.

When Saskov finally cut through the cord completely, it sprayed a transparent liquid onto his right arm. He yelled out in pain, but continued to hack at the finer threads until there was a gap in the net large enough to accommodate him. As he clambered through, drops of the liquid spread across his clothing.

"Jesus, Delgado. It's eating into him."

"It is also making it difficult for him to move," said Cowell. "See how the liquid is setting."

One of the thicker threads was stuck to Saskov's leg. He stooped and tried to cut it loose, but it was difficult for him to move his arm, as the liquid had virtually solidified across his sleeve and back. His clothes seemed to be smouldering, and he was clearly in great pain.

As one of the scorpions rushed towards him, Saskov turned and thrust the knife towards it, but it merely glanced off the shell and fell to the ground.

Saskov stumbled. As the creature reared and prepared to impale the Structure officer on its tusk, Saskov managed to bring his sidearm to bear and fired at the scorpion's soft underside. The creature's chest exploded across him and it fell to the ground, its mandibles slowly opening and closing as it died.

"Shit." said Ash. "Come on. We've got to help him."

"Wait," said Delgado—but it was too late; Ash and the others were already running towards the injured man.

As they ran forwards, the remaining scorpions became more agitated, stirred by both the approaching threat and the death of one of their number. As they reached the broken net, Saskov began pushing himself to his feet. But as he crouched another of the scorpions rushed across to him, and although at the full extent of the cord that attached it to the wall, the creature managed to gore Saskov, driving its tusk through one side of his body at the waist.

He cried out and rolled to one side. Blood stained the rough surface of the tunnel floor. As the scorpion charged again, Delgado fired a shot, but it hit the net stretched across the tunnel, which seemed to absorb the energy.

Now that they were closer they could see that the side of Saskov's face was badly burned. His left ear seemed to be dissolving.

"Keep away from the net," said Cowell. "We must not allow it to touch us." The *vilume* reached forward and stretched the cords with the blade of his knife. The threads had a strange, rubbery consistency.

"Cut them, Cowell," said Delgado. "We have to make the opening larger. Ash, Miskoh: keep firing at those creatures."

The tunnel was filled with noise as Miskoh and Ash fired at the scorpions through the gaps in the net. Meanwhile Delgado helped Cowell to cut the threads, careful to avoid them springing back and splashing the corrosive substance onto their skin or clothing.

"The shots are just bouncing off their shells," said Ash.

Delgado looked across as Miskoh fired a long burst at one of the scorpions. It stopped the creature from advancing for a moment, but did not seem to harm it: once the firing stopped, it continued to lumber towards them. Ash fired at another of the creatures; although the weapon was powerful, the shot did not even appear to damage the shell.

"Try hitting them around the neck, where it enters the shell," said

Delgado. "The skin looks softer there, see? If you can hit that, you might damage them internally."

Delgado sliced through more of the cords until there was a ragged hole that seemed large enough for even the tall Seriatt to get through.

"Go on, Cowell, you first." As the *vilume* stooped and passed through the opening, Delgado turned, brought his weapon to bear, and knelt next to Ash. "You two next," he yelled. He fired a burst at one of the scorpions as it rushed towards Cowell. "I'll cover you. Go. *Now!*"

Ash and Miskoh followed Cowell through the net while Delgado fired at the scorpions. He hit one of the animals at the neck. As the creature shrieked and thrashed its head from side to side, Delgado took careful aim, and instead of firing a scattered burst he focussed on a specific area just behind one of its antennae.

The shots passed easily through the leathery skin. The scorpion screamed and danced. Its huge shell attained a luminescence, glowing from within; then huge cracks appeared in its surface. The scorpion shrieked and expelled a thick green substance from its underside; then its spindly legs gave way. Large pieces of shell fell from the creature, revealing a complex internal structure all but obliterated by Delgado's ordnance.

"One down, five to go," he said as he passed through the net. "The others can't reach us here." As they approached Saskov one of the scorpions rushed towards them. Delgado fired several shots at the animal. The first hit it in the face, and although it did some damage to its mandibles and one of its claws it otherwise had little effect. As the creature reared onto its hind legs Delgado fired several more shots, this time aiming at its underside. Like the scorpion Saskov had hit, the creature's belly virtually exploded, spattering corrosive gore along the tunnel.

"Guess that's a weak spot," said Ash as they dragged Saskov to the other side of the tunnel.

"Yeah. If we could make them stand up on their hind legs on command, we'd be laughing. Lucky none of that stuff hit us. Saskov doesn't look too good."

They put Saskov in a sitting position, leaning against one of the tunnel walls. One side of his face was a single, large burn; much of his hair was gone, his scalp raw and peeling. One side of his mouth was contorted, pulled out of shape by scarred tissue. All that remained of his left ear was a stippled nub of boiled flesh. His right hand was caked in the solidified gel from the net, and his arm seemed to be frozen into position.

Delgado winced at the strong odour that hit him as he pulled away the clothing around the point at which Saskov had been gored. "What do you make of that wound, Cowell?"

"It is not good," replied the *vilume*. "The blood has clotted quickly, but the flesh is already rotting."

"Looks like it's eating him alive," said Ash. "What'll we do with him?"

"You can do just whatever you like," whispered Saskov, hoarsely, his words slightly distorted by his misshapen mouth. "Cute little ass like yours." He looked at her with one eye; the other refused to open.

Ash snorted. "Jesus Christ, this guy just doesn't know when to stop."

"Are you in great pain, Saskov?" asked Cowell.

"Well let's just say I now have a good idea what it's like to be skinstripped and salted. I feel like I've had all the blood drained out of me, too," he said.

"Must be some kind of poison in that stuff," said Ash. "We need to get you some medication." She pulled a capsule from one of the pouches at her waist. "Here." She slipped it into his mouth. "It's an analgesic. All I've got, but it might help."

"You should have been a nurse," he murmured. "You'd look just great in a nice tight uniform, too."

Ash stood and spoke quietly to the others. "He's still Saskov inside, all right. But those wounds are nasty. Unless we can get him some kind of treatment soon, he's going to go downhill fast."

"Hey, no talking behind my back," said Saskov weakly.

"We could put him out of his misery," said Delgado. "Right here, right now. Or we would use him as bait to draw those scorpions."

"Goddammit, Delgado," cried Ash, "you can't be serious."

Delgado shrugged. "He's Saskov. He's Structure. Not so long ago you'd have jumped at an opportunity like that." He glanced back at the creatures; although they had retreated, they were squatting just outside their hollows, watching, waiting. "What do you think, Cowell? Miskoh?"

"Ashala is correct," said Cowell. "Whatever Saskov is to you, we have to bring him with us."

Delgado sighed heavily. "So now we have to get to the *basillia* and kill it while carrying him along? Give me one good reason, Cowell."

"Because, Delgado," said Brandouen, "he is human—and so are you."

Delgado didn't reply, but turned and assessed the situation in the tunnel. As he looked at the *basillia*, it expelled another new Sinz.

"Do you think those scorpions can reach all the way across the tunnel?" asked Ash.

Delgado looked at the creatures that remained, particularly those on the opposite side of the tunnel. "You're thinking that if we can kill the ones on this side, then we might be able to reach the *basillia* without having to fight them all, right?"

"Something like that."

Delgado looked at the Seriatts. "What do you think?"

"Ashala's reasoning is sound," said Cowell. "If we stick to this side of the tunnel, it is unlikely the scorpions on the other side will be able to reach us."

"I don't like the sound of 'unlikely,' even from you. We need to be sure." Delgado looked at the tunnel floor; there were deep scratches around two-thirds of the way across, at the point at which the scorpion had gored Saskov. He assessed the distance, and with the eyeless faces of the remaining guardians turned eerily towards him, began to walk across the tunnel.

As he walked the scorpions to his right and on the opposite side became increasingly agitated: their antennae waved more rapidly; gigantic pincers snapped and clashed; mouthparts jittered and frothed.

When he reached the point at which the tunnel floor was scratched, the nearest of the scorpions began to edge forwards. The others were also increasingly animated, fidgeting in their gel-filled hollows.

"Be careful, Delgado," Ash called after him.

As Delgado reached the middle of the tunnel and drew his gun and knife, the nearest scorpion lunged forwards, snarling and spitting globs of gel. Delgado quickly stepped back to get beyond its reach, but at the same time another of the scorpions rushed forwards.

Ash yelled a warning and Miskoh fired a long burst at the creature—but it loomed up behind Delgado and he cried out, his weapons tumbling to the floor as the scorpion grasped him firmly in one set of its great pincers and raised him up into the air.

The creature's head nodded as if in agreement with something Delgado had said while it tried to skewer him on its curved tusk. But his writhing and kicking made it impossible for the creature to make contact with him, and the appendage merely clashed against its claw.

Ash snatched Cowell's knife and sprinted across the tunnel. As she ran the other scorpions rushed forwards to the full extent of the cords attaching them to the walls. As the scorpion lifted Delgado into the air once more, Ash leaped up and grasped a hard ridge of its shell just below the mandibles and pulled herself up.

As the creature tried to shake her off she plunged Cowell's knife into the joint where the claw entered its body, careful to ensure that the knife was angled upwards so that the creature's corrosive fluid would not come into contact with her skin. With the blade penetrating the creature up to the hilt, she wrenched at the handle to cause as much damage as possible to nerves and muscles within. With a final, firm twist of the blade, the scorpion let out a raucous squeal, then involuntarily dropped Delgado to the ground.

He hit the floor heavily. As he scrambled for his weapons he heard Miskoh's voice calling for him to get out of the way. He looked across and saw the *mourst* preparing to fire at the scorpion again. As Ash stabbed the creature repeatedly in the soft tissues surrounding its antennae, claws, and mandibles, it reared up in an attempt to throw her off. Miskoh fired at the creature's exposed underside and it fell to the ground, sending Ash sprawling across the tunnel floor.

Delgado helped her up.

"Thanks," she said, breathing heavily and eyeing the slain scorpion.

"I think it's me who should be thanking you," he said as they walked back to the others.

"Don't worry about it, Delgado." She slapped him on the back. "I mean let's face it, if I didn't look after you, who the hell would?"

"You are both brave and foolish indeed," said Miskoh.

"Yeah, maybe. Although sometimes it's difficult to differentiate between the two." Delgado looked down at Saskov. "How's the patient?"

Ash knelt next to the wounded man. She pulled a face at the sight of his wounds. He looked like a corpse. His skin was continuing to dissolve where it had come into contact with the corrosive fluid; the shape of his teeth was visible through his cheek it was now so thin, and the side of his face was merely a rough surface where his left ear had once been. He was leaning slightly to one side, his head angled slightly towards his left shoulder.

They looked along the wall at the scorpions on the same side of the tunnel, which had again returned to their gel-filled pods now that the immediate threat seemed to have passed.

"At least we now know that if we can deal with the scorpions on this side of the tunnel, those on the other side won't be able to get to us," said Delgado.

"Deal with 'em, sure," said Ash. "But I still don't see an easy way to do that. I mean, sure, we can kill 'em if they'll be so good as to stand on their hind legs, or if we can get close enough to shoot 'em in the neck, but I don't think they're likely to jump for snacks."

"Not that we have any snacks," Delgado observed

"There is perhaps another way," said Miskoh. He plucked one of the bombs from his belt and tossed it from one long *mourst* hand to the other. "If two of us approach the creatures, I could attach a bomb near the neck with a short delay. When the bomb detonates, the creature will either be killed or disabled."

"The risk is too great, Miskoh," said Cowell. "The one who has to attract the scorpion's attention would be in grave danger, as would you."

"Your concern is touching, Cowell, but what choice do we have? Come. We have wasted time enough here. We do not know what fate may have befallen our colleagues in the palace above. Who now is with me?"

"I'll do it," said Ash.

"No." Delgado and Cowell spoke the word simultaneously, and glanced at each other.

"You should let Ash do it, Delgado," murmured Saskov. They turned to look at him. "If I was one of these bugs, I'd sure keep my eyes on her more than I would on you." He looked at her with his one good eye. "Juicy little ass like that."

"Jesus Christ, don't you ever give up, Saskov? You *are* a bug, goddammit."

"Ashala is courageous as well as wise," said Brandouen.

"No, you can't do it, Ash." Delgado shook his head.

Ash folded her arms. "Why? Because it's too dangerous? Because I'm not strong enough?"

"Because if anything happens to you, who's going to save my ass next time it's on the line?"

She did a bad job of trying not to smile. "Yeah, well. I guess you may have a point there, Delgado."

Delgado looked at Miskoh. "How about me and you?"

The *mourst* gazed back at him, his dark eyes bright. "We will work well together, Delgado."

"Yeah, well Delgado's already demonstrated his ability to attract the scorpions," said Ash.

"That's settled then. I'll draw the nearest scorpion first. Do your thing whenever you feel the moment's right."

"I still believe this is a foolish course of action, Delgado," said Cowell. The *vilume* looked along the tunnel towards the restless creatures.

"Well, maybe you do, Cowell, but this is where it's at. We need to deliver the poison to the *basillia*, and to do that we've got to get past the scorpions. Come on, Miskoh, let's get this thing done. Set your timers short so the bombs go off quick. Just make sure you get your ass out of the way before they do. Ash, you get Saskov's gun. When I wave you forward, you join us. Not before. Got it?"

"Sure, Delgado, I think I can understand that."

"Brandouen, you make sure she does as she's told, okay?"

"We will comply with your wishes, Delgado," replied the *mourst*.

"Okay. Come on, Miskoh," Delgado said. "Let's get this done. We'll split up. You stick near the wall and come at it from the side, and I'll go around in front. We need to make sure we keep all weapons out of sight for as long as possible. Once they see 'em, things'll get real hot."

"They don't have any eyes, Delgado," stated Ash.

"Yeah, well, you know what I mean." He took his sidearm from its holster and stuck it in the back of his waistband, along with the knife. "You concentrate on the bombs; I'll just carry my sidearm and a blade. Cowell, I know they're pretty resistant to it, but when things get hot, I'm sure a few hits with the ripgun will attract their attention. Just watch who it is you're shooting at, okay? Remember to aim for the soft tissues around the back of the neck, and if one of them rears up, make sure we're not so close that we get spattered with whatever that corrosive gunk is that's inside them."

"It will give me great pleasure, Delgado."

As Delgado and Miskoh began to walk along the tunnel, Ash turned and knelt next to Saskov once more. "You better give me that gun of yours," she said. "You're not going to get to use it yourself now."

Saskov shook his head. "No way," he hissed. "The only way you'll get this gun off me is if I'm dead. I came here to do a job, and I'm going to see as much of it through as I can. Besides, the grip's coded to respond to my DNA. You wouldn't be able to do anything with it anyway."

"Goddammit, Saskov, does Structure brainwash you during training or something? You're in no state to do anything much but breathe. Now *recode* the grip and give me the gun."

Saskov shook his head weakly. "No can do."

She swore and reached forward to take the weapon from him—but he grabbed her wrists with surprising speed, gripping them with a strength that belied his apparent state. He pulled her close to his hideous, rotting face. "I tell you what. I'll give you additional user status." He pressed her palm against the gun's butt, then released her and rapidly touched a series of tabs on the weapon's small screen. "If I get killed or can't see this thing through," he said, "then it's yours. But for the time being it stays with me, and you give me a fair chance to complete my mission. Deal?"

She shrugged and nodded. "Deal," she said. "For what good it'll do you."

She stood and turned. Delgado was almost at the centre of the tunnel, keeping one eye on the scorpions on the other side, while Miskoh stuck close to the tunnel wall, heading directly for the two nearest creatures. As they approached them, the strange animals began to chatter, as if arguing with each other about strategy. The one directly ahead of Miskoh was particularly agitated, its small head rocking. As it sensed the approach of both the human and the Seriatt, the creature's pincers snapped repeatedly and a strange white froth began to seep between its delicate mandibles. Sensing their counterpart's increasing excitement, and with the pungent aroma of the already slain scorpions thick in the air, the disquiet of the other blind creatures also increased.

As some of them began to edge from their pods, Delgado looked at Miskoh. "We don't have long," he said. "They're starting to get twitchy." He altered course, heading directly for the same scorpion as Miskoh.

As he walked away from them, two of the scorpions behind Delgado scurried forward. They snapped at him with their giant pincers and dug their tusks deep into the tunnel floor. Although he was just out of reach, Delgado instinctively drew his weapons, but the scorpion just in front of Miskoh suddenly rushed forwards.

As the creature loomed up in front of Delgado, he was aware of the fearsome sound of the ripgun firing, explosions behind him as the weapon's ammunition tore into the tunnel wall. The brilliance of its discharge cast slight grey shadows across the pale floor. Between these blasts he could also hear Ash yelling something but was unable to distinguish the words, or tell towards whom they were directed.

The scorpion reared up in front of him, but not enough for either him or Cowell to get a good shot at the creature's underside. But as it lunged back towards the ground, Delgado thrust up with the knife and buried the blade into the scorpion's jaw up to the hilt. The creature squealed and staggered to the right, pulling the knife from Delgado's grip. As it shook its head and tried to reach the source of the pain with one of its claws, Miskoh leaped up onto one of the creature's brittle legs, then grasped one of its antennae and pulled himself up onto the scorpion's shell. He sat astride it, gripping the shell's thin rim just behind the head as the creature lurched and staggered, then reached behind himself to pluck one of the small explosive devices from his belt.

As the creature lunged at Delgado once again, the *mourst* leaned forward, almost falling from the creature's back, and planted one of the bombs on the soft leathery skin at its neck. As the scorpion frantically danced across the tunnel floor, Miskoh jumped from its back. He gripped Delgado by the sleeve and pulled him back up the tunnel towards the others. Ahead of them the strange grey light of the tunnel was turned a brilliant white as Cowell continued to fire at the other scorpions.

"Quickly," he called. "Detonation will occur in a few seconds only."

They sprinted away from the creature back up the tunnel, then threw themselves to the ground. Behind them the tunnel was filled with a muffled explosion followed by a dull cracking sound.

Delgado raised his head and looked behind him; the headless scorpion lay almost at the centre of the tunnel, its shell oozing the thick gel-like substance through large cracks. He jumped to his feet, offered a hand to Miskoh, and found himself laughing as his head spun on a nobic-fuelled cocktail of adrenaline and endorphins. "Christ, this is just like the old days on Buhatt. That was some kind of rodeo ride, Miskoh. Come on. Let's just keep the momentum going."

As they ran back down the tunnel, Delgado looked at the steaming piles of organic material that now littered it. The acrid vapours they gave off as a result of some kind of chemical reaction with the floor possessed an ammonia-like odour, and the atmosphere within the tunnel was becoming increasingly unpleasant. He looked back to warn the others not to inhale too much of it, but they were too focussed on the scorpions.

As Delgado and Miskoh approached again, the remaining *basillia* guardians writhed and thrashed and ran to the extent of the cords that linked them to their pods, their screeching and the sound of their claws digging into the tunnel floor intermittently drowned out by the raucous sound of the ripgun's immense firepower.

As they approached the final scorpion on the same side of the tunnel, Delgado fired several shots at it, but they either missed or simply glanced off the creature's armoured exterior. He called to Miskoh: "I've lost the knife. Give me one of the bombs. We'll see if we can confuse it. Plant one of these things if you can."

Delgado turned and looked back up the tunnel again. He beckoned urgently to Ash, but she gestured towards Saskov, who was slumped against the tunnel wall.

"I don't care," Delgado yelled. "Leave him there."

Ash shook her head, unable to hear him above the noise of the scorpions and the sporadic fire of the ripgun. She slapped Cowell on the back. The *vilume* stopped firing and stood, and they ran after Delgado and Miskoh down the tunnel, followed by Brandouen.

As Cowell kept back the scorpions behind him with suppressing fire, Delgado circled in front of the last of the creatures that remained on the nearest side of the tunnel. When the scorpion lurched towards Delgado, Miskoh ran towards the creature's rear, eyeing a ridge of armour protruding from the back of its shell to use as a way of clambering up on top of it. The scorpion seemed to sense Miskoh and turned, but as it did so Cowell released a torrent from the ripgun that hit the creature full in the face. Much of the ammunition simply seemed to be absorbed by its protective shell, but a couple of rounds penetrated the tissues at the base of the antennae.

The scorpion screeched and staggered backwards. Its rear legs gave way beneath it, and the creature adopted an odd squatting posture. Its counterparts on the opposite side of the tunnel were frenzied, lurching back and forth, but Delgado was uncertain whether this was due to the fact that the creature seemed to be on the verge of being overcome, or because they knew the *basillia* was about to be exposed to danger. He noticed that their umbilical cords were becoming detached, a thick brown liquid seeping from around the point with which the cords entered the wall. What would happen should they suddenly become free, Delgado was uncertain.

Miskoh scrambled onto the scorpion's back while the opportunity presented itself. The *mourst* struggled to gain purchase on the creature's shell, but as it was partially incapacitated, and with its attention switching from Delgado directly in front of it, to Cowell as he continued to fire the ripgun, Miskoh managed to get to the front of the shell within a few moments. He quickly adopted the same position as he had when tackling the previous creature, straddling the scorpion's neck as he prepared to arm and attach the bomb to its neck.

As Miskoh released his grip on the ridge of shell in front of him and prepared to prime the device, the scorpion screeched and attempted to stand, lashing out at Delgado with one of its gigantic pincers. Miskoh toppled forwards. As he fell he grabbed at one of the antennae. He swung from it and tried to kick himself up to plant the bomb on the scorpion's neck but, agitated by both Miskoh and the presence of Delgado just a few metres in front of it, the creature lurched violently from side to side, and Miskoh fell to the tunnel floor.

The Seriatt landed heavily, and although he remained conscious he was clearly dazed, struggling to get to his feet. Delgado rushed forwards to drag the *mourst* clear, but before he could reach Miskoh, the scorpion let out a piercing bellow and lunged forwards. The scorpion's single, curved tusk penetrated the *mourst*'s body at the waist.

Miskoh cried out and arched his back in pain. As the creature snapped at Miskoh with its huge pincers, Delgado grasped the tusk to pull it free, but it was embedded into the tunnel floor. Miskoh was still conscious. While Cowell looked for an opportunity to fire the ripgun at the scorpion in an area where it might do some damage, Ash tried to help Delgado pull the tusk from the floor.

"It won't come free," Delgado yelled.

"Leave it, Delgado." Miskoh managed to get the words out, although the effort required was great. He was clearly in agony.

"We can't leave you here: you'll die."

"It matters not, Delgado," said Miskoh. "Cowell, Cowell! *Mentatt-riok mett al-mur cos.*"

Cowell looked down at his comrade. "*Scental.*" It appeared to be a question.

"*Gatarba.*" Miskoh grimaced and moaned. The scorpion's tusk twisted in the floor with a raw grinding sound.

"Come *on*, goddammit," yelled Ash, hacking at one of the scorpion's claws with her knife as it continued to snap at them.

"*Mentatt-riok mett al-mur cos!*" repeated Miskoh. The *mourst* was clearly insistent.

The scorpion was regaining its strength with every moment, digging its legs into the tunnel floor, snorting and puffing in an effort to pull its tusk free. Its counterparts on the other side of the tunnel were frenzied.

"*Deltek manatt,*" said Cowell. The *vilume* stooped and took one of Miskoh's hands in his. As the creature's claw hammered into the ground carving a deep gash in the floor, Cowell kissed Miskoh gently on the cheek; despite his bravado the gesture seemed to give the *mourst* comfort.

Cowell stood. "Come, Delgado, Ashala." The *vilume* grabbed Ash's sleeve and pulled her towards him.

"But we can't just leave him."

"He has instructed us. It is a *mourst* right we must honour, so leave him we will. The scorpion will die by his hand. Come now. We do not have time to debate the matter."

Cowell pulled Ash back up the slope towards Saskov. Delgado followed, then paused and looked down at Miskoh.

"Go, Delgado. Go now," said Miskoh. Delgado hesitated momentarily, then knelt next to the *mourst*. With the scorpion's rancid breath hot on his face, Delgado took Miskoh's hand and kissed him as Cowell had done. "*Mertiniat misso*," uttered Miskoh. "Thank you, Delgado," he said. "You are a good man."

As Delgado left the *mourst* and followed the others, Miskoh primed the bomb that was still clutched firmly in his hand. As he muttered the ancient Seriattic words spoken by all *mourst* when facing death in combat, the bomb detonated.

The explosion was considerable, but contained between the scorpion and Miskoh. The *mourst*'s body was vaporised by the explosion, but his head and chest remained virtually undamaged. In its death throes, its guts spilling from the rent the bomb had torn in its underside, the scorpion impaled what was left of Miskoh on its tusk and flung the *mourst* across the tunnel towards the scorpions opposite. The creatures became frantic as they tore Miskoh's scant remains to pieces, snipping and slashing at his body with surgical precision.

"We should've tried to save him," said Ash.

"Do not be concerned, Ashala," said Cowell. "Miskoh wanted this. He knew he could help us. He did an honourable thing." The *vilume* turned and looked down the tunnel. "Now nothing remains between ourselves and the *basillia*. Soon Seriatt will be free."

"You got the gun?" Delgado asked.

"No. He wouldn't give it to me."

"What?"

"He wouldn't give it to me. He's a mess, but he's determined to see this part of the mission through."

"But he's too weak. How does he expect to—"

Ash held up her hands. "Don't ask me, Delgado. He gave me access to his gun in case he gets killed, but he's not going to hand it over unless he really has to."

Delgado cursed. "Okay. Let's go talk to him."

They walked back up the gentle slope to Saskov. Delgado crouched next to him. Ash was right: he was a mess. Much of his face was misshapen, like overheated wax. One side of his face wore an inhuman smile, most of his teeth now visible.

"Ash says you're determined to complete Myson's orders."

"You're surprised? There was a time you'd have done the same in my position, Delgado." Saskov paused, wincing as he swallowed. "I'm on my way out, Delgado. I know that. But I'd like to go with my pride intact, knowing I did my best." Saskov turned his head to look at the other man. "That too much to ask?"

Delgado looked around. The *basillia* was no longer producing Sinz; the other scorpions had retreated to their pods, but still looked agitated. What little remained of Miskoh was a dark smear across the floor.

He looked up at Ash. "What do you think?"

She shrugged. "If he wants to do it, that's fine by me. But he better not screw up because we've only got one shot, remember?"

Saskov began to move, pushing against the wall as he tried to stand. Cowell moved forwards to offer assistance, but Saskov shoved the *vilume* away. When he was standing, he leaned forward slightly, gasping for breath. He was trembling visibly.

"You can't do this, Saskov," said Ash. "You can hardly support yourself, let alone go into a combat situation."

"Your concern's touching," the Colonel wheezed. "But nobics and natural adrenaline are a powerful combination, trust me. Besides, you need all the help you can get. You three are good to go—but I'm dying." He paused and blinked at those words, as if assessing their true import for the first time. "I'm dying," he repeated quietly. "Might as well let me do what I need to do."

After a few moments Saskov took several deep breaths and stood upright, trying not to let the discomfort he felt show on his face. He checked his gun, opened the safety catch, and depressed the switch to load the poison vial into the breech. The weapon clicked faintly in his hand, and there was a smooth mechanical movement within. "Okay," he said. "It's ready."

Delgado pursed his lips, glanced down the tunnel and then back to Saskov. "How'd you want to work it?" he asked.

"We go down nice and easy, spread out. Then while you three distract it, I'll get in close and deliver my gift."

They paused a short distance from the *basillia*. The strange organism was moving slightly, a gentle ripple running through its moist, bloated skin. The pale wall behind it also seemed to shudder occasionally. The young Sinz squirmed in their opaque pods like unborn chicks.

"It looks different," whispered Delgado. "The liplike structures are less pronounced. And its skin looks tighter."

"It's also stopped producing Sinz," said Ash. "It knows we're coming."

Delgado looked at Saskov. The Structure officer was trembling visibly; yellow pus oozed from fissures that had appeared on the side of his face. "You sure you're up to this?"

"Don't worry about me, Delgado," he said. "We should spread out more. I'll go to the right. Ash: you come with me. The rest of you split into two groups. One group approaches it from the front, the other from the left. When I see a chance to administer the poison, I'll take it, so be prepared."

As they got closer to the *basillia*, the ripples and undulations in its rubbery surface slowed.

"Hold it here," said Delgado quietly. The group paused. Delgado glanced at the strange shadows within the pods; they were also less active than before. He looked across at Saskov and Ash on the opposite side of the tunnel and gestured to them. The officer nodded, checked that the vial of poison was loaded, then he alone began to move closer.

As he took another step forward, one of the pods in the wall exploded, dispersing stinking gel and releasing the creature it had contained.

From the remnants of slimy grey skin a sinewy figure stood: a naked, humanoid Sinz, not yet fully developed, yet obviously powerful. It leaped towards Saskov, but Cowell fired the ripgun and shredded the creature in midair.

But before its remains hit the tunnel floor, more of the pods were bursting open. The wiry Sinz figures they released rolled along the floor, then jumped up towards those threatening the *basillia*.

Cowell blasted any of those he could get a clear shot at, then began spraying the wall behind the *basillia*. Those pods that remained sealed exploded, releasing fetid slime and broken Sinz bodies. While Ash and Delgado used their sidearms, Brandouen engaged in ferocious hand-to-hand combat, bladed weapons clutched in both large hands.

Pods continued to explode, expelling more naked, leathery Sinz to protect the *basillia*. As Delgado killed one Sinz, another threw itself at him, wrapping its arms around him and sinking its needle-sharp teeth into his neck. The force of the impact knocked Delgado's gun from his hand, and it skidded across the floor towards the *basillia*. Brandouen rushed to Delgado's aid, stabbing the Sinz in the neck up to the hilt of his blade. The *mourst* then used the knife to pull the creature off, throwing it to the ground and stabbing it repeatedly in the chest.

Brandouen stood and turned to Delgado, pulling a small machete from one of the pockets he had created in his scartex overskin. He thrust the weapon into Delgado's hand. "Take this," growled the *mourst*. "For close combat a fine blade is always preferable to a firearm."

Before Delgado could reply, he saw two more Sinz rushing towards them. He smashed one of the creatures in the head with the rear edge of the machete's blade, then immediately swung the weapon in the opposite direction at the second creature; it decapitated the Sinz, whose small head bounced across the floor towards the *basillia* like a coconut.

Delgado hacked at more of the Sinz as they rushed towards him. Blood spattered his face and clothes as he cleaved limbs and heads.

He heard Ash shout.

He turned and saw that a long, dark pink muscle had unfurled from the *basillia*'s now-gaping mouth like a tubular tongue, and had wound itself around Saskov. Some of the tentacles that had plucked the newly delivered Sinz from the floor and placed them in their pods had also extended from throbbing glands, binding Saskov's limbs and wrapping his head, and held him several metres in the air. His right arm extended between the sinews that ensnared him, the gun containing the poison vial still clutched in his hand.

With great precision the tentacles conveyed Saskov towards the *basillia*; its slimy orifice trembled slightly, as if in anticipation of receiving this tasty morsel.

Although Saskov was clearly alive and struggling to escape from them, the appendages merely tightened their grip, and were joined by more, which sprouted rapidly from other glands around the *basillia*. Saskov was unable to overcome the strength and number of the muscular tentacles, and the sinister organs smothered his body until only his forearms, feet, and the top of his head remained visible.

As well as those that wrapped themselves around Saskov, others attacked Ash, Cowell, Delgado, and Brandouen. Shots fired from the sidearms caused the tentacles to shrink back, but only briefly: a few moments later they would snake outwards again, regrowing, seeking out. And almost as quickly as Delgado or Brandouen could chop at the sinews with their blades, the wounds they inflicted healed, or new limbs grew in replacement.

Cowell redirected the ripgun towards the *basillia*, but the bolts of energy seemed to have little effect.

"It is useless," the *vilume* yelled. "It seems to be absorbing the energy."

"Doesn't matter," Delgado replied, hacking at a tentacle that was snaking towards him across the tunnel floor. "Just keep firing. You might weaken it."

Only when Brandouen got close to the glands and cut one of the tentacles from the tunnel wall at the root did it become evident how to prevent them from regrowing. Delgado joined him as he set about carving hunks of gelatinous flesh from the wall; they clutched blades in both hands, swiping at the few remaining Sinz that continued to attack them, and the tentacles they had yet to amputate.

"Why doesn't he drop the goddamn gun?" yelled Ash as Saskov continued to be pulled closer to the face of the *basillia*.

"He probably thinks that if he gets pulled inside that'll be his opportunity to hit the sweet spot. I'd do the same."

Suddenly the sinews that had extended from the glands in the wall began to unfurl, loosening their grip as Saskov neared the *basillia*'s mouth. His scartex covering glistened with slimy residue and was impressed with the tentacles' shape, indicating the amount of pressure they had exerted. The mouthlike slit in the *basillia*'s face widened, its grotesque lips pursing and puckering. But as the tentacles that extended from the wall released their grip, writhing tongues slid from the *basillia*'s mouth to replace them, continuing to pull Saskov towards it.

As the last of the external tentacles released him, and more tongues slithered up and around his body, twisting around him and pulling him between the organism's swollen lips, one of the sinewy muscles tightened its grip around his wrist until he could hold the gun no longer and it fell to the tunnel floor.

Brandouen and Delgado rushed towards the *basillia* as the last of the Sinz was defeated. They sliced through tough sinews in an effort to free the Structure officer, who had by this time been dragged into the *basillia* up to his chest.

Cowell grabbed Saskov's forearms and tried to prevent him from being completely consumed. "We must pull him free," the *vilume* cried.

"Why?" said Delgado. "So he can die out here? Leave him in there. The goddamn thing might choke on him."

"*Help me!*" demanded the enraged Cowell.

As Delgado grudgingly stepped forwards and gripped Saskov's legs to try to pluck him from the *basillia*'s mouth, Ash plucked the PS4 from the floor and pushed past him.

"What the hell are you doing?"

"This thing's gotta be beat," she said. "Guess I'm the one to do it now."

Before Delgado could say anything more, Ash leaned forwards and pushed her body between the *basillia*'s fat, slimy lips, next to Saskov.

She almost vomited at the stench inside. From the small amount of light passing into the *basillia* between its lips, she could see a wide, throatlike pipe leading downwards in front of her. There were numerous tubes and a clutch of cone-shaped structures at the rear, just in front of her face, that seemed to vibrate gently. To her right, protruding like a cancer, was a large pulsating organ thick with veins and a skein of smaller ducts, with red nodules and weals. Other fat pipes, engorged with fluid, snaked towards it from the *basillia*'s inner walls.

As she aimed the gun at the organ, she heard a sickening, slick sound and saw more narrow tongues rising up at her from the depths of the *basillia*'s throat. Before she could react, one had wrapped itself around her left arm. It was immensely strong and immediately tried to pull her down into the darkness from which it had emerged. As she was dragged towards the throat that gaped before her, the other muscle wrapped itself tightly around her right arm, its pointed tip probing for the gun.

It took all her effort to bring the weapon to bear. She was aware of Saskov sliding from beside her as he was pulled from the *basillia*'s mouth. Forced to relinquish their grip on Saskov, the sinews that had previously been wrapped around him wound themselves around her upper body and face. The pressure they exerted made it difficult for her to breathe. One of the tongues slid inside her mouth. She gagged as its narrow tip slid quickly down her throat, but she bit hard on it and the muscle withdrew.

She had only moments left. As she felt herself being pulled farther inside the Seriatt *basillia* and its tongues found the weapon in her hand, she fired.

There was no recoil from the PS4, and other than a slight tremor in the throbbing mass of muscle at which she had aimed the weapon, no damage seemed to have been caused. She was unsure whether the weapon had fired at all.

The *basillia*'s strong muscles pulled her deeper and deeper, the dark sidewalls of the throat rippling in front of her. She felt someone behind her grab her calves and lift her feet from the floor. As they pulled, the *basillia*'s tongues tightened, becoming so firm around her upper arms that she thought her shoulders were going to pop from their sockets. The gullet in front of her expanded and contracted like some kind of receptive sexual organ, gasps of hot, foul air pushed onto her face as the tendrils tried to pull her in.

Then the structure to her right began to throb rapidly. For a moment it seized completely before resuming its increasingly erratic rhythm. Ash felt the tongues begin to slacken; then abruptly they seemed to wither, and as she was pulled back out of the putrid organism, she saw them shrivel back down into the *basillia*'s throat.

Ash turned away from it and staggered forwards a few steps before falling to her knees and being sicker than she could ever remember. She turned her head to look back at the *basillia*. The tongues that remained outside the organism writhed and squirmed like bisected earthworms. Its skin was also covered in stipples and wrinkles, with discoloured sunken patches like rotting fruit spread across its surface. The *basillia*'s mouth shuddered, and expelled gobs of reeking brown gunk across the tunnel.

Ash turned and threw up again, although there was little of substance now left inside her stomach.

As she recovered, gasping for breath, she felt a hand on her back. She glanced up, wiping her mouth on the back of one sleeve: it was Cowell. Just beyond the *vilume* she saw Saskov, lying on his back on the tunnel floor.

"Is he still alive?" she asked.

Cowell glanced towards the Structure officer. "Just," the *vilume* replied. "But Delgado says that he has broken bones and is bleeding inside. I have given him an analgesic injection, but it will dull his pain only slightly."

"But he's got high-level nobics," she said. "Won't they get him back into shape? Something like that saved Delgado's life once."

"Delgado says they should, but they do not appear to be doing anything to help him. We believe that for some reason Saskov's nobics are not functioning as they should. If we can get him to the surface quickly, we may be able to find medical supplies that may help him."

Delgado walked over to them. "You okay, Ash?" he asked, crouching next to her.

"Sure. No sweat. I just wish I could get the stink of that thing out of my nostrils."

"I guess that's the price you pay for killing the *basillia*," he said. "If the shield's down, half the Structure fleet is probably on its way down here right now."

She looked back at the *basillia* again. It seemed to be decomposing, collapsing in on itself. It made a wet, flatulent sound, and one side of it collapsed completely. Two of the tonguelike structures that lay like dead snakes on the tunnel floor suddenly slithered back into the organism as if seeking sanctuary within. The tunnel walls had also started to secrete a thick grey slime, like slowly melting wax. "But the gun didn't fire," she protested. "There was no damage inside."

"Well, I don't know about that, Ash, but it sure doesn't look too healthy to me. And this *is* how Saskov said it would react if the poison had worked."

"Cowell says he's got broken bones and internal bleeding."

"Yeah, I think so. He sure doesn't look too good."

"But he might have a chance if we can get him back up top?"

"Yeah. I guess he might."

"Cowell, Delgado." It was Brandouen who was calling to them. The *mourst* had walked along one of the tunnels that curved away from the end of the main tunnel on either side of the *basillia* and was looking up at the wall. "Come, you must see this."

"You sure you're okay, Ash?" Delgado asked.

"Sure," she said. "It was just like being hauled through someone's guts in there. Happens every day."

"Great." He stood, smiled, patted her on one shoulder, and offered a hand to help her to her feet. "Come on. Let's go see what our *mourst* friend's found."

As they neared Brandouen, Ash and Delgado slowed, then came to a stop next to the *mourst*. For several moments they simply gazed at the sight before him.

Suspended in the thick opaque gel that formed the tunnel walls were ghostly Seriattic figures. They appeared to float a metre or so from the ground. Some of them held their arms outstretched as if seeking help, while the arms of others were down by their sides.

Many were set so far back in the wall that they were no more than dark shadows, their features impossible to distinguish. But some were nearer the surface. Delgado recognised the Seriattic Administrators—and the Oracles.

Tubes like distended veins linked them, penetrating eye sockets, ears, nostrils, and mouths in fat bunches. Their skin looked crystallised, purple, frozen lips pulled back to reveal dark, cracked teeth. Their bodies seemed somehow shrunken, skin pulled tight across bones as if they had been slowly consumed, every nutrient sucked from them.

Like the other bodies, most were suspended deep within the strange opaque substance from which the tunnel was formed, emaciated figures in a state of stasis, if they were alive at all.

Among them Delgado recognised Oracle Entuzo.

Most of the Oracle's long, thin body was just below the surface of the wall, but the *vilume*'s face protruded slightly. Bunches of narrow veinlike tubes spread through the gel to the Oracle from the eye sockets of those behind her like angel hair. Entuzo's completely black eyes remained untouched, however, the strands instead forming tight spirals on her forehead and temples. And unlike her counterparts, Oracle Entuzo was semiconscious, mumbling unintelligibly in an apparently delirious state.

The moment he realised who it was, Brandouen began hacking at the wall around Entuzo. "We must release the Great Oracle of this torment," said the *mourst*.

"But this stuff might be keeping her alive," said Ash. "You might kill her. Can you risk it?"

"Entuzo is the greatest Oracle out planet has known," said Cowell. "The Sinz obviously recognised the power and value of this important Scriatt. See how she is linked to the others. She is clearly being used as a focal point to channel their combined powers. It is a technique used when deep Sight is required, but a skill Oracle Entuzo mastered more completely than any other. But now Entuzo must be freed, even if the lesser Oracles perish as a result."

"Okay, well I guess you should know what's going on here." Delgado joined the others in their efforts to cut the Oracle free, slicing at the strange rubbery substance and scooping it away with their knives. As more of the material was removed, Entuzo began to fall forwards.

They released that which remained below her waist and around her arms, then Brandouen sheathed his knife and held the *vilume* in place while Delgado freed the Oracle's legs. Cowell reached up and carefully prised the narrow tubes from her head. They did not appear to enter the *vilume*'s body, leaving only a faint pink pattern on the skin.

When Entuzo was finally free, they supported her weight and lowered her gently to the floor. Despite the fact that the material they had removed from the wall to free the Oracle had dissolved to clear liquid, there was no residue on either the Oracle herself or her long black gown.

"Oracle Entuzo," said Cowell, leaning towards the *vilume*. "Can you hear me?"

Entuzo gradually became more lucid. Despite her malnourished state and obvious exhaustion, the Oracle retained an air of supreme serenity. Her pure black eyes seemed to suck in light. "I thank you for releasing me," she said, her voice little more than a whisper. "Too long have I been held captive." The Oracle looked at Cowell. "Gracious *vilume*, tell me who you are, and how you come to set me free."

"I am Cowell." The *vilume* bowed her head. "I am your honoured servant, Great Oracle. The Sinz *basillia* has been overcome. Now we have struck at the very heart of the Sinz, and our planet will soon be free."

"The *basillia* is fundamental to the Sinz existence," said Entuzo. "If the organism has been destroyed, then they are already virtually defeated. This is surely a time to rejoice."

Delgado looked down at Entuzo. "You're saying that all the Sinz we've seen, the humanoids, the birds, the amphibians—they're all dependent on that pile of meat."

"That is correct," replied the Oracle. "But it was more powerful than you appreciate. The *basillia* breeds and nourishes the Sinz. They are part of it, and it is part of them. Its power was sufficient to generate the force field that has isolated our planet for so long. This is why they protected it so well."

"Yeah, we knew about that. But there must be millions of Sinz on Seriatt. Those habitat towers they've built are huge. They'll still take some beating."

"The towers? They are not habitats, human. The *basillia* used them to absorb oxygen and sunlight to maintain itself in this subterranean environment. It has extended roots even farther underground to draw water for nourishment. Many have even reached the ocean."

"That explains all the dry rivers," said Delgado. He looked in the direction of the *basillia* and saw Ash walking along the tunnel, gazing at the other figures suspended in the wall. He looked back down at the Oracle.

"The Sinz have plundered our world," Entuzo stated. She paused and looked at Delgado; the gaze of her penetrating black eyes was disturbing. "We have met before," she said. "I feel it."

Delgado nodded. "Yeah. Long time ago. Longer for you than for me, though, I guess. And not just because you've been imprisoned here for so long. I'm surprised you haven't gone insane. But then, you're an Oracle. I guess you knew you'd be rescued someday, right?"

"Do not be impudent, Delgado," snapped Cowell, suddenly fierce. "The Oracles have greater mental capacity than any human can comprehend. Do not judge them by your own standards."

Entuzo gave what was as close to a smile as it was possible for an Oracle to achieve. "Calm yourself, Cowell. Delgado does not understand." She addressed Delgado once more. "An Oracle's power of foresight offers many abilities," Entuzo said to him, "some of which can be advantageous. I am sorry that the Sinz did not feel that my counterparts were as valuable as I. We were all given the nutrients we needed to survive, but my mind was kept at a higher level than those of my fellow Oracles because the Sinz realised my capabilities, and wanted to use my gift of Sight to help them in their plans." Entuzo looked back at the other Oracles, who were still suspended in the gel. "The others were less fortunate. While I was kept on the cusp of sleep and wakefulness, they descended into coma and now verge on death. If you cut them free now, they will die. It is to be expected given the length of time they have been imprisoned. For a short time after they are released they may join us once more, but they will not survive for long."

"What of the Royal Household, Great Oracle?" asked Cowell. "Are they here?"

"No. They were murdered when the Sinz first came to our world. I fear their lack of real power and usefulness was evident. The Sinz took what they needed. They simply disposed of that which offered them nothing." The Oracle looked at Cowell. "But now, with our new saviour to guide us, our planet can be rebuilt again."

Cowell looked uncomfortable. "The Great Oracle is generous indeed. But, with respect, I feel it inappropriate to suggest I am worthy of such an exalted title."

"Come, Cowell," said Entuzo. "You must accept your destiny. Long ago I saw the coming of a new saviour, but at that time I could not predict with accuracy who it would be, or the circumstances in which you would rise. But now it is clear beyond doubt. You have served Seriatt for a long time, and have earned this honour with your sacrifices."

"But it cannot be," protested Cowell.

"The Oracle speaks the truth," said Brandouen. "You have devoted your life to fighting the Sinz since their invasion, and have now been instrumental in liberating our world. Ashala administered the poison to the *basillia*, but you were key to enabling her to do so." Brandouen knelt before Cowell, bowed his head low, and held his arms outstretched, hands palm-upward. "I live now only to serve you."

Cowell looked increasingly unsettled. "But I have not—"

Oracle Entuzo held up one long-fingered hand to silence the *vilume*. "Your protestations are futile, Cowell. There is nothing but certainty in what I see. You will lead us now."

each of those around her. "I do not feel deserving of
vilume said, "but neither would I dare to argue with the
 ᵣ this is truly what is destined, then I will serve Seriatt to the
 ᴀbility."

 ᵣcle Entuzo placed one of her long-fingered hands on the back of Del-
 ᵣs neck. "And what of you, Delgado?" the *vilume* asked quietly. "Where
 ᵣoes your destiny lie?"

"Shouldn't you be the one to tell *me*?" he responded quietly.

"That is not the way, Delgado. This you know."

"Yeah, sure. There's only one thing I want now, Entuzo. I need to find
the time gate."

"Why do you seek this, Delgado?"

"Because Myson wants it. If the *basillia*'s dead and the shield's down,
then I'd bet Structure's on its way here in force. If you want a peaceful relationship with Earth, you need to destroy that gate. Whatever else he might
want, you can't let Myson get his hands on it. Do you know where it is?"

"Yes," said the Oracle. "I can tell you where it is located. But denying
Myson is not your only motive."

Delgado shrugged. "Maybe not."

He looked to his left and saw Ash running towards him; there was something strange in her expression. "What's up, Ash?" he asked.

"You've gotta come see this, Delgado," she gasped. "One of the people in
the wall . . . I think it's Michael."

The figure was smaller than the Seriatts—undeniably a human form. As Delgado peered up into the cloudy substance, his heart began to beat a little
faster: Ash was right.

"Michael," he whispered.

"Do you think he's alive or dead?" Ash asked.

"I don't know," said Delgado. "According to what Entuzo was saying,
they're in some kind of deep coma, put in there just after the Sinz invaded.
She says if we pull them out they'll die."

Ash leaned forwards and peered at Michael's vague shape. "So what are
you going to do?"

"I'm not sure there's anything I can do."

"But he's your son."

"Well, technically, biologically, yes. But some would say that that's the least important part of being a parent. And I've had no other part in his life. He also killed Cascari, who was my true son. In every way."

"But he *is* still your son. And that's one of the main reasons we've come this far. Isn't it?" Ash gazed at the shadowy figure, then took a step closer and leaned forward, squinting. "Hey, Delgado," she said quietly. "I can't see through this stuff too good, but . . . I think he's moving."

"What?" He stood next to her.

"Look at his neck. It's like he's trying to move his head. It looks like . . . I think he's in pain, Delgado."

Delgado peered briefly into the wall, then produced his knife and began to cut into it, slicing away great chunks of the strange material. Within moments he was frantically hacking and chopping with far more force than was actually effective. "Help me, Ash," he said. "Let's get him out of there, come on."

"But it'll kill him."

"That may be, Ash, but that's probably preferable to whatever torture he's been experiencing in there for who knows how long. Now give me a hand, will you?"

Although Ash helped him, it still took many minutes of hard work to cut Michael free. They supported his weight as he fell forwards, cutting the tubes that linked him to the wall; unlike those they had found on Oracle Entuzo, these actually entered his body, penetrating his facial orifices. They then let him down gently, turning him around to lie on his back.

He was incredibly thin; by Delgado's estimation he probably weighed less than fifty kilos. His skin was shrivelled and wrinkled and grey. His lips were shrunken and purple, his teeth like fragments of cracked stone. The white tubes they had cut hung down the sides of his face like empty veins, a thin grey mucuslike substance dripping from the severed ends.

Delgado knelt next to him. He raised Michael's head to rest it on his thighs, pulling the rubbery strands from his ears and nose. Michael coughed, bringing up thick, red-tinged fluid, choking and gasping for several seconds.

When he was breathing more normally and was more relaxed, Delgado gripped a bunch of the tubes that had spread into his right eye, but then decided against pulling them free, and let them fall against Michael's cheek.

"Michael," he said. "Michael. Can you hear me?"

Michael's head lolled to one side. Delgado shook him.

"Michael. Michael!" Delgado grasped him by the shoulders and shook him more violently, but the younger man simply moaned. Delgado turned Michael's face towards his own and slapped him across the cheek.

"What the hell are you doing, Delgado?" cried Ash.

"I'm trying to wake him up, goddammit!"

Michael groaned softly and turned his head towards the sound of Delgado's voice, but it was a slow, pained movement. "Who's that?" he whispered. His tongue was swollen, making it difficult for him to speak clearly. "Delgado? *Alexander* Delgado?"

"Yeah. Alexander Delgado."

Michael half coughed, half laughed. "Shit. Have you come to take your reven—" Michael suddenly gasped in pain, his back arched, his limbs in spasm for a moment before gradually relaxing again. He drew his tongue across his dry lips, gasping for breath. "It's still got things inside me," he explained. "Parasites. Now I'm out of there I guess they don't know what to do." He moaned and squirmed in invisible torment. "Have you saved me from oblivion just to finish me off?" he asked when the discomfort had abated slightly. "I'm not sure whether that's cruel or merciful."

"We thought you looked as though you were suffering, so we cut you free," Delgado explained. "Besides, you *are* my son . . . no matter what."

Michael turned his unseeing face towards Delgado; for a few brief moments he appeared reluctant to accept the older man's statement. But the truth was undeniable.

"You've left it rather late to make a point of *that*," Michael said. "You should have left me in there with the nightmares. After all this time I was finally getting used to the—" He moaned and writhed, as though something was eating him from within, and coughed up more bloody fluid. He was sweating heavily, and his breathing was becoming increasingly laboured. Ash looked at Delgado with concern.

"You know, I always knew I wasn't Myson's son," Michael gasped. He had to pause to catch his breath before continuing. "But I never knew anything else. Not about where I came from. My mother, or anything like that. If I asked about it when I was a kid, Greer would beat me. Among other things. I didn't think it'd take as long as it did to find out the truth."

"I didn't know you were mine," said Delgado. "If I had, I would've come to get you. I just thought you were some poor kid Myson had had doctored by his biotechs to appear half-Seriattic to get what he wanted. I just didn't know. Ash and a friend of ours called Bucky saved Cascari from Myson's chamber just after he was born. But you must've been born and taken away already. If I'd known you were really mine, well, maybe things could have been different."

"But only maybe. Nothing we can do about it now. . . ." Michael sat up a little and coughed violently, expelling more, even redder fluid. He heaved, gripped Delgado's sleeve with surprising strength, and gasped for breath. He sat up stiffly, his vein-choked eyes staring at Delgado's. "I'm sorry," he hissed. Then Michael's withered face became momentarily taut, and he fell back.

Delgado heard a noise and looked over his shoulder. Cowell was helping Oracle Entuzo along the corridor towards them. Farther along, Brandouen was kneeling next to Saskov.

"Help me down," said Entuzo. "I must see this human child."

Michael turned his head towards Entuzo's voice. "Is that an Oracle?" he wheezed.

"Yeah," Delgado replied. "The only one left."

Michael's head lolled to one side; he was clearly weakening. "Strange company you keep."

Cowell helped Entuzo to kneel next to Michael and Delgado. The Oracle placed one of her long-fingered hands on Michael's forehead and closed her eyes. He sighed deeply as the Oracle examined his past, his fears, his hopes.

"You are fearful, Michael," she said quietly. "Do not be. You simply approach another part of your existence. A different plane. Once there you will be free, and this life will seem like a dream to you, if you remember it at all."

"I don't believe in all that afterlife crap," he said. He coughed and gasped. "When you're done, you're done. End of story."

"You must believe whatever gives you comfort, Michael."

"I admit I'm kind of curious to know what it's like, though," he said. "Death. You know what they say: just like sleep but without waking up." He swallowed and licked his lips. He seemed to be in increasing pain. "I wonder if that's how it really is. Guess I'll know soon enough." He turned his unseeing face towards Entuzo again. "Can you do something for me?" he asked. "Before I . . ."

"Of course, Michael. You seek answers."

"I want to know the future," he said. "And all the answers to all the questions. What happens to the Seriatt and human races?" He laughed briefly, but it dissolved into a coughing fit. "Why are we here?" he gasped eventually. "Is there a God? All of it. Do you understand?" He turned his head and weakly spat gobs of blood.

The Oracle clasped Michael's hands in her own. "I do," she said. "Such are the questions that haunt all intelligent creatures."

"Can you give them to me?"

"I do not know. And you must know that even if I can, the answers to such questions are not always welcome."

"What difference can it make? I just want to know the things I've always wondered about. My knowing them won't change anything now."

"Very well," said Entuzo. "If it is your wish, I will try."

Entuzo took Michael's face in her hands and stooped until their foreheads were touching. Michael's mouth opened slightly. He drew a sharp breath and gripped the Oracle's forearm.

For a few moments Michael and Entuzo were motionless as they shared the Oracle's insights and visions. Then, as Michael relaxed, and his last breath escaped from his body, a single tear fell from the side of his face.

Entuzo drew her face from Michael's and placed one long-fingered hand on his chest. "Be calm, Michael," the Oracle murmured. "There is nothing to fear."

Entuzo looked at Delgado. "He had great potential," she said quietly. "I saw many possibilities. But his life took the least desirable course."

Delgado just looked down at Michael's body.

"How d'you feel, Delgado?" asked Ash gently.

He thought about it. "Guilty," he said. "Guilty and angry and sick." Delgado heard footsteps and looked to his right: Brandouen was approaching them.

"It is Saskov," the *mourst* called. "He wishes to speak to you, Delgado."

Whatever poison had covered Saskov was eating away at his flesh with incredible speed. There was little soft tissue remaining on his face. His eyeballs goggled loosely in sockets virtually bare; his eyelids were almost gone. His lips were misshapen, cheeks sunken and black as if rotting, and there was little left of his ears or nose. The man looked like a zombie. Now the corrosive substance was working its way down the rest of his body.

"Saskov," Delgado said. "Brandouen says you want to speak to me. Although I'm not sure why." When Saskov replied, Delgado had to lean forward a little and cock his head to one side to hear what the other man was saying.

"Ash says the *basillia*'s dead." His breathing was laboured, his voice a rasp.

"That's right. So you can die happy."

Saskov tried to shake his head, but was able to manage only a slight movement. "Not finished yet. I've got to find Michael, and the time gate. You've got to help me get out of here, Delgado. I might be able to get some treatment up top, get me back on the road. Can't let Myson down." Saskov swallowed, slowly, painfully. "Will you help me? You used to wear a Structure uniform, too. Long time ago."

Delgado looked back along the corridor. Brandouen had stopped with Cowell, Ash, and Oracle Entuzo. The Seriatts were fussing over the Oracle. Ash was looking down at Michael; she seemed to be crying.

Delgado leaned forward, and spoke to Saskov through gritted teeth. "I've lost both of my sons because of Structure." He reached down and pulled his knife from its sheath on his thigh, glancing back to make sure no one was watching. "You're all scum. Even after all this time I'm still ashamed I once wore that uniform with pride." He brought the knife around and placed its tip against Saskov's chest.

"What are you doing, Delgado? Come on. Help me get out of here. We can work something out. You're just like me."

Delgado began to apply pressure.

"Delgado!"

As the knife sank into his chest, Saskov whimpered. His hideous eyes watered. He tried to move but was too weak.

"Delgado!" he gasped once more.

"Sorry, Saskov," said Delgado, his mouth tight, "but I'm enjoying this too much. Besides, now I've got pretty much everything I want, I don't need you around anymore."

Saskov's eyes widened. He grasped Delgado's arm and raised his head from the floor so that their faces were almost touching. "Go to hell, Delgado," he rasped. "Go to hell!"

As the knife entered Saskov's chest up to the hilt, he fell back, moaned gently, then sighed his last breath.

Delgado drew the blade from the body, wiped it on the inside of Saskov's tunic, and slipped it back into its sheath.

He stood and looked down at the body for a few moments. When he turned, he found Brandouen standing just behind him. He was unable to read the *mourst*'s expression.

"He begged me," Delgado said calmly as he walked past the *mourst*. "He was in agony. It was the kindest thing to do."

Deep within the birthships, snugly cocooned in moist pods that bristled with sensitive nerve endings and smooth, pulsing glands, the Sinz birthship pilots were becoming increasingly tense.

This exacerbated an already difficult situation.

Extensive training enabled the pilots to maintain a delicate touch in even the most stressful of situations, and they were encouraged to form intimate, almost sexual bonds with their carriers.

Yet although handling the gigantic vessels occasionally required a particularly delicate touch and considerable persistence, a ship completely refusing to comply with its pilot was unheard-of—even when the inexperienced wrestled with the adolescent.

But every birthship pilot in the fleet had recognised changes in their craft, a determined resistance to their attempts at persuasion.

Stimulation of different gland clusters in an effort to produce the necessary chemical changes was proving ineffective. The ships were simply ignoring the increasingly desperate and indelicate efforts of those they carried to maintain the trajectory towards Seriatt.

The huge vessels were altering course, determined to shepherd their offspring to a safer place, where they would not have to face a life of pain and torment.

Realising their pilots were on the verge of losing control, the Sinz captains hastily consulted each other and, realising there was little alternative, ordered the use of the Influence Rods.

When inserted between major gland junctures, with correctly applied pressure, the long rods of bone carved from the hulls of ancient, long-dead birthships would cause the ships to become docile and compliant once more.

Although it was a crude, last-resort method to rein in wayward ships that, due to advances in the Fabricators' rearing skill, had not been implemented for many hundreds of seasons, the crews responded with well-drilled efficiency, sliding the rods from their storage racks and slicing open the necessary access points.

But the birthships were prepared for this eventuality. And although it went against their desire for a nonconfrontational resolution, tolerance of those within had finally waned.

As they felt the clumsy fumblings of their occupants attempting to insert the rods into the apertures so brutally created, the craft manipulated some of the gigantic muscles their occupants had worked so hard to ensure were healthy and strong.

As muscles tightened and relaxed, immense openings appeared in the birthships' vast outer surfaces, and as their interior vacancies decompressed, the unwanted material was evacuated into the void.

Relieved of their irritation, invigorated by their new freedom, and followed by the rest of the Sinz fleet, the birthships began to accelerate away from Seriatt, leaving a scattering of minute detritus behind them.

Nine

The time gate looked fake, its dusty, dormant form like some kind of cheap replica of the vibrant, sparkling device the two of them had stepped through in some former time.

"This doesn't look good, Delgado," said Ash.

"Do not concern yourself, Ashala," said Entuzo. The *vilume* reached out and placed the palm of one hand on the gate's brittle frame. It immediately became illuminated from within, a deep amber glow that quickly grew to a brilliant luminescence. The appearance of the area within the frame changed from matte black to become a vibrant shimmering skin.

"Now tell me what you really desire, Delgado," the Oracle said.

"I want to go back. In time. I mean, I came forward easily enough."

"I see. But 'back' is a very broad term. Which part of your life troubles you?"

He snorted. "The part between birth and now," he said. But Delgado's thin smile was short-lived. When more words were not forthcoming, Oracle Entuzo stepped forward and placed her forehead against his. Delgado neither resisted nor attempted to move away.

After a few moments Entuzo stepped away from him again.

"There is much darkness in you, Delgado. And many layers. But I do See. I fear what you want is not possible, however. Time runs in many lines. Sometimes these lines cross, and at such points there are innumerable possibilities, any permutation of realities. These are the nodes, and are key to the framework of existence. Certain events must occur for the framework to retain its integrity. You wish to return to the moments before the death of your child Cascari. You want to see if you can save him. But I fear that given the events that have since transpired, Cascari's death was one such node."

Delgado shook his head. "No, no. I want to go back farther than that. I want to go back to a time on Earth."

"To what point, Delgado?" asked Ash. "Where do you want to get to?"

He looked at her. "I want to get back to Lycern," he said. "I didn't see her again from the time I handed her over to Myson on *Elixiion*. I just want a few moments to talk with her. To explain. If I can. All that's happened since then—none of that can be changed. Much as I'd like to. But if I can just see her, for a few moments, then at least I'll feel as though I've put something right. Do you think that's possible, Ash?"

"Well, yeah, sure, I guess," she said. "Anything's possible. Right, Entuzo?"

The Oracle was hesitant. "I do not know. With the power of the gate I could put you back to a point in time on Seriatt, but a point on Earth . . . Although never before attempted, it is theoretically possible. If you can give me sufficient information, I may be able to put you there for a limited time."

"All I want to do is speak to her. Just for a few minutes."

"But there is the main problem, Delgado. I can only obtain familiarity with events through you, and your recollection will not be precise, and thus my placement can at best be approximate."

"I can remember every moment," Delgado asserted. "Every second that passed. Everything I said and did and all that happened. It's burned into my memory."

"No, Delgado," said Entuzo softly. "You remember *your* version, *your* history, *your* experience of the events that took place. Ashala's recollection will be different, as will that of anyone else who was present."

"That's because she experienced different things. She's not me."

"No. Ashala experienced the same events, yet her recollection of them will differ from yours." The Oracle became thoughtful, and began to speak quietly. "Yet it is possible that if we combine them, then I may be able to build a sufficiently distinct picture. And through that and the time gate, I may be able to place you at a point close to that you desire. But you must understand that I cannot guarantee to put you at any exact moment, and neither can I guarantee that such a journey will be without problems."

"I'm prepared to take that risk," he said. "I just want a shot at it."

"Very well. But remember this: if I can do this for you, I will be able to maintain a link for a limited period. I should be able to establish a temporal gate at the destination through which you are able to return if the situation in which you find yourself is not desirable. But I will not be able to maintain this link for long. Therefore, when you join the historical time stream, I must allow the link to close almost completely to conserve my energies. After a few moments I will open it fully again. If the situation is not as you wish it, you will have the opportunity to return immediately, before the link closes once more. If you do not, then it will be almost impossible for me to open the link again at that same juncture. Then you will be stranded."

"I understand."

"You sure you want to do this, Delgado?" asked Ash. "You could get stuck in the wrong place at the wrong time. And what if you do something wrong, something that you didn't do last time? How can you expect to repeat everything exactly?"

"You do not understand, Ashala," said Entuzo. "He will not replace himself at any point in the past. He is already there. He will merely be a visitor."

"So there'll be more than one of him? Shit. What if he meets himself? And what if he comes into contact with anyone who knew him? They won't recognise him."

"If the theories of the Continuity Scientists are correct, then his appearance will change according to his position on a given stream. As for meeting himself, then yes, that is a possibility. I cannot advise on the consequences of such an occurrence. Delgado, this is something you must avoid at all costs. Should such an event occur for whatever reason, you will have only your instincts to guide you." The Oracle looked at him. "Are you sure you understand the seriousness of this, Delgado? The events of which you speak are almost certainly close to a node. They are too important, affect the lives of too many individuals to merely be occurrences along differing streams. There is clearly a convergence, and any changes to the fundamental sequence could have disastrous consequences. I believe there is great danger in what you wish to do and would advise against it."

"You should listen to Entuzo, Delgado," said Ash. "Who knows what might happen?"

"No," he said. He looked at the gate. "I've got to give it a shot."

"Very well," the Oracle said. "The choice is yours. But remember that your actions could affect us all."

The Oracle closed her eyes, placed her hand back on the gate's frame, and breathed deeply. The gate pulsated gently, becoming increasingly bright each time.

Delgado took a step towards Ash and took her hands in his. "You know I have to do this alone," he said.

"Sure. Of course." She nodded and smiled weakly. Tears threatened to well.

"But I'll come back for you. Maybe when I've done this, Entuzo can put us two someplace else. Somewhere we can take it easy, huh?"

She smiled more broadly, and a tear rolled down her cheek. "Yeah. Sure. Sounds great."

Cowell looked at Ash. "You should not trust him, Ashala."

"What?"

"I ask you to join with me Ashala. I need someone to help me bring my world back to its once-glorious position. Seriatt would benefit from your honesty and foresight. Too often my race becomes lost in debate and cere-mony. Your openness would be of great value to us as we rebuild our world." Cowell took a step closer to her. "And I need your support, Ashala. I cannot reject the task with which the Great Oracle honours me. But I need someone with your strength to help me achieve all I must." Cowell grasped Ash's shoulders. "*Timauna driss guar nim cor*," said the Seriatt gently.

Ash looked up at the tall *vilume*. "I'm not sure what that meant, Cowell, but I can't be with you," she said. "I'm not as strong as you seem to think. And besides . . . me and Delgado . . . it's kinda complicated. Especially since we met you. But we've been through a lot, me and him." She glanced over her shoulder at Delgado. "And I have a feeling there's a lot more to come. You're gonna have to find someone else."

Cowell's expression changed, and her arms dropped to her sides. As the *vilume* took a step away from her, Ash suddenly saw something different in the Seriatt.

"Very well," the *vilume* said. "If your future lies elsewhere, then I cannot prevent it. But I would advise you to be wary of Delgado, Ashala." The *vilume* looked at him. "I do not believe you know him as well as you may think."

Ash looked at Delgado again. "Yeah," she said. "I know."

"Okay. Let's get this show on the road. You better move back," Delgado said. "Just in case something goes wrong."

Ash stepped forwards, kissed him gently on the cheek, and whispered in one ear: "You be careful, Delgado."

"Sure. See you later, Ash." And before she could say anything more, he stepped into the gate.

There was a loud pop, followed by a deep, resonant sound and a warm wind, and Delgado was gone.

Delgado stumbled from the gate and fell to the floor at Entuzo's feet, coughing and wheezing. Ash knelt next to him and tried to help him up, but he shrugged her off.

He looked up at the Oracle. "What's going wrong?" he gasped. "Things are okay for a while; then there's this flashing light and events start looping over and over again. Only they don't just repeat. It's like, there's slight differences each time. Why can't you get me to the right point?"

"I am trying, Delgado," said Entuzo calmly, "but as I explained, the references are vague and the details inconsistent. Each time you have returned the timeline has been a different one, but I suspect that each point is so close to the node that your presence is causing early convergence of the time streams. There may even be several node events. the survival or death of you or Lycern, the birth of your children. There may also be other events of which we are unaware that are having an effect, resulting in the instability in the time streams. I do not know, Delgado. Even my knowledge of such matters is incomplete. Perhaps you must accept that this is something you simply cannot do."

Delgado coughed and spat a glob of blood to the floor. He stared at it for several moments, then looked up at the Oracle again. "I want to go back," he said. "One more time. I was so close."

"I fear you must not. There is too much at stake. We may be weakening the framework, placing stress upon the node."

"Just once more, that's all I ask."

"But look at you, Delgado," said Ash. "You look like a ghost. Another trip might kill you." She placed her hand on his, but Delgado flinched, as if his skin was sore.

"Just send me back, goddammit," he snarled. His face was ruddy, and white spittle collected in one corner of his mouth. "I need to get to the right point. That's all."

"Jesus, Delgado," said Ash, "Entuzo's just concerned, okay? We both are."

"The risks are great indeed, Delgado," Entuzo said. "I do not wish to be responsible for whatever fate befalls you."

Ash stood as Delgado struggled to his feet. He stood with his hands on his knees for a few moments, desperately trying to regain his breath. "I'm not asking you to be responsible for anything, Entuzo," he gasped. "I just want you to do what I ask."

Ninth chronological displacement
Earth, September 18, 2350

Delgado fell to all fours. Racked by stomach cramps, his body heaved as he gasped for breath. He retched and coughed so hard he almost pissed himself. His limbs trembled violently. His hands were ash white against the cold marble floor, covered in sores and riddled with deep red cracks. His nails were the colour of dried blood.

The dancing limbs of energy cast by the temporal gate behind him gilded the glossy marble; they looked like a halo of flames around his faint reflection in the floor's smooth surface. The image was of no one he recognised.

Perhaps this time he had gone to hell.

Perhaps that was all he deserved.

As the gate faded and the flames around him died, the sense of isolation pierced him like a blade.

He looked to his left: the domed window remained undamaged, but Myson's flier was gone. This was as close to the point he sought as he was likely to get.

He scrambled to his feet. As he staggered across the chamber, limbs heavy and aching, head spinning, two timid nymphs scurried behind Myson's throne; they peered at him with a combination of curiosity and anxiety.

When he reached the bed, he looked down at Lycern. It was clear that Michael's birth had already taken place, but she remained alive—the cyborgs had not yet returned to fulfil Myson's order to kill her.

And that meant that Cascari had yet to be born.

He leaned forwards and turned her face towards his. He sank to his knees and moved his face close to hers. He could feel the heat radiating from her skin. Looking at her then, it was as if no time had passed since they had last been together.

But the feelings surging through him were not completely expected.

"Lycern," he whispered. "Lycern, can you hear me?" She did not respond. He clutched one of her hands in his. "I'm sorry," he whispered. "So sorry." He did not know what else to say. Now he was finally here, nothing seemed appropriate.

He stood and looked around the chamber. Behind one of the pillars on the far side of the room lay another Delgado, the one whose body Ash and Bucky would soon find, so damaged that they would assume him dead. The Delgado whose body would be restored by the nobics of a cyborg that had yet to be killed.

And the presence of that other Delgado meant he could not remain.

Delgado raised his gun and ran one hand across its muzzle. It had served him well. But now he needed it to free him from the torturous existence that had been his life, the memories of all the things he had done, the pain and the guilt he was forced to suppress.

Gorth el miass the Seriatts would call it—the honour of self-atonement.

Delgado set the weapon to max power on the narrowest spread: the highly focused setting would result in the almost total obliteration of his body while damaging little else around him. In the destruction that resulted from Ash and Bucky's return in Myson's flier, nothing would be found of his second self.

He placed the barrel to his head and closed his eyes.

This was not how he had expected the end of his life to come.

Somewhere inside, he felt ashamed.

As he adjusted his grip on the weapon and took his last breaths, he heard a loud snap, followed by a deep and resonant drone and a vibration that he felt through the soles of his feet.

He opened his eyes and saw a bright glow: the portal had opened again. Golden arcs leaped and danced from the shimmering halo that had appeared. All around it the dark marble burned.

As he looked into the gate, a figure began to appear, hazy and indistinct. Behind it he could see vague shapes, and recognised the room where the time gate was located. The figure gradually became clearer.

It was Ash.

She fell from the gate and staggered forwards a few steps, coughing as she supporting herself on one of the marble pillars nearby.

"Ash! What the hell are you doing here?"

"Entuzo said you weren't going to come back, Delgado," she said breathlessly. "What was I supposed to do? She said if I went quickly enough I'd arrive at the same point. So here I am. She said she'd keep it open as long as she could, but she's weakening, Delgado. This stuff is really taking it out of her. You don't look so good yourself. Come back with me now, before it's too late." She looked around, and saw the bed on which Lycern lay. "Have you spoken to her?"

"Yeah. But she's unconscious. Besides, I now know that what I really wanted to do was try to change things. But I can't, Ash. No one can. All that's to come just has to happen. By my reckoning Michael's been born and taken away. But she hasn't delivered Cascari yet. This is why we didn't know about Michael, though, see? You rescued Cascari after he was born, but no one who saw Michael knew about the second birth, and you and Bucky didn't know about Michael. If there'd been some crossover in these few minutes, if someone other than the nymphs had known about both of them, it all could've been so different."

"So what are you going to do? We don't have long."

"I don't know. I just don't know."

Delgado heard a noise and looked towards the door: it was the guards, returning to the chamber to fulfil Myson's order. He reacted instinctively.

"Get behind the pillar," he barked.

"What are you going to . . . ?"

"Just get behind the goddamn pillar, Ash!"

As the first cyborg entered the room followed closely by its two counterparts, Delgado opened fire. The first guard took several shots to the waist. It bent double and turned as it fell. Its primary weapon fired involuntarily as it hit the ground; the shots hit the second cyborg in the chest and the third in the shoulder. With all three of the guards severely wounded, Delgado strode forwards and maintained a rapid stream of hits to prevent them from recovering.

He paused. He could see the cyborgs' nobics spread across the marble floor in a silvery sheen; but there was still movement in them as they gravitated towards each other, trying to reconstitute whichever of their hosts was most likely to survive. He felt a strange sensation in his own nobics, as if they were particularly agitated.

Delgado altered his weapon's settings and fired again, spraying the three bodies with a wide spread. He stopped only when they were dispersed across the floor in a stinking slick of organic material, and the nobics burned to little more than dry residue.

The chamber was suddenly filled with rapid flashes of light. The room began to shudder. There was a deep rumbling sound.

Certain events must occur for the framework to retain its integrity.

Entuzo's words suddenly began to loop in Delgado's head.

The realisation was stark.

Ash approached him through the increasing turmoil. The ramifications of what had happened were not lost on her. "What have you done?" she yelled above the noise. She pointed at the cyborgs' bodies. "One of them should have killed Lycern, right?"

Delgado nodded.

"You've changed it, Delgado," Ash shouted. "It's all different now because she's not dead. Don't you remember what Entuzo said about changes having disastrous consequences?" She gripped his tunic in both hands and shook him. "What the hell have you done?"

The flashes of light increased in frequency, a cranked-up strobe. A myriad of familiar events looped all around them.

"The time streams have become unstable." She thumped his chest in frustration and anger. "What the hell are we going to do now?"

Delgado looked towards the window. Through the fragments of light he could see that it was slightly damaged. A cyborg stood near it, a rugged figure bathed in grey light. One arm was raised as it pointed at a distant shape in the sky.

There were more flashes. The cyborg was gone. Myson's flier was suddenly in the air above the platform, a lumbering white block. Just moments before it hit the flashes increased in intensity and the flier vanished. The cyborg appeared again, pointing stolidly through the damaged window.

To Delgado's left a shimmering golden shape appeared and grew bright. A figure emerged and fell to all fours, retching and coughing, then both disappeared in a series of blinding but silent explosions. It was followed a few moments later by a smaller figure in another portal as Ash's arrival looped.

"The node's at risk," Ash yelled. "You have to put things right, Delgado."

Delgado pushed Ash away and crouched next to Lycern. He leaned close to her. Despite the flickering light, he could see that her skin was flushed, the *assissius* glands around her body increasingly moist as Cascari's birth approached.

He said nothing for a few moments, then whispered to her: "*illios nim guar ehil moe.*" Live to give life. But the words felt hollow, insincere, and his clumsy human accent did their Seriattic beauty no justice.

He glanced up and saw the flier dropping rapidly towards the platform. A moment before impact it vanished and the cyborg reappeared, arm extended as if in some fascist salute. The sparkling portal appeared to his left but dissolved before his double hit the marble floor.

Delgado stood and looked down at Lycern. She moaned, raised her knees, and clutched her distended belly. "Cascari still has to be born," he said to Ash. He looked towards Myson's throne and beckoned urgently to the nymphs. "Come here," he called. "Come *on!*" The nymphs cowered, scared as much by

Cowell looked at each of those around her. "I do not feel deserving of such honour," the *vilume* said, "but neither would I dare to argue with the Great Oracle. If this is truly what is destined, then I will serve Seriatt to the best of my ability."

Oracle Entuzo placed one of her long-fingered hands on the back of Delgado's neck. "And what of you, Delgado?" the *vilume* asked quietly. "Where does your destiny lie?"

"Shouldn't you be the one to tell *me*?" he responded quietly.

"That is not the way, Delgado. This you know."

"Yeah, sure. There's only one thing I want now, Entuzo. I need to find the time gate."

"Why do you seek this, Delgado?"

"Because Myson wants it. If the *basillia*'s dead and the shield's down, then I'd bet Structure's on its way here in force. If you want a peaceful relationship with Earth, you need to destroy that gate. Whatever else he might want, you can't let Myson get his hands on it. Do you know where it is?"

"Yes," said the Oracle. "I can tell you where it is located. But denying Myson is not your only motive."

Delgado shrugged. "Maybe not."

He looked to his left and saw Ash running towards him; there was something strange in her expression. "What's up, Ash?" he asked.

"You've gotta come see this, Delgado," she gasped. "One of the people in the wall . . . I think it's Michael."

The figure was smaller than the Seriatts—undeniably a human form. As Delgado peered up into the cloudy substance, his heart began to beat a little faster: Ash was right.

"Michael," he whispered.

"Do you think he's alive or dead?" Ash asked.

"I don't know," said Delgado. "According to what Entuzo was saying, they're in some kind of deep coma, put in there just after the Sinz invaded. She says if we pull them out they'll die."

Ash leaned forwards and peered at Michael's vague shape. "So what are you going to do?"

"I'm not sure there's anything I can do."

"But he's your son."

"Well, technically, biologically, yes. But some would say that that's the least important part of being a parent. And I've had no other part in his life. He also killed Cascari, who was my true son. In every way."

"But he *is* still your son. And that's one of the main reasons we've come this far. Isn't it?" Ash gazed at the shadowy figure, then took a step closer and leaned forward, squinting. "Hey, Delgado," she said quietly. "I can't see through this stuff too good, but . . . I think he's moving."

"What?" He stood next to her.

"Look at his neck. It's like he's trying to move his head. It looks like . . . I think he's in pain, Delgado."

Delgado peered briefly into the wall, then produced his knife and began to cut into it, slicing away great chunks of the strange material. Within moments he was frantically hacking and chopping with far more force than was actually effective. "Help me, Ash," he said. "Let's get him out of there, come on."

"But it'll kill him."

"That may be, Ash, but that's probably preferable to whatever torture he's been experiencing in there for who knows how long. Now give me a hand, will you?"

Although Ash helped him, it still took many minutes of hard work to cut Michael free. They supported his weight as he fell forwards, cutting the tubes that linked him to the wall; unlike those they had found on Oracle Entuzo, these actually entered his body, penetrating his facial orifices. They then let him down gently, turning him around to lie on his back.

He was incredibly thin; by Delgado's estimation he probably weighed less than fifty kilos. His skin was shrivelled and wrinkled and grey. His lips were shrunken and purple, his teeth like fragments of cracked stone. The white tubes they had cut hung down the sides of his face like empty veins, a thin grey mucuslike substance dripping from the severed ends.

Delgado knelt next to him. He raised Michael's head to rest it on his thighs, pulling the rubbery strands from his ears and nose. Michael coughed, bringing up thick, red-tinged fluid, choking and gasping for several seconds.

the presence of the two strangers as by the chaotic conditions around them. Although he was forced to shout, Delgado forced himself to address them calmly. "Please," he said, a quaver in his voice. "She needs your help."

The nymphs initially remained reluctant, but then moved towards the bed, jabbering excitedly; their movements looked stilted in the strobing light.

But the moment they reached Lycern and began to assist and comfort her, the flashes of light slowed perceptibly. There was no sign of the temporal gate or either of their doubles, but when he looked towards the window again, he saw the flier nosing towards the platform.

This time the craft hit.

There was an immense bang and the room shuddered violently. The craft slid along the platform in a shower of orange sparks as the mesh panels comprising the deck's surface exploded into the air.

With a deep grinding sound the flier turned broadside and ploughed into Myson's chamber.

Pillars toppled, metal girders contorted, slabs of marble shattered and fell, crushing the cyborg guard that reappeared near the window. The floor beneath them trembled.

But Delgado saw little of the destruction as, right in front of him, a child was born.

His son.

As the craft ground to a halt and quiet fell, sheets of dust cascading in the sudden stillness, Ash clasped one hand to her mouth. "Oh my God," she gasped. "It's Cascari."

One of the nymphs held the baby while the other cut the umbilical cord. Delgado leaned forwards, and the nymph turned the infant towards him.

The child's features were perfect and beautiful. Delgado smiled. He gazed at its tiny nose and eyes, the fingers and nails of the hand that gripped one of the nymph's fingers.

Ash peered over his shoulder. "Look at him, Delgado," she said quietly. "He's perfect."

"Yeah. He looks human right now, but that's Cascari all right."

"Scari," repeated the nymph. The fragile creature smiled and looked down at the baby. "Scari."

There was a sudden noise behind them, and the chamber was doused in golden light.

"Delgado," said Ash. "Entuzo's reopened the gate." She peered through the portal; there were unfamiliar shapes; there seemed to be trees and fields. "I don't know where it leads," she said, "but we can get out of here if we're quick." She gripped his arm and stepped in front of him. "But you know that Cascari's birth isn't all that has to happen here."

Delgado searched for options. There were none. He looked at Lycern, and Cascari, and in that moment realised both his true position and the pointlessness of what he had been trying to do.

There was no escaping the truth.

The nymphs took a few steps away from him when he drew his gun. The one holding Cascari turned away, raising one thin arm as if this would somehow shield the child. "No Scari," it said.

"It's okay," said Delgado quietly. "You don't need to worry." He checked the settings on his weapon. "Where did you find him, Ash? We have to make sure he's in the right place."

She glanced around and saw a triangle formed by a marble column that had fallen against the wall. "It was there," she said.

"You're certain?"

"Absolutely. No doubt about it."

"Put him in there," Delgado ordered the nymphs, gesturing urgently towards the space with his gun. "Put him in there, then get the hell out of here. *Do it!*"

The nymphs started, and gabbled to each other as they placed Cascari where they had been instructed. Although clearly reluctant to leave the child, when they were satisfied he was safe, they rushed past Delgado and out of the chamber, careful to avoid the remains of the dead cyborgs.

Ash went and crouched next to Cascari for a moment, then returned to Delgado's side. "You ready?" she asked.

Delgado did not reply. Instead he primed his gun; it began to vibrate gently in his hand.

Certain events must occur for the framework to retain its integrity.

"Good old Entuzo," he said. "Grim, but accurate."

Delgado raised the weapon and pointed it at Lycern's belly. He felt sick, dizzy. His hand trembled. He let his arm drop to his side again and gazed down at her. Was this what his life came to? Or was it some form of retribution for all he had done? Lycern would love that. He tried to determine what he felt. He wasn't sure he felt anything. He wasn't sure what that meant.

"You've got to do it, Delgado," Ash whispered. "She has to die here. You know I'm right."

He looked at Cascari, who was kicking and shaking his hands as if attempting some kind of escape.

Ash looked towards the flier and saw movement through one of the cockpit windows. She touched his shoulder. "Delgado. They'll be here soon. I mean, me and Bucky. And we don't know how long Entuzo will be able to keep the gate open. We need to put things straight."

She was right. He knew she was right. Entuzo was right. Even Saskov had been right when he said Delgado was just like him. Only *he*, Alexander Delgado, was wrong.

But he could not waste time considering what he should or should not have done. There was no time left. There were no choices.

Delgado raised his gun and aimed at Lycern.

But after a few moments he let his trembling hand drop to his side. "I can't do it," he said.

"You have to."

Delgado looked at her.

"You know it has to happen," she said.

"I can't. I can't kill her. She's Cascari's mother. And Michael's."

They heard a faint rumble as the door on the other side of the flier slid open.

"She has to die here, Delgado," said Ash. "You know what Entuzo said. Things are almost right now. There's just this one last event." Ash looked at Lycern, then moved close to Delgado. "You want me to do it?" She produced Saskov's HiMag PS4 from inside her tunic. The black weapon glistened. "I've even got a Structure gun."

He thought for several moments, then nodded once, turned away, and walked a few steps towards the portal.

A moment later he heard the dull sound of a single shot.

Ash grabbed him by one sleeve. "It's done," she said. "Come on, Delgado. It's time to leave."

As Ash pulled him through the glowing gate into the unknown world that lay beyond, Delgado glanced back. He was uncertain then whether he would now be free of his troubles, or burdened forever by all that had happened.

Then the two figures vanished, and as the golden portal faded, Bucky and Girl began to pick their way through the devastation towards Lycern, the infant Cascari, and all the future held.